Name
of Love

Katie Price is one of the UK's top celebrities. She was formerly the glamour model Jordan and is now a best selling author, successful businesswoman and of her own reality TV show. Katie is a patron of on Charity and currently lives in Sussex with her ee children.

Praise for Katie Price's novels:

'A Katie Price book is one of life's guilty pleasures' *Now*

'You'll love this' *Heat*

'The perfect post-modern fairy tale' *Glamour*

'Glam, glitz, gorgeous people . . . so Jordan!' *Woman*

'A page-turner . . . it is brilliant' *Evening Standard*

'Angel is the perfect sexy read' *New Woman*

'Celebrity fans, want the perfect night in? Flick back those hair extensions, pull on the Juicy Couture trackie, then join Angel on her rocky ride to WAG central' *Scottish Daily*

'Crystal is charming. Gloriously infectious' *Evening Standard*

'Peppered with cutting asides and a directness you can only imagine coming from Katie Price, it's a fun, blisteringly paced yet fluffy novel.' *Cosmopolitan*

Katie Price x

In the
Name
of Love

arrow books

Published by Arrow Books 2013

4 6 8 10 9 7 5 3

First published in Great Britain in 2012 by
Century
Random House, 20 Vauxhall Bridge Road,
London SW1V 2SA

www.randomhouse.co.uk

Addresses for companies within
The Random House Group Limited can be found at:
www.randomhouse.co.uk/offices.htm

The Random House Group Limited Reg. No. 954009

A CIP catalogue record for this book
is available from the British Library

ISBN 978-0-099-56475-1

The Random House Group Limited supports the Forest Stewardship
Council® (FSC®), the leading international forest-certification
organisation. Our books carrying the FSC label are printed on FSC®-
certified paper. FSC is the only forest-certification scheme supported
by the leading environmental organisations, including Greenpeace.
Our paper procurement policy can be found at
www.randomhouse.co.uk/environment

MIX
Paper from
responsible sources
FSC® C016897

Typeset in New Baskerville BT by
Palimpsest Book Production Ltd, Falkirk, Stirlingshire

Printed in Great Britain by Clays Ltd, St Ives plc

Prologue

Then

It was one of those days that Charlie adored, where summer felt as if it was finally here and the air was like a warm caress on her bare arms. After a week of twelve-hour days working flat out as a TV researcher, it felt like such a treat to be riding in the countryside. She and Ace, her beloved black horse, were just finishing a two-hour ride and on the homeward stretch back to the stables. Charlie had burst into song on the narrow country lane and was singing 'Ain't No Mountain High Enough' at the top of her voice. She loved soul and always had a good old sing when she was out on her own. But by the way Ace was twitching his ears, it wasn't clear if he loved it as much as she did. Charlie laughed. Loosening her hold on the reins, she leant forward to pat his neck. 'Sorry, boy, I'll shut up now.'

Suddenly a souped-up black Golf roared by, music pumping out from its massive speakers and blue lights under the chassis flashing in time to the beat. The passenger was holding a white scarf out of the window and it was fluttering wildly in the breeze. Afterwards Charlie thought it must have been that which spooked Ace, who was usually calm in traffic. He reared up in terror, causing the reins to slip out of her hands, and bolted along the road with her clinging on to his mane for dear life. He was desperate to get back to the stables, to safety.

It all happened so quickly. Ace was galloping round the bend, just before the stables, so tantalisingly close to home. He was going as fast as he could. The driver of the oncoming 4x4 didn't even have a chance to brake. There was a terrifying impact, a confusion of noise, screams and shattered glass. Charlie was thrown from the saddle and ended up on the grass verge. She briefly blacked out.

It was the appalling, heart-rending noise that brought her round, the sound of Ace screaming in pain. He was writhing on the ground, blood pouring from his shattered front legs and the deep wound in his chest. The shocked middle-aged driver was standing next to his car, calling an ambulance. Later Charlie would discover that she had broken her collarbone and wrist and had severe concussion, but somehow she managed to drag herself over to her critically wounded horse. She cradled his noble head in her arms, oblivious to the blood seeping over her. 'I'm sorry, boy, I'm sorry,' she kept repeating, until mercifully he died.

Charlie was in hospital a day and a night. The physical wounds didn't take long to heal. But after the accident she suffered panic attacks and flashbacks, recurrent nightmares of seeing Ace dying in agony and being powerless to help. She never rode again and couldn't even talk about riding.

Sometimes it felt as if something in her had died along with Ace on that country lane . . .

Chapter 1

Charlie considered the piles of holiday clothes and accessories scattered across her bed – bikinis, dresses, shorts, skirts, tee-shirts, underwear, sun cream, hat, make-up, flip-flops, sandals, gym kit, toiletries, and books. That was everything, wasn't it? And frankly if it wasn't she could always borrow something from her clothes-obsessed friend Zoe, who would no doubt have taken enough outfits to last a month. Charlie had been so busy at work that she had had left packing until the last minute.

She checked the time. An hour should be more than long enough to get to Heathrow as she only lived fifteen miles away in Chiswick, West London. But suddenly she realised that something crucial was missing from her packing – her passport! 'Shit!' she exclaimed, rushing around her flat, frantically trying to remember where the hell she had left it. She wasted over half an hour until she located it in her handbag where she had put it for safekeeping. Now she was cutting it fine.

*

'Going anywhere nice, love?' the taxi driver asked as he turned out of her road.

'I am actually, I'm going to Barbados!' Charlie grinned in spite of her rising anxiety about getting to the airport on time.

'All right for some!' the cabbie joked, switching on the wipers as icy rain splattered against the windscreen.

In spite of the heat blasting out in the taxi Charlie shivered and turned up the collar of her fake-fur leopard-print coat. It was mid-January and bitterly cold. The UK was in the grip of a big freeze, which felt as if it was never going to lift. The trip to Barbados – to the exclusive five-star Sandy Lane resort – had come at the perfect moment. What a way to beat the January blues!

Charlie offered a silent thank you to Zoe's Premiership footballer boyfriend, Nathan, who had committed the ultimate sin of forgetting her birthday, and to make up for it – one of many making-up gifts, in fact – had paid for Zoe to go away on a luxury holiday with a girlfriend. Charlie, who always liked to pay her way, had offered to pay for half but Nathan just looked at her and said, 'Charlie, I earn a hundred grand a week. Relax. Make me one of your wicked curries when you get back and we'll call it quits.'

She gave up trying to argue. A Thai chicken curry for a five-star holiday had to be the best bargain ever.

'Plus you can go out for dinner with Kyle.'

Now this was a deal-breaker. Kyle was one of Nathan's team-mates. There was no way she was going on a date with him. She had a strict no-footballer policy ever since a disastrous five-month relationship with Aaron, a player from West Ham, to be known ever more as Total Fucking Bastard or TFB. 'I don't go out with footballers. Ever. Again. Remember?'

'Shit! Sorry, Charlie, I forgot,' Nathan had said quickly. 'The curry it is then.'

'I've seen you on the TV, haven't I? You're really good.' The cabbie interrupted her thoughts. She was sure he had been about to say 'for a woman'.

Since landing her dream job as a sports news presenter a year ago on the digital channel Total Sport this often happened to Charlie. On the one hand it was thrilling to be recognised for doing a job that she absolutely loved, and on the other it could be the cue for someone to bore on about sport – usually football – in the belief that they too were an expert with unique insights. The cabbie was one of them. He launched into a ten-minute rant about the state of the Premiership, FA and the England squad. Charlie started off by smiling politely and putting in the odd 'Yes I know', but then felt herself glazing over and becoming aware of how slowly they were moving. The traffic was horrendous. At this rate she would miss the flight and lose the chance of the first proper holiday she'd had in over three years. Why hadn't she packed the night before instead of rushing to get everything done at the last minute? She was an idiot. She could just imagine Zoe waiting for her in departures, wanting to kill her. And in a minute she would kill the taxi driver who was jabbering on at her about where he thought Chelsea were going wrong. He hadn't drawn breath since he began his rant. She couldn't bring herself to check the time.

*

But then, hallelujah! He finally stopped talking and turned off the motorway and headed towards the drop-off point at Heathrow's Terminal 3. Charlie leapt out of the taxi as soon as he pulled up, practically dancing on the spot in frustration while he lifted her suitcase out of the boot in what seemed like slow motion. 'Thanks so much!' she exclaimed as she thrust the money into his hand, grabbed her suitcase and legged it.

The check in area was packed and Charlie scanned the vast hall with a rising feeling of panic. Had Zoe given up waiting and gone through without her? She wouldn't blame her friend if she had. Then a flash of brilliant red caught her eye and she saw Zoe surrounded by three scarlet Louis Vuitton monogrammed suitcases, dressed in a floor-length white coat, a white fake-fur Cossack hat and an enormous pair of dark glasses. She looked wildly glamorous. Instantly Charlie ran towards her, pulling her suitcase behind her, aware that one of the wheels was making an annoying squeak. Great, Zoe had designer luggage while Charlie's suitcase sounded like a distressed hamster! She knew she should have bought a new one in the sales . . .

'Zoe! I'm so sorry I'm late,' she panted as she came to a halt.

Her friend seemed serene. 'Not a problem, I've already checked us in online, but we are missing valuable champagne-drinking time in the Business Class lounge, so can you shift your arse?' She raised her dark glasses as she took in Charlie's battered blue suitcase. 'Is that really all the luggage you've got?'

'You know me, I like to travel light. Anyway, I can borrow anything I need from you, can't I? You'll have packed way more than you need.'

The two women made their way over to the Business bag drop, which was deserted. Charlie glanced over sympathetically at the long queue of people waiting to check in their bags to Economy. That's where she usually was when she went away. But Business or Economy, they still had to go through security and there it was the usual scramble of ensuring phones and laptops were out of hand luggage, that coats and boots were taken off and liquids were stashed in plastic bags. Zoe very nearly threw a hissy fit when she realised she'd forgotten to put her favourite perfume and her hairspray in her suitcase and as a result had to hand over both bottles and watch as the security officer chucked them unceremoniously into the bin.

'We'll get some in Duty Free,' Charlie soothed her. 'It's no big deal.'

'You can't get my perfume anywhere but Harrods!' Zoe wailed. 'It's an exclusive Chanel!'

Charlie had a sudden vision of Zoe tackling the security guard and getting them both banned from the flight. So she linked arms with her friend and quickly marched her away. 'Let's go to the lounge.' Champagne would make everything better.

Zoe insisted on buying three new perfumes (Miss Dior Chérie, Agent Provocateur Maitresse and Gucci's Guilty) as she couldn't decide which one she liked best and claimed she needed different scents for different times of day. High-maintenance? You bet. Plus she bought two giant cans of Elnett hairspray, in case she ran out. Charlie resisted the temptation to point out that they were going on a beach holiday. Zoe had a thing about her hair – it had to be perfect at all times. Let nothing come between her and her glossy auburn locks . . .

And then the two women were kicking back in the exclusive lounge. Ah, the bliss of sipping champagne, nibbling strawberries and succulent slices of cantaloupe melon, sampling delicate canapés and delicious sushi, and flicking through the piles of glossy magazines. This was a world away from the heaving departure lounges beyond, where people queued for McDonald's and the loo, and tried in vain to find somewhere to sit. Here, in the lounge, Charlie and Zoe sank into soft-as-butter leather armchairs. There was the aroma of expensive perfumes mingling with the smell of money and success. Charlie breathed it all in. She had to resist the temptation to swipe some of the food into her handbag for later; the sushi would probably end up stinking and she'd be thrown out of Business Class for lowering the tone. She now had a well-paid job but simply wasn't used to this level of luxury. Everyone else appeared to be taking it in their stride, though, the businessmen and women glued to their phones or their laptops, the men in their bespoke Savile Row suits, the women in their designer clothes, handbags costing thousands of pounds cast casually at their feet. After all, they had plenty more at home . . .

'I can't believe you've never travelled Business Class

before. Didn't you go anywhere with TFB?' Zoe commented, stretching out her long legs and admiring her brand new fur-trimmed ankle boots.

'No, because, if you remember, any time I wasn't seeing him, and he wasn't training or playing in a match, he was shagging someone else!' Three months on the humiliation was still searing. Charlie had really fallen for Aaron and had been completely unaware that he had cheated on her with a lap dancer. Unaware that is until Karly, the lap dancer, chose to tell all to the *Sun*. And even though it seemed the biggest, tackiest cliché in the world for a footballer to be caught out with a lap dancer, it still hurt like hell. Charlie had ended the relationship there and then. Even though Aaron had begged her to forgive him, told her it had been a mistake and he'd never cheat on her again . . . all the usual clichéed excuses, she had refused to see him.

The betrayal had felt even worse because she had met Aaron just after her accident, a time when she was feeling incredibly vulnerable and low. He had felt like the one good thing that had happened to her since, and being with him had helped her to block out the horrific event of a year and a half ago, when her life had changed for ever . . . But she wouldn't think about that now.

'Anyway, I'm glad he never took me anywhere expensive or I'd feel like he had something on me.' Charlie sounded so certain but Zoe knew how badly Aaron had knocked her confidence.

Charlie glanced at her friend's boots. 'Won't your feet get really hot on the flight?'

'I'm changing into my ballet pumps. These were just to walk from the car to the plane.'

Charlie shook her head, marvelling again at Zoe's dedication to fashion. She herself quite liked clothes, appreciating that they could make her look and feel good, but she wasn't a slave to fashion. At work she had to be ultra-feminine yet businesslike – wearing the smartly tailored suits and silk shirts that were bought for her by the wardrobe department – but out of work she nearly always wore jeans. And so this afternoon she was in black skinny jeans, a slouchy blue-and-white-striped jumper, and black biker boots.

Zoe caught the look, 'We can't all be like you and get away with anything! Some of us have to make the effort on a daily, no, hourly basis!'

Another shake of the head from Charlie, and Zoe had to smile. It never ceased to amaze her that Charlie didn't realise just how beautiful she was. She was drop-dead gorgeous, in a league all of her own. She was mixed-race and had inherited from her mother striking green eyes that looked clear as crystal against Charlie's caramel skin, and were fringed with sweeping lashes. As if the eyes weren't mesmerising enough, she also possessed full sensuous lips to rival Angelina Jolie's and razor-sharp cheekbones like the model Helena Christensen's. Plus she had a knock-out figure, enviably slim yet with curves in all the right places. Zoe had already noticed all the men surreptitiously checking out Charlie, but her friend was oblivious. Zoe never felt a smidgen of jealousy. Charlie was such a one-off, you could only admire her.

The two girls had first met aged eleven at secondary school in Manchester, and it was a friendship that had lasted all through the years of Charlie going to university there and Zoe moving down to London with her mum when her parents divorced. Now Charlie lived in London too, they saw each other every week.

Two glasses of champagne later the girls were well on the way to feeling pleasantly tipsy, and it was time to board the plane. Charlie took one look at the comfortable seat that could fully recline, the ample space around it, the complimentary bag of toiletries and her own private entertainment console, and grinned at Zoe. 'This is the bollocks! Thank you so much, Zoe. And thank you, Nathan. Please can you forget Zoe's birthday every year!' She blew a kiss out of the window at the miserable lead-grey skies over Heathrow. 'Barbados here we come!'

She settled down in her seat, wrapping herself up in the blanket provided, which was of very superior quality to the thin scratchy ones you got in Economy, and watched in amusement as Zoe carefully removed her make-up, which must have taken ages to apply, and slathered Crème de la Mer all over her face and neck.

'What?' she demanded, catching Charlie's amused expression. 'Long-haul is so drying on the skin, I have to be fully hydrated.' She held out the pot. 'D'you want some?'

'No, but I'd love some more champagne.' And at that moment, as if he had heard her, a beautifully groomed steward with eyebrows to die for walked up to them carrying a silver drinks tray.

'Good morning, Miss Porter. My name's William and I'll be looking after you on the flight. May I offer you something to drink? Orange juice, apple juice or champagne?'

There was no contest. 'I'd love a glass of champagne, thanks,' Charlie replied.

'Love the eyebrows,' Zoe couldn't stop herself from commenting, She did appreciate a well-shaped brow.

'Threading, got to love it,' William said discreetly, offering Charlie the drinks tray.

She thanked him again, then glass in hand spent a very contented few minutes checking out the menu, which was full of delicious-sounding dishes, and the extensive list of films on offer. She was loving it! This was going to be like a very expensive girls' night in, three thousand feet up in the air.

She would have to remember every single detail to tell her mum, Lori, who had never travelled Business Class before either and would love to hear all about it. But thinking of her mum inevitably made her think of her brother Kris. Charlie sighed as she wondered what he was doing right now. Then she couldn't help feeling guilty because here she was surrounded by all this luxury, with people – specifically William of the perfect eyebrows – to cater to her every whim.

She tried to shake off the feeling of sadness that lately accompanied any thoughts of her brother. Even though they were twins she had always seen Kris as her baby brother, whom she looked out for, which had made it all the more painful when she hadn't been there for him. Four months ago he'd been jailed for receiving stolen goods after the riots in Manchester. He'd done it as a favour for one of his best mates, a lad who already had a criminal record. It had been a stupid thing to do, a one-off, and boy, was he paying for it now. Kris had never been in trouble before. He'd been trying to make it as an actor and showing great promise. Charlie and her parents had been devastated when he was arrested. They were all terrified that this one mistake was going to ruin his life . . .

'Are you okay?' Zoe asked, her face shiny with expensive moisturiser.

'Yeah, I was just thinking about Kris.'

'He'll be fine, Charlie. Your brother is strong. It will be over soon and then he can get on with his life.'

She sighed, 'I know.' She didn't add that every time she went to visit him in prison, he seemed more diminished as a person and more deeply depressed.

The captain announced that they were preparing for take-off and William and his eyebrows made a last-minute seat-belt check and whisked away the glasses of champagne. Zoe looked across at Charlie and grinned. 'Maybe you'll have a holiday romance. It's about time you moved on from TFB. Your vergina must have cobwebs from lack of use.'

'Cheers for that lovely image!'

'And did you get a Brazilian? No problem if you didn't, they're bound to do them at the hotel spa. I had a Hollywood, so I'm good to go.'

Charlie rolled her eyes. 'No, Zoe, I'm going to hit the beach with a full bush and terrify all the other guests.'

Zoe giggled. 'It'll be Revenge of the Neglected Bush.'

'The Bush strikes Back,' Charlie retorted, to be countered by Zoe's, 'Night of the Living Bush!'

'Evil Bush Two,' Charlie shot back.

'Return of the Living Bush.' Zoe was giggling so much she could hardly get the words out.

'Okay, enough already,' Charlie managed to say. 'Or we'll be sent back to Economy. And FYI, I had a Brazilian.'

'Thank God for that! Let's hope your landing strip gets some action.'

Charlie pulled the blanket up, as if shielding herself from the comment. 'I'm not bothered at the moment. I've got my career and my friends, what more does a girl need?'

Zoe's arched eyebrows said that there was plenty, plenty more.

After eight hours of the most blissful journey . . . really Business was the only way to fly . . . Charlie and Zoe stepped out of the plane and into blazing sunshine. It was like walking into a wall of heat. Charlie shook back her hair and tilted her face up to the sun. To feel its warmth on her body after the freezing English winter was like a blessing. She couldn't wait to get into her bikini and hit the beach.

'Hiya!' Zoe exclaimed, waving at a chauffeur in a smart white uniform and white peaked cap, who was holding up their names on a placard as they sauntered through arrivals.

'Good afternoon, Miss Martin and Miss Porter.' The

chauffeur bowed slightly as he greeted them, which made Charlie feel slightly uncomfortable. Sure, she was used to good service by now but she didn't expect people to bow before her!

'I am Kofi and I will be driving you to the resort. Please follow me. Your luggage will be taken care of.'

Charlie had been expecting a flash car, but what awaited her and Zoe outside on the tarmac made her open her green eyes wide in astonishment as she took in the silver Rolls-Royce Ghost.

'Oh, baby!' she exclaimed, walking towards the sleek motor. 'Come to Mama!'

Charlie absolutely loved cars. Even as a little girl she had known more about cars than her brother, and she would be the one watching *Top Gear* with her dad, while Kris and Mum grumbled about wanting to watch *Holby City* or something else.

'Happy?' Zoe asked as they sank back into the plush leather seats and the Roller pulled smoothly away from the kerb.

'You bet! I can't imagine it will get any better than this.'

Zoe, who had been to Sandy Lane twice before, smiled knowingly. 'Just you wait and see.'

The half-hour drive took them along roads lined with vivid green sugar-cane fields, and every now and then they would drive past shacks which seemed to be local stores with groups of men sitting outside playing checkers. Charlie hadn't realised how poor much of Barbados still was. The contrast with the five-star resort could not have been greater as they swept through the imposing iron gates, along a tree-lined drive, past an immaculately maintained golf course and gardens and up to the elegant white-pillared hotel. Staff were immediately on hand to greet them. They were offered an ice-cold flannel from a tray to freshen up with, and after that a delicious fruit cocktail. It certainly beat checking into a Travel Lodge.

Once they were checked in, Charlie stood on the balcony of her luxurious suite and gazed out at the glittering expanse of the Caribbean Sea, the crescent of white sand beach fringed with palm trees. She turned to Zoe who was standing next to her, and threw her arms around her, exclaiming, 'Thank you so much, Zoe! I hate to say this but it was so worth Nathan forgetting your birthday!'

Zoe gave a wicked grin. 'Yeah, I know! I'd pretty much forgiven him the moment he apologised as he looked so cute.'

'The diamond necklace must have helped,' Charlie deadpanned.

'It didn't hurt,' Zoe replied, lovingly touching the diamond star pendant round her neck. 'But this,' she held out her arms wide to take in the breathtaking view, 'is the business!'

'And now,' Charlie declared, 'I have to get on that beach before the sun sets.'

Typically Zoe took ages getting ready. Charlie had showered and changed into her bikini, tied her long hair into a ponytail, put on sunscreen, lip balm and a flick of mascara. She'd finished off with a pair of black Chanel sunglasses, tiny denim shorts and gold flip-flops before Zoe had even decided which of her many new bikinis to wear.

'I'll meet you out there, babes,' Zoe told her, still in her white towelling robe when Charlie knocked on the door of her suite.

She quickly agreed, not wanting to waste another moment of her holiday.

Outside she had to stop herself from bursting into song. Everywhere was just so perfect: the elegant Colonial-style buildings, the gardens with their brightly coloured tropical flowers and palm trees, the irresistible flash of blue ocean she kept glimpsing. All the hotel staff she passed smiled warmly at her and said, 'Good afternoon, Miss Porter.'

How on earth did they remember all the guests' names? she wondered. Was there a list of names next to a photograph of each guest that they had to memorise?

'Call me Charlie,' she kept telling them, but they just smiled and she was pretty sure they wouldn't.

She was just walking past the stunning swimming pool, which even had a bar set at one side, so you could sip cocktails while you were in it, and a miniature waterfall, when her attention was captured by the tall, dark-haired man sprinting towards her. Check him out! she thought, admiring his broad shoulders, muscular physique and very handsome face. He was so focused on running that he failed to notice a waiter carrying a tray of drinks, and knocked straight into him. There was a resounding crash as the tray slipped out of the waiter's hands and the cocktail glasses shattered on the marble tiles. Charlie was shocked when the handsome man simply muttered 'Sorry' to the waiter, who was already apologising profusely, and carried on running towards her. Incensed by such bad manners, Charlie barred his way, hands on her hips.

He came to an abrupt halt, towering over her. He could have stepped out of a men's style magazine in his turquoise board shorts as blue as the swimming pool and white shirt, unbuttoned to show off his tanned skin and ripped abs. It was hard not to stare. Very hard.

'Excuse me, señorita.' He spoke in slightly accented English, and looked Spanish with his dark brown hair, strong chiselled features and high cheekbones. She was aware of his gaze burning into her. He might be male-model gorgeous but he seemed arrogant and that was not a quality to endear him to Charlie.

'Is that it?'

He looked puzzled. 'Sorry, I don't know what you're talking about?'

'You barely apologised after charging into that poor guy!'

He seemed slightly taken aback by the criticism. 'I'm sorry, I had an important call to take in my suite.'

'Of course you did,' she said sarcastically.

Charlie had once worked as a chambermaid and remembered only too well what it felt like being on the receiving end of such dismissive behaviour. There was plenty more she could say on that subject. But instead she took a deep breath. She was on holiday; she would let it go. And so, throwing him her most disdainful *You're not worth it!* look, she moved out of his way and went over to the waiter who was on his knees, picking up shards of glass with his hands. 'Here, let me help you,' she said, kneeling down next to him.

'Oh, no, Miss Porter, please, do not trouble yourself.'

'But you've cut your hand!' She turned round and gave handsome arrogant man a filthy look. He seemed to be in two minds about how to react, then walked over decisively and said to the waiter, 'I must apologise for bumping into you. I wasn't looking where I was going.'

'Oh, please, Señor Castillo, it was entirely my fault . . .'

Charlie was about to pipe up that of course it bloody wasn't when another waiter joined them, armed with a dustpan and brush, and set to work sweeping up the fragments of glass.

'I feel that we got off on the wrong foot. May I buy you a drink to show that there are no hard feelings?' handsome arrogant man asked Charlie. He held out his hand to help her up. She ignored the gesture and stood up unassisted, shaking her head. 'No, thanks. Just make sure you don't treat anyone else like that. Everyone deserves respect, whatever they do.' Oops – she sounded pompous! He had said sorry, she should have left it there. The never-ending supply of in-flight champagne from William and his lovely eyebrows had taken its toll on her.

There was another moment when he seemed to be taken aback but then he smiled broadly at her, giving her the full benefit of his brown-eyed gaze. Was he checking her out? Cheeky bastard! He wasn't her type, even if he was ridiculously handsome. And muttering something about meeting a friend at the beach, she turned on her flip-flopped heels and continued on her way. She could feel his eyes on her as she walked off, so added an extra swing to her hips for good measure.

Charlie took a moment to take in the glittering sapphire-blue ocean. A member of staff greeted her, asked her where she would like to sit and then proceeded to arrange a sun lounger, parasol and table just for her, adding that that if she wanted anything, anything at all, she should stick a flag into the sand and someone would come and take her order. Charlie thanked him. All she wanted to do right now was hit the water that looked so inviting. She slipped off her shorts and ran into the ocean. Diving under the clear blue water, she swam out to sea. The water was blissfully warm, crystal clear and as calm as a swimming pool. She lay on her back, floating. This was paradise. She felt as if all the stresses of her life were drifting away. She half wondered whether she would see handsome arrogant man again . . . maybe, maybe not.

She looked back to the beach where she saw that Zoe was finally putting in an appearance and looking fabulous in a bronze metallic bikini and bejewelled sandals, her hair looking as if she had just stepped out of the salon. Zoe was not a woman who ever did understated. Charlie waved at her and then swam back to shore.

For the next two hours the girls sunbathed, swam

and chatted until a spectacular orange-and-red sunset blazed across the sky.

'We should get ready for dinner,' Zoe commented.

'I can't move, I'm so relaxed,' Charlie protested from her lounger. 'Then again, I bet you need to spend the next three hours getting ready, so come on, let's make a move.'

Chapter 2

Charlie breezed into her suite. Her skin had that lovely tingly feeling from swimming in the ocean, and as she checked out her appearance in the mirror she noticed that she already had a glow about her from being in the sun. She turned on the shower and was about to step under the powerful jet of water when there was a knock at the door. She grabbed a fluffy white robe and slipped it on. It was bound to be Zoe. Instead, it was one of the hotel's clerks, holding a huge bouquet of flowers, almost bigger than he was. 'Sorry to disturb you, Miss Porter, but Señor Castillo asked us to deliver these to you. Where would you like them?'

For a second Charlie wondered who on earth they could mean, then she remembered. Señor Castillo was the handsome arrogant man.

'Oh, put them wherever you can, thank you . . .' she checked out his name-tag . . . 'Benson.'

He smiled and handed her an envelope on his way out.

Charlie ripped open the thick paper and pulled out a note: *Dear Ms Porter, I would like to apologise for the earlier incident and to invite you to have dinner with me tonight. Shall we say 8.30 at L'Acajou? Yours, Felipe Castillo.*

The cheek of the guy, assuming that (a) she would want to go out for dinner with him, and (b) she would drop everything to go out with him tonight! Señor Castillo was in for a surprise because she had no intention of joining him at L'Acajou. Or anywhere else. For all he knew she was here with her boyfriend. He must be used to women falling over themselves to be with him and his ripped abs. Well, not Charlie, however tempted she was. And, yes, she was prepared to admit that she was tempted . . . But he would have to try much harder than a bunch of flowers and a dinner invitation if he wanted to impress her.

She phoned up Reception and asked them to pass on a message, thanking him for the flowers and the invitation but declining as she had other plans for dinner. There were advantages to having other people to do whatever you asked them, she decided.

Then Charlie hit the shower. She knew that Zoe would still be ages getting ready, so she took her time as well. She blow-dried her long brunette hair so that it fell in glossy waves over her shoulders instead of being tied back as normal. She went for a smoky sultry-eyed look with bronze eye shadow that accentuated her green eyes and a sheer caramel lip-gloss that gave her the perfect pout. It was far too hot for her usual skinny jeans, so she went for a short flared white skirt and emerald green silk vest. Knowing that Zoe would have a go at her if she wore flip-flops, she put on a pair of tan sandals that made her long legs look even longer. A spritz of her favourite perfume, Chanel's Coco, and she was good to go.

Miraculously, when she knocked on Zoe's door her friend was actually ready, looking gorgeous in a white maxi-dress with brightly beaded straps.

'I've booked us a table at L'Acajou,' Zoe told her. 'But let's have cocktails first at the Monkey Bar. It's so chic – all old-school colonial. I always feel like such a lady there.'

Damn, that might be awkward if handsome arrogant man saw them. 'Does it have to be that restaurant?'

'It's fab. You'll love it, I promise.' Zoe noticed the frown on Charlie's face. 'What's the problem?'

'It's just that someone asked me out for dinner there tonight.' Charlie hadn't so far mentioned the incident with Señor Castillo. It was a matter of pride to her that she hadn't accepted his offer of a drink. That she could resist his charms perfectly well, even though she had thought of him more than once while she sunbathed on the beach. Now she quickly related her chance encounter with him.

'You should have said yes!' Zoe exclaimed. 'That would be such a result, copping off with someone in the first hour of arriving on holiday! Was he fit?'

Charlie thought of those dark brown eyes, so dark they were almost black, the powerful, muscular body . . .

She shrugged. 'He was okay, if you like that sort of thing. But the point is, I'm not here to have dinner or anything else with some random bloke, least of all a random arrogant bloke.' She linked arms with Zoe. 'I'm here with you. Now come on, it must be cocktail hour.'

The Monkey Bar was every bit as chic as Zoe had said, and the hotel had certainly gone all out for the monkey theme – there were monkey artefacts and sculptures everywhere and even a monkey-themed mural. Charlie nearly got the giggles when Zoe whispered that one of the elderly male guests had a scrunched-up face exactly like the monkey lamp base on their table.

'I don't think they do Sex On The Beach or Screaming Orgasm or Slippery Nipple,' Charlie commented, flicking through the leather-bound cocktail menu.

Zoe rolled her eyes. 'You can take the girl out of Manchester but you can't take Manchester out of the girl.'

'Don't come all posh on me!' Charlie shot back. 'I know you're dying for a Cock-sucking Cowboy.'

The waiter appeared at that point and both women quickly ordered Bellinis.

'I wonder if your guy is going to be here,' Zoe commented as they arrived at L'Acajou. The restaurant was open-air on the beachfront with stunning views of the ocean and star-lit sky. Out in the Caribbean, with no light pollution to obscure them, the stars were phenomenally bright. The maitre d' led them to a table overlooking the sea, shimmering purple and silver in the moonlight. The gentle lulling sound of the waves could still be heard over the classical piano music.

Charlie shrugged. 'He's not my guy, and I'm not bothered.'

'God, I am! I really want to see what he looks like! As I said before, it's about time you saw some action.'

Charlie ignored the comment and considered the menu. 'I am never going to be able to eat at Nando's again,' she joked. Everything looked absolutely delicious. 'I'm going to have scallops, then yellow-tail snapper.'

'I'm going to have the salmon, then the lobster tortellini, and I know I won't be able to resist the dark chocolate soufflé. It's so yum!' Zoe groaned. 'I'll have to hit the gym big time tomorrow. I don't think Nathan will appreciate me coming back a porker.'

'I'll come with you, I've got to stay in shape.'

That earned an eye roll from Zoe. 'You're in amazing shape. You can afford to ease off for a week.'

Charlie shook her head. 'Don't be mad! There are lots of thinner, younger girls out there, gagging for my job.' Which was precisely why she ran four miles every day on the treadmill, and worked out with a personal trainer once a week.

The waiter approached carrying a silver ice bucket complete with a bottle of Cristal.

'Oh, there must be a mistake, we didn't order this,' Zoe commented.

'It is with the compliments of Señor Castillo. He is sitting over there.' The waiter gestured to a table across the room. Charlie swivelled round and saw Felipe sitting with another man. He caught her eye and raised his glass. Bollocks, she couldn't get away from him!

'Is that him?' Zoe exclaimed, craning her neck to

have a good look. 'He's totally lush. What were you thinking of, saying no to dinner? He looks like that model, David Gandy.'

'He's not all that,' Charlie lied. 'I'd better go over and say thank you. In fact, I'll return the champagne while I'm at it.' She reached for the bottle, but Zoe stopped her.

'Don't be so ungrateful! Just smile sweetly and thank him. And fix up a date. In fact, why don't you ask them both to join us for dinner? Go on, it'll be fun.'

Charlie ignored the last comment and walked over to Felipe's table. For some reason she felt a flutter of butterflies in her stomach as she became aware of his dark brown eyes fixed on her. It must be hunger pangs, she tried to tell herself, but she knew it was something altogether different . . .

Both men stood up politely when she reached their table. So Felipe had good manners apart from with the staff. Charlie flicked back her hair, and tried to act casual. 'Thanks for the champagne and the flowers, but you really didn't have to. There was no need.' Usually a very direct, confident person, she was finding it incredibly hard to look him in the face.

'There was every need. I would hate you to think that I don't treat people with respect.'

Charlie could feel herself blushing as she remembered her outburst. Maybe she had been a little over the top. She managed to meet his gaze and saw that he was smiling.

'Oh, Charlie's forgiven you! She's a very forgiving sort of person.' Zoe had joined them. 'Anyway, we wondered if you wanted to have dinner with us? I'm Zoe, by the way.'

Charlie shot her friend a WTF look, which Zoe ignored.

'And I'm Luis,' Felipe's friend said, kissing Zoe on each cheek, and then greeting Charlie in the same way. Luis had wild black curly hair that tumbled across his forehead, and a friendly open face.

'And you all know who I am, the man who was rude but who very much wants to make amends,' Felipe said, kissing Zoe then Charlie. There it was, that flutter again as his lips touched her skin and she caught the aroma of a deliciously musky aftershave. 'And, yes, we would like very much to join you for dinner. Maybe it would be best if you came to our table as it is already set for four.'

He raised his hand and signalled for the waiter, catching Charlie's eye as he did so. He grinned. 'Don't worry, Charlie, I promise to be very polite.'

While Felipe spoke to the waiter, Charlie and Zoe returned to their table to collect their bags. 'What did you do that for?' Charlie demanded. 'I told you I didn't want to have dinner with him.'

'Oh, come on, live a little. You're on holiday!' Zoe gave a cheeky grin. 'And I reckon Felipe likes you. I saw the way he was checking you out. Got to love a hot Latin!'

Charlie admitted defeat, she was never going to get Zoe to change her mind, and actually, if she was honest, she was secretly looking forward to dinner with Señor Castillo.

'Okay, but please don't tell them I'm a TV presenter. I don't want to talk about work. If it comes up, I'll say that I work in your boutique.' In the past Charlie had found that if she talked about her career it tended to dominate the conversation, and right now she wanted time out from that.

'As if I would ever let you near any of my customers with *your* dress sense,' Zoe teased. But she agreed.

Felipe Castillo de Rivas, internationally renowned event rider, middle child of one of the oldest and most aristocratic families in Spain, watched with admiration as Charlie gathered her things. Now this was a woman he would like to get to know better. He hadn't been annoyed by her earlier outburst; on the contrary, she had aroused his interest. He had been rather bored on this holiday so far as he wasn't used to relaxing. Usually every minute of every single day was taken up with riding, but two months ago he had sustained a serious shoulder injury when his horse fell during a cross-country course and the doctors had advised rest, sun and physiotherapy – especially if he wanted to be fit enough to compete in the London Olympics. A brief affair with a beautiful, fiery woman could really liven things up for him . . .

He saw Luis shaking his head. 'How is it that you always, *always* get your own way?'

Felipe shrugged, and gave a wicked grin. 'It must be down to my charisma. But, Luis, just one thing. I don't want to tell Charlie what I do. This is supposed to be a holiday, I don't want to get sucked into a conversation about riding.'

'Or about coming from a super-rich family? How sweet, you want her to like you for yourself,' Luis teased.

'That too. If it comes up, just say that I've got a web-design company with you.'

Luis chuckled. 'That the best you can come up with? You can barely use your iPhone and you have to call me every time there's a problem with your broadband connection!' Luis was Felipe's oldest and best friend. They had known each other since the age of six, and Felipe was well used to Luis teasing him. And as Luis did run a web-design company, Felipe supposed he could fill in for him if there were any awkward questions.

'Just don't let her see you without your shirt on, because you hardly look like someone who spends hours at their computer.' Luis looked ruefully at his own slight paunch, while Felipe couldn't resist slapping his solid abs and grinning. 'I guarantee it won't be long before the lovely Charlie sees much more of me than just my chest.'

Luis rolled his eyes.

'Anyway,' Felipe continued, 'I'm sure we'll have plenty of other things to talk about. I think Charlie is someone with strong opinions on things. I'm very much looking forward to dinner.' He looked up as Charlie and Zoe returned. Zoe was an exceptionally pretty woman, but Charlie was the one his eyes were drawn to. She was beautiful, a one-off, and incredibly sexy. She was very slim and yet had delicious curves and particularly fine breasts from what he could see . . . just the kind of figure he worshipped in a woman.

This week was supposed to be one of complete rest and relaxation. When he returned to Spain, training for the Olympics would kick off in earnest, as well as the start of the eventing season in February. Surely getting to know Charlie better counted as the very best kind of relaxation?

He wondered when would be the best moment to ask her to come back to his penthouse suite after dinner. *When* rather than *if*, because although Charlie seemed a little tense, he imagined her unwinding when they were alone together, imagined slipping off her clothes, showering kisses on her skin, sliding his hands between those long legs . . .

Charlie found herself sitting opposite Felipe at dinner. She was pretty certain that Zoe had engineered it.

'So, is Charlie short for Charlotte?' he asked her, crumbling his bread into pieces and never once taking his eyes off her.

People always assumed this. 'Nope, it's not short for anything. I'm a twin and my mum was told she was having two boys so she and my dad had already decided on Kris and Charlie for names. And when I was born they didn't want to change that.'

Felipe treated her to his killer smile. 'It suits you. I can't imagine you as a Charlotte, you've got too much attitude.'

The compliment pleased Charlie, not that she was going to let on. 'And is Felipe a Spanish name?'

He bowed his head. 'Yes, I'm Spanish and so is Luis.'

'Are you a couple?' Zoe asked cheekily.

Luis gave a deep laugh. 'He keeps asking me but I am very happily married to my beautiful wife who is up to her eyes organising her sister's wedding, which is why we are here together.'

'So you're single?' Zoe addressed Felipe. Charlie wondered why her friend had never considered a career in journalism with such an ability to ask direct questions.

'Yes. And in case you were wondering, I am not gay.'

'Didn't think so.' Zoe grinned. 'I've got pretty good gaydar. I have a boyfriend myself but Charlie's single. She's not gay either.' Charlie nearly choked on her scallops. And she couldn't bring herself to look at Felipe. She would bloody kill Zoe later!

In fact, she felt unusually tongue-tied in front of the handsome man sitting opposite her. She was acutely aware of his gaze on her and couldn't resist stealing glances at him from time to time when he thought he wasn't looking. But then his eyes would lock with hers and she would find herself quickly looking away. Since TFB she felt as if she had lost her flirting mojo. However, meeting Felipe made her feel as if it might be coming back . . .

It was down to Luis and Zoe to keep the conversation flowing over dinner, and when the subject of work came up Zoe talked about her boutique and mentioned that Charlie worked with her – her friend was going to owe her for that one. Charlie made sure she quickly changed the subject, as she didn't want to elaborate on the lie.

She found out that Felipe and Luis owned their own web-design company, which surprised her as Felipe definitely didn't have the look of someone with an office job. They both spoke exceptionally good English and Charlie felt slightly guilty that she only knew how to ask for '*dos cervezas por favor*' in Spanish. Still, two beers were better than nothing . . .

'So what do you most want to do while you are here?' Felipe asked her.

She shrugged her slim shoulders. 'Swim, maybe have some treatments, take a boat out. Just relax and enjoy myself.'

Felipe smiled. 'I'd be very happy to help you enjoy yourself.'

Charlie suppressed a smile. He sounded way too smooth, as if delivering a line he had used many times in the past. No doubt he was expecting her to flutter her eyelashes at him and reply in her best flirtatious voice, *Why, thank you. Shall we go to your suite now?* In his dreams!

He seemed to realise his mistake and quickly added, 'For instance, I could take you out on a boat or we could go riding.'

'A boat trip maybe. Riding definitely not.'

She instantly felt herself tense up at the mention of riding. Any flirtatious thoughts went straight out of her head as she struggled to control the fear that was already taking over.

'You don't like horses? You can't ride?' Felipe continued. 'I can teach you, and I guarantee you will love it.'

Charlie shook her head. She could already sense the onset of a panic attack. Her chest felt tight, she couldn't breathe properly, couldn't get enough oxygen into her lungs. She picked up her glass of water, but her hand was shaking so much she had to put it back down.

Felipe was looking at her in concern. 'Charlie, what is it?'

Zoe and Luis had stopped talking and thankfully Zoe spoke up now. 'Charlie was a brilliant rider but she had a bad fall last year. She doesn't ride any more.'

'Ah, but you should have got straight back on again!' Felipe declared. 'I ride myself and have lost count of the number of times I have fallen off. But I always get back on, I never let it defeat me.'

He had no idea . . . Charlie couldn't even reply. Nightmare images were flooding her mind; her beloved Ace screaming in agony as she tried to reach him. Suddenly it was too much for her. She stood up and pushed her chair violently from the table, knocking it over in her haste to get away. Before anyone could stop her, she sprinted out of the restaurant.

Felipe made to follow her, appalled that he had upset this beautiful girl, but Zoe stopped him. 'It's best if you leave her. I'm not sure that she'll want to see you.'

'I had no idea that mentioning riding would cause such pain to her. Please could you tell me what happened?'

Zoe sighed, reluctant to re-tell the story of how she had nearly lost her best friend.

'*Please,*' Felipe urged her.

'Just over a year ago Charlie was out riding. She was

on a country lane when a car went by too fast and spooked her horse. He bolted and careered straight into an oncoming 4x4. It was a miracle that Charlie survived. The people in the car were okay but her horse died. It wasn't her fault, but she's never forgiven herself and has never ridden since. She can't even talk about riding or horses. She still has panic attacks and flash-backs about what happened.'

Felipe ran his hands through his hair. How could he have been so insensitive! He had been so caught up with wanting to impress Charlie that he'd said the one thing guaranteed to push her away. He was an idiot. He looked back at Zoe. 'When you see her, please tell her how very sorry I am. I never intended to upset her.'

'Sure. In fact, I'm going to see how she is right now. I don't like to leave her on her own.'

Felipe quickly scribbled down his mobile number on a piece of paper and held it out to Zoe. 'Would you text me to let me know how she is?'

'Of course, and I'm sorry about dinner,' she replied. She smiled ruefully. 'I guess it's not quite the night you had in mind.'

'It's no problem,' Luis said quickly. 'In fact, why don't we arrange to have the meal sent to your room?'

Zoe wasn't at all sure that Charlie would have any appetite, but it was a kind offer so she accepted, then hurried back to check on her friend.

Luis looked at Felipe. 'Of all the women here, you choose one with a phobia about riding. How ironic is that, my friend?' He'd intended to raise a smile from Felipe, but his friend seemed to be lost in thought.

'I wonder if she can possibly forgive me, and if she will ever want to see me again,' Felipe replied. He couldn't believe that he felt like this after such a brief time. All he knew was that he had to see Charlie.

Chapter 3

Charlie was curled up on her bed. Even though it was a humid night she was shivering uncontrollably and in the grip of a major panic attack as she relived the terrible events of the accident in her head. Ace bolting, her own desperate struggle to control him, the terrifying impact with the 4x4 . . .

She wrapped her arms around herself now as sobs wracked her body. To see her beloved Ace dying in agony had been indescribably painful, the single worst experience of her life. There was an urgent knock at the door. 'Charlie, it's me, Zoe, can I come in?'

Charlie was too short of breath to answer, but she managed to drag herself over to the door and open it. As soon as Zoe saw the state of her friend she raced over to Charlie's handbag and pulled out a paper bag – Charlie always carried one with her, breathing into it was the one sure cure for a panic attack. Zoe ran back to her friend and handed it to her. She sat down next to her on the bed, rubbing her back. 'You're

going to be okay, Charlie. Breathe in and out slowly
. . . remember what the doctor taught you. I'll do it
with you.'

It took a good few minutes for Charlie to regulate
her breathing. 'Okay now?' Zoe asked, as she finally
took the bag away from her face.

She nodded. 'I'm so sorry. I bet you're wishing you'd
brought Amber away instead of me.' Amber was Zoe's
sister.

'Don't be mad! She's even more high-maintenance
than me! She'd still be getting ready for dinner now.'

Charlie managed a small smile. She felt completely
wiped out. She got up to wash her face, and nearly
collapsed back on the bed as her legs felt so wobbly.
When she reached the bathroom mirror she saw that
crying had smudged her mascara and her eyes were
blood-shot. She splashed water on to her face, then
called out, 'Wonder what Felipe would think of me
now?'

Her friend came into the bathroom. 'He told me to
tell you how sorry he was, and I think it was genuine.'

'Hah! He was probably thinking that he'd blown any
chance of a shag.' Charlie sniffed. 'Not that I was going
to anyway. He's far too full of himself. He's probably
lined up the next girl as we speak. Promising them a
ride on his big boat.'

Zoe shook her head. 'Don't be so cynical! I'm going
to text him that you're okay now.'

'Really? You've got his number?'

'Yes, why? Do you want it?' Zoe teased her.

'Nope.'

Whatever Zoe said, Charlie was pretty sure that Felipe would have moved on to someone else. She felt a flash of regret at the prospect. In spite of him bringing up such a painful subject, he intrigued her.

Another knock at the door interrupted her thoughts. Surely that wasn't Felipe? There was no way she was up to seeing him in this state.

'Relax, it's just the waiter with our dinner,' Zoe said, going to answer the door.

'I don't think I can face anything rich right now,' Charlie replied, the thought of fish making her feel queasy.

'D'you want me to order you a cheese and tomato toasted sandwich?'

Charlie nodded gratefully. Her friend knew her so well, suggesting her favourite comfort food. 'Oh, and a hot chocolate.'

'In this heat! You must be the only woman in Barbados who wants to drink that,' Zoe commented. She hesitated and added, 'Don't you think you should see your GP about having therapy when we get home? I mean, Felipe only mentioned riding and you had a panic attack.'

Charlie shook her head. 'No way, it won't help.' She'd had one disastrous session with a therapist a few weeks after the accident, but instead of helping, it had only made things worse. The therapist had suggested that Ace dying symbolised something from her childhood and had implied that she might have been abused then – a ludicrous idea, as if being involved in a terrifying accident wasn't significant enough in itself! Charlie had found the so-called therapy session so traumatic that now she was resistant to the whole idea of therapy. She insisted to her family and close friends that she would get better by herself.

'And I haven't had a panic attack in a while.' She didn't say anything about the recurrent nightmares she had about the accident. She hadn't told anyone about those.

Zoe looked as if she had more to say, but Charlie added, 'Please, Zoe, let's forget this happened.'

Felipe paced the polished wooden floor of his penthouse suite, the phone clamped to his ear, as he listened to his mother Vittoria. As usual it was a fairly one-sided conversation. He had barely had a chance to ask his mother how she was before she launched into a series of complaints, starting with asking him why he hadn't been home for ages? His reply that it was only four weeks fell on deaf ears.

And then, why hadn't he taken Paloma away with him?

'Because she's my ex-girlfriend!' Felipe protested. 'It's over between us. Remember?'

'She is the best thing that ever happened to you. Are you crazy!'

Felipe gritted his teeth. This was precisely why he hadn't been home for a month. His mother had adored Paloma and been devastated when Felipe broke up with her. She had already married him off in her own head, and was welcoming the thought of grandchildren. Felipe's elder brother was gay, so Vittoria had few expectations that he would provide her with a grandchild, and even if he did it wouldn't be from any conventional marriage. Their spoilt younger sister, Gisela, was too busy living the life of a jet-setter and had declared she had no intention of having children until she was in her late-thirties. She was only twenty-five.

Felipe held the phone away from his ear as Vittoria continued to nag. He wandered out to the balcony, from where he could look out over beautifully maintained gardens and beyond to the sea. He wondered what Charlie was doing now, and if there was anything he could do to make amends for having upset her so much.

'And I hope you are behaving yourself on this holiday . . .' His mother's acid tone dragged him back to the present. 'Your father and I don't want to read any more stories about your antics. You're thirty now, Felipe, not a teenager. It is most unbecoming and reflects so badly on the family name.'

He gave a rueful smile; his mother was referring to a recent story in which a certain soap-star actress he'd had a brief affair with, post-Paloma, had decided to tell all to the press . . . It had been one more in a very long line of kiss-and-tells. Felipe had come to loathe journalists with a vengeance. It was true that he had been wild in his early-twenties but in the last two years he had become more settled, give or take the odd fling. But the press were a little too attached to his playboy label and wouldn't let him forget his colourful past, relishing every opportunity to bring it up. 'I'm behaving myself perfectly. In fact, I am about to play cards with Luis. Just the two of us and a bottle of wine. Can you picture a more innocent scene?'

Vittoria let out a sigh of exasperation. 'Let's hope you spend all your evenings like that while you're away.'

Felipe thought of the beautiful Charlie and sincerely hoped not.

Charlie woke up the following morning determined to put the panic attack behind her. It helped that Zoe had booked them in at the luxurious spa for a morning of pampering treatments – a pedicure that left her with baby-soft feet, and an Indian head massage that seemed to ease away the painful memories. While Zoe was having further treatments Charlie wandered down to the beach. She couldn't get enough of the breathtaking view of the ocean before her. She loved living in London and feeling part of such a vibrant and exciting city, but she also loved the feeling of space that being by the sea gave her.

She half wondered if she might see Felipe, but most likely he was on a yacht, giving some other girl the benefit of his intense brown eyes. Charlie didn't like the flash of jealousy such an image aroused in her. *Stop thinking about him!* she ordered herself, not wanting to waste her precious holiday pining after a man she barely knew. Instead she swam, sunbathed, then ordered a Caeser salad and tropical fruit smoothie for lunch, savouring every delicious mouthful and sip. Back at work she would be bolting down a sandwich at her desk washed down with a Diet Coke as she never had time for proper lunch breaks.

The hotel had laid on a boat to take people out snorkelling and on the spur of the moment Charlie decided to go on the trip. As she walked along the wooden jetty to the gleaming white speedboat, she saw Luis was already sitting in it, cutting a colourful figure in pink board shorts with a floral pattern and a pink-and-white-striped polo shirt. Her stomach flipped in anticipation. Did that mean Felipe was also going to be here? Suddenly Charlie wished she'd made more of an effort with her appearance. She was wearing her white bikini, with faded denim shorts, a black vest, and the barest minimum of make-up.

Luis smiled warmly at her as she stepped aboard.

'How nice to see you, Charlie. Are you feeling okay now?' He held out his hand to steady her.

'I'm fine, thanks, Luis. I'm sorry about running out like that last night.' She sat down next to him.

'And so is Felipe, he never meant to upset you.' Luis paused. 'He'll also be very sorry that he turned down my suggestion of snorkelling.'

'Oh, and why's that?' Charlie could guess but she wanted to hear Luis say it.

'He is very taken with you, of course! You have captivated him with your bewitching green eyes.' Luis's formal English made Charlie smile.

'You mean he's after a holiday shag,' she whispered cheekily.

Luis put his hand over his heart. 'Charlie, where is your sense of romance? Felipe really likes you.'

'And I'm sure he really liked the girl he met up with last night after Zoe and I left.' She couldn't help herself;

she wanted to know, even if the truth would sting a little. No girl wanted to be forgotten that quickly.

Luis tutted. 'What a horribly low opinion of men you have, young lady. Felipe played cards with me – which reminds me that he lost and owes me money.' He beamed at Charlie. 'And he talked about you non-stop, which is undoubtedly why I won.' He glanced down at his outfit. 'By the way, is this combination a bit too much? Felipe told me I looked like a prawn.'

Charlie tried not to smile, as Luis probably had OD-ed on the pink. 'I think you look very stylish. A little on the pink side, but why not? You're on holiday.'

'I look like a prawn, don't I?' he said ruefully.

'I like prawns,' Charlie replied, giving him an affectionate pat on the shoulder. She wasn't usually so open with people she didn't know, but Luis was so easygoing and friendly that she felt completely relaxed with him.

And then the speedboat's engine roared into action and the boat shot out to sea, cutting through the clear water and leaving a gentle swell in its wake. 'I'll have to bring my wife here,' Luis commented as they looked back at the white sand beaches and the lush green vegetation beyond. 'She would love it.'

'She doesn't mind that you came away with Felipe?'

'Not at all, she needs to focus on the wedding plans – her sister is very demanding, and she knew that I would only get in the way. Besides, Felipe needed a break from . . .' Luis hesitated slightly '. . . work.'

'It's funny,' mused Charlie, thinking of Felipe's exceptionally fit, athletic body, 'he doesn't have the look of a web designer.'

'No? Well, he works out a lot. Quite obsessively actually.' Luis patted his own slight paunch. 'As you can see, I could do better. In fact, I promised Mariana I would go to the gym while I was here. I haven't been yet. How about you?'

'Yep, I do the gym thing. Have to because of work. Do you know how much weight the . . .' Shit! She'd been about to say 'the camera puts on'. 'I mean, working in a boutique, you get to see yourself in the mirror all day and so if you have a fat day there's no getting away from it.' She was starting to regret ever having coming out with her lie.

The comment raised a smile from Luis. 'Charlie, you have no reason to be insecure. You must know that you are a beautiful woman. A little too slim for my liking, but perfect for Felipe.'

'Who says I want to be perfect for him?' she bantered back, not wanting to give away how much the compliment had pleased her.

'And you seem just as strong-willed as him too. I think you are very well matched. How about having a drink with us tonight, to show that there are no hard feelings about what happened?'

'I'll think about it,' Charlie replied. 'But I'm not promising anything.'

It was only when they were returning after a blissful couple of hours spent snorkelling amongst tropical fish of every colour that Luis brought the subject up again. 'So have you decided about the drink?'

It was just one drink and she did want to see Felipe again . . .

'Okay,' Charlie replied. Then she added impulsively, 'I'm going to swim to shore, will you take my things?'

She stripped down to her bikini and dived gracefully off the side of the boat. As she stepped out of the waves, water cascading from her body, she heard a loud wolf whistle, and someone shouted, 'All right, darling! You look like one of them Bond girls in that white bikini!'

It was Zoe, taking the piss as usual. Charlie flipped her the middle finger and only then noticed Felipe lying beside her friend, staring intently at her.

Instantly she felt self-conscious. She tried to smooth her hair back. It was stiff with salt. God knows what she looked like after swimming in the sea for the last two hours! She was bound to have red marks on her cheekbones from wearing the snorkel mask. And Felipe looked male-model beautiful in a pair of white shorts, accentuating his darkly tanned olive skin. He really must work out all the time – his body looked as if it had been sculpted, it was so perfectly muscled and so perfectly in proportion. Her gaze lingered on his strong forearms, tightly defined biceps, taut six-pack, the line of dark hairs running from his navel into his shorts. Lucky, *lucky* Zoe being treated to such a vision for the afternoon.

As soon as she reached the lounger Felipe sprang up and greeted her with a kiss. 'I know Zoe has already apologised for me, but let me say it in person. I am so very sorry for upsetting you last night. It was the very last thing I wanted to do.'

'Thank you, but you could hardly have known about

what happened to me,' Charlie replied, suddenly feeling a little shy.

'How about we have a drink now? We could go to the beach bar.'

Charlie looked across at Zoe and Luis. 'Are you going to join us?'

'Nope. I'm heading back to the room to Skype Nathan,' Zoe replied, getting up from the lounger and slipping on her flip-flops.

'And that reminds me, I need to make an urgent work call, I'll come with you,' Luis added. He handed Charlie her bag and then he and Zoe practically jogged off the beach in their eagerness to leave Charlie and Felipe alone. Charlie gave a rueful smile at their complete lack of subtlety.

'Can I meet you at the bar?' she asked Felipe. 'I need to dry off and get dressed.'

She waited until he had put on a tee-shirt and walked away before she quickly dried off and slipped on a cute purple mini-dress over her bikini. She combed out her wet hair and tied it into a ponytail, then dabbed on some lip balm. That would have to do, though it didn't seem nearly enough given that she was having a drink with the most handsome man at the resort. Scrap that – one of the most handsome men she had ever met!

'I suppose you're used to this kind of luxury, Mr Five Star,' Charlie teased as she took a seat opposite him, her gaze taking in the swanky beach bar, the bottles of champagne lined up behind it, the ever-attentive bar staff . . . and coming to rest on him, as if daring him to deny it.

Felipe shrugged. 'I admit I've stayed in many luxurious hotels. But, believe it or not, I don't take any of it for granted.'

Charlie arched an eyebrow; she was somewhat doubtful of that, given his initial dismissive treatment of the waiter.

'The web business must be going very well if you can afford to stay in places like this. So you haven't been affected by the recession?' she commented.

For some reason Felipe looked slightly awkward as he replied, 'Not too badly. It's tough for everyone, of course, but we're doing okay. So have you ever been somewhere like this before?'

'I haven't had a holiday for three years.' Shit! What did she say that for? Now her story about working at Zoe's boutique was going to sound even more lame; she never should have lied in the first place.

'Zoe must be a slave driver if she never lets you take time off. Is this holiday to make up for it?'

Charlie hated lying, and knew that she was hopeless at it, so garbled the story about Nathan forgetting Zoe's birthday and footing the bill for the luxury trip, adding that she had been helping her friend get the boutique off the ground and therefore couldn't take any holiday until now. A line her mum was fond of quoting whenever she discovered any lies popped into her head then: 'O, what a tangled web we weave when we tell great fat

porky pies.' Charlie was going to get into a proper
tangle if she wasn't careful. She would say as little as
possible about the boutique.

'Generous boyfriend,' Felipe commented. 'But I
imagine Zoe is the kind of girl who always gets what
she wants when it comes to men. She has that look
about her.'

He'd got the measure of Zoe all right. 'Always,'
Charlie agreed.

'And your boyfriend didn't mind you coming away
without him?'

Charlie had the feeling that they were weighing each
other up, acting out a ritual dance of attraction. She
took a sip of her frozen strawberry Mojito before replying,
'As Zoe told you last night, I'm single.' The words
seemed to hang in the air between them.

Felipe smiled, showing off white, even teeth. 'Good,'
he said softly. 'I just wanted to make sure.' He paused.
'So am I. Just to be clear.'

And Charlie wanted to come out with a feisty reply
about how she was perfectly happy being single, thank
you very much, but found that she couldn't. Sitting
opposite Felipe she was aware only of the pressing
reasons why she wasn't happy being single, of how
attractive she found him, of how much she wanted
him. And suddenly she felt reckless. She could have
a holiday fling with him, couldn't she? She had
nothing to lose. She wondered what it would be like
to kiss him, to feel that powerful body . . . It was
surely the cocktail going straight to her head. And
then just as suddenly she thought back to last night,

and the panic attack, and felt some of her confidence desert her.

Felipe seemed to sense her change of mood. He reached out and put his hand over hers. She felt a flicker of desire at his touch.

'I know you must still be upset because of the accident. Six months ago I had to have one of my horses put down. I'd had him for twelve years. And, yes, I know you can't compare that with what happened to you, but it broke my heart all the same.'

Quite unexpectedly Charlie's eyes filled with tears. She never usually let her guard down like this, especially in front of people she hardly knew, but there was something about Felipe that invited her confidence and made her feel that she could open up.

He gently brushed away the tears. 'So, you see,' he said gently, 'I do understand.'

He gazed at her and Charlie found that she couldn't tear her eyes away from his. At that moment it seemed anything could happen.

'Will you have dinner with me tonight?' A beat. 'I could arrange for room service in my suite.'

Charlie hesitated, tempting as the offer was; it sounded as if Felipe had all the moves mapped out. Dinner, then they would inevitably go to bed. Then he would most likely make a move on the next girl at the resort who caught his eye.

'Actually, I'd rather eat out, and we must ask Luis and Zoe, too. I don't want to exclude them.'

Felipe frowned, and again she got the sense that this was a man who was used to getting his own way. 'Luis won't mind. I'm sure he and Zoe will find something to occupy themselves with. Maybe Zoe can give him some fashion advice, to stop him dressing like a prawn. He looked like a prawn, didn't he?'

'A little,' Charlie admitted. 'But it's dinner with the prawn and Zoe or I can't make it.'

Felipe looked set to argue, then seemed to think better of it. 'Very well, the four of us it is. I'll make a reservation at Bajan Blue. If you're sure that's what you want?'

Charlie stood up. 'It is. I'll see you and Luis later.'

Felipe also stood up and lightly kissed her on the mouth. His lips tasted deliciously of rum and salt from his margarita. Charlie tried not to think about how good they felt on hers and how that briefest of kisses had sparked a chain reaction of lust inside her . . .

'I'll look forward to it,' he murmured and, chancing his luck, kissed her again.

Charlie was the first to break away. The cocktail, the sun and Felipe had definitely gone to her head.

Chapter 4

'So how did you get on?' Zoe asked some time later when she'd nipped into Charlie's room for a chat. She sat cross-legged on the bed, eagerly waiting to hear the juicy details.

'Okay.' Charlie wasn't sure exactly how she felt. She was torn between thinking that she should have a holiday fling with Felipe and seize the moment . . . and his gorgeous body . . . and the feeling that if she did she would only end up getting hurt.

'That's all you've got to say!' Zoe exclaimed. 'Come on, you have to give me more than that, girlfriend! He is *so* good-looking, and he's got a bit of an edge to him. If I were you, I'd definitely be saying "*hola*" to him and not "*adios*".'

'Hmm, I guess. Anyway you'll be seeing him again later, so you can say "*hola*" to him then yourself.'

'Oh? I thought the two of you would be having a romantic dinner together . . . and the rest.' Zoe grinned.

'Nope, there's going to be the four of us – you, me, Luis and Felipe.'

'Great, I'll go and get ready. What are you going to wear?'

Charlie shrugged; she hadn't given it any thought. But Zoe had already shot off the bed and was flipping through the clothes in her wardrobe.

'No, no, no, no, no,' she commented after each garment she considered. 'You can borrow something of mine. Back in five.' She whisked out of the room, a woman on a fashion mission. Charlie touched up the red nail varnish on her toes (Chanel's Rouge Fatal – Zoe had given it her seal of approval) and wondered what Felipe was doing. Somehow she doubted that Luis was putting him under the same pressure as Zoe – not that Felipe would ever take advice from a man who dressed like a prawn . . .

Zoe returned holding up a silk mini-dress with a racer back, in block colours of black, coral and red. It was bold and stylish and suited Charlie down to the ground. 'Gotcha!' Zoe declared, holding it up against her friend.

'Isn't it a bit short?' Charlie protested. She'd been thinking more along the lines of her black maxi-dress.

'You've got the legs for it. One day you'll have cellulite, your knees will be wrinkled, you'll have varicose veins, your arse will be saggy, and you'll look back and think: "Why didn't I wear that mini-dress when I had the chance?"'

Zoe was a persuasive saleswoman, and the picture

she painted was so disturbing Charlie didn't resist any more.

After Zoe returned to her own suite, Charlie spent a very happy hour getting ready, taking a leisurely bath, spending longer over her make-up than usual, and all the while feeling a growing sense of excitement at the prospect of seeing Felipe. She took one last look in the mirror. The racer-back dress gave a glimpse of her shoulders and its short skirt flaunted her long brown legs. All dressed up with somewhere to go. Good enough for Mr Five Star?

She knocked on Zoe's door, fully expecting to be kept waiting for the next half-hour while her friend finished straightening her hair, curling her lashes, or doing any one of the many beautifying rituals she deemed it essential to perform before a night out. But Zoe was even further behind than usual as she opened the door in her white towelling robe, without a scrap of make-up on. It would be a miracle if they got to the restaurant before midnight. Charlie was about to tell Zoe to pull her finger out when her friend groaned and said, 'I'm not going to be able to make it, I've got terrible period pain.' She really did look awful.

'Oh, babes,' Charlie exclaimed, 'I won't go then. I'll stay with you and we'll watch a film.' She sounded sympathetic but actually she was thinking, *Bugger! I really want to see Felipe!*

'No, I've taken some strong painkillers and I'm going to crash.'

'Are you sure? Maybe I should stay in case you need anything.'

'For Godsake, it's period pain, not a life-threatening illness! Go to dinner.' Zoe hobbled over to the bed and lay down. 'Dress looks good . . . I knew you'd rock it. It's designer so I will kill you if you spill anything on it. Now get out of here!'

Charlie blew her friend a kiss as she left.

She took a deep breath before she walked into the beach-front restaurant. It had been a long time since she'd been out on a date. TFB had made it hard for her to trust men. There is nothing so crushing to the self-esteem as being cheated on, but meeting Felipe made Charlie feel that it was definitely time for her to move on. Immediately the attentive maitre d' led her to the table where Felipe was sitting alone. As Charlie walked over she was suddenly gripped with self-doubt. Was the dress too short? Would Felipe think it slutty? Did she *want* him to think it was slutty? And where was Luis?

'You look beautiful,' Felipe told her as he kissed her twice in greeting.

So did he, in a long-sleeved white linen shirt and black cotton jeans.

'Where's Luis?' asked Charlie as she took her seat, tugging down the dress as far as it would go.

'He has some urgent work to attend to. He sends his apologies.' Felipe paused. 'And where's Zoe?'

'She's not feeling very well.'

Felipe seemed to be trying not to smile and Charlie got the distinct impression that she had been set up. She bet Zoe had just pretended to be ill! She glared at him.

'What?' he asked. 'Is it so very bad that it is just you and me?' He poured her a glass of champagne.

'No,' Charlie conceded. 'It's not. It's just that I'm out of practice at all this.'

'This?'

'Going out for dinner with a man.' She hesitated. 'The whole flirting thing.' Shit! She could actually feel herself blushing!

Felipe raised his eyebrows. 'So you are flirting with me then? And there I was thinking we were just friends.'

'Don't tease me!'

At that Felipe reached for her hand and lightly kissed it. 'For you, anything. But tell me why are you out of practice? You must have men falling over themselves to be with you.'

Charlie sighed, reluctant to bring up the subject of TFB, but if she didn't her attitude would appear odd. 'My ex cheated on me. It was humiliating and hurtful.' She bit her lip. 'I thought I was in love with him. Apparently he didn't feel the same way. And since then . . . I haven't met anyone I even wanted to go out with.' *Until now*, she thought.

'Ah, Charlie, not all men are like that. And he was an idiot to do that to you.'

'Yeah, I know.' And she smiled at him.

Felipe took the smile as a sign that she wasn't going to run away from him – not just yet anyway. He could see such strength and resolve in her character, and yet he had also glimpsed a vulnerability that intrigued him. Paloma, his ex-girlfriend, had been supremely confident, breezing through life as if nothing affected her. Their relationship had been frustratingly one-dimensional, but with Charlie he could sense hidden depths. He longed to be alone with her, away from other people, but knew that he had to be patient and let her take things at her own pace.

The waiter came over for their order and Felipe realised that food was the last thing on his mind. He got the impression that Charlie felt the same as she skipped ordering a starter and went for a light choice of miso-roasted black cod. Usually Felipe would have had a ribeye steak from the grill but now he went for salmon.

'I noticed your tattoo on the beach this afternoon. Whose are the initials? Not your ex's, I hope?'

'No, thank God!' Charlie turned in her chair and showed off her left shoulder where there was a small tattoo. 'It's my twin brother's initials and mine. We both had them done for our eighteenth birthday. My mum went mad. She hates tattoos, thinks they're dead common and that we'll regret it. I haven't so far.'

Felipe felt a tug of desire. All he could think of was how much he wanted to kiss the skin that she had revealed, but he managed to say, 'You must be very close to him then.'

'I am but I don't see much of him as he's in Manchester and I'm in London.' She seemed reluctant to say any more, and Felipe didn't want to push it.

The waiter approached their table and re-filled their champagne flutes.

'So, have you upset any more waiters lately?' Charlie asked.

'I have been on my best behaviour and treated everyone with respect, whatever they do. Everyone deserves respect, Charlie, didn't you know that?' He repeated her words to him. She looked faintly embarrassed.

'Sorry, I guess I'm extra-sensitive. I worked as a chambermaid in a hotel when I was a student and was treated like shit by so many of the guests.'

'A chambermaid? What kind of uniform did you have? Let me guess – a short black dress? A frilly white apron? Stockings?' Felipe teased her.

Charlie pouted. 'That's exactly the kind of comment I had to put up with from all the pervert men!'

'But come on! I'm sure it cuts both ways. For instance, I bet you like a man in uniform? Say . . . a fireman?'

What woman didn't? 'Okay,' Charlie conceded, 'but I didn't like the way the men felt they could say anything to me, and it wasn't just about the uniform. They thought they were superior to me because of the job I was doing. But people shouldn't be defined by what they do.' She gave him a challenging stare and he was aware of the grit and determination within her.

'I completely agree.' He raised his glass, and clinked it against hers.

Their meal arrived and they continued their flirtatious banter as they both picked at their food – far more interested in each other than in dinner. She was feisty, opinionated and passionate; he liked that. Paloma only seemed to get fired up about Prada's latest collection. Charlie made a refreshing change.

When the waiter cleared away their half-empty plates

59

Felipe made a point of thanking him. Hell! He would have offered to clear the plates away himself and do the washing up for the entire restaurant if it helped win him Charlie. And just as he thought he was doing well on that score, he nearly blew it with his next suggestion. 'We could have dessert in my suite?'

Charlie shook her head. 'You never give up, do you?'

'No, you will find that I am very persistent. And that I nearly always get my own way.' But sensing he was in danger of not getting it this time, he added, 'How about a walk on the beach?'

He felt as if he'd won first prize in a race when Charlie agreed.

It was a beautiful night with a full moon casting a shimmer of silver across the ocean. The air was fragrant with the scent of jasmine, and a slight breeze caused the palm trees to sway slightly and their huge leaves to rustle gently. Charlie stumbled slightly in her heels as she walked down the stone steps and Felipe reached out and held her hand. His grip felt warm and strong. He didn't let go when they reached the beach and she realised that she didn't want him to.

The beach was deserted; the sun loungers had been stacked up and the parasols all folded away into ghostly white spikes. Charlie kicked off her sandals. The sand felt refreshingly cool under her feet as they walked along the shore away from the resort. 'It's so beautiful here,' she declared. She felt a wonderful sense of freedom and excitement at being alone with Felipe.

'Being here with you makes it perfect,' he replied.

And he moved towards her and kissed her. At the feel of his mouth, his beautiful mouth, on hers and the delicious probing of his tongue, Charlie felt tendrils of lust unfurl within her body. Now all she could think of was how much she wanted him. She kissed him back. She felt reckless . . . on fire.

'I have a dare for you, Charlie,' Felipe murmured. 'We should have a moonlight swim. It's like this whole beach is here just for us – what do you say?'

'I think we might need to go to the next beach,' she replied, noticing the two hotel staff patrolling the shore. They were on the look out for any would-be thieves attracted by the resort, but Charlie knew skinny dipping would be frowned upon.

'You're on.'

A scramble over some rocks and they discovered a deserted cove.

'Race you in,' she challenged.

'But I have more clothes than you to take off,' he protested. 'You should give me a head start.'

'Okay, shirt and shoes off and then we're even.'

She moved closer and unbuttoned his shirt, loving the feel of his warm skin, and then she couldn't resist further exploration and brushed her hand over his rock-hard abs. He was watching her all the time as if daring her to go further. She unzipped the dress and let it tumble on to the sand. Felipe didn't take his eyes off her as she unclipped her bra and threw it down.

'You are so going to lose!' she taunted, naked except for her lace briefs.

'Believe me, it will be worth it,' he replied, blatantly

checking out her body. She contemplated turning away from him and then thought, What the hell? and slipped off her underwear. She raced into the sea and dived in. The water felt like silk against her skin.

By the time she'd surfaced Felipe was in the water beside her. Damn, she'd missed out on the view. 'Loser!' she taunted, swimming away from him.

'Not so fast!' he called out, quickly gaining on her with an impressive front crawl. Reaching out for her arm, he pulled her to him. Charlie contemplated resisting, and then gave up and curled her arms around his neck and her legs around his waist as he stood up. She shivered with pleasure as she encountered his naked body, which was every bit as muscular, defined and hard as she had anticipated. Felipe kissed her on the mouth and then her breasts, the moonlight glistening on her naked skin. She felt incredibly powerful, sexy and turned on. Ready for anything.

But then she noticed a couple walking along the beach and wriggled out of Felipe's embrace. He was about to protest, then registered they were no longer alone.

'I think we should go somewhere a little more private, don't you?' he commented, mirroring her thoughts exactly.

'That's a very good idea, Mr Five Star,' Charlie replied as she quickly swam back to shore.

Checking that the couple weren't looking their way, she raced out of the water and slipped on the dress. She would most likely have to buy Zoe a new one as she wasn't sure the designer number could take the salt water. Then she couldn't resist watching Felipe bounding out after her. He made no attempt to cover his very prominent erection.

'I'm surprised there hasn't been an eclipse,' she teased. But secretly she was very, very impressed . . .

And she was even more impressed when they finally made it back to his penthouse suite. Without a trace of inhibition he pulled off his clothes and fell on to the bed with her. 'Now where were we?' he murmured, expertly unzipping her dress and sliding it off her body . . .

Charlie woke up exactly where she had fallen asleep, with Felipe's arms around her. Last night felt like a dream, a wonderful dream . . . except judging by the evidence of Felipe lying next to her, it had been real. She carefully slipped out of his embrace and nipped to the bathroom. As she might have predicted her hair had been transformed into wild curls but everything else seemed in pretty good shape – her eyes seemed to have an extra sparkle and her skin had a glow about it. She felt amazing! She had forgotten how good sex could be . . . good sex, that was. Actually, forget that, amazing, orgasmic, mind-blowing sex where she had lost count of how many times she had come . . .

She quickly showered and cleaned her teeth. Wrapped in a towel, she crept back into the bedroom, intending to slip back into bed, but Felipe was already up and sitting on the terrace, dressed only in a pair of white boxers and Ray-Ban Aviator sunglasses. He was outrageously handsome, even first thing in the morning. He waved at her. 'Charlie, I've ordered room service. I wasn't sure what you'd like so there'll be a selection of fruit, pancakes, eggs, juice.'

She padded over. 'You know, you would make a very lovely boyfriend.'

He put his arm around her and pulled her on to his lap. 'Is that a proposition?'

'Actually, I just want you for sex and breakfast, if that's okay?' she teased.

'Fine by me,' he deadpanned, then cheekily whipped the towel from her body and threw it out of her reach.

'I'm sure the resort has strict rules about this kind of thing,' Charlie told him, attempting to cover herself up with her arms.

'You're right,' Felipe murmured. 'I was going to make love to you in the sunshine, starting perhaps like this . . .' He gently moved Charlie's arm away and kissed and sucked at her already-hard nipples, causing ripples of desire to pulse through her body, which intensified when he slipped his hand between her legs and began caressing her with his fingers, causing her to sigh with sheer pleasure and forget about the possibility of anyone being able to see them.

But then he stopped. 'Let's go inside.' While Charlie lay on the bed, he put the Do Not Disturb sign outside the door before joining her. He brought her to another trembling orgasm with the delicious flicking of his tongue, and while she was still quivering with ecstasy he pushed inside her and fucked her with an intensity that had them both gasping for breath . . .

*

They finally had breakfast around midday.

'Really, every day should start like this,' Felipe told her as they once more sat outside on the terrace, this time dressed in their robes.

'Agreed.' Charlie grinned at him. And then she felt a pang of guilt. She was supposed to be on holiday with Zoe. She didn't want to abandon her friend just because of a man, even a man as gorgeous as Felipe.

'I should go,' she added. 'I need to catch up with Zoe.'

'There's no rush. I've told Luis and Zoe to meet us at the beach in an hour. We're taking a boat out.'

'Oh?' Charlie was surprised that Felipe had thought of this.

'I didn't think you would be the sort of girl to drop a friend, and even I would feel bad about leaving Luis to his own devices.'

Charlie was impressed by his thoughtfulness. TFB would have sulked in such a situation, expecting her to drop everything for him. Felipe was altogether more mature. She appreciated the difference.

Once she'd finished breakfast Charlie tracked Zoe down by the pool. Her friend was reclining on one of sunbeds beneath a blue parasol and looking the epitome of beach chic in yet another of her bikinis – this time a vivid purple number – and an over-sized pair of sunglasses, sipping a healthy-looking fruit smoothie.

'Good night?' Zoe enquired.

'It was all right, if you like that kind of thing.' Charlie tried to sound low-key, but couldn't stop an enormous grin from spreading across her face.

'And what kind of thing would that be?'

Charlie flopped down on the sunbed next to her friend. 'Hot sex, hot sex and more hot sex, with a hot man, who is gorgeous! And clever and sexy and gorgeous . . . did I already mention that?'

Zoe laughed; she didn't think she had ever heard Charlie speak like this about a man before. Nor had she seen her looking so relaxed. Since her accident it had been as if part of Charlie had shut down and she had no longer been her old carefree self.

'So what did you do last night?' Charlie went on.

'I spent a great evening with Luis, playing cards and watching the football. And checking out his wardrobe and telling him what to wear so he doesn't end up looking like a crustacean. His wife is *so* going to thank me.'

'I knew you were only pretending to be ill!'

'Yep, all part of my scheme to get you to go out with Felipe. Weren't you impressed by my acting skills? Oscar potential, I reckon.'

Charlie gave a rueful smile, partly at her friend's cunning plan and partly at the idea she had needed any encouragement to see Felipe. The only thing she was going to find hard was not seeing him.

'And I got the lowdown on Felipe,' Zoe continued. 'He broke up with his girlfriend four months ago, which I think seems like a decent length of time, so he's not on the rebound. And *he* ended it with her.' She glanced over at her friend who was gazing up at the sky.

'I think I really like him,' Charlie said dreamily. Then she looked at Zoe. 'I might have to buy you a new dress. We went skinny dipping and it got wet.'

'No problem, I don't think it suited me anyway. So come on, tell me, out of ten, how would you rate him?'

'Off the scale.'

'Oh, yeah, baby!' Zoe exclaimed, adding cheekily, 'Aren't you glad you had that Brazilian?'

'The Spaniard was a lot more fun,' Charlie replied, grinning.

It turned out to be an idyllic day. Felipe had hired a catamaran skippered by a local man called Captain Jack, who insisted he'd been called that long before the *Pirates of the Caribbean* movies existed and that he'd had the dreadlocks and gold tooth before Johnny Depp was even born. He also had the loudest laugh Charlie had ever heard, which he put to good use when he found out that Zoe and she were enjoying this holiday at her boyfriend's expense.

'I would never dare to forget my wife's birthday. She'd be likely to cut off my balls and wear them as earrings!' Captain Jack declared, causing Felipe and Luis to look a little uncomfortable at the image.

'Oh, no, I'd never do that,' Zoe said sweetly. 'I much prefer my diamonds. They're from Tiffany's.' Prompting another guffaw from Captain Jack.

They motored along the coast for an hour to an area popular with turtles. There they spent several hours snorkelling and swimming with the graceful amphibians who were well used to humans and seemed unconcerned by their presence, and were happy to allow the swimmers to observe them at close quarters.

Charlie had wondered if it might be awkward seeing

Felipe again after their passionate night and equally passionate morning. But she felt completely at ease with him as they chatted to their friends, swam together and sat next to each other on the boat, he with his arm around her. Charlie loved that he was so affectionate with her in public, kissing and hugging her. She felt treasured and desired. Felipe was a wonderful contrast to TFB who had only ever seemed to show any affection in the bedroom.

For a late lunch Captain Jack steered them to a tranquil bay and served up a delicious picnic of miniature crab cakes, shrimp salad, slices of watermelon, and mango and lime sorbet. Felipe made a point of thanking him for everything he did and helping out wherever he could, and Charlie smiled, wondering if he was only on his best behaviour in front of her.

'Your wife has a beautiful smile and beautiful green eyes. You're a lucky man, Señor Castillo,' Captain Jack commented as he topped up everyone's wine glasses with ice-cold white wine.

Felipe smiled. 'I agree entirely, but she's not my wife.'

Captain Jack froze. 'Well, I would change that pretty soon, my friend!' he exclaimed. 'You two are meant to be together, that is obvious. I can see that. Anyone can see that. And I am never wrong about these things. I can show you many, many photographs I have been sent over the years by couples who got married after I had predicted it.'

'Actually we only met two days ago,' Charlie put in, feeling slightly embarrassed by the way the conversation was going.

But Captain Jack was an unstoppable force. 'Pah! What is time when true love is at stake? I knew from the first moment I set eyes on my wife that she was the one for me. We got married within two months and we've been together for thirty-five years.'

Luis, realising that this might be awkward for Charlie and Felipe, took over. 'That is wonderful. I hope I can be as fortunate with my own wife Mariana.' And he insisted on Captain Jack showing him photographs of his wife and children.

'And you think I'm a matchmaker,' Zoe whispered when Captain Jack was in full flow about his youngest son going to university. 'Captain Jack ought to get his own website!'

But even as Charlie smiled at her friend's comment, she wondered if Captain Jack was on to something. It seemed crazy, but the fact was she had never felt like this about anyone before.

They arrived back at the resort beach just as the sun was setting with another brilliant display of colour, turning the sky to flame and the sea to golden silk. The perfect ending to a perfect day. As Captain Jack helped Charlie out of the boat, he said, 'You know, you should definitely come back here for your honeymoon. Send me a message when you do, I'm on Facebook, and you can come over for dinner and meet my wife. She runs a beach-front café along the coast and makes the tastiest fish curry on the island.'

Clearly he wasn't a man to give up on an idea.

Chapter 5

Five days and nights of total loved-up bliss followed. It couldn't have been a better start to a relationship. There were hours of lazing on the beach, swimming, talking and sunbathing, then they would escape to Felipe's penthouse suite to make love in the afternoon. They were passionate, sensual lovers, who felt they had found the key to their own secret paradise. Usually it took Charlie some time to feel relaxed with a lover . . . but with Felipe she felt a great sense of release, free from any inhibitions. They were a perfect match in every way.

They were in that 'can't keep their hands off each other' phase, when every moment in each other's company was precious and charged with significance, when every second apart made them long for each other. Fortunately their two friends understood, and while the lovers were locked away in their suite, Zoe and Luis would be off playing golf, for which they had discovered a mutual passion, having spa treatments or playing cards. Every evening the four of them would meet up for dinner. The more Charlie got to know Luis, the more she adored him. He was so charming and easygoing. He made a good foil to Felipe who was far more fiery. She still teased him about being arrogant. They went on another boat trip with Captain Jack, where he repeated his prediction that Charlie and Felipe were destined for each other.

Charlie had never experienced such an intense connection with someone before. She felt happier than she had ever been since the accident, almost back to the confident, optimistic girl she had once been. But in spite of this there were still some things she held back. She didn't tell Felipe about her brother being in prison and nor did she reveal that she had lied about working in Zoe's boutique, figuring that all this could wait until after the holiday. The subject of riding was not mentioned again by either of them. High on desire, she wanted to keep things light and happy and didn't want anything to spoil their time together.

On the penultimate day Charlie woke up and instantly felt a pang of sadness at the prospect of saying goodbye to Felipe. She had been naïve to think that she could simply have a holiday romance and then forget all about him. She was pretty sure she was already falling in love with him . . . not that she was going to let on to him. It must be the idyllic place and Captain Jack's over-the-top comments getting to her.

'You look sad,' Felipe said quietly, gently stroking her hair.

She had thought he was asleep.

'No, no, I'm fine,' Charlie replied, aware that she sounded falsely bright, speaking in the kind of voice you put on when you don't want people to know your true feelings.

'Well, you should be sad! *I'm* sad! Sad that we only have one more day together. Aren't you going to miss me at all?' He nimbly rolled on top of her and began kissing her neck.

'Some parts more than others,' Charlie teased, enjoying the feeling of his body against hers and wiggling her hips provocatively.

'You mean you don't want me for my mind? Just my body?' He ripped off the sheet and revealed her naked body. His lips grazed against her already-erect nipples as he kissed her breasts and then continued further down. By the time he had arrived between her legs, Charlie was incapable of thinking about anything . . .

After a leisurely breakfast Felipe suggested that they go to the beach. There they swam and sunbathed. They both felt blissed out after making love, dreamily content. Captain Jack was preparing to take another group out on a trip and, catching sight of Felipe and Charlie, gave them a big wave. He then tapped meaningfully at his ring finger.

The couple laughed, but Captain Jack's comments had given them both pause for thought. Felipe had never imagined he would get married, despite his ex-girlfriend's best efforts to try and get him to propose.

He had never seen the point of marriage and had always doubted he would ever meet someone he would want to marry. He was convinced that he would feel suffocated by the very idea. But maybe that was because he hadn't met the right person until now . . . Meeting Charlie had caused him to question those beliefs. He could see that there was something wonderful about loving someone so much you were prepared to make a life-long commitment. Not that he was going to say that to Charlie just yet, it would most likely make her run a mile!

Charlie, meanwhile, was wondering what Felipe thought of Captain Jack's prediction. Did he think it was something the captain came out with to any couple he met, all part of his larger-than-life skipper act? Or did he think there was more to it than that, as she did? She looked over at Felipe. His hands were folded behind his head, showing off his fine profile. She wanted to drink it all in, so she could remember this moment when she was apart from him. He caught her looking and said, 'I'm tied up with work for a couple of weeks when I get back, but I promise to come over to the UK as soon as I possibly can.'

'Sure, that would be great.' She sounded casual, when already she was thinking it would be torture not to see him every single day. It seemed crazy to admit this, after merely a week, but Felipe was wrapped round her heart. She couldn't imagine not being with him.

He reached out for her hand. 'Hey, I promise I'll come over. I really want to see you again, Charlie. I'm not like TFB.'

'I know,' she said quietly. 'It's just, I think I'm going to miss you.'

'You think!' Felipe exclaimed, sitting up. 'How can you lie there so cool, so offhand, so calm? I *know* I'm going to miss you.' And he ducked down and kissed her hard, leaving Charlie in no doubt of his sincerity.

'Let's go back to the room,' he murmured, 'I must have you again.'

Laughing, Charlie gathered up her things. But the smile was erased from her face as they ran off the beach and slap into an ex-footballer and close friend of TFB. There was, unfortunately, no way that Charlie could ignore him as Greg had seen her and, as usual, had a good old leer at her body.

'Charlie Porter, what a surprise! You're looking good, babe.' He kissed her and she received a blast of his aftershave; its full-on citrus scent was exactly like his in-your-face character. She had never liked him. He was a cocky jack-the-lad who was routinely unfaithful to his wife.

She managed to say hello and to introduce Felipe. But Greg was far more interested in talking to her. 'How's the TV gig going? I'm always watching you . . . I reckon you're really going places. You should have your own show, especially as you're a proper journalist. I've always thought you can hold your own against anyone. And your looks don't hurt either, do they?'

Charlie could hardly bring herself to look at Felipe. She had imagined breaking the news of her actual career to him gently, maybe when they were in bed together or over a bottle of wine. She hadn't factored in a wanker like Greg blowing her cover.

Felipe dropped her hand as if she was toxic. She looked at him. The happy-go-lucky grin had gone from his face. He looked brooding, silently furious, dark brows drawn together.

'Come and have a drink, they do wicked cocktails here, don't they?' Greg babbled on, oblivious to the tension between the couple.

'No, thanks, Greg. We've got plans.'

'Well, maybe see you later,' he replied. Charlie sincerely hoped not.

Felipe nodded curtly and marched off towards the hotel. Charlie had to practically jog to keep up with him. 'Please, Felipe, I can explain,' she told him.

But he refused to answer. It was only when they were in his suite that he slammed the door shut and glared at her, eyes blazing with fury. 'I take it you don't work in a boutique. So what the fuck do you do?'

'I'm a TV presenter, I work for a sports channel. I'm sorry I didn't tell you but I wanted to get away from the whole TV thing. In the past it's been an issue for the men I get involved with.' Charlie sighed. 'I just wanted some time out from all of that. But of course I was going to tell you.'

He gave a disbelieving laugh. 'How perfect for your career that you should meet me. I wonder when your story is going to come out about screwing me – in every sense of the word.'

Charlie had absolutely no idea what he was talking

about. She had expected him to be surprised when she told him what she actually did, but not this level of rage.

'What story?' she asked in bewilderment.

'The story that you are bound to be writing for the press, hoping to boost your own pathetic profile through me. Let me tell you, Charlie, that you are not the first one.' He ran his hands through his hair and muttered bitterly, 'I genuinely thought you were different, someone special. I never fucking learn, do I?'

Charlie was confused, but they could sort this out, couldn't they? 'Felipe, I don't know what you're talking about. I'm very sorry I lied to you, but it didn't seem like a big deal. And I was going to tell you.' She took a step towards him, but Felipe gave no sign that he took her apology seriously.

'I hate lies and I hate journalists,' he shot back. 'Now go, I don't ever want to see you again. You're not the person I thought you were.' His voice took on a cruel edge that she had never heard in it before. 'You were a good fuck, one of the best, but maybe you're just a talented actress. And maybe that's a polite way of calling you a whore. For a while you had me believing that you actually felt something for me, but I suppose you do this kind of thing all the time. Either way, I want you to go.'

For a second Charlie stood rooted to the spot in complete shock. Felipe couldn't possibly mean the terrible things he'd just said, could he? He couldn't be throwing away what they'd had as if she meant nothing to him, or worse than nothing – he'd actually called her a whore. She stared at him, willing him to realise that this was all a mistake, but there was no warmth or tenderness in his face. He looked hard and unyielding. And to underline his words, he walked over to the door and flung it open. This was really happening. Making a huge effort to hold herself together, Charlie walked out with her head held high. Felipe slammed the door shut behind her.

Fuck! He couldn't believe he'd walked right into her trap. She would have enough material for at least ten articles! He marched on to the terrace and lit a cigarette, inhaling deeply even though he was supposed to have given up. Then he stormed out of his suite and hammered on Luis's door.

His friend was stunned to hear about Charlie and wouldn't believe that she was capable of selling a story about their whirlwind romance.

'But she seems so genuine, such a warm and loving person,' he insisted, after Felipe had come out with his tirade against her. 'And I believe she genuinely has feelings for you.'

Felipe gave a bitter laugh. 'What I can't believe is how successfully she deceived me, pretending not to know who I was, playing hard to get, leading me on . . . when all the time she was going to rip me apart in the press.'

He paused, fighting to hide just how upset he was underneath all the bravado.

'Can you arrange flights for us this afternoon? I want to get as far away from this place and Charlie Porter as possible.'

'But, Felipe, you didn't tell her who you were and what you did!' Luis protested.

'I think she knows very well who I am and what I do,' he snapped back, unwilling to concede anything.

'Come on! I've never seen you so caught up in a relationship before. If you walk away now, you'll regret it, I'm sure.'

But Felipe was reeling from his sense of betrayal. Nothing his friend said would make any difference. 'Please book those flights, Luis. This paradise suddenly seems like hell.'

Charlie was too shocked to cry when she relayed what had happened to Zoe. Her friend was, for once, unable to put a positive spin on events and could only keep repeating that Felipe had got hold of the wrong end of the stick, that it had to be a mistake and Charlie must call him or see him to explain. That it could surely all be resolved.

'You wouldn't say that if you'd heard him,' Charlie replied, feeling as if all the happiness had drained out of her. 'He sounded as if he hated me.' She winced as she remembered Felipe calling her a whore; she couldn't bear to tell Zoe that. The stunning view of the bold blue sky and glittering ocean visible from the balcony seemed entirely the wrong setting to be experiencing such depths of despair.

'Of course he doesn't hate you! The guy was totally besotted with you. I'm going to call him right now and sort out this bollocks.' Zoe reached for the phone but Charlie stopped her.

'Please don't, Zoe, I don't think it will do any good, and I already feel humiliated enough.' Charlie wanted to leave this luxurious resort, go back to the UK, back to her own life where she felt in control. She wished she had never met Felipe bloody Castillo.

She longed to lock herself in her bedroom and cry her eyes out, but she owed it to Zoe to pull herself together and Charlie had always been adept at putting on a brave face. She forced herself to do it now. 'Let's go to the beach. We're leaving tomorrow and it's minus-one back home. We need to make the most of the sun.'

'Are you sure you wouldn't rather stay here?' Zoe asked, sounding surprised that Charlie was up to doing anything after the shock of Felipe dumping her so brutally.

'I'm not going to let that man ruin my holiday,' Charlie said defiantly. 'Just let me get my things and I'll come and knock for you in five minutes.'

It didn't make sense, Charlie thought when she returned to her room. Why would Felipe assume that she would sell a story on him? Who was going to be interested in the private life of a man who ran his own web-design company? It wasn't like he was Bill Gates! There had to be something that Felipe wasn't telling her. She switched on her laptop and Googled Felipe Castillo. There was no hit for someone with that name, but plenty for Felipe Castillo de Rivas.

She clicked on an official website and to her growing amazement saw a picture of Felipe, dressed in white breeches and a black jacket, mounted on a magnificent chestnut stallion. The site was written in Spanish and English and she read that he was an international event rider, likely to be picked for the Spanish Equestrian team for the Olympics. No wonder he had made that comment about riding.

Charlie had to close her eyes briefly and take a few deep breaths, trying to avoid the feeling of nausea that any reference to riding triggered in her. She clicked through the pictures of his amazing equestrian centre in Andalusia. Saw the beautiful horses he bred, the photographs of him jumping his way to victory in one event, performing dressage in another, and looking incredible on the chestnut stallion as horse and rider moved as one . . .

But why had he kept his sport a secret from her? Why did he think anyone would be interested in a story about a TV presenter in the UK having a romance with him? It was only when she clicked on some other sites that she gathered Felipe must be a major heart throb and celebrity in Spain as there were fan sites dedicated to him, and from what she could just about understand, not speaking a word of Spanish beyond *hola*, *adios*, *gracias* and *dos cervezas, por favor*, he seemed to be a member of an aristocratic family too. So maybe that was the reason for his rage with her; he didn't want Mummy and Daddy to find out he'd been getting his end away with a common English girl. Shock then amazement had now given way to anger at the fact that Felipe had been lying to her! No wonder he had looked so awkward when she'd asked him about his work. How dare he turn on *her* for being economical with the truth?

Charlie grabbed her bag and raced out of her room, determined to confront him. She slowed down when she reflected that he would doubtless say that she'd been pretending not to know who he was, then pressed on, determined to have it out with him. But when she reached the door to his suite it was ajar and two maids were hard at work inside stripping the bed.

'Can I help you, Miss Porter?' one of them asked, midway through pulling off a pillowcase.

'I was looking for Felipe Castillo de Rivas.'

'Oh, I'm sorry, miss, but he has checked out of the hotel. Is there anything else we can assist you with?'

Charlie shook her head, trying to fight back the tears that were threatening to spill at the realisation she was more than likely never going to see him again.

Charlie spent a very subdued afternoon with Zoe on the beach, trying her best to hold herself together. But it was hard. The last time she had been here it had been with Felipe, and they were making plans for his trip to the UK . . . Zoe insisted she should text Felipe and tell him that she really didn't know who he was, but Charlie refused. Why would he believe her? She couldn't deal with any further humiliation. Besides, he was the one who should be apologising to her.

'Listen,' she told Zoe, 'I've had fun. It was a holiday fling, the sex was great, and now I'm moving on.'

Zoe looked as if she had plenty to say on that score, but seeing the determined, hurt expression on Charlie's face, buttoned it. It didn't help when Captain Jack returned from one of his boat trips and, noticing them, walked over to say hello.

'Ah, my favourite ladies!' he declared cheerily. 'So has your man proposed yet? He'll have me to answer for if he doesn't do it very soon.' He beamed at Charlie and she thought for a horrible moment she might burst into tears. Somehow she managed not to.

'Actually, Captain Jack, he's gone back to Spain and I don't think we'll be seeing each other again. It was just a holiday romance.'

Instantly Captain Jack looked pained. 'I can't believe it. I'm never wrong about these things. Like I told you, all the other couples I predicted would get married, have got married.' He seemed set to want to find out all the details, but fortunately some other guests came over and wanted to book him for a trip and Zoe and Charlie were able to slip away to the beach bar.

'Make mine a strong one,' Charlie said gloomily, sitting down at one of the tables and feeling completely drained. But there was to be no escape, as a red-faced, sweating Greg strolled into the bar, 'Well, hello, girls! Let me buy you both a cocktail.' He fanned himself with his cowboy hat. 'I think I might have had too much sun.' That was an understatement – the man was scarlet!

'No, you're all right, thanks,' Zoe said, clearly as desperate as Charlie not to have to engage with him.

But he insisted and Charlie could still see Captain Jack on the beach. Faced with the prospect of ten minutes of Greg the wanker or Captain Jack the relationship counsellor, she felt in this instance it would have to be the wanker. And what a wanker he was! After he'd boasted about the yacht he was buying, he told Charlie how much Aaron, aka TFB, regretted cheating on her, and how he wasn't over her. 'Would you see him again, Charlie?' Greg asked hopefully, and, from Charlie's point of view, hopelessly. 'The boy knows he done wrong. He hasn't been himself since you left him.'

'Yeah, right – has he been staying single then? Pining for me? Spending every night in on his own?'

'Er, well, not exactly . . .' Greg looked guilty as hell. 'He's been going out a lot, to deal with the pain. He can't be on his own – you know what he's like. But he wants you back, I know that much.'

No doubt TFB was proving his devotion by shagging anything that moved, Charlie thought bitterly.

She was about to voice that opinion when Greg's trophy WAG wife Sammi tottered up in heels more suited to a club than a beach. She had a full face of make-up on, a scouse brow and false lashes. Charlie had met Sammi several times before and had zilch in common with her. She was vain, lived to shop, turned a blind eye to Greg's infidelities . . . all in all gave other WAG a bad name. She was also ferociously jealous of other women, especially prettier, younger women like Zoe and Charlie.

'Hiya, how great to see you guys,' she said insincerely, air kissing both of them and enveloping them in her exotic overpowering perfume, nearly taking Zoe's eye out when she swished back her long black hair extensions.

'Why don't you join us for dinner?' Greg suggested, ignoring the look on Sammi's face that said *over my dead body.* He obviously couldn't bear the thought of dinner for two and now Charlie remembered that there had been a story a couple of weeks ago about him cheating on Sammi *again.* This was clearly their make-up break. By the end of it Sammi would no doubt be pregnant again and pictures would have appeared in the tabloids of the pair of them cavorting in the sea like new lovers, and making everyone who saw them want to throw up.

'Thanks,' Charlie replied, 'but it's our last night. We're leaving first thing so we just want to chill in our suite.'

'Text me if you change your minds. And I'll let Aaron know that I've seen you.'

Charlie couldn't trust herself to reply, so shrugged as if to say, *Whatever!*

'Yuck!' Zoe muttered once they were out of earshot. 'That man makes me want to take a shower, he's such a grease-ball letch. And she's such a bitch! They're perfect for each other. So where shall we go for dinner? The gruesome twosome are going to the beach restaurant.'

Charlie had no appetite. 'D'you mind if we don't go out? I don't think I can face anything.'

'No probs, why don't we have room service and champagne? We can eat on the terrace.'

'Sounds good to me,' Charlie lied. She wanted to crawl into bed and forget the day had happened. Most of all forget that she ever knew anyone called Felipe . . .

Chapter 6

Charlie loved her two-bedroomed garden flat in Chiswick. It had felt like such a massive achievement, being able to buy it. She had enjoyed gradually doing it up, carefully choosing the colour schemes; she liked bold strong colours, so the living room was painted mulberry and her bedroom was a warm garnet. But now as she opened her front door and dragged her suitcase inside she only felt that the flat seemed small and dark after the stunning space and light of the Caribbean. And that she had nothing to look forward to except work. On the flight back she had watched *Bridesmaids* and cried practically all the way through. Charlie rarely cried at sad movies, let alone one that was a comedy.

'It must be PMT,' she had told Zoe.

'You're allowed to be upset about Felipe,' her friend replied.

'Why? Do you think he gives a flying fuck about me? I refuse to be upset about him.' Bold words, but she felt wretched inside.

Now she shivered as she walked into the living room; the heating wasn't on and the flat was cold. She had picked up her post from the entrance hall, but couldn't be bothered to go through it now and slung it on the coffee table where she noticed the red light on the answerphone was flashing. For a fleeting second before she pressed Play she wondered if there would be a message from Felipe, a ridiculous thing to think as he didn't have her landline number and she wanted to forget all about him, but she couldn't help it. Stupid, stupid Charlie . . .

The messages turned out to be from her mum. Charlie hesitated before calling her back; she needed to sound upbeat otherwise her mum would instantly know that something was wrong, and Charlie didn't want to tell her the sorry story of Felipe. She left it until she'd had a shower and put on a pair of PJs, a big sweater and her UGGs, and had a glass of wine in her hand.

'Hiya, it's me,' she said as brightly as she could when Lori answered the phone.

'Well, hiya, how was the holiday? We Googled the resort and it looked amazing!' Her mum sounded so happy for her that Charlie could feel tears pricking her eyes. If only she knew how it had all ended . . . No! Charlie was not going to cry again. She took a deep breath and launched into a rundown of the week, omitting any mention of Felipe and ending with, 'I'll post my pictures on Facebook later and then you'll be able to see for yourself.'

'Ah, Charlie, I'm so glad you had such a good time.

You deserved it, sweetheart. And we can't wait to see you tomorrow.'

Charlie usually told her parents pretty much everything, but she had found the experience with Felipe so intense and then so humiliating that she needed to keep it to herself, at least for the time being. It wouldn't be easy as she was going up to Manchester the following day to see them and her brother, but she would try her hardest.

After the call she couldn't stop herself from clicking through the holiday photos on her camera. There were so many that she wouldn't be able to put on Facebook – shots of her and Felipe, arms round each other at dinner, walking hand in hand on the beach, lying side by side on sun loungers deep in conversation, the two of them swimming with turtles, kissing in the swimming pool under the waterfall . . . Zoe had taken it on herself to be the official photographer of their romance.

Charlie paused at a photograph of Felipe gazing at her while she smiled at something Luis had said. How could he have looked at her with such longing – and then rejected her? She selected delete, all set permanently to erase the photo, but then couldn't go through with it.

She knew that even if she deleted every single one of the photos the images were burned into her consciousness, ready to be gone through again and again. And then, because she couldn't stop herself, even though she knew it would hurt, she switched on her laptop and looked up images of Felipe – Felipe urging his horse over an almighty jump in a cross-country competition, triumphantly holding a trophy over his head, leaning against the door of his stables and looking broodingly handsome in jeans, at some red-carpet event holding hands with a stunning woman called Paloma . . . Until seeing his handsome, unobtainable face became unbearable and Charlie slammed the lid shut.

It was just a holiday romance, she tried to tell herself. But if it had been, why couldn't she stop thinking about him?

Felipe picked up his phone and selected Charlie's name; he had not been able to forget about her. Fuck! What was he doing? He pressed Cancel and flung his phone on the sofa in frustration. This was not the first time he had come close to calling her, but he had to stop. She was a journalist and had lied to him; he couldn't possibly trust her or see her again. In a week or so she would have sold her story to *Marca* or one of the other Spanish tabloids and he would be pursued by reporters wanting to feast on the juicy details of his private life, distracting him from his all-important training. Other women had sold stories on him and he had never cared – or rather he had cared about the consequences of the story, but from the women themselves he'd felt detached. Thinking of Charlie writing up their romance cut him like the worst kind of betrayal. He had really felt something for her. At first it had been an intense physical attraction, but the moment she had broken down in tears about the accident, it had blossomed into something more. She had got to him, got under his skin. He didn't think any woman had ever had that effect on him. She consumed his thoughts when he wasn't riding and distracted him, which was precisely why this Saturday night he was going to be late for dinner with Luis and Mariana.

His friends were already at the restaurant and engrossed in conversation. Felipe watched them for a moment as the waiter took his jacket. They looked so happy and so very much in love, even after five years of marriage. Felipe felt a stab of longing as he remembered how good it had felt being with Charlie. Mariana caught sight of him and waved enthusiastically. She was a beautiful woman, who bore a striking resemblance to Penelope Cruz with her rich brown eyes, curvaceous figure and luxuriant jet black hair, but Felipe had always seen her as a friend, which was just as well as the usually mild Luis would have killed him if he had ever made a move on her.

'I'm sorry, I didn't realise what the time was,' Felipe said after they had all kissed each other in greeting.

'I expect you were thinking about Charlie.' Mariana winked at him. 'I want to hear all about this English beauty.'

It was typical that Luis had told her what had gone on; he was incapable of keeping anything secret from his wife. Felipe rolled his eyes, but couldn't be annoyed.

'She is certainly beautiful' – he paused – 'on the outside. You can judge how beautiful she is on the inside when you read what she has to say about me.'

Luis looked at Mariana as if warning her not to say anything, but she leant forward and put her hand affectionately on Felipe's arm. 'Have you considered that you might have got this all wrong, and that Charlie is not and never was going to write a story about you? I know you believe that you are the centre of the universe, but really it is entirely possible that she had absolutely no idea who you were!' She held up her phone. 'This doesn't look like the kind of woman who would write a kiss-and-tell.'

It was Charlie's publicity picture for her TV channel. She was smiling, and looked every inch the glossy, professional presenter: confident, in charge, in control.

'No, she doesn't, but what is she supposed to look like? Now, please, I know you enjoy talking about my love life because you are married and boring and have no excitement any more, but can we stop and order something to eat? I'm starving.'

Conversation turned to the financial state of his equestrian centre. As well as having a string of his own horses, Felipe and his team of riding protégés trained and competed on ten horses belonging to wealthy clients, who owned them as an investment and for the prestige. Felipe also bred horses and provided a livery for a further ten animals whose owners rode them in competitions. He had built the centre up from nothing and its reputation and renown had grown alongside his success as an event rider.

But the economic downturn was having an impact on even his very wealthy clients and he had just lost two who had been forced to sell their horses. If things didn't improve he would have to ask his mother for another loan, and he didn't want to do that. It was a depressing sign of the times and usually Felipe would have had plenty to say on the subject but tonight he couldn't concentrate. His thoughts kept drifting back to Charlie.

He wondered what she was doing now. The UK was an hour behind. Was she out with friends in London? Or with another man? Was she at home? Alone? Or with someone else? Was she thinking about him? He remembered the look of sheer incomprehension and shock on her face as he had laid into her about lying to him. He had said some terrible things to her. Was it possible that she hadn't set out to deceive him, as Mariana suggested? But then why else would she have lied about what she did?

Mariana clicked her fingers in front of his face to get his attention. 'You are miles away, Felipe. Maybe skinny dipping on a deserted beach in the moonlight? Or caressing your lover with ice-cold strawberries and licking champagne off her toned stomach?' She gave a cheeky grin. Luis really did tell Marina everything . . .

'And can I say that I entirely approve? I know Charlie is younger than you, and I like to promote the older woman in a relationship.' Mariana was five years older than Luis. 'But she sounded more than a match for you.'

Felipe shrugged. 'I'm sorry to disappoint you, Mariana, but nothing is going to happen between Charlie and me. Really, it would be for the best for this story to come out and then I could deal with it and forget all about her. It's just the waiting that is distracting me.'

'Just the waiting?' Mariana teased. 'Not all those delicious memories?'

'Just the waiting,' he repeated firmly.

A phrase which rang especially hollow at 2 a.m. when he was unable to sleep and found himself at his computer, studying all the images of Charlie Porter he could find and then looking once more at the photographs he had taken of her. He couldn't bring himself to delete them. Deep down he felt that he and Charlie had experienced a once-in-a-lifetime connection, and although he tried to tell himself that it never could have worked because of her riding phobia, he didn't believe that.

Charlie overslept the following morning and as a result it was a mad dash to get ready. She was about to race out of the door when she remembered the post and ran into the living room to shove it in her bag, figuring she would go through it on the train. She only just made it in time and leapt on the train with two minutes to spare. She intended to use the journey to catch up on the sports news, and pulled out her laptop. The three other passengers already had their laptops out as well and it was a tight squeeze to fit hers on the table.

'It's like a laptop stand off,' she joked, raising a flicker of a smile from the businessman opposite her, nothing from the young woman next to him or the lad with headphones on beside her.

Before she got down to work she flicked through the post in her bag. There was a depressing number of bills which she ignored. But when she came to a cream envelope with a handwritten address she opened it and pulled out what seemed to be a photograph. She turned it over and saw with a shock that it was one of her publicity photos for the TV channel, and that someone had scrawled *Bitch, you don't deserve this job* in black marker pen across her face. For a few seconds she stared at it, stunned that someone could be so nasty about her.

Then she shoved the photo back into the envelope. She was sure that people had written horrible things about her before, but those letters would have gone direct to the TV studio and been dealt with before they got to her. The studio wouldn't give out any personal details, so how had this person known where she lived? Had they followed her? Charlie felt a flicker of fear at the thought. She was about to get up and throw the letter in the bin, and then on second thoughts decided to hold on to it in case she received any others. It might be evidence. She, like all the presenters, had her own Twitter account, and there had been the odd snide comment before about her looks getting her to where she was. But someone else always posted a positive reply, making the hater look small. This comment felt like a personal attack.

She switched on her laptop and her hands shook slightly as she checked out the sports news pages and blogs. But Charlie was a fighter and it wasn't long before fear was replaced by anger. How dare someone write such a thing? She bloody well did deserve her TV job. She had worked her arse off for it!

She had always loved sport, and had wanted to be a sports presenter since she'd started her GCSEs, telling every careers teacher that it was her dream and ignoring them when they suggested she might be aiming too high, that those jobs were few and far between, and hadn't she better concentrate on working behind the scenes? She'd confounded their expectations by getting a place at Manchester University to study Broadcast Journalism and finishing up with a 2:1. After uni she had worked as a runner – which basically meant earning practically nothing and being treated like a complete dogsbody, for six months, then landed a job as a researcher on a morning TV show for two years – better pay but she was still treated like a dogsbody and worked flat out. She was seriously beginning to doubt that she would ever make it as a presenter, but then Zoe had sent her friend's showreel off to Total Sport without telling her and they were so impressed that they invited Charlie to come in for a screen test. They'd offered her a job on the spot. It was an amazing break but it hadn't been a lucky fluke; it was what Charlie had worked towards for the last six years. The person who had sent the photo was jealous and bitter.

Charlie was still seething about it when the train drew in to Manchester Piccadilly station, but managed to file it away when she saw her dad, Ray, waiting patiently for her beyond the ticket barrier. She'd told him that she would get a taxi, but it was typical of him to want to pick her up himself. At well over six foot tall he stood out as easily the most stylishly dressed man on the platform, in a navy overcoat and trilby. He liked dressing well when he wasn't working.

'Dad!' she called out, thrilled to see him, then threw her arms around him. Now she worked in London she didn't get to see as much of her parents as she would have liked.

'How is my star daughter?' he asked, hugging her back. 'Prepare yourself but I don't have a Roller waiting outside, it's at the garage. You'll have to make do with the Ford Mondeo. But it'll be good for you to see how us non-celebs live. There's no complimentary champagne or fancy canapés either, but you could share my Dr Pepper and packet of Twiglets, if you play your cards right.'

Charlie knew she shouldn't have mentioned the Rolls-Royce that had transported her and Zoe to and from the airport; her dad was never going to let her live it down. He was always on the alert for anything she said that seemed to flaunt her newfound TV success, and when he detected something, he would invariably tease her, so that she didn't, as he said, 'forget her roots'.

Her parents lived in Chorlton, a few miles out of the city centre, in a Victorian terrace. They had worked hard to give Charlie and her brother the things they themselves never had as kids, both coming from relatively poor backgrounds, especially her mum. Ray worked as a plumber – the world's nicest plumber, Charlie was always teasing him. He would regularly undercharge pensioners or single mums, which was probably why they still lived in the terrace and not in a large house like some of his contemporaries. Her mum worked at the Clinique counter at John Lewis's in the Trafford Centre in Manchester. Lori could sell anything to anyone. Really she was wasted in cosmetics, she should have been working for Sir Alan Sugar. She had the gift of the gab.

They chatted all the way back to the house, catching up on each other's news. But when Charlie asked how her brother was, conversation ground to a halt. Her dad frowned. He had been devastated when Kris was sent to prison, and would only go and visit him if Lori pushed him into it. He found it impossible to comprehend how his son, the boy on whom he had lavished so much love and attention, and who'd had all the advantages that Ray himself hadn't, had ended up in such a mess. He blamed Kris and he blamed himself.

'Out in another two months, and then God knows.'

'Oh, Dad, I'm sure he'll be okay. It sounds like such a cliché but he's learnt his lesson.'

'Has he? Here's another cliché for you: only time will tell.'

'I'm going to see him tomorrow with Mum. Will you come too?'

Her dad shook his head. 'I'm working.' He sounded hard, totally unlike his usual easygoing self.

Ray pulled up outside the house, then turned to Charlie. 'Come on, don't let's upset your mum by talking about your brother.'

'Sure,' she replied. She wanted to tell her dad to let it go, to forgive Kris, but she knew it had to come from him.

Her mum had seen them pull up and had already opened the front door. At forty-six, Lori could easily have passed for someone ten years younger. She had a knock-out figure, an exceptionally pretty face with the same striking green eyes as Charlie, and long blonde highlighted hair, which she refused to have cut just because she was over forty. 'Do Madonna, Courtney Cox or Elle Macpherson have short hair?' she was fond of saying, adding, 'I'm not getting old without a fight! The hair stays, and if it falls out, I'll get a wig. I'd rather be mutton than mumsy.'

'So good to see you!' Lori exclaimed, hugging Charlie tightly. She breathed in the familiar scent of her mum's perfume, Clinique's Happy mixed in with fabric conditioner. Now she knew she was home.

Home. The place where she had always felt so secure and loved, where she could drop her guard. Charlie loved her TV job, but boy, it was tough sometimes. She could never have an off day, always had to be on top form, aware of how many other women wanted to step into her shoes . . . At home she could let go, relax.

Lori had made one of her legendary roasted Mediterranean vegetable *lasagne* and they sat round the kitchen table eating, chatting and drinking wine. They were halfway through the meal when she exclaimed, 'By the way, who was that gorgeous man in your holiday photos? He looked like a male model.'

Shit! Charlie hadn't realised she had posted a picture of Felipe.

'Er, not sure who you mean,' she blustered, not fooling anyone.

Lori reached for her laptop and clicked on to Charlie's photos. Sure enough, there was a picture of Felipe and Charlie standing on the beach, talking to each other. It was one of Zoe's more artistic shots, taken when Charlie hadn't realised they were being photographed. Felipe had his arms round her waist, holding her close to him. They certainly looked more than good friends; they looked like lovers, with eyes only for each other.

'Oh, him,' she muttered.

Her mum looked at her expectantly and Charlie knew she would never get away with not saying anything – her mum had ways of making her talk . . . 'He's called Felipe, and he lives in Spain so I'm not likely to see him again.'

'Loads of cheap flights to Spain,' Lori persisted. 'You could go for the weekend.'

'I often work at weekends, remember?'

'Not *every* weekend.'

Charlie sighed; she would have to 'fess up. 'Actually, Mum, I'm never going to see him again.' And she went on to tell them about Felipe believing that she was a journalist about to sell a story on him.

'That is totally out of order!' Lori exclaimed. 'As if you would ever do something like that! What a bastard tosser! And there was I, thinking how lovely he looked.'

Hell hath no fury like a mother whose daughter has been dissed . . .

'Well, now you know,' Charlie replied. She raised her glass. '*Hasta la vista*, Felipe.'

Chapter 7

It didn't matter how many times before Charlie had been to visit her brother in prison; every time it got to her. Her mum was falsely cheerful on the drive over but Charlie knew how much she hated seeing her son there. True to his word, her dad hadn't come.

It didn't help that it was a freezing cold day with bursts of sleet and that Lori had to park a good ten minutes' walk away from the prison. As they drew closer her conversation dried up, and by the time they arrived they were both silent as they took their place in the line of visitors waiting to go in. No one looked happy; everyone had lowered heads, hunched shoulders, and were shivering in cheaply made coats that weren't warm enough to keep out the bitter cold. Plumes of cigarette smoke spiralled into the air. Signals of the lost, Charlie always thought. Several places in front of them a toddler was crying. Poor child, having to see their dad here.

'It's at times like this that I wish I smoked,' Lori

remarked grimly. The usual sparkle was missing from her eyes; her mouth was set.

'Think of the wrinkles you'd have,' Charlie tried to joke. Her mum didn't reply.

One of the doors to the prison was opened and the queue shuffled forward. It took over an hour to get through security. Everyone, including the children, was searched for drugs and all bags had to be locked away in lockers. No one could take in mobile phones. By the time Charlie and Lori made it to the depressing visitors' room, with its peeling pale blue paint and CCTV cameras mounted on the walls, they felt as if they were the criminals.

Kris was already sitting at one of the tables, which was bolted to the floor, on a plastic chair, which was also bolted to the floor. Like all the other prisoners, he was wearing a red bib over his prison clothes of a grey sweatshirt and trousers, the colours chosen so all prisoners could be quickly identified. There was something about the bib that particularly upset Charlie – it was just like the sports bib he used to wear for five-a-side football and was a reminder that Kris wouldn't be doing that again for a while. It broke Charlie's heart to see him here, hands jammed in his pockets, head down. He looked as if he couldn't be less bothered about seeing them. She supposed that it was all part of the tough act he had to put on to survive here.

'All right,' he said, as they took their seats across the table from him. His skin looked grey and unhealthy under the harsh fluorescent lights and he had bags under his eyes. *Please let him not be taking drugs*, Charlie prayed.

She knew that for all the searches of visitors, drugs were rife in prison. The temptation to take them, to escape in your head, must be overwhelming. As far as she knew Kris had only ever smoked dope, but God knows what went on inside here.

Lori reached out and put her hand over his. 'How are you, love?' Kris couldn't meet her gaze. Instantly one of the prison guards gave them the evil eye. Touching between inmates and prisoners was strictly forbidden, in case anything illicit was passed to the prisoner. Next time he would shout at them.

'Never better. This week I've been on a spa retreat, sampling some haute cuisine and fine wines.' Kris was sarcastic and bitter, his words hiding a world of pain.

'Don't be mean,' Charlie said quietly. 'You know how much Mum worries.'

'And Dad?' For a second a flicker of hurt flared in Kris's eyes.

'And Dad,' Charlie repeated.

He sniffed as if he didn't believe her. 'So how was Barbados?'

Charlie thought of her luxury holiday, where her every whim had been catered for, the beauty of the scenery, her passionate encounter with Felipe . . . How could she describe it here, surrounded by so much poverty and despair, broken families, broken people? 'It was great, thanks,' she said quickly.

Fortunately he didn't press her for details.

'Look, I've been thinking,' Charlie carried on, 'you've only got another two months to go and you should be thinking about the future. Why don't you move in with me for a while? You could try and get back into acting again.'

Kris shook his head, and put on a mock-posh voice. 'I don't think my agent's going to be returning my calls, do you? And the acting possibilities aren't so good in here.'

He had always been a talented actor. At school he was the lead in all the productions. He studied drama at college and had a few TV roles. Just before he'd been arrested, he'd been up for an audition in a major drama series and had got the part. He was arrested the day after.

'We could try and get you another agent. Come on, you've got a great CV. We could start by contacting that director again. He really liked you.'

'Well, I fucking blew that one, didn't I? And there's no point in contacting him. He won't want to know. You'd be wasting your time.'

Lori winced.

'Please don't talk like that,' Charlie pleaded with him. 'You've got to have hope. You know that we're all here for you, Kris.'

He hung his head. 'Yeah, I know. Thanks.'

They managed to muddle through for a further twenty minutes, Charlie babbling on about Zoe, who Kris knew, and about work; Lori updating Kris on what had been going on at home. It was only when the buzzer rang, signalling the end of visiting time, that they got a glimpse of the Kris they knew and loved.

'Sorry,' he mumbled to Charlie, 'I'm just a bit crap at the moment. It's been getting to me, being in here.' His eyes, when he looked up at her, were full of tears.

Charlie longed to give him a hug to reassure him. 'It's going to be okay, I promise. Let me help you? I know you'd do the same for me.'

'Yeah, I know,' he managed. And then he was walking away from them and Charlie was having to comfort her mum who was silently weeping.

Two days later Charlie was back at work. She had contacted the director and left a message, as she had promised Kris, but hadn't heard back. She felt that she had to do something, *anything*, to help her brother. Felipe was never far from her thoughts either but she welcomed the distraction of work. There it was the usual frenzy of planning meetings, going through the studio running order, checking the research notes and adapting the scripts before she went on air. But she loved it, thriving on the high-pressure atmosphere.

Being in front of the camera felt as natural to Charlie as chatting to a group of friends. It helped that she got on so well with Aidan, her co-host. He was ten years older than her, and a total sweetheart. Charlie knew he was gay, but he wasn't 'out' at work. The world of sport still lagged behind as far as sexuality was concerned – sure, there were exceptions, but Aidan had chosen to keep his secret while at work and Charlie respected his decision.

'Does it feel like you've never been away?' he asked after they came off air.

'Yes, but I'm glad to be back.'

'Well, you're looking good, Charlie. Liking the tan – you can always tell when it's for real and not fake.

You look expensive and classy.' He sighed and pulled back his shirt sleeves to consider his own pasty forearms. 'If I get any paler, I'll be auditioning for a part in one of those vampire series.'

'Can you act?'

'No, but when has that ever stopped quite a few actors I could name?'

They were heading for the canteen to grab something to eat, when Darcy, one of the production assistants, caught up with them. Charlie got on with most people at work but had never seen eye to eye with Darcy, who in her view was a superior rich girl and a total bitch. 'Arsey Darcy' she called her behind her back. In spite of the sulky expression almost permanently on Darcy's face, she was stunningly pretty with long blonde hair, almond-shaped blue eyes, perfect skin, and the super-slim figure of a model. She was a terrible PA, though, and always acted as if doing any actual work was beneath her. And Charlie loathed the way she flirted with all the male presenters. It was such a cliché.

'Hey, guys, there's a planning meeting now about Olympic stuff in the conference room,' Darcy drawled, as if it was too much effort to actually speak clearly.

'Really?' Aidan asked sharply. 'There wasn't an email about it.' He didn't like Darcy either.

'But I sent one out.' Darcy pouted, looking innocent. Charlie was pretty sure she hadn't. 'Anyway, Nicky told me to come and round you both up as you're late.' She turned and sauntered along the corridor, treating Aidan and Charlie to a view of her pert bum in a pair of expensive leather trousers, and swishing her shiny hair.

Charlie had heard from one of the other PAs that Darcy had her hair blow dried at a salon at least twice a week. Lucky her to be able to afford it . . . Charlie didn't know anyone else who could on a PA's salary.

'We wouldn't be late if we'd known,' Aidan muttered to Charlie.

The two of them were the last to take their seats round the huge white table in the conference room. Nicky, the Channel editor, a fiercely ambitious and bright woman in her mid-thirties, raised her eyebrows at them as they sat down, but didn't break off from talking. She hated anyone being late to meetings. She was busy outlining the various big sporting events that were coming up, the biggest of all of course being the Olympics. The BBC had sole rights to cover the events themselves so the sports channel was going to do a series of special reports and interviews with the athletes in the run-up to the Games.

'I'd like each of the presenters to specialise in a couple of sports for this,' Nicky explained. 'It will mean going out on location to record the films.'

Please let me get athletics or football, Charlie thought. This felt like being back at school, waiting to hear who was being picked for the sports teams, as Nicky reeled off who was doing what. Suddenly Charlie had an appalling thought. What if she was assigned to cover the riding? She had been lucky so far in her work and had never had to report on any equestrian events. The very thought of being around horses and riders was too much. She knew she wouldn't be able to cope with it. Charlie's mouth suddenly felt dry and she could feel sweat breaking out on her forehead. It was the insidious onset of a panic attack. Already her breathing was becoming more shallow.

Nicky looked over at her and Aidan. 'You two are going to be covering the gymnastics and swimming. Is that okay?'

Thank God! But the announcement came too late to stop the sickening onrush of a panic attack.

Nicky looked at her expectantly, clearly waiting for Charlie to say something positive as she usually did at such moments. Instead Charlie put her hand up to her mouth, muttered something about feeling unwell and bolted from the room.

'Are you okay?' Nicky called after her, but Charlie couldn't reply. She had to get away.

Somehow she made it to the Ladies where she locked herself in a cubicle and rifled frantically through her handbag for the paper bag. It took over ten minutes for her to compose herself and regulate her breathing. Back in the newsroom she found Nicky perched on one of the desks, chatting to Aidan. Both of them looked at her in concern.

'I'm sorry, Nicky, I think I must have eaten something dodgy.' It was a feeble excuse, but the best one Charlie could come up with.

'Poor you, and you look dreadful,' Nicky told her. 'Go home, your shift's finished anyway.'

Aidan grabbed his jacket. 'I'll come with you.'

'Oh, before I forget, I meant to give you both these invitations to the Sports Relief charity dinner in two weeks. I'm sorry it's such short notice but I really need both of you to go, it's good PR stuff. And bring a plus one if you want.' Nicky handed each of them a black envelope with their name written on it in elegant silver handwriting. 'It's on the thirteenth of February, so please tell me you haven't got romantic mini-breaks planned?'

Both Aidan and Charlie shook their heads. *Fat chance of that,* Charlie thought.

They headed out of the office and Aidan waited until the lift doors had closed before saying, 'I'm going to have to come straight out with it . . .' Usually that would have been the cue for Charlie to shoot back some cheeky innuendo, but his next comment totally wrong-footed her. 'Are you pregnant, Charlie?'

'Oh my God, no!' She hesitated. 'At least . . . I don't think so.' Like she needed that on top of everything else! No, she was absolutely sure that she wasn't.

'I didn't even realise you were seeing anyone. You kept *that* one quiet.'

She had hoped not to mention Felipe, wanting work to be her escape. 'I'm not. I was sort of seeing someone, but it's over. *So* over. So so over.' She knew that she didn't sound as if she thought it was over, and sure enough the look Aidan gave her showed he wasn't sure he believed her. Maybe it would be good to confide in him; she had always trusted him. 'Have you got time for a coffee?'

'With you, absolutely.'

They walked out of the office and headed to a nearby café which was one of their favourite haunts. It was run by Annie, a straight-talking South Londoner who made the best toasted *panini* and coffee in the area. Aidan ordered the skinny lattes while Charlie found a table in the corner.

'Get this down you,' he said, putting the drink in front of her. Charlie clasped her hands round the mug, grateful for its comforting warmth. She hated feeling so insecure and on edge.

'*So?*' Aidan asked, his handsome face full of concern. His black hair was going grey at the sides and it suited him. Charlie was always teasing him that he was a silver fox.

'*So*, on holiday I had a fling with someone but it ended badly. *Very* badly.'

'I need more than that to go on, girlfriend!' he replied. Away from the office he was always more teasing, and allowed himself to be a tiny bit camp.

Charlie took a sip of coffee before launching into the story of her doomed romance with Felipe.

'Bloody hell, Charlie, you have worse luck with men than me!' Aidan commented when she had come to the end. 'And that's saying something . . . So you haven't heard from this Felipe at all? Great name, by the way.'

'God, no! And I don't want to either.' That was a super-sized lie but Charlie didn't want to admit that, in spite of Felipe treating her appallingly, she couldn't stop thinking about him.

'Are you sure about that? Maybe by now he's calmed down and realised that he got it all wrong.'

The chances of that seemed a million to one. Charlie shook her head. Aidan knew better than to push her. Charlie might come across as confident and able to deal with anything but he knew she was more sensitive than that.

'And what happened to you in the meeting?'

Charlie hesitated. She had always hoped to keep the riding accident a secret from people at work, but now she desperately needed Aidan's advice on what she should do. She couldn't keep it to herself any longer.

'So you had a flashback?' he said after she'd told him everything.

Charlie picked up a sachet of sugar and fiddled with it. 'A panic attack. It's pathetic, I know, I should be over it by now.' She shrugged. 'Maybe it's for the best things didn't work out with Felipe. I mean, if I can't be around horses and he's a horseman . . . how incompatible can you get? It's like the universe is playing the ultimate joke on me.'

'Have you ever had therapy?'

'I went to see someone once, but it didn't work out and actually made me feel worse. They just wanted me to talk over the accident and my feelings about it. It was horrible, like reliving it all over again.'

'That was very unlucky, but don't write off all therapy because of it. I seriously think you need to see someone.' Aidan was looking through his wallet. He pulled out a business card.

'This is my therapist's card. Dr Rosie Mackay. She's brilliant. I saw her when I was suffering from anxiety attacks a few years ago, after my flat was burgled. She totally sorted me out. *Please* go and see her, it's the only way. It's not an admission of failure. If you'd hurt your leg you'd go and see a doctor, right?'

'Yeah, I suppose,' Charlie muttered reluctantly. She picked up the card and slipped it into her bag, but knew she had no intention of using it. That bad experience had put her off for life. She would have to get over the accident all by herself.

Aidan gave her an encouraging smile, clearly believing that he had won the argument. He picked up the invitation, 'So will you be my plus one at the dinner if the lovely Felipe doesn't get in touch?'

'He won't. And I would love to be your plus one.'

Chapter 8

'Keep still,' Mariana ordered as she attempted to do up Felipe's white bow tie, while he fidgeted with his mother-of-pearl cuff links. 'Honestly, you are worse than a teenager!'

'I still cannot believe I let you talk me into going to this waste-of-time event. It's an entire weekend out of my schedule!' he grumbled. He, Mariana and Luis were over in London, staying at the exclusive Brown's Hotel in Mayfair, getting ready for the charity dinner.

'It's important for your profile,' Luis told him. 'And a great chance for you to promote the equestrian centre. There are going to be many, many wealthy people there.'

'I don't need their money,' Felipe said abruptly. 'Haven't you finished yet, Mariana? Christ! I feel like a prize stallion being groomed for a show. Are you sure you don't want to brush my hair and check my nails?'

'You *do* need their money,' Luis corrected him. 'You said yourself that you didn't want to rely on handouts from your parents. So you are going to do your very best to smile and look pretty tonight.' He patted his friend affectionately on the shoulder. 'And if you're good I'll give you a carrot . . . maybe even a sugar lump if you're extra good.'

'And who knows who we'll meet?' Mariana put in, winking at her husband.

She was looking gorgeous in a fuchsia-coloured silk-chiffon evening dress that made her olive skin glow. Felipe noticed the wink, and wondered what Mariana meant by it. Going to a charity dinner was the very last thing he felt like doing. He hated the thought of making small talk all night with people he didn't care about, when the one woman he did care about was lost to him . . .

It had been three weeks since they had flown back from the Caribbean, and so far no story about his ill-fated romance with Charlie had come out in the press. By now Felipe realised that she was not going to sell a kiss-and-tell; she never had been. She had been telling the truth when she said she had no idea who he was. She must surely loathe him after he had humiliated her like that. He had well and truly screwed things up.

Charlie pulled a face at her reflection in the mirror while Zoe gave her a last-minute pep talk. 'You look gorgeous, stop stressing! You're going to have a great time.'

Charlie remained to be convinced. Since Felipe had turned on her, she had suffered a crisis of confidence. After work she'd barely gone out, other than to the gym or for a quick drink with Zoe. She definitely wasn't in the mood for this night out. She had far too much on her plate to want to dress up and socialise with people she hardly knew. She was worried about her brother as the director still hadn't called her back. And in spite of everything he had said, Felipe was never far from her thoughts.

'Are you sure this dress will stay up?' she asked, tugging at the daringly low neckline of the bodice. She was wearing a red satin strapless gown closely fitted to her curves, the fishtail skirt fanning out in elaborate ripples at the back. She wasn't entirely comfortable with the amount of cleavage revealed by the dress and it had taken all Zoe's powers of persuasion to get her to choose it. Charlie had wanted to go for a black number. In fact, given the choice, she would have been far happier in black skinny jeans and a black jacket.

'Yes, it will stay up,' Zoe said through gritted teeth. 'God! I thought I was used to high-maintenance clients at the boutique, but you take the bloody biscuit!'

She picked up a Valentine card that was lying on the dressing table. On the front was the drawing of a cutesy brown bear holding up a love heart. It was exactly the kind of thing Charlie loathed. 'Who is this from?' she asked, opening the card. The handwriting looked like a twelve-year-old's and there was a biro-drawn love heart over the i of Charlie.

'No idea. Someone who doesn't know me at all.'

'Well, I'm guessing it's not from Felipe. He didn't seem like the kind of man who would send a woman a card with a picture of a bear on it.' Zoe warmed to her theme. 'His card would be dramatic, passionate, and sexy. Say a black-and-white photograph of himself lying naked on a bed scattered with rose petals, with maybe a rose . . . No! Not big enough . . . a bunch of roses held in a strategic position.'

Charlie glared at her. 'Why did you have to mention him?'

For some reason Zoe looked a bit shifty. 'Sorry, I didn't mean to.'

Charlie didn't have a chance to pursue this conversation as the doorbell rang then. It was Aidan, who had called round in a taxi to collect her. Zoe answered the door while Charlie grabbed her bag – a red satin clutch to match her dress – and a black feather bolero. Charlie grimaced as she draped the feathers round her shoulders. It was barely above freezing outside and there was no way this flimsy bolero was going to keep her warm. She'd have to smuggle her black leather jacket out of the flat, away from Zoe, aka the Style Police. But just as she was walking out of the flat, Zoe caught her red-handed and confiscated the jacket.

'Perhaps you'll meet a handsome man who'll lend you his jacket, if you're cold.'

Aidan buttoned up his own jacket protectively, and joked, 'Don't look at me, Zoe, I'm freezing my nuts off out here.'

'Oh, I didn't mean *you*!' she replied. 'It's just that you *never* know who you'll meet at events like these, do you? Think of Cinderella!'

'What are you on about? It's a dinner, not a ball,' Charlie called out.

'Oh, you know what I mean!' Zoe blew the pair of them a kiss as they got into the taxi.

'I think Zoe may have overdone it on the Mojitos, she's been talking complete crap,' Charlie commented to Aidan who was holding the taxi door open for her. 'You look totes hot by the way.'

'And you look beautiful,' he replied, then sighed. 'I'm not looking forward to tonight. I could really do without it, if you must know.'

'Oh?' It wasn't like Aidan to be negative; he generally threw himself into social events and was the life and soul of the party.

He lowered his voice so the taxi driver couldn't over-hear. 'I received something in the post this morning and I don't know what to do about it.' He pulled out an envelope and handed it to Charlie. She instantly recognised the handwriting on the front. Silently she pulled out a publicity photo of Aidan that he had autographed. Scrawled across his face in thick black marker pen was written: *When are you coming out?*

'I don't want anyone to know at work. If it does get out, forever after I'll be known as the gay sports presenter. I want to be known for what I do profession-ally, not for my private life. Why would anyone send something like this? It's so needlessly spiteful.'

Aidan was wound up and stressed. Again this wasn't like him. But Charlie knew that the comment on the photograph would have hit a nerve. Aidan's ex-boyfriend was always going on at him for not being out at work. It was one of the main reasons they'd eventually split. Aidan had been devastated.

'Actually, I had something like this sent to me the other week,' she told him.

'Are you a lesbian now then?' Aidan tried to joke.

'No, mine said, *"Bitch, you don't deserve this job"*.'

'Nice,' he said sarcastically.

'So what do you think we should do about it? Is there anyone we could speak to at work? Say someone in Security?' Charlie slid the photograph back into the envelope and handed it to Aidan.

He shoved it into his inside pocket. 'I'd rather not. Let's hope someone's got their nasty little digs out of their system. But keep your note, just in case there are any more.'

Charlie patted his shoulder. 'Tonight we could pretend that we're an item, if you like? That will disrupt their mean little scheme, if they see any pictures of us together. Not that I can believe anyone is that interested.'

The comment raised a smile from Aidan. 'Don't you realise you're going places? You're beautiful and smart and great on TV. People are definitely watching you, Charlie.'

'You too,' she told him, as ever finding it hard to take a compliment.

'I'm pushing thirty-five, remember? My TV days are numbered. I'll be on the presenter's scrap heap soon, forced to appear in a humiliating reality show where I lose all dignity.'

'Don't be silly, you'd be great in something like *Strictly Come Dancing*,' Charlie replied, trying to cheer him up.

Aidan shook his head. 'Too classy. It'll be *Celebrity*

Big Brother for me. I'll get drunk and snog someone in the hot tub.'

Oh, dear, he really was on the downward spiral. 'Listen, you're a silver fox like Swoony Clooney, and I don't see his career stopping any time soon.'

That at least raised a smile from Aidan.

The dinner was being held at The Dorchester on Park Lane. Charlie could still remember going on a double-decker bus tour of London as a child and marvelling at this grand avenue with its expensive hotels, little imagining that one day she would be sweeping up the red carpet herself. Hordes of photographers were milling around expectantly, eager to capture the stars, and it had been rumoured that David Beckham was turning up. Aidan helped Charlie make an elegant exit out of the taxi and the two of them linked arms as they walked up the red carpet and posed for a couple of pictures.

'Charlie Porter and Aidan Shepherd, have you got something to tell us?' one of the paps called out cheekily.

The couple laughed and shook their heads and Aidan whispered in Charlie's ear, 'If there ever could be a woman, I swear it would be you.'

'I'm not sure that's a compliment,' she whispered back. Then, laughing, they swept into the grand hotel foyer together.

Inside the lavishly decorated ballroom, with its gold pillars and glittering chandeliers, Felipe stifled a yawn. He had been up since half-past four this morning, wanting to fit in a ride in the indoor school before catching the flight to London. So far he hadn't met anyone who could help with the financial crisis the stables were in. He would have been better off staying at home and continuing his training. Luis and Mariana were in high spirits, though. He smiled as he watched them across the room, chatting together and drinking champagne. He was on his way to join them when a very pretty young woman passed by him and stumbled, her foot catching in the hem of her cobalt blue gown. Ever the gentleman, Felipe reached out his hand to steady her arm.

'Thank you so much!' the young woman exclaimed breathlessly. She really was exceptionally pretty with long blonde hair and striking blue eyes. 'It's my own stupid fault I can't walk in these ridiculous shoes.' She raised her skirt to reveal the culprits: diamanté sandals with five-inch heels.

'It was my pleasure,' he replied, dragging his eyes away from her slender ankles and long tanned legs. A white-jacketed waiter was circulating with a tray loaded with champagne flutes. 'Can I get you a drink?'

'Oh, yes, please. I'm Darcy by the way.'

He clinked his glass against hers. 'Felipe. Pleased to meet you.'

Maybe tonight would not be entirely wasted if he could spend it with this attractive woman. Later they might possibly go back to his hotel room. It had been nearly a month after all and Felipe felt he needed the release that only sex could give him . . . However, within ten minutes he had scrapped that idea. He was bored out of his mind. Darcy might be stunning but he found her dull. There was no spark there for him as they talked about where he was from and what he thought of London. He found himself remembering his first encounter with Charlie. She had instantly intrigued him. As well as being beautiful and sexy, she was so feisty and refreshing. But there was little to be gained from thinking about her.

Once Darcy found out he was an international event rider she had endless questions about his training and horses. Felipe could feel the energy draining out of him. It didn't help that he had got through four glasses of champagne very rapidly. He perked up when she mentioned that her parents owned a stables. So he could add rich to the list of pretty but dull. At least that might be useful.

'You'll have to come down and visit, if you're here for long enough. There's plenty of room in the house for you to stay.' She was gazing at him provocatively, leaving him in no doubt whose room he'd be sleeping in. The blatant offer didn't arouse even a flicker of interest in him.

'Thank you, but I'm leaving on Monday.'

'That's a pity, but maybe we can meet up in Spain. I'm always flying over there. We have a villa in Marbella.'

The stables, the big country house, the villa . . . Felipe couldn't get excited about any of them. After all, he had those things himself. 'Of course,' he replied, and smiled politely. He was about to make an excuse about needing to find his friends when he caught sight of a woman in a show-stopping red dress. He caught his breath – it couldn't be, could it? But even from a distance he knew it was Charlie. And as if to banish any doubt she tilted her head to the side and he saw her beautiful profile.

Darcy was still chatting away but he had no idea what she was saying; all his attention was focused on Charlie. An older, handsome man had his arm round her and the two of them were laughing about something. They seemed very close. Were they a couple? Charlie hadn't wasted any time, he thought bitterly, conveniently forgetting that he was the one who had pushed her away.

'I'm sorry?' he said to Darcy. 'I didn't quite catch what you said.'

Darcy glanced over in the same direction as Felipe and noticed Charlie and Aidan, the two people at work she loathed the most. Charlie for being so popular with everyone and for calling her Arsey Darcy behind her back – one of the other PAs had let that slip – and above all for being a presenter, the role Darcy herself coveted. Aidan she disliked for the way he always seemed to look down on her. She glanced back at Felipe who seemed riveted by the sight of Charlie. He hadn't looked at *her* like that. Darcy experienced a hot flash of jealousy. Even at the ball it seemed she was going to lose out to Charlie. Well, she wasn't going to give up without a fight.

Charlie and Aidan were having a fine old time pretending to flirt with each other. The glasses of champagne they'd knocked back had helped and Aidan had perked up considerably since the taxi journey. They had chatted to various sporting stars, including Andy

Murray and Victoria Pendleton, and all in all had done their duty.

'Can I just say what a cute boyfriend you make?' Charlie whispered. She was feeling far more relaxed as well after her earlier blues.

Aidan grinned and kissed her cheek. 'That's what all the boys tell me.'

While he went off to talk to a cricketer he knew, Charlie took the opportunity to glance around the room. It was like a *Who's Who?* of the sporting world and their partners. Fingers and toes crossed TFB wouldn't be here. This wasn't his kind of scene at all. He was much happier in a club, flirting with the many girls who made it their mission to seek out wealthy footballers. She saw Gary and Danielle Lineker, Zara Phillips and Mike Tindall, Steven and Alex Gerrard, Jamie and Louise Redknapp. And then she noticed Angel and Cal Bailey. Wow! They were such a good-looking couple. Angel had just had a baby boy but you never would have known from her slender figure. She looked radiantly beautiful. Her long honey-blonde hair was in an elegant ballerina-style up do and she was wearing a gorgeous black lace evening dress. Cal, who seemed to get better-looking with every passing year, had his arm protectively around her. Charlie couldn't wait to tell her mum, who had a massive crush on Cal, along with most of the women in the country.

Charlie took another glass of champagne from a waiter and gazed at the women swishing by, so colourful with their glittering jewels and bright dresses. For an instant they reminded her of the tropical fish she'd seen in the Caribbean. Men looking suave and sophisticated in black tie were cruising by. Even old boot-faced uglies were improved by black tie, and good-looking men became staggeringly handsome in it. She noticed Darcy deep in conversation with a tall, dark-haired man – and then nearly dropped her champagne glass when she saw it was Felipe. Fuck! What he doing here? Instantly she felt breathless, giddy and light-headed. How pathetic! She was like a schoolgirl seeing her first crush.

'Hello, Charlie, my darling girl!' Another surprise. It was Luis, arm-in-arm with a beautiful woman who resembled Penelope Cruz. At this precise moment it wouldn't have surprised Charlie if it had been Penelope Cruz.

'Luis, how great to see you, but what are you doing here?' It seemed an astonishing coincidence. She thought of Zoe's OTT Cinderella comment – had her friend known that Felipe was going to be here?

'Oh, we had some business meetings in London, which coincided with the dinner. And this is my wife Mariana.'

'It is wonderful to meet you, Charlie, I've heard so much about you. And you are in every way as beautiful as Luis told me. Have you seen Felipe yet? I know he is dying for you with all his heart.' Clearly Mariana's English, which she spoke in a husky voice with an adorable Spanish accent, was not quite as good as her husband's.

'Are you sure about that?' Charlie said dryly, instantly becoming defensive.

'Oh, yes! And it is so romantic, is it not? The night before – what do you call it here?' She rattled off something in Spanish to Luis, who said, 'Valentine's Day.'

'Yes! Valentine's Day!' Mariana gushed, and then waved enthusiastically to catch Felipe's attention. Charlie thought she might need to sit down to cope with the surge of emotion that came rushing through her as Felipe saw them and strode straight across the ballroom, with Darcy in pursuit.

Charlie's mouth felt dry and her heart was racing wildly. It wasn't just from the shock of seeing Felipe. She realised that she was still absolutely furious with him. This was the man who had brutally rejected her. And now he was standing in front of her, a vision in black tie, so devastatingly handsome . . .

'Good evening, Charlie.' He was cool, polite, seemingly unaffected by meeting her again. He could give TFB lessons in how to be a bastard! The hours and hours she had spent thinking about this man, and now he was talking to her as if she was a slight acquaintance. It was outrageous!

'So how do you two know each other?' Darcy butted in. God, she was annoying. Mind your own business, Charlie wanted to retort. Instead she bit her tongue and let Felipe do the talking. Choosing not to look at Darcy, his gaze still fixed on Charlie, he replied, 'We met on holiday in Barbados.'

'How exciting,' Darcy drawled, sounding very unexcited about it.

'And then Felipe decided that he didn't want to know me and basically told me that he never wanted to see me again.' Charlie was not doing so well at keeping her cool. 'Oh, and that I was a whore! It's hard to forget that kind of comment.'

'He realises he was a complete idiot and that he made a monumental mistake, Charlie, one he deeply regrets.' Now Luis was getting involved.

'Too fucking right!' she burst out, causing other guests to look over, raising their eyebrows at the bad language.

'I do realise that I made a mistake, and I'm sorry,' Felipe put in, but to Charlie's mind he still sounded too smooth and arrogant. And he couldn't have been that sorry or he would have got in touch with her before now.

'How's the website company by the way?' she added, sounding sarcastic and spiky. Felipe didn't answer but bowed his head to acknowledge that he had screwed up.

By now Aidan had joined the group. Sensing that something was amiss, he put his arm protectively round Charlie's shoulders. 'Everything okay?'

She pointed at Felipe. 'This is Felipe, the man who dumped me because he thought I had lied to him – when all the time he had lied to me. And this is lovely Luis and his lovely wife Mariana.'

'And you are?' Felipe asked, glaring at Aidan.

He stuck out his hand. 'Aidan Shepherd. I'm lovely too, and it's lovely to meet you.' He had clearly fallen under Felipe's spell; he was bloody flirting with him!

'And you're a friend of Charlie's?' Luis asked.

'Yes, a very good friend,' Charlie replied, giving

the word 'good' extra emphasis and sliding her arm round Aidan's waist. Felipe frowned as he took in the gesture.

She felt she was in the middle of a farce, which would have been funny save for the fact that seeing Felipe again had triggered so many emotions in her, foremost of which was that, however angry she still was, she was also head over heels in lust with him.

'I'm Darcy Stratton-Hensher by the way,' Darcy said, moving forward and shaking hands with Luis and Mariana.

'And I'm sure you are lovely too,' Luis said gallantly.

I wouldn't count on it, Charlie thought, wondering why Darcy was hanging around, and then realising she most likely had her eye on Felipe. The two of them were certainly a perfect match when it came to sheer arrogance and feeling entitled to do exactly as they wanted. They could get married and combine their two posh double-barrelled names. Bastards.

A gong sounded, signalling the start of dinner.

'I guess we'd better take our seats,' Aidan said. 'Perhaps we can meet afterwards for a drink? I'm sure Charlie and Felipe have plenty of catching up to do.'

'Actually I checked the seating plan and we're sitting at the same table. That's a coincidence, isn't it?' Luis put in.

It certainly was . . . Again Charlie got a funny feeling that Zoe and Luis had known she and Felipe would be meeting tonight.

'Oh, fab, I'll see if I can join you,' Darcy added. 'It looked like I was on a table with some complete bores and I would much rather sit with you guys.' She was gazing adoringly at Felipe as she spoke. He was looking at Charlie, but she wouldn't meet his eye. Acting as if it was entirely irrelevant to her where Felipe was sitting, she took Aidan's arm, theatrically swept back her long skirt and began walking into the dining room, head held high. She was the Queen of Mean and nothing could touch her.

'What are you doing, you total loon!' Aidan whispered. 'Why are you pretending that we're an item? Do you think men like that grow on trees? Let me tell you, they categorically do not. He's divine, go get him!'

'He also dumped me and lied to me, remember?' Charlie hissed back. 'I want you to pretend that we're together. So stop looking at him with your tongue practically hanging out.'

'I can't help it. He is, as all you youngsters say, well fucking fit. I'd love to see him in a pair of tight white jodhpurs and riding boots! Maybe with no shirt on . . . or, if not, a jacket, undone to show off his chest . . . I've always been more into rowers and tennis players. Who knew that riders were so delish? The ones I've met before all had faces like pickled walnuts. But Felipe is like a god! The abs that man must possess . . . the muscular thighs. In fact, you can tell me. Don't spare me any details. Giddy up! I'll have to check out some websites when I get home. Happy days are here again!'

Charlie punched him. Aidan was slightly drunk, and his camp alter ego was coming out. That didn't suit her plan of making Felipe jealous at all.

'Ouch,' Aidan protested, rubbing his arm.

'Don't moan, I know you like it rough. And FYI, men wear breeches while riding, women wear jodhpurs.'

'Whatevs! I need another drink if I've got to pretend to be straight. I had no idea that you ladies were so macho.'

The circular tables with their crisp white cloths each seated ten people and it was pretty near impossible to have a conversation with the person opposite, so Felipe was disappointed to discover that was exactly where Charlie was sitting, sandwiched between Aidan and another man. He urgently needed the chance to talk to her, to put things right. Instead he was trapped next to Darcy, who was making her attraction to him embarrassingly obvious. Go away! he wanted to say, longing to be left alone with Charlie. Now he had seen her again he realised that any idea he could ever forget about her was absurd. He was seized with a powerful desire for her . . . he remembered how smooth her skin had felt when he had caressed her . . . remembered kissing the tattoo on her shoulder, her silky-smooth thighs . . . He gazed over at her, willing her to understand. For a second her eyes locked with his, then she quickly looked away.

Darcy's incessant chatter intruded on his thoughts. 'I had no idea Charlie and Aidan were an item. I wouldn't have thought he was her type at all.'

'And what is her type?' Felipe asked, pushing smoked salmon to the side of his plate. He wasn't hungry.

Darcy gave a sly smile. 'Oh, with the exception of you, she tends to go for the rougher sort. Her last boyfriend was a footballer. He could barely string a sentence together, but I guess he had *other* attractions for Charlie.'

If Darcy thought she was doing herself any favours by slagging off Charlie, she was very much mistaken. With each new barbed comment she sank lower and lower in Felipe's estimation. Now he could add bitchy to the list of things he knew about her.

'Then again, I imagine Charlie's used to that kind of man, given her background.'

And now he could add snob. He stifled a yawn.

Darcy, realising that she was losing him, went for the kill as she whispered, 'Did you know that her brother's in prison?'

Felipe recalled Charlie not wanting to talk about her twin. He sighed. 'That's hardly her fault, is it? I'm sure we all have things we are not proud of in our lives.'

'Of course. I only said it because I feel sorry for her.'

Felipe didn't believe that for a second. He glanced at Darcy's smooth pretty face. It showed no sign of sympathy. Then he noticed Charlie getting up from the table and, muttering a hasty 'Excuse me', took the opportunity to follow her. They had to talk.

Charlie felt shaken up and jittery. She couldn't eat, and nor could she keep up the pretence that she and Aidan were an item. All she could think about was Felipe. She was so intensely aware of him across the table from her. She had felt his gaze on her and it had taken every ounce of self-control to tear her eyes away. She needed to get out of here, to clear her head and decide what to do. She quickly left the ballroom, heading in the direction of the Ladies. She was halfway down a long corridor with mirrored walls when Felipe called after her. She stopped and spun round. He was a few feet away. God, why did he have to be so handsome! Even more handsome than she had remembered. It wasn't fair. She wanted to hate him for what he'd done, to run away from him, but she couldn't.

'Charlie, please wait, I need to talk to you.'

'What makes you think I want to listen to anything *you* have to say! Why don't you go back and carry on flirting with Darcy? She's much more your type. You're both arrogant, rich and spoilt!'

Felipe shrugged off the insult. 'You're the only woman who interests me, Charlie.'

It was unfortunate that Darcy had chosen that moment to go to the Ladies and heard their comments as she passed by. Charlie would almost have felt sorry for her but for the intensely hostile look the other woman shot her. Felipe barely seemed to register Darcy. He stepped closer to Charlie. 'Please give me the chance to talk. We can go in here.' He pointed out an empty room off the corridor, that was being used to store tables and chairs.

Charlie hesitated, then followed him. Once inside the room he shut the door behind them. Charlie stood, with arms folded, trying to keep her expression as neutral as possible, while all the while emotions battled inside her. Lust, anger, longing, hurt pride, all vying to be the most powerful . . .

'What do you want to talk about? You've already

apologised. What more can you have to say to me? Oh, I know, how about the fact that you didn't tell me who you were and what you do? Talk about hypocritical!'

Felipe had his hands in his jacket pockets, and seemed less sure of himself. 'I should have been honest with you from the start, it's true. I get the feeling that you don't take my apology seriously?'

'Oh, I do apologise, my lord,' Charlie said sarcastically, making a curtsey to him. But even as she sounded so uptight, all she could think about was how much she wanted him . . . it was fucked up, but she couldn't help it.

Felipe moved closer. 'Please, Charlie, do we have to fight? I was a fool, a complete idiot, just as Luis said. I should have believed you, but past experience has made me mistrustful of journalists. The fact that you didn't tell me what you do caused me to be defensive and too quick to jump to conclusions. The wrong conclusions.'

'Why has it taken you so long to realise your mistake?' Charlie still sounded hard but she was softening, his dark brown eyes were very persuasive . . . and he was close enough that she could smell his delicious musky aftershave, a scent that triggered memories of lying in his arms and making love in the afternoon.

'I told myself that I could forget you. I didn't want to admit that I was wrong. But seeing you tonight has changed all that, made me realise that I can't forget you, Charlie. I can't forget how good we were together.' Felipe moved closer still. Reaching for her hand, he raised it to his lips and kissed it. 'And I don't think you have forgotten either.'

Charlie shivered at the feel of his lips on her skin. She wasn't sure who made the next move but suddenly they were in each other's arms and he was kissing her, and instead of being outraged, she was kissing him back for all she was worth, an intense, passionate, must-have-you kiss. His hands slid over her shoulders, down her back. She remembered what it felt like when they made love, and realised that was what she burned to do now. She pressed her body against his, boldly ran her hand over his chest. She had to have contact with his skin. She pulled open the buttons of his shirt, then dipped lower still. She dared to unbutton his fly and caressed him.

'What are you doing to me?' Felipe murmured.

He bunched up her skirt and his fingers circled her inner thigh . . . tantalising, teasing, brushing over her lace briefs. She was melting at his touch. Her body was screaming for him to possess her . . . But suddenly a vivid image came into her mind, a memory of the look of disdain on Felipe's face when he had told her he never wanted to see her again. He had made her feel so completely worthless. That look had burned into her consciousness. It was also a brutal reminder of the way TFB had cheated on her. If she made love with Felipe now he would only turn round and hurt her again. However much she ached for him, she could not, *would* not, allow herself to be vulnerable again.

'D'you want me?' she murmured, knowing perfectly well what the answer would be.

'So much,' came his reply, in a voice that was husky with desire.

With an immense effort Charlie pulled herself away from him. 'Well, you can't have me!' And before Felipe had the chance to stop her, she raced out of the room and carried on running all the way out of the hotel, where she jumped straight into a waiting taxi, knowing that if she didn't get right away from Felipe, this minute, she would do something she regretted.

Chapter 9

Luis could not stop laughing when Felipe told him what had happened back at the hotel.

'You really are a complete idiot, my friend. And it's entirely your fault. You needed to woo her, romance her, make her feel special . . . not leap on her like a randy schoolboy.'

Felipe undid his bow tie and dropped it on the floor. No woman had ever left him in that situation before. His pride was severely dented, and other parts much deflated . . . He flung himself down on the sofa and put his head in his hands. How could he have blown it with Charlie twice? He wasn't used to failing like this with women. It was humiliating. *Very* humiliating. He looked up at his friends.

'I thought she wanted me. I'm misreading everything. I don't know what I can do.' This was quite an admission from a man who had always thought he knew exactly what women wanted.

Mariana picked up the bow tie and handed Felipe a

cup of black coffee. 'It's not as bad as you think. But you do need to put more effort into winning her back. After Charlie left, I had a very interesting talk with Aidan. Charming man. He and Charlie are most definitely not together. I'm almost one hundred per cent certain that he's gay. They are simply friends and work colleagues – whatever Charlie was trying to make you believe. He is convinced that she still has feelings for you but doesn't want to admit it. No doubt because of the appalling way you treated her. And because of her horrid ex who cheated on her.'

Felipe winced at the reminder, but at least Mariana wasn't laughing at him. He drank some coffee and started to feel slightly more optimistic about his chances.

'I've also been finding out about what Charlie is doing tomorrow. In the morning she coaches a girls' football team at a school in Wandsworth, which is in South London. In the afternoon she will go to the gym, and in the evening she has no plans. So there are more than enough opportunities for you to charm her tomorrow. And it being Valentine's Day, what could be a more perfect time for your reconciliation?'

'What makes you so sure she will be charmed by me?'

'Because she still has feelings for you, believe it or not, that much is obvious to everyone.' Mariana handed him a piece of paper on which she had written down Charlie's itinerary for the following day. 'If you don't try and win her back you will regret it for ever. And for ever, my dearest Felipe, is a very long time.'

He looked at his two best friends and suddenly realised that it was far too much of a coincidence he had ended up at the same event as Charlie. 'That dinner wasn't about meeting new clients. You planned for me to see her, didn't you?' he said accusingly.

'Yes, we did, along with Zoe,' Luis replied cheerfully. 'We've been in contact since Barbados. You've no idea how complicated it's been playing Cupid – like a military campaign.'

Felipe threw a cushion at Luis's head, but his friend ducked and laughed.

'Why the hell didn't you tell me?' Felipe exclaimed. 'That way I might have been more prepared and not fucked it up again.'

'You have many good qualities, but you're also the most stubborn man I know. I thought you were more than likely to refuse to come to the dinner if I told you.'

That silenced Felipe. Luis continued, 'We all know that the feelings you and Charlie have for each other go far deeper than a holiday fling.' He looked at Mariana and smiled. 'And as you introduced me to my wife, the love of my life, I felt it was about time I repaid the debt.'

Mariana kissed her husband and then blew Felipe a kiss. 'I know you're not really cross with us. You must go to bed, you need to be super-fresh for tomorrow. And no pressure, but you really can't afford to blow it this time.'

Then, taking Luis's hand, she led him off to their next-door suite.

Felipe slumped back on the sofa. He felt as if he'd been put through the mill emotionally. Was there possibly a way to win Charlie back? He fervently hoped so; he was starting to believe he couldn't be happy again without this beautiful woman in his life.

Charlie was in bed, but unable to sleep. Her mind was still buzzing from the after-effects of seeing Felipe. And not just seeing him . . . she had never before experienced such intense desire. A few minutes longer with him and she knew she would never have been able to pull away. But she had to forget about him. He was a one-way ticket to heartbreak and she had been there before. And yet . . . how could she forget him?

Her phone vibrated with a text message. Who would be texting her at half two in the morning? For a second she wondered if it was Felipe. Maybe he too couldn't sleep and was writing to tell her that he had to see her again. Instead it was an automated reminder that she had an appointment at the dentist on Tuesday – how romantic. Felipe was probably sleeping soundly. Or maybe he had gone back with Arsey Darcy and done the deed with her. Though maybe not, since he had said he wasn't interested in her. Then again, he was very charming and could probably talk his way out of that one. Darcy had certainly seemed very interested in him, and although she was annoying she was also stunning . . . Oh, for God's sake! Why couldn't she get this man out of her head? Charlie punched her pillow in frustration – both at herself for caring and at Felipe. At this rate she was going to be knackered for football training tomorrow.

She only fell asleep around four, and as a result

overslept. Fortunately she was low-maintenance, so it was a quick shower, tinted moisturiser, lip balm, mascara, and hair tied back in a pony-tail. Clothes were a tee-shirt, oversized black hoodie and Puffa gilet over baggy tracksuit bottoms and trainers. A complete contrast to the all-out glamour of last night.

Charlie's weekends used to be taken up with riding. But since the accident she'd found that she had to fill up her time in other ways when she wasn't working. So if she wasn't doing a presenting shift, Saturdays were now set aside for a two-hour session with her personal trainer and, once a month, she helped out with a girls' football team on a Sunday.

Brandon, who was one of the team's coaches, met her as she raced into the sports centre. He had a massive crush on her, which Charlie was fully aware of as every time he spoke to her he blushed. He was boyishly good-looking but reminded her a bit too much of TFB with his shaved head and cheeky grin. He had hoped to be a professional footballer but hadn't quite been good enough, so he had given up the dream and trained as a PE teacher instead.

'Hi, Charlie, how are you?' His cheeks flamed as he said her name. He was sweet. Maybe she could experiment with being a cougar? Brandon didn't look like he could break her heart and trample over her self-esteem.

'I'm good, thanks, Brandon.'

He cleared his throat. 'So did you get any Valentine cards?'

Shit! The cutesy bear must have come from him. There was no way she could be a cougar to a man who sent pictures of cutesy bears. He probably still lived at home and his mum ironed his boxers. It was plain wrong.

'Oh, yeah, I did.'

Brandon's cheeks turned a shade redder. 'I was wondering if you had any plans for tonight? I mean, I'm sure you're bound to, but I thought I read that you'd split up with that footballer . . . and if you were free, then I could take you out.'

It was the longest speech Brandon had ever made to her. She would have to let him down gently. 'That's so sweet of you, but I can't. I have plans.' A bottle of Sauvignon Blanc had her name on it, along with an M&S ready meal (because no one should cook their own dinner on Valentine's Day, right?) and *Kill Bill 1*. She was in no mood for a rom-com.

Brandon looked crushed; it must have taken a lot of courage for him to ask her out and Charlie felt slightly guilty. Not guilty enough to say yes, though.

'So how did the girls get on last week?'

'They got well and truly beaten. It was a massacre.' He was a bit sulky now she had rejected him. Charlie could only hope he hadn't spoken in that tone to the girls; it would be too demoralising for them. She sighed. 'Okay, that was last week. Fingers crossed, things will be better this week.'

Charlie stashed her bag in one of the lockers in the communal changing room that always smelt of trainers and sickly floral body sprays. She headed out to the pitch where Dave, one of the girls' dad, was putting them through some warm-up exercises. Dave was the main reason why Charlie had ended up working with the team. He had contacted her at work and asked if she would agree to help out for six months, figuring that having someone like her on their side would inspire the team, which to some degree it had. But Charlie was convinced it was mainly so he could get one up on the rival teams, as Dave was the most fiercely competitive dad she had ever encountered. Given half the chance, he would have had the girls training every single night of the week, appearing to forget they were only ten years old.

It was a bitterly cold morning, the sky was a depressing grey and Charlie shivered, even in her layers of clothes. Since coming back from Barbados she seemed to be cold all the time. In spite of her resolution not to think of him she wondered what Felipe was doing right now. Probably doing Darcy, she told herself. And then an image of his beautiful tanned back came into her head, his broad shoulders, his . . .

'All right, Charlie, could you get us the First Aid box? Charmaine's got a nose bleed again.' Dave's booming voice cut across her thoughts. It was probably for the best, she thought, sprinting back to the changing room.

'At the roundabout take the third exit,' intoned mistress Sat Nav in Felipe's hire car. He promptly miscounted and took the second. He was renowned for being a terrible navigator, even with Sat Nav telling him exactly what to do, plus he'd barely had any sleep, no breakfast, and the two coffees he'd drunk were making him on edge.

'Recalculating,' intoned the Sat Nav. Not for the first time on this journey.

'*Mierda!*' Felipe shouted. 'Where's the fucking school?'

'Take the next left.'

Felipe missed the next left. He should have accepted Luis's offer to drive him. At this rate Charlie would already have left for the gym. Of course he could have texted her and asked her to meet him, but a text seemed too casual and he had a suspicion that Charlie might well not even reply. No, he had to see her face to face.

It was a tense twenty minutes before he finally pulled up outside the school, just in time to see Charlie hugging a hulking great lad in a tracksuit. Felipe felt as if he had been punched. Surely she was not with *him*! Before Felipe had a chance to get out of the car, Charlie had jumped into a cream Fiat 500 and driven off, with the lad staring wistfully after her. Triple *mierda*! Felipe slammed his hand against the steering wheel in frustration.

'You have reached your destination,' the Sat Nav informed him, the computerised female voice sounding smug.

'I know, you stupid woman! But it's too fucking late!' he shouted, startling a young mum pushing a pram across the road in front of him, who gave him a funny look and increased her pace, keen to get well away from the ranting lunatic.

In fact Charlie was too physically exhausted to go to the gym and far too emotionally wound up about Felipe. What she needed was a heart-to-heart with Zoe. She decided to drop in on her friend's boutique. Seeing

Felipe again had shaken her. She realised that she had been sleep-walking through these past three weeks, pretending not to care, when all the time the truth was staring her in the face – she still wanted him. Oh, God, she wanted him so much! In spite of running around in the freezing cold on a muddy football pitch, having to mop up a nosebleed, calm down twelve hysterical girls who had won . . . the memory of last night and Felipe was still burning away inside her.

Once she'd arrived in Wimbledon Charlie managed to squeeze her car into a tiny space just off the High Street. In contrast to Felipe she was a great driver, with a brilliant sense of direction. She checked her phone; there was still nothing from him. Bastard! Surely if he wanted to see her again he would have called or texted. Charlie failed to take into account the fact that she was the one who had run out on him last night. She bought a couple of take-out lattes and chocolate croissants from the patisserie near Zoe's boutique. Frankly she could have done with a drink, but coffee and croissants would have to do.

Zoe was in the middle of serving a customer when Charlie walked into the chic but cosy boutique. Zoe hated those designer stores that had big open spaces and three garments on display while haughty sales assistants looked down their noses at anyone who wasn't a size zero and sporting the latest designer handbag. Her staff were the complete opposite, all friendly, charming girls who knew how to make the clients feel good about themselves, whatever their age, shape, size or bank balance. The store itself was painted an inviting chocolate brown with dark wooden floorboards and richly patterned rugs. And when clients went into the fitting rooms, they found flattering lighting and mirrors that made the whole experience a pleasure and not a form of punishment devised by a sadist who liked people to suffer while they tried on clothes.

Mouthing 'Hiya' to Zoe, Charlie nipped into the office-cum-staff rest area at the back of the store, and sat down on the comfortable sofa to await her friend. She checked her phone again. Nothing. She thought of her mum, who was fond of saying that back in her day there was none of this texting, Facebooking malarkey, and life was more straightforward. Though Charlie imagined that it must still have been torture if you were waiting for a telephone call or a letter. She sipped her coffee, picked at her croissant and tried to distract herself by flicking through *Grazia*, but it was hopeless, her thoughts kept returning to Felipe . . . It had been hard enough not to think about him when he was in Spain, but now he was out there in London, it was impossible.

'Hiya, babes.' Zoe breezed in, looking polished in a cream silk pussybow blouse and black leather pencil skirt. 'Come for a makeover?' She took in Charlie's mud splattered trainers and sportswear, and visibly shuddered.

Charlie ignored the good-natured dig. 'I hope you don't mind me turning up when you're working? I just had to talk to you.'

'I thought you would after last night.' Zoe sat down next to Charlie and kicked off her heels. 'And, yes, we do need to talk, starting with why did you run out on Felipe like that? Luis has told me everything. D'you have any idea how long it took him to persuade Felipe to go to the dinner?'

Charlie looked at her friend in disbelief. 'He *arranged* for Felipe to be there? I knew it seemed like too much of a coincidence!'

'Yep. And before you have a go, remember how well you two got on before Felipe found out what you did. Any idiot can see that . . .' Zoe paused and then grinned. 'Any idiot except you two, which is why Luis and I had to step in. Like your Fairy Godfather and mother.'

'Pity Felipe isn't such a Prince Charming . . .' Charlie muttered bitterly. 'First he was flirting with Darcy, then he practically jumped on me.'

Zoe tutted. 'Stop rewriting history, Cinders. I have it on good authority that he did not flirt with Arsey Darcy, and that you gave as good as you got.'

Charlie stretched out her long legs and shoved her hands in her hoodie pockets. 'So what do you suggest?' she asked sulkily.

An eye roll from Zoe. 'I bet Cinders never put out that attitude to her Fairy Godmother! Listen up, Charlie, because you're going to get it right this time. Tonight you and Felipe are going out for dinner, and you are going to sort things out between you once and for all. I've already made a reservation at Antonio's. I had to offer Toni a massive discount at the boutique for his wife. It's Valentine's Night and his tables have been booked up for weeks.'

'You didn't have to do that!' Charlie exclaimed, suddenly feeling guilty that her friend had gone to so much trouble.

'It's only because I know how good you two could be together. And that's why you're here, isn't it? Because you can't stop thinking about Felipe.'

Charlie bit her lip and nodded.

'So all you have to do is go home, pour yourself a glass of wine, have a bath and put this on.' Zoe stood up and reached for a dress on the rack behind her – a cute, sexy, skater-style dress in coral.

'Can't I wear jeans?'

'You'll wear this and thank me for it.'

God, Zoe was so bossy! 'Now who's got the attitude?' Charlie retorted.

Zoe responded by flipping a finger. Definitely not in a Fairy Godmother's repertoire.

Felipe had got so hopelessly lost as he attempted to drive back to the hotel that he ended up abandoning the hire care in Hammersmith and taking a taxi back to the hotel. He just had time to pour himself a glass of water before Luis and Mariana knocked on his door, desperate to find out how the big reunion with Charlie had gone. They couldn't believe that he hadn't even talked to her.

'I knew I should have driven you!' Luis declared. 'You're a sublime horseman, but an idiot behind the wheel. A clear case of four legs good, four wheels bad.'

Felipe glared at him. Like he needed a critique of

his driving right now. He wasn't sure that his ego could take much more of a hammering . . .

'Never mind his atrocious sense of direction!' Mariana cried. 'There are more important things at stake. So tonight Zoe has booked a table for the two of you at a restaurant near Charlie's house, and there you can finally tell her how you feel.'

'How do you even know she will come to the restaurant?' Felipe demanded. 'She's more than capable of standing me up.'

'She certainly likes standing up a certain part of you!' Mariana said cheekily.

He never should have told them what had happened last night; his friends were not going to let him forget it in a hurry.

'But she probably feels she made her point then,' Mariana added, trying not to laugh.

Felipe shot her a warning look; he did not want another innuendo made at his expense.

Mariana smiled sweetly and continued, 'And don't forget, we have her address. If she doesn't show up, you can always go round there.'

'Assuming she will let me in,' came Felipe's sulky reply.

Mariana threw her hands in the air. 'Felipe Castillo de Rivas, you would try the patience of a saint!'

Finally Felipe grinned at his friends. 'I'm sorry. Of course I will go tonight. Thank you for arranging it, but don't expect to hear all the details . . . I think you two are enjoying this a little bit too much.'

'And promise you will get a taxi?' Luis added.

'And what about flowers?' Mariana put in. 'You must take flowers. It's Valentine's Day. Do you want us to arrange a bouquet for you?'

'I am perfectly capable of buying flowers,' he replied. Did his friends think that he was a complete imbecile? It was probably best if he didn't ask them that, given what had happened so far with Charlie.

'Zoe has already told me that Charlie's favourites are oriental lilies, white roses, and freesias. Definitely no carnations or chrysanthemums.' Mariana was actually reading from a list. 'Oh, and she hates red roses . . . something to do with an ex sending her two dozen after he was unfaithful. What a worm! Who would ever cheat on beautiful Charlie?'

'And to think that I was going to stop off at a service station and buy a bunch of pink carnations or red roses or both.' Felipe couldn't resist teasing them.

'Don't worry,' he added, seeing their serious expressions, 'I promise I am not going to blow it this time.'

Chapter 10

Charlie had toyed with the idea of being late for Felipe and keeping him waiting, but in the end she was only ten minutes late and to her dismay discovered that she was the first to arrive. Great, so now he was most likely going to stand *her* up . . . And on Valentine's Day of all days! Take the shame!

The cosy restaurant was packed with couples all doing their best to seem as loved up as they could, but at least half of them looked as if they had nothing to say to each other and would so much rather have been out with their mates. It was nauseating. Charlie had never liked going out on Valentine's Day. So far hers was the only table for one.

She was about to order a glass of wine when the waiter brought over a bottle of champagne. 'A gift from your friends,' he told her when she explained that she hadn't ordered it. Charlie shook her head and smiled. You couldn't accuse Luis and Zoe of not having tried their best . . . now it was up to Felipe and her. 'Would you like a glass now?' the waiter asked.

She wondered if she should wait for Felipe before she had a glass, then figured she would go ahead without him. She needed something to help with the nervous anticipation fizzing away inside her as frantically as the champagne bubbles. 'Yes please,' she replied. Her hand was shaking so much when she picked up her glass that it overflowed on to the table. She checked her phone. No messages. Five minutes went by. She checked her phone again. He wasn't coming, she convinced herself, disconsolately snapping a breadstick in half. She would give it another five minutes and then go. She fiddled with the single red rose in the vase, pulling off several petals. Served it right, she loathed red roses. But then Felipe walked into the restaurant, and Charlie's heart raced that little bit faster. He looked so handsome in a dark brown leather jacket and black jeans. He smiled at her and walked over to the table. He was holding a beautiful bouquet of flowers – all pale pinks and whites, not a red rose in sight.

'Charlie, I'm sorry I'm late, the traffic was bad.'

The traffic! That was hardly up there with the most romantic lines of all time, was it?

He lightly kissed her cheek and instantly Charlie started analysing the kiss. Surely it had been too polite, the kind of kiss you would give a friend. It didn't compare with their passionate kiss the night before. Was this dinner simply going to be about him apologising and that would be it? Something to make his conscience feel better before he moved on to the next woman?

'You haven't been waiting long, I hope?' Felipe asked. Polite again. What had happened to the reckless, intense passion?

'Oh, no, I've only just got here.' She hoped he didn't notice that her champagne glass was almost empty. Either he would think she was a desperate saddo who'd been waiting ages, or a drunk. She didn't know which was worse . . .

'Would you like a glass of champagne? It's a present from Luis and Zoe.'

Felipe smiled. 'How like them. These are for you, of course.' He handed her the bouquet.

'Thank you,' she replied. The flowers were promising. There was nothing worse than bad flowers, but these were elegant lovely blooms. She started to feel a little more hopeful.

He reached for the bottle of champagne and topped up her glass without comment then filled his own. He held it up. 'To no running away this time.'

Charlie could feel herself blushing when she thought about last night and the state she'd left him in . . .

She clinked her glass against his. 'Okay. Deal.'

Conversation was then further stalled by the arrival of the waiter to take their order. Charlie was far too nervous to think about food and ordered spinach and ricotta cannelloni as that was what she always had.

Once the waiter had gone, Felipe leant forward. 'So, Charlie, will you let me explain my behaviour? I don't think I can bear for you to think badly of me for another second.'

Now he was sitting opposite her, his handsome face

so serious and intense, his brown eyes imploring her to believe him, Charlie didn't think she would ever think badly of him again. She nodded and listened as he filled her in on a side to him she had only known about through stories on the web. He came from a wealthy, aristocratic family; he was an international event rider and ran his own equestrian centre. In a month's time he would find out if he had been picked to compete in the Spanish Olympic eventing team, which was something he had dreamt of doing all his life. He had missed out on the last Olympics because of a broken wrist.

Charlie had wanted to hear his side of the story, but with every detail he seemed to be moving further and further away from her. She suddenly felt as if they were a completely lost cause. This relationship could be nothing more than a holiday romance; there were too many obstacles in the way. She wished he was simply a business-man. That way they might have stood a chance . . .

He finished, 'So now you know everything about me, Charlie.' He was smiling and seemed relieved to have told her the truth, unaware of the impact on her.

She gave a brittle smile. 'So you come from a posh family, mine's working-class. You ride and I can't do that any more. I can't bear to watch anyone ride, and I can't even talk about it, that's how bad it is. And I know that riding must be your whole life, especially in the run-up to the Olympics. You live in Spain and I live in England. I think we should face facts. We only worked as a holiday fling.'

He frowned; this was not the outcome he had expected, but he had reckoned without Charlie's vulnerability. He reached for her hand and clasped it in his, fearing that he was about to lose her again.

'You make too much of things that aren't important. What my family thinks does not matter – besides, they will all love you.' Everyone except my mother, he thought, though he wasn't going to tell Charlie that.

'And I'll do whatever it takes to help you overcome your fear of riding. You can overcome it, I swear. Yes, I wish we lived in the same country but we are not so very far away. I once made the mistake of throwing away what we had. Don't do the same thing, Charlie, I beg you. What I feel for you, I've never felt for any woman before. Never.'

He could see that she was struggling to stay composed. He had to make her see that they could make this work. But right then the waiter appeared with their orders and suddenly Felipe saw that if they remained in this restaurant he was going to lose her again. He turned to the waiter.

'I'm sorry. Would you be able to box up the meal? There's been a change of plan.'

Charlie looked up at him questioningly.

'We are going to your place,' he said firmly, 'I don't think I can sit here another moment.'

Back at the flat they didn't even make it to the bedroom as he took her in his arms and they kissed with a fierce intensity. They fell back on to the sofa driven with a passionate need to possess each other. The flowers and boxes of food were abandoned on the floor.

'I want you so much, Charlie,' he told her in between

kisses. 'You are all I can think about.' He pushed up her dress, ripped her tights as he pulled them off her. She didn't care. She only wanted to feel him inside her.

He had barely caressed her when Charlie felt an orgasm take hold of her, shuddering through her in delicious waves that made her yearn for more. 'Fuck me then,' she implored him. As he slipped off his jeans, his rock-hard cock was ready for her. She pulled him down to her, gasping with pleasure as he slid inside her. And then it was a feverish, frantic fuck as the lovers were reunited.

'I'm sorry that was too quick,' Felipe told her afterwards, 'I was so desperate for you.'

'Well, we have all night,' Charlie murmured, lightly kissing him. She still couldn't quite believe that he was here, lying naked in her arms on the sofa. If it was a dream, it was the most bloody fantastic one she'd ever had.

He gazed at her. 'I really want us to be together, Charlie. I know there are many things that seem to be against us, but we are both strong, we are both fighters, we can make it work, I know we can.'

She curled her arms around him. 'It's what I want too. More than anything.'

Morning came too soon for them. Charlie longed to keep the curtains closed and stay in bed with Felipe; the thought of being apart from him again seemed too brutal. They'd only had one night together; it wasn't nearly enough. But she forced herself out of his embrace, showered and prepared to face the day, because that's what you did, even if you longed with all your heart not to . . .

She was sitting at her dressing table and brushing her hair, when Felipe returned after his shower. He had a white towel wrapped round his waist and the sight of his beautiful body and gorgeous olive-brown skin, made her want him all over again. And yet now, in the daylight, there was something that bothered her . . . Felipe came straight over to her and went to kiss her, but Charlie put her hand on his chest to hold him back. 'Tell me the truth. If Luis and Zoe hadn't set up our meeting, would you have got back in touch with me?'

'I couldn't go on much longer without seeing you. I thought of you all the time. And if you don't believe me, look at this.' He picked up his phone from the bedside table and showed her his recent search history. All the pages were to do with her.

'And I still had these pictures of you.' Now he selected the photographs on his phone, which were all of her or of the two of them on holiday. 'And these.' Finally he selected the draft folder of his email. There were ten unsent messages to Charlie, all expressing his longing to see her again and deep regret for his behaviour.

'You could have sent them,' Charlie said, thoroughly charmed by what he had shown her, and also regretting that they had wasted all this time. 'You're too stubborn. I bet you hate saying you're wrong. Admit it?'

'You're right, of course, but in this case I am delighted to say that I was wrong.'

Charlie wound her arms round his neck and pulled him to her. 'Say it again,' she demanded, kissing him.

'I can do better than that.' And picking her up easily, he swung her back on to the bed.

There was definitely something to be said for having a world-class sportsman for your lover, Charlie thought as she pulled off the towel to reveal Felipe in his full impressive naked glory.

'I love making love with you in the morning,' he told her afterwards.

'Only in the morning?' she teased.

'And in the afternoon, and in the evening. When you come over to Spain we can stay in bed all weekend and fuck like crazy.'

'Don't say that,' Charlie told him. 'You make me want you all over again.'

'Good, that's the idea,' he replied, kissing her. They couldn't get enough of each other.

It was nearly lunch-time when they finally managed to tear themselves away from each other and get ready to go to the airport where Luis and Mariana were meeting him. They wanted to spend every minute they possibly could together. Time had suddenly become incredibly precious.

As they were about to go out of the front door Felipe noticed the post had arrived. He picked it up and handed it to Charlie. She winced as she recognised the handwriting on one of the envelopes.

'What is it?' he asked, seeing her expression.

'Nothing important. Some saddo who's been sending me nasty messages.'

Felipe held out his hand. 'Don't look at it. Give it to me and I'll throw it away.'

But Charlie had already ripped open the envelope, determined to deal with the note herself. This time it wasn't a photograph but a print-out of a *Manchester Evening News* article reporting on her accident. There was a picture of her riding Ace, taken some months before the accident. *Murderer* was scrawled over it in blood-red ink. How could anyone be so twisted? She felt a wave of nausea and pressed her hand over her mouth. Felipe grabbed the cutting from her.

'Bastards!' he exclaimed, screwing it up. He took her in his arms. 'It's all right,' he told her, gently stroking her hair. 'It's just someone who is jealous of you. You mustn't let it get to you. It wasn't your fault that Ace was killed.'

Charlie buried her face in his shoulder, breathed in his delicious scent and felt the warmth of his body envelop and comfort her. For a few minutes they remained in the embrace. Then she looked up at him, 'I'm okay now. Let's go.' She didn't really feel okay, but had become good at hiding her feelings.

'Are you sure?'

She nodded, 'I'm not going to let it get to me. Come on, we'll get a taxi.' And, grabbing his hand, she ran out of the house as if wanting to escape.

It had to be one of the saddest feelings in the world, saying goodbye to your lover at an airport, Charlie thought, watching Felipe go through to departures along with Luis and Mariana. Felipe blew her one last kiss through the glass and then Charlie turned and walked out of the airport as quickly as she could. Two weeks is not a long time, she tried to tell herself as she stepped outside and got in line for a taxi. Her phone beeped with a message and she smiled as she read the text from Felipe: *Miss you already beautiful Charlie xx*

She was still glowing from being with him as she walked into the office later that afternoon. The only desk available – as they all had to hot desk – was one opposite Darcy and even that didn't bother her. Charlie felt as if she had an invisible force field of happiness around her that not even Arsey Darcy could disturb. As ever she was hard at work playing Solitaire.

'Hi, Darcy, how are you?' Charlie said, sitting down, keen to log in to the computer and check her emails. She felt slightly guilty, knowing that the PA had overheard her critical comments to Felipe, and hoped they could both pretend the incident hadn't happened.

Darcy managed to drag her eyes away from the screen long enough to drawl, 'Oh, hi Charlie. The same as ever. You know, arrogant, rich and spoilt.'

Oops. 'Er, I'm sorry. I was a bit drunk, I didn't mean it.' Charlie hesitated, not in the habit of talking about her personal life in front of Darcy. 'It was quite emotional for me, seeing Felipe again, but I shouldn't have said those things about you.'

She shrugged. 'Sure. Whatever.'

'So did you have a good weekend?' Charlie asked, hoping to draw a line under what had happened.

'Fab. I've just found out that my parents have bought me a horse for my birthday. He's a divine grey called Mischief.' A smile played over Darcy's lips and for a second Charlie wondered if the other woman knew about the accident and was taunting her. Then she dismissed the thought; she was just being paranoid because of the newspaper article. She had known for ages that Darcy was a keen rider.

'When's your birthday?' Charlie managed to say, really hoping that was the end of the conversation.

'On Wednesday. It looked to me like you and Felipe had a lot to talk about at that dinner. Did you see any more of him afterwards?'

Quite a bit, Charlie thought, as an image of his beautiful naked body stretched out on her bed came into her mind, not that she was going to share that with Darcy. 'I did actually,' she said, adding briskly, 'but now he's back in Spain and I must get on with some work.'

She kept her head down after that as she went through some research notes and the running order for the night's show. It was a relief when Darcy got up and slunk out of the room, no doubt going for a fag.

Aidan turned up next. Throwing his leather messenger bag on to the desk he said expectantly, 'Well?'

Charlie looked around the newsroom; she wasn't about to tell all in front of a pack of reporters and researchers, who had hearing like bats and no discretion.

'Coffee?' she suggested.

*

Aidan was hugely excited at the news she had finally got back together with Felipe. 'I never thought TFB was in your league quite frankly, darling – forgive the footie reference – but Felipe is a different proposition alto- gether. The man is a god!' His excitement was prompting his camp alter ego to come out again. He pronounced 'darling' exactly as Craig Revel-Horwood did.

Charlie pouted. 'I suppose you think he's slumming it by being with me?'

'Don't be crazy! I only meant that he's gorgeous. And *you're* gorgeous,' Aidan appeased her. 'You make the most gorgeous couple. You'll have beautiful babies, who'll be bilingual. You'll divide your time between your London pad and his massive *cortijo* – that's house to you, sweetie, with its extensive *finca* – that's land. See, I'm not just a pretty face, I can speak the lingo. There, happy now?'

He was much less happy when she revealed that she had been sent another message by their mystery stalker.

'How could they have known about the accident?'

'I suppose they must have Googled me,' Charlie replied. It was horrible to think of someone digging into her past like that and then putting their own nasty twist on it.

Aidan shook his head. 'What a vicious little shit they must be.' He paused then asked, 'So have you phoned my therapist yet?'

'I haven't had time, but I will do it,' Charlie lied. She knew that if she told Aidan she had no intention of making the call, he would be on her case all the time.

He sighed. 'Make time, sweetie. You're dating an internationally famous horseman. You've got to start that therapy.'

'Sure,' she replied, not quite meeting his eye.

Chapter 11

Felipe walked into the busy restaurant and looked around for Eduardo, his brother. It was Friday night and they were meeting for dinner. It was the end of a long week where Felipe had been training hard and missing Charlie. Talking on the phone or texting was small compensation. He was counting the days until he saw her again. Eduardo was already at the table, frowning with concentration as he checked his emails. His only concession to its being Friday night was that he had undone the top button of his shirt and loosened his tie. Felipe smiled to himself. His brother the lawyer was always working. He reached the table, wondering if Eduardo would even notice his arrival, but his brother immediately put down his phone, stood up and warmly embraced him.

'I'm going to switch your phone off while we have dinner,' Felipe told him. 'You work too hard.'

'You can talk. How is training going?'

The two brothers chatted easily about what they had

been doing and Eduardo wanted to hear all about Charlie. They had always got on well and Eduardo's sexuality had never been an issue for his younger brother.

'So what have you bought Mama for her birthday?' Eduardo asked, halfway through the seafood risotto. He was always the member of the family who remembered important events.

Felipe slapped his hand to his forehead. *'Joder!* I keep forgetting.'

'Too tied up with the beautiful Charlie?' Eduardo grinned at him. 'Well, you have over a month to get her something extra-special. You know what she's like. She might say that she doesn't want anything, but woe betide anyone who takes her at her word. I've bought her an antique jewellery case.'

'Show off,' Felipe teased.

His brother sighed. 'It's all pointless, it won't make her any more accepting of Ricky.' Last year he had married his long-term American boyfriend. To avoid any family tensions they had held the ceremony on a beach in Malibu with only two friends present. But in spite of the commitment Eduardo and Ricky had made, his mother still didn't see it as a 'proper' relationship.

'And then there's her birthday party on the twenty-fifth. She's planning a huge event at the house.'

'I wonder if I could get out of it by claiming I need to train . . .' Felipe loathed those big parties where his mother acted like a queen and all the guests sucked up to her.

Eduardo shook his head and added, 'It gets worse, I'm afraid.'

'Oh, Christ, how can it?'

'She's asked Paloma.'

Felipe slammed down his hand on the table. 'Fuck! Why can't she let it go? I told her that there is no chance I will ever get back with Paloma, but she can't resist meddling, can she?'

'That's Mama. All her hopes are pinned on you.' Eduardo smiled sympathetically.

'Maybe Paloma won't come.' Felipe was clutching at straws. He knew it was almost certain that his ex would accept the invitation. She had always got on well with Vittoria and Felipe knew Paloma still wanted him back. She had been sending him texts every couple of days asking if they could meet up. Felipe always made an excuse. And then only three nights ago, she had turned up at his house late at night. She was slightly drunk and had pleaded with him to get back together with her. At one point she had put her arms around him and suggested they go to bed together. He hadn't been tempted for a second. Gently moving out of her embrace, he had called her a taxi and she had reluctantly and tearfully left.

'Your love life is very complicated, brother. You should get married like me.' Eduardo grinned at him, clearly expecting Felipe to come out with one of the cynical comments about marriage he had so often made in the past. Instead Felipe hesitated and said, 'I might just do that.'

Eduardo looked astonished. 'My God! Charlie really has changed you. I never thought I would hear you say that.'

'Nor did I,' Felipe replied.

'Well, I cannot wait to meet her. She must be a remarkable person to have made you change your mind so completely.'

'She really is.' Felipe couldn't help smiling.

'By the way, did you know there's a young woman over there who keeps staring at our table? I'm assuming it's at you, as I would hate her to be wasting her time on me.'

Felipe looked over in the direction Eduardo indicated and to his astonishment saw Darcy sitting there with another young woman. He remembered her mentioning that she often came to Marbella, but why did she have to be at this restaurant? He wondered if he could get away with pretending he hadn't seen her. However Darcy saw that he had recognised her and strutted over in her tight fitted dress, looking like a runway model. She obviously revelled in the admiring looks she attracted from male diners.

'I thought it was you!' she drawled. 'But I wasn't sure. What a lovely coincidence.'

Felipe forced a smile. Had she forgotten that he had said he wasn't interested in her? 'Darcy, hello. This is my brother Eduardo.'

'Would you both like to join us for some champagne? It's kind of a belated birthday celebration. I was supposed to be meeting up with some other friends but they got held up at work in London and missed the flight. What total party poopers.'

Felipe wanted to decline politely, but the fact that Darcy had mentioned it was her birthday put him in an awkward position. He didn't want to be a complete shit. 'Of course, Darcy, but let me buy the champagne. And Happy Birthday.'

She looked coy. 'Don't I get a birthday kiss?'

She was pushing her luck now, but Felipe got up and lightly kissed her on the cheek.

'Just one glass,' he whispered to Eduardo as they made their way to Darcy's table. But it proved harder to get away than Felipe had anticipated. Darcy's friend India had organised a birthday cake, which involved everyone in the restaurant singing Happy Birthday to Darcy – or rather *Feliz Cumpleaños*; India then insisted on taking photographs of Darcy cuddling up to Felipe and Eduardo, but mostly Felipe. India seemed to be a sweet enough girl but neither Felipe nor his brother had anything in common with the two women and Felipe was itching to get away.

'So are you and Charlie an item now?' Darcy asked. She was giving Felipe her full flirtatious attention, looking at him from under her lashes. He had no idea how much Charlie would have said but guessed correctly that she wouldn't choose to confide in Darcy.

'It's early days, but yes.'

Darcy bit her lip. 'I don't want to speak out of turn, but you're so lovely that I hope you don't end up getting hurt. Charlie has a bit of a reputation for getting through men. She's very tough.'

She clearly hadn't learnt the lesson from their last encounter that bitching about Charlie was going to do her no favours at all.

'Good, then we are well matched because I am just

In the Name of Love

as tough,' Felipe said briskly. He looked at his watch. 'And now I am going to have to say goodnight. I have an early start tomorrow.'

'Really? I was about to suggest going on to a club. I thought all Spaniards stayed up late. It's only midnight!'

She was the most thick-skinned woman he had ever met. And those pouting lips did nothing for him at all. 'I really do have to be up early,' he insisted.

As soon as the two brothers had left the restaurant Felipe suggested they go for a brandy at Barrica. This was a bar the two brothers often went to in the old town. It tended to be frequented by locals and didn't attract wealthy tourists such as Darcy. Felipe felt the need to unwind after the hour spent in her company.

'So long as you don't think the girls are going to track us down,' Eduardo joked. 'I mean India seemed nice enough, but Darcy was so intense and desperate to please you, it was painful to watch. I think the woman has issues.'

'Agreed. But I felt I had to be polite as she works with Charlie.'

'Darcy must be fiercely jealous of her as she clearly fancies you like crazy. She couldn't keep her eyes off you.'

Felipe grimaced. 'I was simply being polite.'

Eduardo laughed and slapped his brother on the back. 'Poor Felipe, it's not your fault that you are such a babe magnet!'

'I'm not the only one. I could see India eyeing you up . . .'

'Let's get that brandy.'

*

165

Darcy drained her champagne glass and then asked the waiter for a brandy. She was royally pissed off that Felipe had so obviously made an excuse to leave; this was not the outcome she had imagined. No, her plan had involved dancing, and then going back to his place where she would show him exactly what he was missing by seeing that arrogant bitch Charlie. Darcy had been planning this encounter for the last week. It had been easy to discover where Felipe liked dining out. She had done her online research and he was frequently spotted in this restaurant. Plus she had overheard Charlie chatting to Aidan about what Felipe was up to this weekend. In the two weeks since the charity dinner, she had found herself obsessing about Felipe, creating all kinds of scenarios where he realised his mistake in choosing Charlie over her. All it would take, Darcy had convinced herself, was just one more meeting away from Charlie. As her parents' villa had been free it had seemed liked the perfect opportunity to run into Felipe, accidentally on purpose. Coincidence had nothing to do with it.

'What the fuck was that all about?' India exclaimed. 'All that bollocks about people not turning up for your birthday. You had your party last week!'

Darcy shrugged. She didn't like being put on the spot, and wanted to rewind back to Felipe joining them, missing out the parts that didn't add to her fantasy of how good they could be together.

'Well, I felt like having another one, especially since Drew forgot it – again.'

Drew was her ex-boyfriend. They had gone out for the best part of two years then six months ago he had dumped her by text, claiming he wasn't ready for commitment. Darcy had been devastated. It had brought to the surface all her insecurities about not being good enough. And so when every now and then Drew suggested a shag, she said yes . . .

'Darcy, what do you expect? The guy never remembered even when you were supposed to be going out!'

She ignored the comment. 'It was so lovely of Felipe to buy the champagne, wasn't it?'

'Yeah,' India admitted. 'He seemed like a really nice guy.'

'And he's gorgeous, don't you think? And a brilliant rider. He's got an apartment here in Marbella as well as his *cortijo* in the Jerez area – I had a look on Google Maps, it's absolutely beautiful. We've got so much in common.' Perhaps if she said it enough times then it would come true . . .

India frowned. 'But he's just started going out with Charlie, hasn't he?'

Darcy could do without the reality check. 'I can't believe that they're well suited. You know what a bitch she is.'

'You don't want to piss Charlie off. She could make your life at work difficult.'

It was typical of her friend India to be so practical.

'My life at work couldn't be any worse,' Darcy said bitterly. She wanted to be a presenter, but while she knew she had the looks – and that wasn't just her being arrogant – the minute she was in front of a camera, she lacked confidence.

She picked up her phone and began looking through

the pictures India had taken this evening, deciding which ones she was going to put up on Facebook. She didn't care what India thought. The fact was she and Felipe would be great together.

'Ready for your spray, Charlie?' asked Fi, the bubbly make-up artist, brandishing the silver airbrush. Unforgiving high-definition TV made airbrushing with liquid foundation essential preparation for appearing on camera.

'Yep, go ahead,' Charlie replied, closing her eyes while Fi got to work, spraying her with a fine mist. It was an experience that always made her want to giggle, even if it did leave her with flawless skin.

Fi had just finished and was dusting on translucent powder when Aidan burst into the dressing room. 'Have you seen these?' he demanded, waving his iPhone in front of Charlie.

She reached for the phone where she saw Darcy's Facebook page, showing a series of pictures of her and Felipe. Darcy was doing her best seductive top-model pout, snuggling up to Felipe, while he was giving a friendly smile and had his arm round her. WTF! Where the hell had the pair of them met up? And why hadn't he told her?

'Where were these taken?' Charlie asked, unable to hide the emotion in her voice.

'In Spain apparently, this weekend,' Aidan said grimly, sitting down next to her.

'That's Darcy's new boyfriend, isn't it?' Fi piped up, craning her neck to look at the pictures. 'She's been going around telling everyone about her night with Felipe the sexy Spaniard. He's an Olympic equestrian. She's a lucky girl, isn't she? I wouldn't mind giving him a ride!'

Charlie and Aidan looked at each other. 'Now don't jump to conclusions,' he warned. 'Darcy has a reputation for being flexible with the truth. I'm sure there's a perfectly reasonable explanation.'

'If there is then why didn't Felipe tell me he had seen her?' Charlie instantly leapt to the conclusion he was cheating on her. After all, that was exactly what TFB had done to her. And she hadn't heard from Felipe today when usually he called first thing in the morning. She ripped off the tissue round her neck, protecting her shirt from the make-up, and stormed out of the room, with Fi calling after her that she hadn't finished.

She had to go outside in order to get some privacy. It was March. Although the sun was making an appearance there was a bitter wind blowing. Charlie was only wearing a silk shirt and skirt, but she was oblivious to the cold. Felipe's phone went straight to voice mail, his sexy-sounding voice only added to her torment.

'Why didn't you tell me about Darcy? I trusted you!' The words tumbled out. Charlie was twisted up with frustration and hurt that he wasn't there to talk to. She stomped back into the building, barely able to reply to Barry the security guard's cheery hello as he let her in. Great. Now she was becoming as rude to other people as Felipe. There was no time to make any further calls as she was due on air with Aidan.

'Okay?' he asked as she took her seat next to him in the studio.

'I'll be fine,' she said curtly, checking through her script. In front of them the three remote controlled cameras clicked into place. Jim the sound guy clipped on her microphone. In the gallery Ruby, one of the PAs, was counting down the seconds until they went on air. Charlie could hear the signature tune playing and then the red lights lit up on the three cameras indicating they were live. She plastered a huge smile on to her face. Her personal life was not going to affect her career. No one watching her, not the viewers at home, not the production team in the gallery, would ever have known that only minutes before Charlie had been an emotional wreck.

As soon as they were off air Aidan was on her case. 'I'm sure Darcy is blowing things out of all proportion. Why don't we find her? She's not going to lie to your face.'

Charlie had already fished her phone out of her bag and discovered Felipe had not called back. That surely meant only one thing. He was guilty and didn't have the balls to tell her. She shook her head. 'I don't want to see her. I've got some pride, Aidan.' And refusing his suggestion that they go out for a drink, she headed to the car park. If Felipe was playing around then they were finished. She was not going to be a victim. Not again.

She got into her car and immediately called Nathan, Zoe's boyfriend. 'It's Charlie. I know it's short notice, but can you see if Kyle is up for meeting me tonight?'

'What? I thought you said that you would never go out with another footballer. I remember that look in your eye when you said it, it was well scary.'

Shit! She would have to come up with an excuse that Nathan would believe.

'I want to talk to him about the season and sound him out as a possible contributor.' That was a whopping lie as Kyle was renowned for his prowess on the pitch and for his good looks, but not for his ability to talk about the beautiful game.

'Oh, right. It's for research.' Nathan didn't sound as if he had fallen for that one. She could almost hear his brain whirring as he figured out what to say next. 'Tell you what, I'll text him your number and if he's free he can give you a call.'

Realising that he was trying to stall her, Charlie replied, 'No, just give me his number and I'll call him.' Fury at Felipe was making her completely brazen. She was going to go out with Kyle and flirt outrageously with him, and who knows what else . . .

Two hours later she had showered and was dressed in a belted snakeskin-print shirtdress that she usually wore with leggings. Tonight she had gone for bare legs and wickedly high heels. She was sipping her second cocktail at the exclusive May Fair bar and already feeling slightly tipsy as she waited for Kyle to roll up. Felipe still hadn't called her back, even though she'd left another message, this time telling him that she knew about him and Darcy; she'd ignored all other calls and texts, including several from Zoe and Aidan. They would only try and tell her to be reasonable, and right now Charlie felt like being extremely unreasonable.

'Hey, Charlie.' Kyle had arrived. He fancied himself as something of a fashionista and was wearing a sharply tailored petrol blue suit. His overpowering exotic aftershave made Charlie want to sneeze. He had a big grin on his face.

'Hi, Kyle.' She got up to receive his kiss, and wobbled slightly. God! She'd better slow it down on the alcohol front. She wanted to be in control, not face down in her Passion Fruit Martini.

He sat down next to her on the purple velvet sofa. Already Charlie felt unsettled as she'd expected him to sit opposite her.

'So this was a surprise, you calling me up. A nice one, though, don't get me wrong.' Kyle had a strong Essex accent and the air of a man who was used to getting his own way with women. And if reports in the tabloids were to be believed, he'd got through more than a few . . .

He ordered a Mayfair martini from the waiter. Charlie knew this particular cocktail cost a staggering £150.

'I always have one of them when I'm here, they're well good.' Kyle stretched out his arm along the back of the sofa, almost brushing it against Charlie.

'Is it really worth that much?' she asked. She could just about imagine spending that amount on a very special bottle of champagne, but a single drink? She could almost hear her mum's voice in her head exclaiming, '*What a waste of money! That's more than most families spend on their weekly shop!*'

'Yeah, 'course. You can try some.'

Hmm, somehow she didn't like the thought of putting her lips on his glass.

'So why did you want to see me, Charlie?'

She fiddled with her necklace, and prepared to launch into her lies. 'I've been meaning to hook up with you for ages actually.' Number one. 'I wanted to see if maybe you might be interested in being one of the interviewees when we profile the players.' Number two. 'And to ask if you could present a trophy to the girls' football team I help coach.' Number three. The bullshit was flowing fast now.

'Sure, I can do all that.' He grinned cheekily. 'So it's not because you find me attractive or nothing like that?'

Oh, how she wanted to fancy him! But she felt as if her body had been put into cold storage. He was fit, he was young, he had an amazing body. It meant nothing to her. He wasn't Felipe.

'Don't fish for compliments,' she bantered back. 'I'm not one of those girls who'll run whenever you click your fingers.'

Kyle leant forward, 'Good, cos that's exactly why I like you.' His gaze took in the short dress with its unfastened buttons, giving a glimpse of Charlie's black lace bra. 'Like the outfit. You're always so prim and proper when you're on TV.' He paused. 'I liked your *Extra Time* shoot as well. I had a copy by the side of my bed until the girlfriend, now ex, got the hump.'

Charlie winced inside. When she had just started out presenting, some lingerie modelling shots she had done as a hard-up student had ended up in the press. The photographer had sold them on, cashing in on her newfound fame. The lad's mag *Extra Time* had bought the whole set. Charlie had been mortified then and now felt mortified all over again. She had to resist the temptation to pull down her skirt and cover up some cleavage. She had wanted Kyle to be attracted to her, but now the brazen I-can-do-what-the-fuck-I-want attitude was wearing off. She was left feeling that she looked like a bit of a slut, and she didn't like it. Letting Kyle think he was in with a chance with her wasn't going to solve anything.

'So you weren't supposed to be seeing one of your girls tonight?' she asked, keen to change the subject. She didn't like to think of what he was doing while he flicked through *Extra Time* . . .

'Nah, I'm single at the moment and Tuesday nights are poker nights with the lads, so count yourself lucky that I blew them out for you.'

He was giving her the full eye-contact routine. It would have been successful with so many women, who would be dying to show him a good time by now, but lust was the last emotion Charlie was feeling. Kyle was going to end up wishing he had played poker after all.

'I thought you were off footballers? That's what Nathan told me.'

And here Charlie had to serve up another lie. 'Well, enough water's gone under the bridge. Not all footballers are like' – she stopped herself from saying TFB and managed to come out with his name – 'Aaron.'

'Not when they have a girl like you.' Kyle's gaze was more intense. 'Another drink? Or d'you want to get something to eat?'

'Food would be good, and another drink.' Actually Charlie wasn't sure that another drink was a good idea but it might stop her from thinking too much about everything.

Half a bottle of wine later, on top of the two cocktails she'd had, Charlie was feeling light-headed and drunk. She never usually drank this much in the week, and she had barely managed to eat anything, still furious with Felipe and hurt and confused. And mixed in somewhere with all of that was guilt that she had led Kyle on into thinking she was interested in him. He wasn't as bad as she had expected. She should have gone home after work and dealt with the Felipe and Darcy thing herself, not involved someone else. She felt as if she was putting on an act and at any second the mask would slip.

'I can't believe you've been single since you split up from Aaron,' Kyle commented. They'd done the football talk and then discussed his car and his ex-girlfriend. In that order.

Charlie picked up her wine glass and took a sip. 'There was someone but it didn't work out.' Suddenly the enormity of what had happened hit her. Felipe, the man she was falling in love with . . . no, wait, the man she was still in love with . . . had screwed someone else! Her chin wobbled and, to her deep embarrassment, tears spilt out of her eyes. She was supposed to be transmitting a kick-ass, ice-cool image, not becoming a quivering wreck! Kyle saw his chance to speed things up and moved closer to her, putting his arm around her.

'Hey, Charlie, don't be sad.' He stroked her back as she struggled to keep herself together. 'He's not worth it if he's made you feel like this.' Then he paused. 'Bloody hell, what's *she* doing here?'

Charlie looked up and saw Zoe steaming towards them, with a sheepish-looking Nathan trailing behind. She reached their table and stood glaring at them, hands on hips.

Zoe didn't even bother to say hello to Kyle, just launched straight in with, 'What's going on, Charlie? I've had Felipe on the phone wondering why he can't get hold of you and what your message meant?'

Charlie sniffed and attempted to rub away the mascara that had no doubt smudged under her eyes. 'He's been seeing Darcy, did he tell you that?'

Sensing that he was in the middle of something heavy, Kyle removed his arm from around Charlie's shoulders. 'I'm just going to make a call,' he said, getting up from the sofa.

'That would be for the best, Kyle,' Zoe said, taking his place.

'I'll go with him,' Nathan added, clearly desperate not to become part of the emotional scene.

'Tell me you weren't about to go home with that gash hound!' Zoe exclaimed. 'I mean I love Kyle, but seriously . . . he makes TFB look like a fucking monk!' When she got wound up Zoe's language went to the dark side. She would never swear in front of her clients at the boutique but when she got the chance, she could really let rip.

Charlie shrugged. 'Does it matter?'

'For fuck's sake, of course it matters!' Zoe took in her friend's slightly bloodshot bleary eyes, the too-short dress, the barely touched grilled sea bass. She beckoned to the waiter and ordered a large hot chocolate and a glass of water. 'You need to sober up, because in a minute you're going to be apologising to Felipe for accusing him of shagging Arsey Darcy! I mean, isn't there enough drama in your life without going and inventing this?'

Thoroughly pissed off with Zoe's nagging, Charlie rummaged through her bag for her phone. She went straight on to Facebook where she clicked on to Darcy's page and held the phone up for Zoe to see. 'Well, what's this then?'

'It doesn't mean a thing,' Zoe said, and then proceeded to give Felipe's version of the night he had bumped into Darcy at the restaurant.

'Why didn't he tell me that he'd seen her?' Charlie demanded, stubborn to the last and not ready to concede that she could have been so wrong.

'Because she doesn't even feature on his radar! While Arsey Darcy was fantasising about him, Felipe had most likely wiped her from his memory. He is in training for the Olympic Games!'

The waiter arrived with the hot chocolate and water.

'Right, when you've drunk that, you're going straight home to phone him and apologise.'

God, Zoe was so bossy! Nonetheless Charlie did what she told her, making sure that she paid half the bill and telling Kyle that she would be in touch about him appearing on the programme. A big fib, but she had to say something. Fortunately he was so intimidated by Zoe that he made no attempt to arrange another date, but muttered something about seeing if he could join the lads for a last poker hand.

Back home, by the time Charlie called Felipe, she was very nearly sober and very contrite as she listened to his description of meeting up with Darcy.

'Charlie, please can we get this straight, I don't have any feelings for Darcy. The woman is deluded. I only want you.' He paused. 'Where have you been tonight?'

Oh, God! Now she was going to have to 'fess up to seeing Kyle. 'Um . . . I met up with this footballer. I wanted to sound him out about appearing on the show.'

Felipe laughed. 'That is crap, Charlie! You just wanted to make me jealous. I know, because it's exactly what I would have done.'

She tried to deny it and then gave up.

'I was never going to do anything,' she admitted.

'Charlie, you have to trust me. I know that you had a bad experience with your ex, but I am not like him. There will be times when you can't get hold of me, but that is not because I am seeing anyone else, I swear. You want this to work, don't you?' Felipe continued, an edge of anxiety to his voice.

'Yes, more than anything,' she admitted, wishing they were together so that she could feel his arms around her. She wanted to forget all about her ill-fated evening with Kyle . . .

'Then we're even,' he said softly. 'And now have a glass of water and two Paracetamol and go to bed. And don't bother to say anything to Darcy. I get the feeling that she is very insecure. I feel sorry for her actually.'

'Insecure? That snooty cow! She could have been responsible for breaking us up!'

'That was never going to happen,' he replied. 'Now go to bed!'

Charlie didn't want to say anything else about Arsey Darcy, but secretly she intended to have it out with her at the very first opportunity. She didn't feel sorry for her at all.

Chapter 12

As luck would have it, the first person Charlie saw when she walked into the office was Darcy. She tried and failed to summon up Felipe's measured words of advice. Just one look at that sulky pouty face enraged her. This was the woman who had nearly destroyed her relationship with him. *Insecure, my arse!* Charlie slammed her bag down on the desk, causing Darcy to glance up from the computer screen, where for once, miraculously, she appeared to be doing some actual work.

'What have you got to say for yourself then?' Charlie was pointing her finger accusingly and her Manchester accent had become noticeably stronger. Everyone else in the office paused in their work and looked over, riveted by the drama.

'I don't know what you're talking about, Charlie,' Darcy protested, looking quite taken aback. Charlie noticed that there were tears in her eyes – all part of the innocent act, no doubt.

'You know exactly what I'm talking about . . . going

around telling everyone that you were seeing Felipe and that you spent the night together. Posting up pictures on Facebook. God, you're pathetic! Women like you make me sick, thinking that flirting with every man you meet is the only way to get ahead. Well, don't ever fucking pretend that Felipe is your boyfriend again, do you understand?'

She had expected Darcy to retaliate and give as good as she got; instead she gave a strangled sob and fled out of the room. Charlie licked her finger and drew an imaginary number one in the air. 'Game, set and match to Charlie Porter,' she said gleefully, then realised that her colleagues looked embarrassed. Shit, she had gone too far.

Suddenly she felt mortified. She should have found a more mature way of dealing with Darcy instead of shouting at her as if they were still in the playground. She grabbed her bag, intending to find Darcy and apologise, but as she walked along the corridor she bumped into Nicky, who was fuming because Darcy had just told her that she felt ill and had to go home.

'She does bugger all when she's here as it is!' their boss exclaimed. 'She's already had one warning from me. Another one and she'll be out.'

Charlie felt even worse then. 'Actually, I think she's been working much harder lately, and there is a nasty bug going round.'

Nicky looked rather surprised. She knew how unpopular Darcy was, but she didn't want to be seen to be picking on someone who was ill, so she replied, 'Okay, well, I'll leave it for now.'

*

Darcy opened the door to her Notting Hill flat, praying that India had already left for work. India was her closest friend but Darcy couldn't face her now. She felt raw with humiliation. She hadn't actually told anyone at work that Felipe was her boyfriend, but when her colleagues had seen the pictures and assumed that he was, she hadn't corrected them. She had been so caught up in the wonderful fantasy that he might be interested in her that she had failed to think about Charlie . . .

The flat was empty. Luckily the cleaner had already been, so all the dirty wine glasses and mugs had been cleared out of the living room, the carpets hoovered and surfaces polished. Darcy and India were both bone idle when it came to housework and relied on their cleaner to keep order twice a week. Darcy knew it was a luxury – the trouble was she was used to luxury. Recently her father had threatened to reduce her allowance and Darcy didn't know how she would cope without it.

She curled up on the midnight blue velvet sofa and clutched one of the cushions for comfort. She lit a cigarette, even though India would freak as she hated Darcy smoking inside the flat. Why was her life such a failure? Nothing she did ever seemed to go right. She was in a dead-end job, she didn't have a boyfriend and she wasn't popular. She knew that people saw her as a confident rich girl, but it was all an act to stop them looking any further and realising what a loser she really was . . . She found herself pulling up the sleeve of her grey cashmere cardigan and looking at the series of pale, silvery scars criss-crossing the inside of her arm.

It had been a while since she had self-harmed, a good therapist and medication had helped, but no one in her family ever talked to her about it. It was Darcy's dirty little secret . . .

Her phone vibrated with a message. It was from Drew, her ex. *Any chance of a shag tonight x?* He didn't even attempt to flirt. That's all she was to him now, a shag when he felt like it. A small part of her said that she should ignore it, or say no, that she was worth more than this, but she was too used to doing exactly what he asked, and longed for any kind of attention. So instead she texted back, *Am at home. How about now? Bring something x* She meant coke. Along with the self-harming there had been drugs. That was the reason she had been expelled from her exclusive private school and subsequently did badly at sixth-form college, failing to get into university. It was one of the major reasons why her parents were so down on her. She had entirely failed to be the successful daughter they thought they deserved.

See u in half an hour, came the reply. He didn't even bother to sign off with a kiss now he was getting what he wanted.

It wasn't even as if she particularly liked having sex with Drew, she reflected afterwards, watching him straightening his tie – he hadn't bothered to take off his shirt or his socks. He was too focused on his own pleasure ever to consider whether she'd had any. She hadn't.

He was whistling as he looked in the mirror. Catching

her looking at him, he said, 'Still the best head girl, Darcy.' Then laughed at his own crude joke.

'Glad I'm good at something,' she muttered. The coke was wearing off and she felt like a drink, anything to avoid getting back to reality.

Drew wandered back to the bed. 'You're good at lots of things, especially in the sack and . . .' He broke off as his phone rang and Darcy never did get to hear what else she was good at as he had to go straight back to the office and do something important with a hedge fund, whatever the fuck that was.

Her phone beeped with a text message. Unexpectedly, it was from Charlie.

Sorry, I was out of order. It's early days with Felipe and I guess I felt insecure. I didn't mean to be such a bitch. Hope you feel better soon. Charlie x

Darcy deleted the message without bothering to reply and poured herself a vodka. She was unlikely to forget being humiliated so publicly. Charlie Porter could go fuck herself.

Felipe had planned to spend his Friday morning going to the deli and buying food and drink, as he didn't plan on venturing out that weekend. Instead his mother had called him and asked him to meet her for coffee as she was in town. Aware that he hadn't seen her in several weeks, Felipe reluctantly agreed. He had been putting off telling his mother that he was seeing Charlie, anything for an easy life, but now as he sat drinking espresso he realised he would have to come clean. Vittoria was banging on about her favourite subject – the one and only Paloma – how beautiful she was, how generous, how clever, how she was organising Vittoria's favourite charity ball, her attributes never-ending . . .

'Mama, I am never going to get back with Paloma.' Felipe cut across her outpouring.

Vittoria Castillo de Rivas paused and brushed a piece of imaginary fluff from her black-and-white-checked Chanel jacket while gathering her thoughts. At nearly sixty-five she was still a striking-looking woman, whose fine bone structure had stood the test of time. Her shiny black hair, which didn't show a hint of grey, was swept into an elegant pleat and as ever her face was immaculately made up. Felipe didn't think he had ever seen his mother looking less than perfect. Of course, when he was a child he had rarely seen his mother before eleven in the morning. A nanny always got the children up and gave them breakfast while Vittoria spent hours getting ready.

'Why do you say that, Felipe? Don't be so stubborn. You must see that you and Paloma are a perfect match. She is beautiful, sophisticated, charming . . . You just need to say sorry for this little blip in your relationship and she will take you back, I am convinced of it.'

Felipe sighed. This was exactly why he hadn't wanted to have this conversation with his mother. He'd better get straight to the point.

'We are not a perfect match. And, if you must know, I have met someone else. Someone who means a great deal to me. And if it is all right with you, I'm going to bring her to your party. She's English and she's called Charlie.'

In her dismay Vittoria swallowed her coffee too quickly and nearly choked.

'Are you okay, Mama?' Felipe asked, already knowing what the answer would be.

'No, I'm not! It's as if my children are all deliberately conspiring against me. First there is your brother, following his unconventional life-style, and then there's your sister who is never going to settle down at this rate. And now you talk about this girl. Well, what does this Charlie do?' she demanded, sounding as if she could hardly bring herself to pronounce the name.

'She's a television presenter, specialising in sport. She is very talented and very beautiful. I am sure you will like her.' Felipe sounded confident but he was certain that Vittoria wouldn't take to Charlie, who was far too opinionated and feisty for his mother's conservative tastes.

'And what about her family? Who are they and what do they do?'

'I have no idea,' Felipe lied, knowing perfectly well that Charlie's dad was a plumber and her mother a sales assistant. That information would have sealed Charlie's fate even before his mother had clapped eyes on her, as Vittoria was an appalling snob. That was one of the many reasons why she refused to see his point of view about Paloma, who came from a wealthy and aristocratic family. A family his mother wouldn't object to linking with the Castillo de Rivas name. Well, she was going to have to deal with the disappointment.

'Does this Charlie have a second name?'

'It's Porter. And this might sound strange, Mama,

but please don't talk about riding with her. She had a horrific accident last year and is still struggling to come to terms with it.'

His mother looked astonished. 'But how can you possibly be involved with someone who does not share your passion for your sport? And at this crucial time in your career! Are you mad? What can you possibly have in common with this Charlie?'

Felipe thought of his passionate connection to her – their overwhelming and intoxicating physical attraction to each other as well as their emotional bond. But there was no point in trying to put this into words for his mother. She would never understand. If she had ever loved Felipe's father, she had kept it very well hidden. Passion didn't seem to figure in Vittoria's world.

She glared at him then pursed her lips. 'I suppose it is all about sex.'

Felipe didn't bother to correct her.

She adjusted her Chanel pearl necklace. 'And does she at least speak Spanish?'

'She's learning,' Felipe replied. And almost smiled as he thought of the words he had been teaching Charlie to say, all related to their bedroom activities along with a colourful collection of swear words. He wasn't about to tell his mother that Charlie knew how to say 'fuck me' in perfect Spanish . . .

His mother arched an eyebrow. 'How typically English. I presume she is capable of eating Spanish food and won't be asking for fish and chips at my party?'

Felipe laughed, even though he knew his mother didn't intend to be funny.

'And I suppose you haven't told her that your uncle is a renowned breeder of fighting bulls? You know what the English are like about animals, so absurdly sentimental.'

Felipe could just imagine Charlie's views on bull-fighting. He didn't think he would be proposing they went on a date to one any time soon.

'I know you think the world revolves around the family estates, but believe it or not we do have other things to talk about.'

And then, because he had had quite enough, he kissed his mother goodbye.

By the time he met Charlie at Malaga airport a couple of hours later, Felipe had forgotten all about the annoying encounter. As Charlie rushed through arrivals to embrace him he was struck again by how very beautiful she was and how much he wanted her . . . He took her straight to his apartment overlooking the sea where they made love for the rest of the evening. He couldn't get enough of his green-eyed girl . . . and nor could she of him.

Charlie stretched her arms above her head, happily blissed out after sex. For the first time she took in the luxurious and spacious bedroom. It had to be the grandest one she had ever been in, with its high ceiling decorated with delicate plaster mouldings, an immense chandelier and an ornate stone fireplace, over which hung an elegant Venetian glass mirror. It was decorated in a surprisingly feminine style, with the walls painted a pale pink, deep pink velvet curtains, and a rococo-style bed covered in silver leaf. As they had raced through to the bedroom she had glimpsed a huge living room, an ultra-modern kitchen, and a flight of stairs that apparently led up to a roof terrace. Felipe had told her he only had a one-bedroomed apartment. This was bigger than most people's houses! Then there was the white Ferrari in which he had picked her up. Charlie hadn't quite realised how wealthy he was . . . or the style in which he lived.

'I wasn't expecting your bedroom to look like this,' she commented. 'But still,' she teased him, 'it's good that you're in touch with your feminine side and manly at the same time.'

Felipe grimaced. 'Not my taste really. Paloma interior designed the whole apartment. It was one of her many projects to improve me.'

'Oh.' Charlie realised that she would rather not have known that the beautiful Paloma had lain in this very bed, contemplating her perfectly designed bedroom. She felt herself coming over all princess and the pea when she said, 'I don't suppose you could get a different bed, could you?'

'For you, anything. So are you hungry? he asked, kissing her shoulder.

'Starving. What are you going to whip up, Mr Five Star?' she joked, knowing that Felipe possessed many fine qualities but cooking wasn't one of them. That was what happened when you grew up with a chef preparing all your meals, including your packed lunch for school.

'I thought we could go out for tapas, and you could sample some local delicacies.'

'Delicious. And when we get back, I'll try another Spanish delicacy.' She lightly stroked his cock and, even though they had made love twice, Felipe felt another stirring of desire . . .

He laughed. This was another very good reason why he was so attracted to Charlie. She loved sex as much as he did. Paloma had always acted as if it was something she knew she had to do, but not appearing to relish it. She was always happier getting out of her rococo bed than tumbling into it with him.

They finally made it out of the apartment around ten. The city was buzzing with people shopping, having dinner, drinking in bars, watching the world go by. Charlie adored seeing everyone out and about with their family and friends so late at night. They ate tapas and drank rosé at a local bar, flirting all the while, then it was back to bed again.

With every moment they spent in each other's company Charlie felt she was getting closer to Felipe. The one thing she felt bad about was the fact he couldn't talk to her about riding. Even the calluses on his hands, from where the reins had rubbed, reminded her of his profession and she had to struggle not to think about it. For so long she had felt trapped by her fear and the appalling memories. She desperately wanted to be free from them; she just didn't think therapy was the answer. Time surely was the best healer . . .

The following day they drove along the coast and

found a relatively deserted stretch of beach to picnic on. Felipe complained that it was too cold, but to Charlie the March sunshine made it feel like summer compared to the low temperatures back home. They spread out a rug and lay on the sand, drinking wine and swapping stories. Before them was the blue expanse of the Mediterranean, dotted with the brightly coloured sails of wind surfers shooting across the water.

'Now you have to tell me something I don't know about you,' Felipe told her. He was being serious, but Charlie chose to keep it light.

'I hate liquorice; it is evil. I can't be in the same room as a piece of it, ever since primary school when Simon Newbury force-fed me a shoelace.'

Felipe frowned. His English was pretty much perfect, but didn't cover every variety of confectionery. 'I don't really know what you are talking about. I'm guessing a sweet?'

They went through a succession of trivial dislikes – they were at that stage in their romance where everything about the other person was fascinating.

Charlie's aversion to Sambuca after a drunken night with Zoe; Felipe's bizarre dislike of cucumber.

'What's not to like?' Charlie protested. 'It's practically water!' Then there was her loathing of clowns, Felipe's of very small dogs . . .

And then the conversation took a more serious shift as Charlie reflected that there were plenty of things Felipe didn't know about her, things that she would rather tell him herself than let him hear them from someone else.

'There's something I have to tell you about my family,' she said, sitting up and hugging her knees, instinctively mirroring the insecurity she felt inside.

'If it is about your brother, then I already know he is in prison,' Felipe said gently. 'I know, and of course it doesn't matter to me. Why should it?'

'It will matter to your family though, won't it?'

Felipe had hinted that his mother was something of a snob.

'I don't care what my family think. My brother and sister, the people I am closest to, will not mind. And I am not prepared to worry about my mother's reaction. Anyway there is no reason for her to find out.'

Charlie gave a wry smile. 'It's not out in the Spanish press yet about us seeing each other but it soon will be, and that's the first thing they'll pick up on – along with my modelling pictures. I'm sure your mum will love those.' She explained how the lingerie shots had ended up in the men's magazine.

Felipe reached out for her hand and kissed it. 'I can live with that, even though I don't like the thought of all those men feasting their greedy eyes on your body. I want you all to myself.' And he pulled her towards him and kissed her. Afterwards he smoothed her hair back. 'Nothing is going to come between us. You shouldn't worry so much.'

'So what about your serious stuff?' Charlie asked him. Felipe seemed so together that it was hard to imagine him being stressed by anything. He sighed and lay back, looking up at the blue sky with white clouds scurrying over it as if off to somewhere more important.

'My family can be a pain in the arse, especially my mother. I feel as if I am a constant disappointment to her. My brother and sister feel the same way. It is hard sometimes, living with the weight of someone else's expectations.'

'I can't imagine how that must feel,' Charlie replied. 'My mum and dad have always loved me unconditionally. I don't understand why you'd want to have a child if you didn't love them in that way.'

Felipe smiled. 'I agree, but try explaining something like that to my mother. She is all about duty and the family name. Sometimes I almost feel sorry for her, and then at other times she is completely infuriating.'

'And what about your father?' Charlie had found it puzzling that Felipe rarely mentioned him. It was almost as if the strong mother had airbrushed him out of the picture.

'He was never really there for us when we were growing up. He was more interested in his business, and my mother has always been the dominant one.'

There was also the question of Felipe's ex. Up till now Charlie had resisted asking any questions about her but she found herself saying, 'And is Paloma over you?' She had seen the pictures of Paloma on the web and knew what an incredibly beautiful woman she was. Just the kind of nightmare ex-girlfriend you didn't want your boyfriend to have . . .

'She would say that she wasn't.' Felipe thought of all the tearful phone calls when she'd pleaded with him to come back to her, the late-night visit – but he didn't want to tell Charlie about that, it would only make her insecure. 'But I think she enjoyed the status and position of being with me more than the relationship itself.' He turned to face Charlie. 'And, in case you're wondering, I am completely over her.' He raised a glass to her. 'To us . . . to our future.'

Charlie lightly clinked her glass against his. She lay back down, and rested her head on Felipe's chest. She felt unbelievably lucky to be with him.

'By the way, I meant to tell you, my mother's having a birthday party in two weeks' time. You're invited, of course.'

Charlie lifted her head to look at him; it seemed very early days in their relationship to be meeting the parents. 'Are you sure?'

'Absolutely, she insisted you come.' What was a little white lie, here and there? Felipe thought.

'And what kind of party is it?'

He shrugged. 'Nothing special. Around a hundred and fifty people.'

That was Felipe's nothing special! Her mum's latest birthday party had started off at her favourite vegetarian Indian restaurant with family and friends. The meal was followed by karaoke in the local pub, where Lori had performed a stunning rendition of 'Holding Out for a Hero' and tone-deaf Aunt Helen had them all cringing with her version of 'Hit Me Baby One More Time'. Somehow Charlie doubted karaoke would be on the agenda at Felipe's mother's party.

'What do I wear?' she asked.

'As little as possible,' Felipe teased, running his hands over her back.

'I'm sure your mother would love that!'

'Okay, a cocktail dress, I suppose, but please don't go to any trouble.'

Charlie was already mentally going through her dresses and discarding each and every one of them. She was going to need Zoe's expert help on this one.

Chapter 13

Darcy still hadn't forgiven Charlie for her outburst. She kept her head down at work, and didn't get into any further confrontations. But all the while she brooded on how to get her own back on the woman who seemed to have everything. Darcy found herself obsessing about Charlie. If she wasn't going out at night she would regularly spend hours on her laptop, checking the web for any stories that had came out about the presenter, clicking through all the images of Charlie she could find, willing there to be a bad shot of her. There never was; Charlie was infuriatingly photogenic.

There was no shortage of news articles on her either. She was starting to make a name for herself as a presenter, and was already known in the tabloids and celeb mags for her ill-fated relationship with the foot-baller. Now it had emerged that she was involved with Felipe, the press had seized on the romance. And, even more galling, every single article was positive, saying how good it was that Charlie had found love again after

Aaron, what a stunning couple she and Felipe made, blah blah, blah . . . It was enough to make Darcy want to throw up, but she couldn't stop herself from reading about it. Everything about Charlie was perfect; it was so unfair. Everything, that was, except her brother Kris, the criminal. The very sexy criminal, Darcy had to admit, when she found a selection of Kris's acting publicity shots on the web during one of her searches. He had the same colouring as Charlie, but his eyes were a deep chocolate brown. He had a handsome face that exuded confidence and, by the look of one of the shots of him stripped to his waist, a ripped body . . .

'He's hot,' India commented, sitting down on the sofa next to Darcy. It was Sunday night and the two flat-mates were chilling out, drinking wine and about to watch a film.

'He is, considering who his sister is,' Darcy replied.

India looked questioningly at her. 'He's not Charlie's brother, is he?'

Darcy nodded. 'And he's in prison. I bet she isn't so proud of that.'

India sighed. 'You've got to let it go, Darcy. Charlie doesn't seem that bad. And I know she laid into you at work, but she was upset about the Felipe thing.'

'What the fuck!' Darcy exclaimed. 'Whose side are you on? She totally humiliated me in public!'

'And she apologised,' India said quietly.

'So? Big of her.'

Darcy's mobile rang then and Drew's name flashed up on the screen. A booty call on a Sunday night? She could ignore it; she should ignore it. She had promised

India that they would have a girls' night in, but then again what if Drew was phoning to tell her he wanted her back? However badly he treated her, she always clung on to that hope. She took the call.

'Is that my favourite head girl? Fancy jumping in a taxi and coming over? And wear something sexy, Darcy. I'm in the mood for a bit of luvvin'.' Darcy hated it when he put on that stupid street accent. He sounded a complete dick. But she still couldn't stop herself from saying yes.

India had been eyeballing her during the call, obviously realising who she was talking to.

'Drew, I'm guessing,' she said, sounding as judgemental as Darcy's old headmistress.

'Yep.' She got up from the sofa, all set to have a shower. 'He's asked me round. You don't mind, do you? I know we were going to watch *Horrible Bosses*, but we can see it tomorrow night.'

'You're not seriously going over, are you? For God's sake, Darcy, he says jump and you say how high!'

'Yeah, well, it's not exactly like that. There is this bond between us . . . I can't explain.'

India looked as if she might actually throw up. 'Oh, *please*, he's just after a shag. It will serve you right if I drink all the wine.' She hesitated, 'I wasn't going to tell you this but I think I should if it makes you see sense. Remember your sister's birthday party last year, when you felt sick and had to go home?'

'Yeah, so?' Darcy wondered why India was bringing this up now.

'And instead of going home to look after you, Drew stayed?' She paused. 'He made a pass at me, Darcy.'

'Oh, come on, he was probably drunk!' Darcy desperately tried to excuse him, just like she always did.

India looked sharply at her. 'When I turned him down, reminding him that he was going out with my best friend, he told me I should be grateful because I was so fat.'

Darcy couldn't look at India; she knew it was exactly the kind of comment Drew would have come out with, and wrong on so many levels. India was size 12. Her phone beeped with another message from him. *Am very excited about seeing you x.* She had to see him. She quickly got up from the sofa in case India decided to reveal anything else. 'I'll tell him that I know what he did,' Darcy said.

India shrugged and pointed the remote at the flat-screen TV on the wall. 'Yep, I'm sure it will make all the difference.'

Darcy had a hasty shower and put on the sheer black underwear and stockings that she knew Drew liked, under a very short dress. She called out goodbye to India on her way out, but her friend didn't reply.

Drew hadn't made any effort for Darcy when he opened the door to his Islington flat. He seemed to have slept in his clothes and hadn't shaved. When Drew didn't shave, he didn't look sexy and rugged, he just looked a mess. He planted a kiss on Darcy's lips and she almost backed away. He hadn't even bothered to brush his teeth. His breath stank of garlic and cigarettes. The flat was a tip as well, with a pizza box on the coffee table, an overflowing ashtray and DVDs scattered across the floor.

'I'm so hungover,' he complained, flopping back on the sofa. 'It was Robbo's stag do last night and we went to a lap dancing club. We only got back at six this morning.'

Ask me what I've been doing, Darcy silently urged him.

He reached for her and pulled her down on the sofa with him, sticking his hand up her skirt. 'Stockings, nice.' Then he slapped her on the bum and said, 'Be an angel and grab a bottle of wine. I reckon I need a hair of the dog.'

Feeling thoroughly taken for granted, Darcy wandered into the kitchen and contemplated the floor-to-ceiling wine rack. Drew fancied himself as a bit of a wine connoisseur and, knowing he was particular about which bottle to drink when, she called out, 'Which one do you want?'

There was no reply. She could hear that he was on the phone to one of his mates, so she took the initiative and reached for a bottle of Pinot Noir. It didn't look that special to her, so she opened it and poured two large glasses. She wondered about leaving the bottle in the kitchen, and then figured what was the point? They were bound to end up drinking the lot, so she put it on a tray along with the glasses.

Drew had ended the call by the time she walked back into the living room and had resumed his position on the sofa. He noticed the wine bottle and exclaimed, 'Fuck! Darcy, why didn't you ask me? That's a ten-year-old bottle, I was saving it for Mummy's birthday.'

Yuck! She couldn't bear it that he still said 'Mummy.' He was twenty-nine, FFS!

'I did ask you, but you ignored me.' *As usual*. She took a sip. To her it tasted like any other half-decent red, and she doubted Drew's mummy would have noticed the difference either.

He groaned. 'My head hurts too much to argue. Take off your clothes.'

Darcy wanted to be made love to, to feel special. Right now, as she stood in front of Drew and stripped down to her underwear, she felt about as special as the lap dancers he had ogled last night, except it was at least in their job description.

'Very nice,' Drew commented. 'We both agree.' He was looking down at his crotch where his erection bulged in his jeans. Darcy took an extra-large sip of wine. Then she put the glass down and knelt on the sofa next to him, unfastening the buttons on his fly. He had already shut his eyes in anticipation. 'Oh yeah, Darcy, you know what I like . . .'

Afterwards he remained sprawled out on the sofa. Darcy lay next to him and tentatively laid her head on his chest. If he would just hold her, she would feel better about so many things.

'Darcy,' Drew murmured, a minute or so later.

'Yes?' she replied expectantly.

'You're squashing me and I've got to take a slash.'

Darcy got dressed while he was in the bathroom. Maybe she could stay over. It had been a while since she had done that, but she could suggest they watch a film and order a takeaway. Drew seemed to be in much better spirits when he walked back into the living room.

'You've totally cured my hangover, babes. Your lips have got the magic touch.' That was the closest he got to giving a compliment.

'What d'you want to do now?' she asked. 'I thought maybe we could watch a film.'

'I wish I could, Darcy, but I promised Rich I'd meet him for a drink tonight. He's having problems with Serena. She's being a complete bitch about him wanting to go on our boys' trip to Thailand.'

Darcy knew better than to ask if she could come for a drink as well, so instead she called a taxi. Drew was on the phone again when she left so she let herself out. She was a fool and she hated herself for giving in to him.

India was in bed by the time she got home. Darcy drank the best part of a bottle of red on her own, didn't eat anything and practically passed out in bed. She woke up feeling hungover and depressed. India was not sympathetic when she saw her in the kitchen, trying to force down a glass of water.

'He didn't ask you to stay over, what a surprise.' And then, because Darcy looked so dejected, she dropped the judgemental act and added, 'Come on, Darcy, you've got to stop seeing him. He's so bad for you; he's just messing with your head. Drew only cares about himself, you're way better off without him.'

Darcy bit her nails, her hands were shaking; she was going to be shit at work today, *again*. 'If I don't have Drew, what do I have?'

India sighed. 'You've got yourself, you've got a good job – whatever you think of it, loads of people want to work in TV – you've got friends. You're stunning-looking.' She didn't mention Darcy's family in the list, there was no point – they had never been there for their daughter.

Low as she felt, Darcy appreciated the comments. She felt bad about yet again choosing to spend time with Drew rather than India. She was weak; she was pathetic.

'How about we go and see a film tonight?' her friend suggested. 'Just us. We could get a pizza first.'

Not for the first time, Darcy silently thanked God for India. She was a true friend, who had always been there for her, and unlike so many other people, saw through the rich-girl façade to the real her. 'Thanks, India, I'm definitely up for that.'

'And no texting Drew,' India added.

'No, I promise.' She only hoped she could keep to it.

Darcy was actually starting to feel better until she saw Charlie at work, glowing from a weekend of sunshine and sex with Felipe. Darcy fetched coffee for the production meeting, and then took notes like a good little PA and tried to avoid looking at Charlie's radiant face. It was like staring at the sun. It hurt. But she couldn't avoid overhearing Charlie chatting to Aidan after the meeting, all about her wonderful time with Felipe. She was talking quietly but Darcy was sitting at the neighbouring desk so unfortunately could hear every single word.

'I had the best news ever first thing this morning,' Charlie said as she and Aidan went through the research notes for their show.

Darcy froze at her computer. How much good luck did one person deserve?

'You remember that director I contacted about Kris? He got back in touch with me and said he would definitely see Kris again when he came out. I can't wait to tell him! It'll give him something to look forward to and he needs that so badly.'

Charlie had taken the decision to be open at work about what had happened. There was no point in trying to hide the fact that her brother was in prison as the press had already reported it.

'When's he out?' Aidan asked quietly.

'Three weeks. I want him to come and stay with me in London, but he hasn't said whether he will or not.'

'It's going to be hard for him being around you though.' Darcy spoke up without thinking and was treated to frosty expressions from Charlie and Aidan.

'I don't think it's for you to comment,' Aidan said pointedly. 'Have you finished the running order yet?'

'Why do you say that?' Charlie demanded, instantly on the defensive.

'I only meant because you're so successful and he'll be feeling down on himself after . . .' Her voice trailed off.

'Prison. You can say it, Darcy!' Charlie snapped. 'For fucksake, it's none of your business anyway.'

Darcy didn't want another falling out with her. 'I'm sorry, Charlie, you're right.' And she put her head

down and carried on typing, though she was aware of
Aidan and Charlie exchanging looks. The two of them
went off for coffee after that.

'Christ, that woman drives me insane!' Aidan exclaimed
once he and Charlie were in the canteen. 'She's always
listening to everyone's conversations. It's like she's just
waiting for them to slip up.' He expected Charlie to
agree with him whole-heartedly, united against Arsey
Darcy. Instead she sipped her coffee and looked
thoughtful.

'Do you think she's right, though, about Kris? I hadn't
thought of it like that. I just thought he'd be glad to
be away from Manchester, to have a fresh start. But
maybe it will be hard for him.'

'Of course she's not! It will be so much better for
him to be with you.'

'Yeah, I think so too. She was probably just trying to
wind me up. That is Arsey Darcy's speciality.'

'Anyway, enough of her.' Aidan lowered his voice to
a whisper. 'I have news about *moi*.'

'Oh?'

'Put it this way, you're not the only one to have
enjoyed a weekend of sex, sex and sex.'

Charlie clapped her hands together. 'Yay! Your sex
drought is over. Who is he?'

Aidan glanced around to make sure no one was in
earshot. 'He's called Felix and he's a barrister.'

'I thought you had a bit of a spring in your step this
morning,' Charlie teased.

'That's not the only place, darling,' Aidan quipped,

prompting giggles from the pair of them. He swore Charlie to secrecy and they both returned to work, ignoring Darcy.

'I need something classy and sophisticated. Something that says, "I am meant to be with your son, so back off, Dragon Lady,"' Charlie told Zoe the following evening at the boutique. It was Operation Find the Perfect Party Dress. The two women had decided to make a night of it and Zoe had cracked open a bottle of Cava; Adele's *21* was playing in the background.

'I don't think you should wear black, it's too boringly safe and shows a lack of imagination,' Zoe commented, flipping through the rails of clothes. She held up a subtly patterned leopard-print dress.

Charlie shook her head. 'She's bound to think leopard print equals slut.'

'The woman clearly has no sense of style,' Zoe replied. 'Okay, give me a few minutes. I'll find you the perfect outfit.'

Charlie relaxed on the sofa, sipping her wine, while Zoe rushed round the boutique picking out dresses. Charlie was pretty sure that Señora Castillo de Rivas was going to be very hard to please and equally sure that the beautiful Paloma would have a wardrobe full of designer numbers to choose from. This party would be the first time Charlie met Felipe's family and she wanted to make a good impression.

Five minutes later Zoe hung the selection of dresses in the fitting room, then held the curtain open. 'Ms Porter, could you step this way? Your garments await you.'

'Liking the customer service!' Charlie teased as she did as she was asked.

None of the dresses felt right, however. They showed too much flesh, or they were too prim and proper. It was that age-old problem of when you needed to buy a dress, you couldn't actually find anything you liked. Charlie was trying to think if she had anything at all in her wardrobe that she could possibly wear. But then Zoe handed her a scarlet Robert Cavalli number. Charlie took one look at the price tag and whistled. It was way more than she usually paid.

'If you like it, I'll give you a discount.'

Charlie half hoped she wouldn't like it because it was so eye-wateringly expensive. But as she slipped on the scarlet silk jersey dress and looked at herself in the mirror, she knew it was the one. The dress showed off her figure without being in any way slutty. It was a sexy, sophisticated, grown-up dress that said, *I mean business and I deserve to be with your son*. She stepped out of the fitting room.

'That's the one. I knew it would be,' Zoe commented.

'If you knew that why did you make me try on all those other dresses?' Charlie grumbled.

'Because you wouldn't have realised that this was your dress until you had done that.'

'Do you play those kinds of psychological games with all your customers?'

'Of course. Why else do you think I'm so successful?' Zoe held out a pair of gold sandals. 'All you need are these and a gold clutch bag,'

'Hair up or down?' Charlie asked, experimenting

with twisting her long hair into a bun and then letting it cascade over her shoulders.

'I would say up if you can. Get it done professionally when you're in Spain.'

Charlie wrinkled her nose, she didn't want to spend precious time away from Felipe in a hairdresser's. 'I'll get it blow dried before I fly out.'

She treated Zoe to dinner at her favourite Thai restaurant as a thank you for her help and for the discount, and returned to her flat feeling happily mellow from the several glasses of wine. The mellow feeling didn't last as she picked up her post from the hall table. There, on one of the envelopes, was the familiar handwriting of the nasty message sender. Her heart sank as she wondered what vicious taunt awaited her this time. She contemplated ripping it up and throwing it into the bin without reading it, but then couldn't stop herself from opening it. Inside was a picture of her brother with *Jail Scum* scrawled across it in black. How low could they get? She angrily screwed up the picture then smoothed it out and put it back in the envelope. It seemed a strange coincidence that she should have received this message just after she had been talking about Kris. She remembered Darcy coming out with her comment about him. Could she be behind the messages? She must have been angry with Charlie for the negative comments she had made about her and for the misunderstanding about Felipe. But Charlie had apologised, and surely even if Darcy didn't like her very much she wouldn't resort to these methods . . .

She let herself into her flat and wandered into the

kitchen to make herself a cup of tea, determined that the message sender was not going to put a downer on her. But she couldn't help wondering what would motivate someone to act like this – it had to be about jealousy, or else someone felt they had been slighted by herself and Aidan, though she couldn't think who, or why someone would feel like that. She shoved the note into the folder along with the others and then tried to forget all about it. She was seeing Felipe tomorrow night and wanted only to think about him, not about someone who was deliberately setting out to upset her.

Chapter 14

'Do I look okay?' Charlie asked, standing in front of Felipe in her scarlet dress.

He gave a low whistle. 'You look more than okay, you look beautiful and very, very sexy.' He was sitting on the bed. He reached out and pulled her on to his knee.

'You're sure I look sophisticated enough? I don't want everyone to be looking at me and thinking I'm your bit of rough.'

Felipe kissed her shoulder, deliciously exposed by the dress. 'That's a pity because I thought that's exactly what you were.' He couldn't resist teasing her. And then he couldn't resist kissing her, and one thing led to another and they ended up in bed again, after only just having got dressed for the party.

'You've ruined my hair!' Charlie protested afterwards as she looked in the mirror and saw that her sleek blow-dried style had now become wild and curly.

'Good, I prefer it like that.' Felipe told her as he straightened his tie. 'Now come on or we'll be late.'

He didn't add that his mother absolutely loathed unpunctuality.

'Great,' Charlie grumbled. 'That'll be a mark against me before I've even opened my mouth.'

She had been anticipating a large house, but even so the sheer size and grandeur of Felipe's parents' country *cortijo* nearly took her breath away. It was a huge seventeenth-century mansion with white stone walls and weathered terracotta tiles on the roof. It had turrets and even its own bell tower. Surely this was a castle and not a house! The impressive driveway was lined with tall poplars, standing straight as guards, and in the distance beyond them she could see extensive olive and orange groves. Felipe pulled up on the wide driveway beside the house and immediately a parking valet appeared to park his car. It was a world away from anything Charlie had experienced before. She suddenly felt on edge . . . and very far from home. She tucked a stray curl behind her ear.

'Don't look so anxious,' Felipe reassured her, holding her hand. 'My mother won't bite, and we don't have to stay long.'

The party was already in full swing when the couple walked inside. Guests in beautiful designer creations were milling around in the elegant drawing rooms which opened on to two courtyards with elegant stone fountains and lemon trees on one side and a sun terrace on the other. There were stunning views over rolling hills covered in the vines the family cultivated for their famous sherry. Attentive white-coated waiters offered glasses of champagne and exquisite canapés: slivers of smoked salmon and caviar, tiger prawns wrapped in Parma ham, seared carpaccio of beef. It was just as well that Charlie wasn't a vegetarian like Lori . . . Mind you, she was so nervous about meeting Felipe's parents that she had no appetite at all.

Beyond the terrace was an immaculately tended garden, full of vivid purple bougainvillaea, bright red hibiscus and palm trees. There was also a tennis court and an infinity pool. Charlie's mum and dad had a patio and a water butt and an allotment where her dad grew vegetables.

As they attempted to locate Felipe's mother, they kept being waylaid by guests wanting to say hello. Felipe introduced Charlie to everyone and she smiled politely and said, '*Hola, encantada de conocerla*', a polite greeting that she had been practising. She continued smiling politely when they took that as a signal to continue speaking Spanish and she didn't have a clue what they were saying. She also managed to down two glasses of champagne very rapidly. Then she switched to water. She didn't want to be pissed when she met the formidable mother.

Eventually they found Señora Castillo de Rivas holding court on the terrace. She was wearing an exquisite violet silk crêpe cocktail dress that showed off her slender figure. Her long black hair was swept into an elegant French pleat, and diamonds glittered in her ears and round her neck. She looked beautiful and very, very scary, definitely the sort to bite. She caught sight of Felipe and immediately launched into a stream of Spanish, kissing and hugging him and stroking his cheek.

'Mama, this is Charlie,' he said when he could finally get a word in.

Vittoria gazed coolly at the beautiful young woman who stood before her, then stepped forward to kiss Charlie. '*Encantada de conocerla.*'

'*Feliz cumpleaños*,' Charlie managed to say.

Vittoria gave a smile that didn't reach her eyes and rattled something off in Spanish. She didn't exactly radiate warmth; 'glacial' was the word that sprang to mind instead. She was the Ice Queen. Usually the mothers of her boyfriends adored Charlie. Vittoria was going to be a tough one to please and Charlie very much doubted she would ever succeed.

'Mama, *please* speak English,' Felipe interrupted. 'I told you Charlie has only just started learning the language.'

Vittoria gave a rather patronising smile. 'Of course, I understand. So, Felipe tells me you work in television? That must be very exciting.' She enunciated every word in perfect English and sounded as if she thought working in television was about as exciting as taking out the bins. Then she proceeded to fire questions at Charlie. Where did she live? How old was she? What had she studied at university? Where did she meet Felipe? Until he intervened again.

'Mama, we're going to say hello to Papa, do you know where he is?'

Vittoria shrugged her slim shoulders. 'You know how much he hates parties, I expect he's smoking one of his cigars somewhere and keeping a low profile.'

Lucky thing, Charlie thought.

'If you find him, do tell him to mingle. It is my birthday after all. It would be nice if he put in an appearance.' She gave another shrug, 'And your sister isn't going to make it. She claims her flight from Bangkok was delayed. She's been staying at some five-star spa and yoga retreat there. Though I don't know what she has to retreat from, she doesn't actually do anything but spend money.'

Charlie wondered if Vittoria had a good word to say about anyone in her family.

Felipe draped one arm round Charlie as they walked away from his mother. 'See, that wasn't so bad, was it?'

Charlie gave him a WTF stare. 'She hated me! I need another drink now.' She reached for a glass of champagne from a nearby waiter. It was telling that Felipe didn't contradict her. Fortunately when they found Señor Castillo de Rivas sitting in a far corner of the garden, under a parasol, contentedly puffing on a cigar, he was a pussycat compared to his wife. He barely spoke English but smiled warmly at Charlie and didn't appear to view her as some slut who had no business being with his son. Maybe the rest of the party wasn't going to be so bad after all.

But then, as they strolled back to the house, a beautiful woman approached them. Charlie instantly recognised her. It was Paloma, Felipe's ex girlfriend – even more beautiful in real life than she had been in the photographs Charlie had studied. Paloma was petite with long, glossy jet black hair, striking blue-black eyes, and a slender but curvaceous figure. Charlie, who was a slim size ten, felt enormous next to her. Paloma addressed Felipe in Spanish and they kissed each other in greeting. Charlie couldn't help thinking what a stunning couple they made. Paloma had such poise, she was so elegant and sophisticated. She belonged to Felipe's world of wealth and privilege. Again, Charlie felt like an outsider.

'And this is my girlfriend Charlie,' he said in English.

'It's a pleasure to meet you, Charlie,' Paloma said in equally perfect English, holding out her hand.

'And you, Paloma,' Charlie replied, wishing that she could reply in perfect Spanish.

'It's a wonderful party for your mother, isn't it, Felipe?' Paloma continued. 'She seems very happy.'

As happy as an Ice Queen ever could be, Charlie thought.

'I'm sure that there will be something not quite right with it,' Felipe replied. He looked at Charlie. 'No matter how much money is lavished on her and how much trouble people have gone to, my mother is always dissatisfied. I think she enjoys feeling like that.'

'Oh, no, Felipe! You're wrong. She only wants the best for you and the family!' Paloma exclaimed.

Pass the sick bag . . . someone was trying too hard to please. And from the adoring way Paloma was gazing at Felipe, it was apparent that she still had strong feelings for him.

He shrugged. 'Unfortunately she pays no attention whatsoever to what people actually want or what makes them happy.' He put one arm round Charlie as he spoke. 'But I'm not a little boy any more who can be told what to do. I know exactly what I want.'

Paloma gave a resigned smile. 'I can see that, Felipe.' She took a moment as if to compose herself before she continued, 'So how is your training going?'

Instantly he tightened his hold on Charlie as if to reassure her. 'Very well, thank you, but let's not talk about that here. It is supposed to be a party after all.'

Paloma did a double take. 'You've changed then, Felipe!' She turned to Charlie. 'I must congratulate you on broadening Felipe's horizons; he talked about riding non-stop to me. I swear I could recite every single rule of dressage, the times of all his cross-country competitions, the number of wins he's had, what his horses ate, when they were off form, when they were on form . . . What was that famous line of Princess Diana's? "There were three of us in our relationship." Me, Felipe and his horse Audaz.'

Charlie felt as if the smile was frozen on her face as she registered what an immense strain it must be for Felipe not to be able to talk to her about his sport at all. She hadn't even known the name of his horse until now.

'There are plenty of other things to talk about,' he said quietly.

'How lucky for you, Charlie,' Paloma replied. 'I mean, I love riding, but I don't want to hear about it,' she wrinkled her perfect nose, 'what is that expression? Twenty-four seven.'

It was a relief when they were joined by Eduardo and Ricky. Charlie warmed to the couple straight away, they were both so easygoing and charming, and she didn't feel as if she was walking on eggshells about to say the wrong thing. She could see the family resemblance between Eduardo and Felipe, though Eduardo lacked his brother's athletic build. When Paloma moved off to talk to other guests, she relaxed still further.

'It's a lot to take on board, isn't it?' Ricky observed, gesturing at the house and the grounds. He was tall and blond and looked like a Californian surfer boy with his golden-brown tan and cornflower blue eyes.

'It is,' Charlie agreed. 'I have a two-bedroomed flat which is probably the size of the hallway here.'

Ricky smiled and lowered his voice. 'And I guess you've met Vittoria? Terrifying, isn't she?'

Charlie nodded, pleased to have found an ally.

'Still, it's harder for you as she had her heart set on Felipe marrying Paloma. She likes to pretend that I don't actually exist, that it's all a bad dream and one day she'll wake up and discover Eduardo has fallen in love with a nice Spanish girl.'

Eduardo overheard him and burst out laughing. 'That is never going to happen. You're stuck with me for life!'

'Good, I was hoping you would say that,' Ricky replied.

They seemed so in love, and so settled; Charlie envied them that. She still felt as if she was on a rollercoaster ride with Felipe. It was passionate and thrilling and it consumed her, but she couldn't help wishing that things were a little more straightforward for them. There was the riding issue, geography, and apparently Felipe's mum, all conspiring against them. She was still musing about this as she walked through one of the courtyards in search of a bathroom.

'Are you enjoying the party, Charlie?' It was the terrifying Vittoria. She stood in front of Charlie, blocking her way.

'Very much, thank you, I do hope you are,' she replied politely, hoping that would suffice and that she could make a speedy escape.

'I must show you some pictures of Felipe. I know how modest he is about his achievements, but it seems to me you can't really know someone unless you understand what they do.'

Charlie didn't like the direction in which this conversation was going, but keen to make a good impression, she allowed Vittoria to link arms with her and lead her to a comfortable living room at the back of the house. It was far less formal than the other rooms, with sofas and chairs that looked as if they could be sat on rather than being antique showpieces. Charlie took in the glass-fronted cabinet stuffed with trophies from Felipe's competition wins and the photographs of him on horseback displayed everywhere. She was already starting to feel a little breathless, and looked longingly at the open door. She could leave now; make an excuse about not feeling well. But she missed her chance as Vittoria reached for one of the silver-framed photos and handed it to her. It showed Felipe sitting on a magnificent thoroughbred which had been groomed to perfection, so that his chestnut coat seemed to glow in the sunshine.

'This is Audaz, one of the horses Felipe will be riding in the Olympics. Have you seen him yet? A magnificent animal, his father was a great champion. We have high hopes of him.'

Black dots seemed to dance in front of Charlie's eyes as her breathing grew more shallow.

'Not yet, but I'm hoping to very soon.' Her voice seemed to be coming from a long way away.

'Ah, yes, Felipe mentioned that you have a "thing" about riding. Such a pity, because he needs all our support at the moment. I've been very worried about him, he's been off form lately and distracted. The Olympics is the single most important event of his career. It is something Felipe has been working towards for years. He missed out on the last one because of an injury. Riding is his life and this competition means everything to him. It cannot be fair to ask him not to talk about it, can it?'

'No, it's not fair,' Charlie managed to reply. 'And I am going to try . . .'

She was going to say that she was trying to overcome her fear, but Vittoria cut her off.

'Yes, yes, you're going to have therapy, Felipe told me, but how long is that going to take? In the meantime, the fact is he has to keep back a significant part of his life from you. How can that be a proper relationship?'

Vittoria's tone was soft and wheedling as if she were talking to a reluctant child but Charlie was hardly listening to her. In her mind she was back to that fateful day. She saw the car speeding towards them, felt the gut-wrenching impact, once more heard the anguished cries of her beloved Ace. She dropped the photograph, causing the glass to shatter as it hit the marble floor, then fled from the room, oblivious to Vittoria calling her name.

Somehow Charlie stumbled up the sweeping wooden staircase and found a bathroom. With shaking hands she managed to lock the door, then she collapsed on the floor, leaning against a wall while the panic attack took hold of her.

Downstairs Felipe was wondering where Charlie had got to. He had checked the gardens and courtyards, the terrace and all the downstairs rooms, but there was no sign of her. He was about to look upstairs when his mother came out of the family living room. 'Have you seen Charlie?' he asked.

Vittoria looked faintly guilty, but her words were typically defensive. 'We were having a perfectly friendly talk when she dropped one of my favourite photographs of you and ran out of the room. She seems most unstable and emotional, really the last person you need around you right now. And did I see a tattoo on her shoulder?' She shuddered. 'So terribly common. I simply don't understand why young women want to disfigure themselves in that way. Paloma wouldn't dream of having such a thing. And just look at this.'

She handed over a folder containing a series of news articles about Charlie – there were stories about her brother and the pictures from her ill-fated modelling shoot.

'She is not the girl you think she is. To be associated with such a person can only drag you down. You could do so much better! And I gather her father is a plumber and her mother a shop assistant.' Vittoria looked expectantly at Felipe, as if imagining he was going to be appalled by such revelations. How little his mother knew him . . .

'I know all of this and it doesn't matter to me in the

slightest.' He slung the folder on to a delicate antique table, causing the papers to slide out and cascade to the floor.

'I want to know what exactly you were discussing with Charlie,' he demanded, fearing that he knew only too well. He should never have exposed her to his mother.

Vittoria gave one of her infuriating shrugs, as if it was all too tedious for her. 'I just pointed out what a difficult time this was for you in the run-up to the Olympics and how you needed all our support.'

Felipe's eyes seemed to become darker as he said quietly, 'You talked to her about riding, even though I expressly asked you not to?'

'I did. You must realise that you simply cannot be with this woman.'

Felipe's only thought was for Charlie, who must have been devastated by Vittoria's deliberately insensitive comments. Ignoring his mother, who continued trying to defend herself, he raced up the stairs and ran along the landing. He tried the door of the first bathroom he came to. It was locked. He hammered on it, calling out, 'Charlie, are you in there?'

There was no reply, but as he listened he was sure he could hear someone crying. 'Charlie,' he repeated, 'please let me in. My mother was completely out of line speaking to you like that.'

There was still no reply. 'If you don't open the door, I swear I'm going to break it down.'

And then he heard the sound of someone walking over and turning the key. He opened the door and Charlie stood before him. Her face was streaked with tears. He went to take her in his arms, but she held up her hands as if to push him away. 'Please don't. You'll only make it harder.'

'What are you talking about?' He couldn't bear to see her looking so anguished.

'Your mother was right. You should be with someone who can talk to you about what you do.'

'What are you saying? You're going to get help, and you're going to overcome this fear. Not for me, but for you.' He took a step closer. 'Charlie, it would destroy me if you left me.'

'Paloma would be so much better for you,' she said quietly.

'She would not.' He moved closer. 'It's you that I want. Only you.' And now he put his arms round her and pulled her close to him, so close that he could feel her heart racing.

They left the party after that. Charlie slipped away and waited in the car while Felipe said goodbye to his parents. She wasn't up to seeing anyone. She felt drained and exhausted as she always did after a panic attack, and couldn't stop thinking about what Vittoria had said. She had no idea that Felipe had been off form in his training – they had never spoken about it. Was Vittoria right? Was she being unfair on him?

Charlie pulled down the sun visor to check her appearance in the mirror, wincing as she took in her smudged mascara and swollen eyes. And she had bitten her lip and caused it to bleed. It was a far cry from the sophisticated, glamorous look she had started out the afternoon with. She was about to repair the damage when there was a rap on the window. She glanced round and saw to her dismay that it was Paloma, looking as polished and chic as ever. Perfect timing. Not. Reluctantly she lowered the window.

'I just wanted to check that you were okay,' Paloma said smoothly.

Charlie felt like a complete wreck next to her.

'I'm fine,' she mumbled.

'I suppose these big parties can be a little intimidating when you're not used to them.' Now she sounded condescending and Charlie felt a return of her old fighting spirit as she replied, 'Oh, I'm used to big parties – less used to someone setting out to undermine me deliberately.'

'Who would do that?' Paloma asked, the picture of innocence.

Charlie ignored the question and continued, 'I have a problem with riding because of something that happened to me, but I am determined to get over it and support Felipe. I know he would do the same for me.'

'Absolutely true.' Felipe had reached the car. He opened the driver's door as he said, 'Goodbye, Paloma, enjoy the rest of the party.' Charlie was secretly pleased he didn't kiss his ex goodbye, especially when he leant across and kissed her instead. 'Let's get out of here.'

She couldn't have agreed more.

Chapter 15

The following day Charlie and Felipe met up with Ricky and Eduardo on their yacht which was moored at the luxurious Puerto Banus marina, playground of the super-rich and famous. It should have been a wonderful day – the sun was shining, the sky couldn't have been bluer, she had the whole day with Felipe before she had to fly back – but Charlie was still feeling subdued after the party. However much Felipe reassured her, she found it impossible to stop thinking about her encounter with Vittoria. Once again she found herself wishing that he was merely a businessman.

'Felipe told us what happened with darling Mama. I'm so sorry, Charlie,' Eduardo told her as she stepped aboard. 'You mustn't worry about what she said. She can be the most tactless woman in the world.'

'It's true,' Ricky told her. 'She has never once congratulated us on our marriage. It really is best to ignore her.'

'Sure,' Charlie replied, and managed a smile. She

was grateful for their comments but wasn't sure she would be able to act on their advice. And being on this gleaming white motor-yacht, surrounded by the evidence of wealth, wasn't helping either. It was a constant reminder that this was not her world . . . whatever Felipe said.

Her spirits lifted slightly once Eduardo started the engine. He steered them slowly out of the marina then turned up the power and shot out to the open sea. She loved the feeling of the sun on her skin and the wind whipping through her hair, the smell of the salt water. She had always adored being outdoors, loved the sense of freedom it gave her, and that had been one of the extra pleasures of riding. Now she felt that she didn't spend nearly enough time outside.

Eduardo and Ricky were brilliant company, great at making conversation flow, joking together and teasing Felipe, creating a relaxed and happy atmosphere. As they moored the boat off a small cove and Charlie helped Ricky arrange a picnic on the table out on the deck she felt some of the earlier insecurity leave her. Maybe she could belong here . . .

'This food is delicious!' she exclaimed, as she tasted the spicy prawns, patatas bravas, bite-sized tortilla and calamari, suddenly realising how hungry she was. After the party she hadn't felt like eating anything at all.

'Ricky's a brilliant cook,' Eduardo told her.

'Not like Felipe then,' she commented, grinning at him.

'I have other skills!' he protested. He had taken off his tee-shirt and was lounging back on a chair in a pair of cut-off jeans. His skin was deeply tanned and he had never looked in better shape.

Charlie couldn't resist leaning over and kissing him.

'Get a room, you two!' Ricky joked.

'Sorry,' she replied, not feeling sorry at all as she reluctantly prised herself away from Felipe.

Eduardo grinned. 'It's nice to see my brother looking so happy.'

They lazed on the boat for the next couple of hours, drinking ice cold rosé, sunbathing and chatting. Charlie was feeling completely relaxed until Felipe murmured, 'Imagine if you lived out here, Charlie. We could do this all the time.'

'Yes, but what would I do? I can't speak Spanish, and even if I did it's very unlikely I'd get a job in TV here. It was hard enough getting one in the UK!' She was aware of how uptight she sounded, but couldn't stop herself. Did Felipe's comment mean that he didn't take her work seriously? He probably thought that she could give it up and spend her days shopping. She would go insane.

'I am not suggesting that you give up work and become a kept woman. I am just saying I would like it if you lived here,' he replied. 'I like the fact that you are passionate about what you do.'

Charlie sighed. 'Sorry, I didn't mean to snap at you.' She bit her lip. 'It's just that sometimes I feel that there are so many things conspiring against us.'

'They are only problems if you make them into problems,' Felipe told her.

Charlie thought they had probably said enough in

front of Eduardo and Ricky, who had been politely pretending that they couldn't hear the exchange. So, instead she stood up and declared, 'I'm going for a swim, anyone else fancy it?'

The three men looked at her as if she was bonkers.

'It will be freezing!' Felipe told her. 'And you haven't got a wetsuit.'

'Wimps! Losers! Weeds!' she taunted them. 'I'm used to swimming in the Channel, the water's always freezing there.'

In fact she hadn't realised the sea would be that cold, but now she had declared her intention to go in, she felt that she couldn't backtrack. And without giving herself the chance to change her mind, she stripped down to her bikini and climbed down the ladder at the side of the boat. Surely it wouldn't be that cold? But as she took the plunge and dived in, she felt as if her body was going into shock. The water was icy. The men looked over the side. 'It's not that cold,' Charlie called back, trying to tough it out.

'Then why are you are turning blue and your teeth chattering, my darling?' Felipe responded.

She stuck her tongue out and managed to last five minutes before she swam back to the boat. Her body felt completely numb. Luckily Felipe was on hand to wrap her up in a huge beach towel. 'You are too stubborn!' he told her, rubbing her back. 'You'll catch a cold.'

'I'm fine,' she replied, and promptly sneezed.

At that moment she noticed another yacht approaching them.

'Isn't that Paloma's boat?' Eduardo commented.

'Yes, it is,' Felipe replied, not sounding very happy about it.

How bloody typical that the gorgeous Paloma should turn up now when Charlie was purple with cold, her hair bedraggled and all her make-up had washed off.

Paloma's sleek yacht drew parallel with theirs and she waved cheerily at them.

'I'm going to get dressed,' Charlie said, grabbing her clothes.

'You can have a shower if you like, there'll be plenty of hot water,' Ricky told her. 'I'll show you where everything is.'

She followed him inside the yacht. The lounge area was furnished with white leather sofas studded with crystals, and glossy black panelling. One entire wall was devoted to the photograph of a naked woman cavorting in the sea while drinking straight from a champagne bottle. Someone had drawn a bikini top and bottoms on her to preserve her modesty.

'Sorry about the décor,' Ricky commented. 'We think the boat was owned by a drug dealer and we haven't got round to having it refurbished yet.'

'It is a bit pimp up my yacht,' Charlie agreed.

He opened a door to a spacious master bedroom, which to Charlie's amusement had a mirrored ceiling. 'Now that is class!' she teased. 'Surely you want to keep that?'

'How do you know we didn't have it put in?' Ricky bantered back. He paused for a beat. 'We didn't. It's coming out. Now prepare yourself for the shower room.'

He opened the door to the en suite bathroom – which was covered floor-to-ceiling in tiny gold mosaic tiles.

'Wowser, that is blinging!'

'And that's coming out too.'

Ricky handed her a towel. 'By the way, you mustn't worry about Paloma. Felipe doesn't have any feelings for her any more.'

'She does for him though, doesn't she?'

Ricky shrugged. 'Perhaps. But as Felipe said, it's only a problem if you make it a problem.'

'So you wouldn't mind it if Eduardo's ex kept turning up then?'

'Are you kidding! I'd go fucking ape!' Ricky grinned. 'I totally know where you're coming from. But don't worry, Felipe adores you and we do too. Paloma is history. So have that shower, slap on some make-up, girlfriend, and join us back on deck.'

It was good to know that Ricky was an ally.

By the time Charlie emerged from the bedroom, Paloma was on board. Her own yacht was moored nearby and she was sipping a glass of rosé and looking as glamorous as ever – today doing boating chic in white jeans and a white halter-neck top worn with huge white sunglasses and a silk scarf by Hermès wrapped round her hair. Mind you, Charlie thought, she had probably spent all morning getting ready.

'I can't believe you went swimming, Charlie. I won't go in until July!' Paloma exclaimed.

'She is very tough,' Felipe said, and put his arm round Charlie as she sat next to him.

Paloma managed a tight little smile; it must have hurt seeing Felipe's gesture. But she was clearly a fighter as she carried on, 'This is my favourite bay too. We used to spend so many afternoons here, didn't we, Felipe? Do you remember the time we entertained your team-mates and Joaquin got so drunk he dived into the water fully clothed? You had to dive in after him to make sure he was okay.'

Charlie felt a twinge of insecurity. There were so many parts of Felipe's life that she knew nothing about. She wondered if Vittoria had told Paloma about her panic attack.

Felipe shrugged. 'I must have been pretty drunk too, because I can't really remember it.' He looked at his watch. 'I think we had better head off soon.'

'Of course, don't let me detain you, I just wanted to say hello.'

'Did you skipper the boat yourself?' Charlie asked; she felt she should say something out of politeness.

Paloma gave a tinkling laugh. 'Oh, no!' She called out something in Spanish and a young man in jeans and tee-shirt emerged from the cabin of her yacht and waved at her. 'I have Mario, he skippers my boat for me. I was desperate for some sea air this afternoon; I'd been sending out invitations for Felipe's mother's charity ball all morning and had a terrible headache.'

How hard could it be to send out invitations? Charlie wondered as Paloma got ready to leave, saying effusive goodbyes to the men and blowing Charlie a kiss.

The rest of the afternoon seemed to go by too quickly after that. Just time to race back to the apartment, to tumble into bed and make love one last time. Charlie had come to dread saying goodbye to Felipe at the airport. It always felt like such a wrench, and especially today, after the events at the party.

'Promise me you will call as soon as you get back home?' Felipe asked. He had his hands on Charlie's shoulders and was gazing at her as if trying to capture every single detail of her face.

'You know I will.' She wanted to tell him that she loved him, but something held her back. Maybe it was too soon . . .

She started walking away towards departures, then stopped and spun around and called out, 'You were right, I'd love it if we lived in the same place.'

Felipe smiled and called out, 'But I'm always right, Charlie.'

Back at his apartment, Felipe couldn't relax. The unmade bed was a reminder of Charlie; the pillow still carried the scent of her perfume. He hated being apart from her. And even as he thought that he had to smile as there had been so many times in the past when he had felt stifled in a relationship. His ex-girlfriends had always wanted to know what he was thinking, all the time. It was ironic that Charlie gave him so much space . . . space he was more than happy to give up for her.

He was sure that he loved her . . . he had never felt like this about anyone before . . . but he was wary of telling her in case she felt it was too soon. In case *she* felt stifled.

It had been a hell of a week. His mother had been

right about one thing. He was off form and training had been going badly; his shoulder was killing him. Spending the weekend with Charlie had allowed him to push all thoughts of competing out of his head, but now they returned with a vengeance – all the negative, pessimistic thoughts that he felt almost powerless to control. He found himself reaching for the whisky, even though he had promised that he would stay off the hard stuff until after the Olympics. Felipe was a brilliant horseman but he was prone to bouts of insecurity.

His bleak mood was interrupted by the ringing of the doorbell. Hoping that it might be Eduardo and Ricky, he was disappointed when he answered the door to Paloma. The woman he couldn't seem to shake off, however obvious he made his feelings for Charlie.

'Felipe, I wanted to see that you were okay. Your mother told me what a difficult time you've been having lately with training.' She had changed into a simple black silk dress and looked beautiful. But her beauty had no effect on him any more. He could appreciate it but it didn't make him want her. She had no hold over him.

He didn't ask her in but leant against the doorframe, arms folded, 'I'm fine, Paloma. You must remember that bad weeks are par for the course.'

'Bad enough to make you start drinking whisky again? You needn't bother to deny it, I can smell it on your breath.'

Damn, he hated being found out; it made him defensive. 'It was just a glass, it's no big deal. And it is nothing to do with you, Paloma.' He knew how dismissive he sounded, but couldn't help it.

Instead of being offended she gave him a sympathetic smile. 'I am only saying it as a friend. You always say that it is only one glass, but then there'll be another . . . and then another . . . until you have finished the bottle. And you'll wake up in the morning feeling wretched and wonder why on earth you did that to yourself. Why don't you let me make you some coffee and we can talk?'

He had been expecting her to put on one of her needy *You must still love me* performances but she seemed totally together. It made a pleasant change not to see her playing the role of spurned girlfriend.

Maybe it would be good to talk to her. God knows he needed to confide in someone who understood how he felt. Felipe nodded and she walked in. She threw her scarf and bag on the sofa and headed straight for the kitchen. Naturally she knew where everything was. A few minutes later she returned with a cafetière of coffee and a selection of tapas. 'I thought you probably wouldn't have eaten since the picnic,' she told him, setting the tray down on the elegant mirror-glass coffee table – one of the many items she had chosen for the apartment.

'So tell me how things are?'

In a way it was a relief to open up to Paloma. She did understand both the pressure of competition and the pressure he put himself under. She waited until he had finished speaking before saying, 'Felipe, you are a great sportsman and this is your time. We all believe in you, we all believe you can do it.' She smiled at him. 'You just have to believe in yourself and you will succeed, I have no doubt.' She paused. 'But you know all this, of course, and I'm sure it's only what Charlie has been telling you all weekend.'

He hesitated. 'My mother must have told you that Charlie has a problem with riding.' He could just imagine the lurid picture Vittoria had painted of Charlie's panic attack the previous day.

Paloma couldn't quite meet his eye as she replied, 'She mentioned it. But that surely doesn't stop you talking to Charlie about your training and your anxieties, does it?'

'I don't need to talk to her about it.' He was lying and was certain that Paloma had picked up on this. He expected her to make something of it, but instead she said, 'I want you to know that you can always talk to me. As a friend, I'm always here for you.'

He thought of his earlier depression. If Paloma hadn't arrived when she did, the chances were he would have hit the bottle and felt even worse for it.

'Thank you, Paloma, that's very good to know.' He smiled warmly at her. She smiled back and said lightly, 'What else are friends for?' Then she reached for her bag and scarf and stood up to go.

'Don't you want another coffee?' he asked, surprised that she was leaving so soon. Usually he had to come up with an excuse in order to get rid of her.

'Actually I have a date.' She shrugged. 'I don't know where it will lead, but I have to move on, don't I?'

Felipe smiled, genuinely pleased that she had met

someone else. He didn't feel remotely jealous. 'He's a lucky man, whoever he is.'

He felt considerably happier after he'd said goodbye to Paloma. She was right, everything would be okay.

Chapter 16

God! It was frustrating having a conversation with her brother on the phone. Charlie could hardly get a word out of Kris, beyond a monosyllabic 'yes' or 'no'.

'Have you told Mum that you're going to be staying with me?' Charlie asked. She knew that Lori had been to see Kris the day before and was really hoping that he had broken the news to her then. He was due to be released at the end of the week.

A sigh from Kris, then, 'I just couldn't do it, Charlie. I know she's going to be really upset.' He paused. 'Can you tell her?'

Shit! Charlie could just imagine her mum's reaction. She knew how much Lori was looking forward to having her son home again. 'Okay.' She tried not to let her reluctance show.

'Anyway Dad will be relieved that he doesn't have to see his criminal son.' He still sounded so bitter that their dad had only visited him once.

'I'm sure that's not true, Kris. Just give him time.'

She heard a prison guard in the background telling them to end their conversation. 'I've got to go, Charlie. I'll see you next week.'

Kris put the phone down before she had a chance to say goodbye properly.

Charlie stared out of her living-room window. She was sorely tempted to go for a run, anything to put off making the call, but if she didn't get it over and done with now it would only make things worse. She selected her parents' number. Lori picked up and immediately launched into an account of how she had redecorated Kris's room in preparation for his release.

'I've gone for a neutral look on three walls with a kind of beige slash taupe, and then made a feature wall over the bed in a rich dark brown. I thought it was sophisticated and masculine, and as far away as possible from that vile pale blue paint he's been surrounded by – I swear I never want to see that colour again. What d'you reckon? D'you think he'll like it?' She sounded so bubbly and excited at the prospect of having him back home.

'The room sounds great, Mum, but Kris is only going to be in Manchester for a day or two before he comes down to London to stay with me.'

'When was this decided? He needs time to find his feet again.' Already Charlie could hear the catch in her mum's voice as she held back the tears.

'He thought it would be best to make a fresh start. You can come down and stay any time and he'll be back to see you.'

'I was so looking forward to having my boy back. It's

been so hard these last five months.' Lori sounded despondent.

'I know, Mum, and Kris has missed you so much. He said he can't wait to see you and to have your home cooking again.'

'Did he? He needs feeding up, poor lad. I was planning to make that vegetable korma he likes. And I'm going to get some bacon in so I can make him a proper English breakfast, even though you know I don't like having meat in the house.'

'He'll really appreciate that, Mum.'

They chatted for a while longer and by the time they said goodbye Lori had rallied and was back to sounding her usual upbeat self. Charlie hadn't mentioned that Kris didn't think their dad wanted him at home anyway. She hoped that if Kris could get an acting job, it might help their father to forgive him, accept that his son was making something of his life and that prison had been a one-off. God, families could be so complicated! Though however difficult her dad was being over Kris, he was nothing like as difficult as Felipe's mother. Vittoria was in a league all of her own.

Apparently she and Felipe weren't speaking after the events of the party. Charlie had urged Felipe to make peace with Vittoria – she might not like the woman, but she certainly didn't want to come between a mother and her son – but Felipe had refused. He insisted that his mother had to apologise for what she had said to Charlie, that it was inexcusable. Charlie didn't believe an apology was coming her way any time soon.

*

A week after her brother's release from prison, Charlie was nervously anticipating his arrival at her flat. She had wanted to go and meet him at King's Cross Station but he'd insisted he would be fine getting the tube on his own. Charlie wasn't so sure. It must be a huge shock being surrounded by so many people after five months of imprisonment. She could only imagine how it felt because Kris hadn't once talked about his experiences inside. They had always been open with each other in the past, but prison had put a stop to that. She felt as if he had closed himself down and was no longer sure how to get through to him.

She wandered into the spare bedroom once more to check that it looked okay. She'd splashed out on a new flat-screen TV for her brother, as well as a brightly coloured stripy duvet cover from Habitat as her old white lace one had looked a bit too feminine. It was a pleasant, light room, with two large sash windows over-looking the long narrow garden. It had to be a million times better than the cell he had left behind, she reflected.

The doorbell rang and Charlie raced out of her flat to open the front door. Kris was standing on the door-step, a rucksack by his side. He still had the hunched defeated look he'd had in prison, the one that made Charlie want to cry. Instead she smiled and hugged him tight.

'It's so good to see you,' she said, trying to keep a check on how emotional she felt.

'You too,' he replied, but could barely raise a smile.

Charlie had imagined a cosy night in, with the two

of them filling each other in on the past five months. She had always been able to talk to her twin about anything. He knew better than anyone else the impact the accident had had on her, though she hadn't told even him about her nightmares. However, after a brief chat about his journey, Kris slumped back on the sofa, switched on the TV, and didn't seem to want to talk, in spite of her best efforts to spark a conversation. Everything she suggested was met with a shrug or a 'Don't mind'.

Finally she asked if he wanted to meet her for lunch the following day and received yet another shrug.

'I just thought it might be good to go out so you get used to being around different people, especially as you're seeing the director at the end of the week.'

'I'll let you know,' came the non-committal reply.

Lori had warned Charlie that Kris was being uncommunicative, but even so it was a shock to find him so hard to talk to. Charlie ended up leaving him to watch the football while she went into the kitchen to make *lasagne* – one of Kris's favourite meals. At one point he wandered in and for a moment she thought he might be about to initiate a conversation. Instead he simply asked if there was somewhere he could smoke.

'Would it be okay if you went into the garden?' Now probably wasn't the time to have a go at him about smoking . . .

'No problem.'

She handed him a saucer. 'You can use this as an ashtray.'

She watched him through the French doors as he

paced up and down the decking. He seemed so down she wished there was something she could do to help him. But he hardly spoke to her over dinner. He did ask how it was going with Felipe, but Charlie didn't feel the moment was right to talk about how her fear of riding was casting a shadow over their relationship. So she told him everything was fine.

Kris picked at his food and hardly ate anything. He usually had a voracious appetite and polished off everything on his plate and then had seconds. He offered to clear up afterwards but Charlie wouldn't hear of it. After turning down her offer of home-made banoffee pie, another of his favourites, he once more went outside for a cigarette.

Later that night when they'd both gone to bed Charlie lay awake, worrying about him. She'd been naively expecting that the moment he came out of prison everything would be okay. It certainly didn't seem that way. Suddenly she remembered Darcy's comment that Kris might find it hard to live with her. Had she done the right thing, asking her brother to stay? Or was her successful career undermining him and reminding him of what he didn't have?

Kris wasn't up when she left for work the following morning, so Charlie scribbled a note telling him to help himself to breakfast and whatever else he wanted, and again suggested he meet her for lunch. She didn't hear from him, however, and ended up being frantically busy before she went on air, so much so that she didn't even get a chance to call him.

*

'Is there anything else?' Darcy asked Nicky, as she sat in her boss's office, twiddling her pen, notepad at the ready like a good little PA. She bloody hoped not. She hadn't stopped all morning.

'Can you confirm the guest bookings for tonight and tomorrow and book their taxis?' Nicky asked, barely looking away from her screen.

'Um . . . I thought Ruby was going to do that? I hoped I could do some research, maybe find some new contributors,' Darcy replied.

'Ruby's away so I need you to do it. And by all means find some new contributors, but that will have to be on top of your other work.'

'I understand, Nicky,' Darcy managed to reply, even though she was fuming. She walked out of the office as if she couldn't be happier about her mundane tasks. But once she was out of Nicky's eye line she stormed along the corridor and slammed her fist against the lift button. She was sick to death of everyone treating her like shit. 'Do this, do that, don't do this, don't do that!'

She marched out of the lift, and through the security barrier into the spacious, minimalist reception area, her heels clicking loudly against the tiled floor. And on top of everything Drew hadn't called her since their last encounter and neither had he replied to the texts she'd sent him. Darcy's promise to India that she wouldn't text him had lasted all of two days and then she couldn't stop herself. She was so lost in thought, intent only on getting outside and having a much-needed cigarette, that she barged straight into the young man who was walking into reception.

'Hey, are you okay?' he asked, sounding concerned. Though in fairness it was a question she should have asked herself, as she had done the barging.

Darcy was all set to mutter 'Yes' and continue out of the door; then she glanced up at his face. Instantly she recognised the good-looking man. This was Charlie's brother. He lacked the cocky expression she remembered from his publicity photos, and was considerably paler with dark circles under his eyes, but it was definitely him. Now this could be interesting . . . She gave him her best flirtatious smile. 'Oh, I'm fine. I'm so sorry I bashed into you.'

'I reckon I'll survive.' He grinned back at her. For a second they held eye contact then Darcy said coyly, 'I think I know who you are.'

Instantly the grin went and he looked defensive. Shit, she hadn't meant to unsettle him.

'You're Charlie's brother, aren't you?' she went on quickly. 'I work with her and she showed me your publicity shots. I'm Darcy by the way.' She could only hope that Kris didn't mention this to his sister, as no doubt that would give Charlie yet further ammunition to have a go at her.

His face softened slightly. 'Surprised you recognised me then, I know how rough I look at the moment.' He certainly didn't seem to have his sister's supreme confidence.

'Have you come in to see Charlie?'

'Yeah, she mentioned something about lunch, but I might have left it too late.'

'She's just gone on air now. She won't be off for another couple of hours, I'm afraid.'

He shrugged. 'Yeah, I knew I should have called her first.' He seemed so despondent Darcy suddenly had an idea.

'I haven't had lunch yet. There's a little café round the corner, if you fancy it? It's nothing special, but the sandwiches are good.'

He smiled, which had the effect of instantly lightening his face. 'That is the best offer I've had in so long. Thanks, that would be great.'

Darcy asked Kris out for lunch primarily because she was curious to find out more about Charlie, but she quickly found herself warming to him. She was too used to going out with Drew, who barely paid her any attention and got bored if she ever tried to tell him anything about herself. Kris seemed genuinely interested in her. He asked her questions, and actually listened to her answers.

'D'you like working in TV?' he asked.

Usually this would be the cue for Darcy to rave about her job, how much she loved it, how important it was. Instead she replied, 'It's different from how I thought it would be. I feel like a dogsbody most of the time.'

'You'll get there. That's how Charlie used to feel, you just need to persevere.'

'And you need quite a lot of luck,' Darcy replied. She didn't add that she thought his sister was a jammy cow; it was unlikely to go down well. 'So what about you?'

He shrugged. 'I guess you know that I've just come out of prison. It's all about making a fresh start. Charlie's got me another meeting with a director I met before it all went tits up.'

'Sounds good,' Darcy commented, wondering why he didn't seem very excited by the prospect.

'Yeah, let's hope so. I kind of don't want to get my hopes up. I know that Charlie is only trying to help, but I don't think she realises that the rest of the world will just see me as an ex-prisoner. I'll be lucky if I get any job, let alone an acting role.'

Darcy smiled sympathetically; she knew only too well how it felt to be down on yourself.

'Charlie's very lucky, everything always seems to go her way,' she couldn't stop herself from saying. She hoped it didn't sound too bitchy.

Kris shook his head. 'It might seem like that, but she's had to work really hard to get where she is, and then she had to cope with the accident . . .'

Hang on, Darcy didn't know anything about this. 'What accident?'

Kris looked as if he regretted mentioning it as he quickly said, 'Sorry, I'd better not say anything if you don't already know. Charlie doesn't like to talk about it.'

''Course. I understand,' Darcy replied smoothly, instantly curious to find out more.

As they left the café, Kris asked if she wanted to go out for a drink sometime. He sounded unsure of himself and Darcy thought it was so sweet. She was also relieved that her comment about Charlie hadn't put him off. 'I'd love that,' she said. And as they swapped phone numbers, she was surprised to realise that she meant it.

When she returned to the office, she had a smile on her face for the rest of the afternoon, especially when she walked past Charlie in the corridor. What would she make of Darcy going out on a date with her precious brother?

Darcy received a text from Kris as soon as she arrived home after work: *Great to meet you today Darcy. How about a drink tomorrow night? Kris x*

That was a first. The men she usually went for would leave it a good few days before getting back in touch with her, keeping her on tenterhooks. They were all from the school of treat her mean, keep her keen. Darcy was all set to reply when on second thoughts she decided that she would keep someone waiting for a change. She poured herself a glass of wine and couldn't resist Googling Charlie to find out about the mystery accident. She was surprised she had missed it before, but there was only one article about it. The reporter said it was a 'miracle' that she had survived. Lucky again, Darcy thought to herself, though she had to admit that, much as she disliked Charlie, the accident sounded horrific and she wouldn't have wished it on anyone. Darcy imagined that it must have put Charlie off riding for life. And now she thought of it, she couldn't recall Charlie ever talking about horses. It must surely put a strain on her relationship with Felipe. So perhaps everything was not so perfect in Charlie's world . . .

Darcy topped up her wine glass and had a long bath. When she picked up her mobile she saw she had another message from Kris. *Sorry, was that too keen? x* She smiled and this time was about to reply when the doorbell rang. She padded over to the entry screen and, to her surprise, saw Drew standing outside, clutching a magnum of champagne. Usually she wouldn't have hesitated to let him in, but now she did. He was only here because he wanted a shag. Impatient at her lack of reply, he pressed the buzzer again. He looked sweaty, slightly pissed. Darcy thought back to her meeting with Kris, the way he had looked at her as if she was someone special and then his sweet texts. Her phone rang. Drew, of course, no doubt wanting to know where she was and why she wasn't entirely at his disposal. She ignored the call and the buzzer and went into her bedroom where she put on Cee Lo Green's *F**k You*, which seemed appropriate in the circumstances, and painted her nails a gothic black.

After pressing the buzzer a couple more times Drew finally gave up. Some ten minutes later India arrived back from work and, after knocking on Darcy's door, walked into the bedroom.

'I've just seen Drew getting into a taxi,' she said. 'Please tell me he wasn't round here? I'll have to get the flat fumigated.'

Darcy held up her hands to consider how the colour looked. 'Prepare yourself, India – I didn't let him in.'

'OMG!' India replied, sitting down on the double bed. 'Tell me you're never going to see that toxic fuckwit again?'

'I'm never going to see him again,' Darcy replied, realising with a rush of confidence that she actually meant it. She was over Drew.

Her phone beeped with a message. It was another

one from Kris. *Did I mention how beautiful I thought you were? x*

'It's not from Drew, is it?' India asked, raising her eyebrows as she noticed the huge smile on Darcy's face.

'Nope, believe it or not, it's from Charlie's brother. We had lunch together today and he's asked me on a date.'

India looked as surprised as Darcy felt by the turn of events. 'So are you going to go?'

'Why not? I've got nothing to lose. Plus he's super cute.' And she quickly texted back that she would love to meet him for a drink.

Chapter 17

Darcy looked at her watch. She was supposed to have met Kris half an hour ago. She had turned up twenty minutes late herself, not wanting to appear too keen, only to discover that he wasn't even there yet. Feeling slightly disappointed, she had ordered a bottle of Sauvignon Blanc and sat down at one of the tables. She got out her phone and checked her Facebook page – anything to give her something to do. She hated being kept waiting like this, it reminded her of all the times that Drew had been late – sometimes even forgetting that he was supposed to be meeting her. Drew had messaged her, wanting to know why she hadn't returned his calls. She hadn't replied.

A glass of wine later and Kris still hadn't shown up. A couple of men in suits sitting at the adjacent table kept looking over at her, obviously thinking that she was out on the pull. Great, that was all she needed. She toyed with the idea of phoning or texting Kris but then dismissed it; she didn't want to seem desperate.

She couldn't understand why he hadn't turned up. He was the one who had pursued her and now he was making her feel like a fool.

One of the suits approached her table: a confident, ex-public school type, the sort of man she knew only too well from being with Drew. 'Hi, we wondered if you would like to join us for some champagne?' Yep, he had the same drawling accent. 'It can't be much fun sitting here all on your own,' he added.

Darcy knew from past experience how her night would pan out if she did that. She'd drink too much, flirt with both men, end up going back home with one of them, then wake up in the morning feeling like death. She'd never see the guy again, even though he'd take her number and promise to call. She wasn't the kind of girl they wanted to see again, but she had been good for one night.

'Thanks, but I'm going now,' she replied, feeling far too humiliated by Kris's no show to want to spend another minute in the bar.

'That's a shame, but maybe you could meet me another time.' And he handed her a card with his mobile number.

'Maybe,' Darcy replied, slipping the card into her bag, thinking, *No way*.

She stood up, all set to leave, and Kris ran into the bar. It was raining outside and he was soaked through.

'Darcy, I'm so sorry I'm late – the Circle line was screwed up and I couldn't get a taxi. I had to run most of the way.' He was out of breath and water was streaming off his face.

Darcy couldn't imagine Drew ever running anywhere to see her but she wasn't ready to forgive Kris yet. 'Why didn't you text me?'

'I did!' he exclaimed, pulling out his phone. 'Look.'

She saw that he had sent her three texts.

'You probably don't get a signal in here. I am really sorry. I hope you didn't think I wasn't going to turn up? I would never do that to anyone, let alone a girl I wanted to impress.'

Now Darcy managed a smile; she wasn't used to men being open about their feelings. It made a very refreshing change. She sat down again. 'Would you like a glass of wine?'

'Sure, thanks.' He beamed at her, clearly delighted that she wasn't going to leave. 'I'm just going to try and dry off a bit, but promise you won't go?'

'I promise,' Darcy replied, pouring him a glass of wine.

Suddenly the night was transformed. From the moment Kris returned from the bathroom, they laughed and flirted together. He was so charming and funny and sweet and sexy, and best of all he seemed really to like her. Darcy basked in the glow of his attention, felt that she could be all the things he seemed to think she was – funny, intelligent, beautiful, nice. He wasn't one of the rich city boys she usually went for, but he was far more of a gentleman than they ever were to her.

In fact the only negative thing about the date happened after they'd left the bar. Darcy lived round the corner and Kris offered to walk her home. They strolled back, holding hands. Darcy couldn't remember the last time she had held hands with Drew. Outside her flat they kissed for the first time, and what a promising kiss it was too. Kris's body felt impressively hard and muscular against hers. Drew could do with hitting the gym and losing weight – too many business lunches and nights out on the lash with the boys had left him slightly flabby around the middle, but Kris's abs felt satisfyingly rock-solid.

'So, do you want to come up?' Darcy murmured, in a sultry voice, fully expecting to spend the night with Kris.

His reply floored her. 'Don't you think we should take things a bit slower?'

Darcy looked at him in disbelief. Typical! She had made her attraction to him obvious and now he was rejecting her. She didn't think she'd ever been on a date with a man where they hadn't ended up in bed together. That was how she knew that they actually liked her.

Immediately she pulled away. 'Okay, I get it. If you don't want to, it's fine by me.'

'That's not what I said at all,' Kris replied. But Darcy was already running up the steps and before he could stop her she had opened the front door and slammed it shut, ignoring Kris who was calling out her name.

She was in a complete state. India was out so there was no one to let off steam with. She felt humiliated and hurt. She poured herself a large glass of wine. She'd even blown her allowance on a new outfit for the night – a tight black dress from Vivienne Westwood that showed off her killer body, complete with expensive new underwear from La Perla in sexy black Chantilly lace and silk. Now she flung the clothes on her bedroom floor, vowing never to wear them again. She had been completely wrong about Kris – he was just as vile as his sister.

After her shower, she noticed she had a message on her phone. She half wondered if it might be from Kris, and even though she had written him off, the disappointment was sharp when she found it was from her mother, reminding her that there was a family dinner in two weeks. So, yet another opportunity for Darcy to feel like a loser as her high-flying sisters boasted about their work achievements and settled relationships. Darcy rifled through her bedside cabinet for the bottle of sleeping pills she kept for emergencies. She knew she wasn't supposed to mix them with alcohol, but the thought of not being able to sleep and re-living the humiliation of Kris turning her down was too much. She took two.

She woke up with a pounding headache and discovered five missed calls and several texts from Kris, all asking her to call him. Well, he could fuck right off! She had been stupid to agree to meet him in the first place; he was obviously just as arrogant as his sister. Darcy wanted nothing more to do with him. Her resolve weakened slightly when she arrived at work and Wendy, one of the receptionists, called her over to tell her she had a delivery. Darcy expected it was most likely a programme insert that had been sent to the wrong place and stood there, arms folded, with a bored expression on her face, which disappeared when Wendy handed her a bouquet of exquisite blush pink roses.

'I didn't know it was your birthday,' she commented. The polite description of Wendy was that she prided herself on knowing everything about everyone. The less polite – she was nosy as hell.

'It isn't,' Darcy replied, wondering if it was a make-up gesture from Drew. But when she opened the card she discovered the flowers were from Kris: *I really want to see you again. I thought we were getting on so well last night. Please call me. I have to see you again Kris x*

Darcy left it a good couple of hours before she made the call. Kris answered on the first ring. She thanked him for the flowers, knowing that she sounded formal and cold, and was completely disarmed by his immediate and heartfelt reply. 'I never thought being a gentleman would backfire on me like that. It wasn't that I didn't want to spend the night with you, because I did.' He paused and seemed to be waiting for her to reply. She let him carry on. 'But I've done that so many times in the past. This is going to sound really sappy, but I wanted things to be different with you. I really want to see you again. Is there any chance you could meet me tonight? I know you probably want to be all cool and say no, but I would love it if you said yes.'

Darcy had been planning to say no to whatever he suggested, but he had won her over. However, she felt she needed to keep the upper hand, so even though she was free, she told him she couldn't meet him until Sunday night. And while she relished the feeling of control it gave her, as soon as she'd said it, she wished she hadn't left it so long.

Charlie couldn't help noticing that Kris seemed much happier. She put it down to the fact that he was finally adjusting to his freedom and feeling more optimistic about his future. It was a relief because Felipe was flying over on Saturday night and she had been dreading that her brother was going to continue being morose and monosyllabic. But Kris told her that he was looking forward to meeting Felipe and agreed to go out for dinner with them, along with Zoe and Nathan, which seemed like a huge step forward.

Felipe had said that he would go straight to the restaurant, but Charlie couldn't resist meeting him at the airport. She watched him stride through arrivals and her stomach somersaulted with excitement, longing and lust. He seemed just as thrilled to see her and swept her into his arms, kissing her passionately. And right at that moment she wished they were going back to her flat and not having dinner. It had been two long weeks. All she felt like doing was falling into bed with him. It was obviously what Felipe was thinking as well, as he murmured, 'Are you sure we can't skip dinner?'

'I would feel bad about letting everyone down,' Charlie replied.

'What about keeping me waiting?' he demanded. 'I have needs.' He lowered his voice. 'Pressing needs.' His arms were round her waist and she could feel exactly how pressing those needs were.

'Me as well,' she replied. 'But it will be all the sweeter.'

Kris, Nathan and Zoe were already installed at a table in the cosy Italian restaurant in Soho when they arrived.

'Ah, my favourite match-maker!' Felipe exclaimed, warmly embracing Zoe.

'Yep, I'll be sending you an invoice for my services!' she teased back. 'You two caused me and Luis no end of trouble.' She pointed at her forehead, 'I think you've given me a new frown line.'

'Hah! You loved every minute of it!' Charlie interjected.

Zoe introduced Nathan and Felipe shook hands with the footballer. 'That's quite a woman you've got there,' Felipe told him.

'The same thing back to you, mate,' Nathan replied.

'And this is my brother Kris,' Charlie put in.

'It's so good to meet you,' Felipe told him, and slightly startled Kris when he shook his hand and then gave him two kisses on the cheek.

'It's a Spanish thing,' Charlie told her twin.

Introductions over with, they all settled down to order. Charlie loved how easily Felipe got on with her brother and Nathan.

'So, Kris, you have to give me all the dirt on Charlie. What was she like when she was growing up? I bet she bossed you around.'

'Cheek!' Charlie exclaimed.

Kris shook his head. 'Nope, we've always got on well,

even when we were teenagers.' He grinned at his sister. 'This is going to sound so corny but she's always been there for me. Totally solid.' He left a pause. 'But until she met you she had the worst taste in men.'

Charlie punched him on the arm. It didn't stop Kris from revealing her roll-call of shame, starting with Liam, the first boy she properly went out with at the age of fifteen, who was appallingly vain and obsessed with his hair. He had a more meaningful relationship with his Lynx hair gel than he did with Charlie. Then there was Simon, who couldn't make up his mind to do anything unless his mates were involved and who pulled out of a holiday to Corfu with Charlie at the last minute because his mates were going to Ibiza. She dumped him and had a much better time with Zoe.

'What about Finlay the vet? He was sweet and he was very good with animals,' Charlie had to defend herself. In fact, although Finlay had been very good-looking and owned an adorable Golden Retriever, he was Dullsville and a great disappointment in bed. No staying power at all . . . talk about blink and you missed it.

'Sweet? I don't know if I like the sound of him,' Felipe put in.

'Don't be jealous,' Kris told him. 'He was the most boring guy I've ever met and Charlie thought so too, which is why she finished with him on her birthday. The poor guy had booked a table at some flash restaurant and bought her expensive perfume!'

'Seriously? That was harsh!'

Charlie grimaced. 'I know, it was really bad, but I

just couldn't face going out on a romantic dinner with him and making forced conversation.'

'And you said you didn't want to make *lurve* with him again.' That from Zoe. 'Even if it did only last forty-five seconds.' She turned to Felipe. 'She timed him.'

God! Talk about being under the spotlight.

Felipe couldn't stop grinning on hearing about Finlay's lack of prowess.

'And then there was Aaron.' As soon as he said the name, Kris realised he had gone too far.

'Let's leave it there,' Charlie said quietly.

'Sorry.'

Felipe put his arm round her. 'I think we should all now confess our worst-ever relationship. I'll start. It was with Dolores. We were both thirteen, but the truth is I only asked her out because I wanted to get close to her big sister, Salma, who was fifteen. I would go round to their house and hang out round the pool and well, stare at Salma in her bikini. She had an incredible body.' He was actually looking quite wistful at the memory of the bodylicious Salma.

'You little pervert!' Charlie exclaimed.

'Yes, that's exactly what Salma and her friends shouted when they caught me and my friends spying on them sunbathing topless.'

Everyone laughed and carried on swapping stories of their early romances. It was the kind of night out Charlie had never had with TFB, who didn't get on with any of her friends and would sit there looking bored or texting. In contrast Felipe was warm and charming to everyone. He was bloody gorgeous and she adored him! But she couldn't help noticing that everyone avoided the topic of what he actually did for a living, including Kris. It was as if one part of Felipe's life was a complete no-go area. And Charlie knew that this wasn't right. She tried to push the thought away; she had to be hopeful that soon this wouldn't be the case otherwise what future could they have together?

Just before the desserts arrived she quickly nipped to the bathroom. When she returned to the table, she overheard Zoe saying excitedly, 'But, Felipe, that is such great news, we have to celebrate!'

And she saw her boyfriend shake his head.

'Celebrate what?' Charlie asked, taking her seat. She suddenly realised how awkward everyone looked. No one would meet her gaze. 'Seriously, what is it? You have to tell me.'

Felipe put his arm round her. 'I found out yesterday that I have qualified to be part of the Olympic team.'

And he felt that he couldn't tell her! Charlie felt terrible, just terrible. 'That is fantastic, I'm so proud of you, Felipe.' She hugged and kissed him, willing the distress not to show on her face. 'Now let's get some champagne!'

Once or twice she caught Zoe looking at her with concern, obviously wondering how Felipe's news had affected her, but Charlie just smiled back. After tomorrow she wouldn't be seeing him for three weeks as he was taking part in two European eventing competitions, one in Portugal and one in Germany, and she didn't want anything to ruin their time together.

Kris tactfully went straight to his room when they

returned to the flat, saying that he was going to watch a film.

Felipe waited until Kris was safely out of the way before he said, 'I was going to tell you about the Olympics. I wanted to wait until we were alone, but Zoe asked me and I didn't want to lie. I'm sorry it came out like that.'

'It's the best news ever. I know what it means to you.'

He looked serious. 'Do you think you might be able to come and watch me compete? I know it's tough for you, and I completely understand if you cannot.'

There it was, the question she had been dreading. Summoning every ounce of strength she possessed, Charlie replied, 'Of course I will. I'll be completely over the riding thing by then, I know it.'

He hesitated, already guessing her response, but felt he had to say it anyway. 'Maybe it wouldn't be a bad idea to have a course of therapy first?'

She shook her head. 'No, I've told you, I can do it.'

He smiled at her. 'My brave girl, I believe you can do anything.'

How Charlie wanted to believe him, but the anxious thoughts were already forming. He put his arms around her and kissed her, a deep passionate kiss, and Charlie tried to submerge herself in the moment, in the desire that burned through her . . .

Felipe broke off to murmur, 'I have to have you now.' His hands skimmed over her breasts . . . how she wanted him.

'I feel the same,' she said breathlessly.

'Come on then,' he replied, taking her hand and leading her to the bedroom, 'What are we waiting for?'

Their passionate love-making was a brilliant distraction, blocking out thoughts of everything else, and they both lost themselves in the moment and in the sheer intensity of their feelings for each other. But afterwards, as they lay in each other's arms, a tangle of hot limbs, Charlie found herself thinking once again of Felipe's big news. The fact was that nothing seemed to have diminished her phobia about riding. She kept thinking it would get easier, but it hadn't happened. Her first feeling when he'd mentioned the Olympics wasn't one of elation for him, it was fear that he would expect her to go. She hated herself for what she felt was weakness. She should be thrilled for him; she should be looking forward to what would be the sporting event of a lifetime.

She turned round and kissed his neck, loving the smell of him mingled with his aftershave.

'Happy?' he asked, gently tracing the outline of her lips.

'Very,' she replied.

But at 4 a.m. she woke up drenched in sweat and shaking from a terrifying nightmare, to find Felipe's arms around her. 'Hey, baby,' he stroked her back. 'What's the matter? You were crying out in your sleep.'

Charlie struggled to surface from the dream – the nightmare images were all from the accident. Ace writhing in agony, bright red blood spilling out from his horrific injuries, covering the rider who seemed to be lying lifeless on the road. She had woken up at the moment she realised the rider was her. She couldn't tell Felipe the truth and taint his amazing news.

'It was only a bad dream . . . one I've had since I was a child. A huge tidal wave is about to break and I'm standing on the beach and can't move.' It had been a recurrent nightmare, that much was true. And Felipe seemed to believe her.

'Poor Charlie, can I get you anything?'

'No, just hold me.'

He quickly fell back to sleep but Charlie was awake for ages, wondering how on earth she would fulfil her promise to watch him compete.

Felipe was flying back early afternoon, so they only had time to go out for a quick breakfast the following morning at a brasserie near Charlie's flat.

'What do you usually do on a Sunday?' he asked, tucking in to his Eggs Benedict while Charlie picked at her croissant. She still felt haunted by the nightmare.

'Go to the gym, chores, shopping, see Zoe. I used to go . . .' she hesitated '. . . I used to go riding. And then when I stopped, I couldn't bear not doing anything. The weekend became these dark days I had to fill with activity.' She gazed at Felipe. 'Tell me the truth, is it very hard not being able to talk to me about riding?'

'Of course not, I have so many other people I can talk to about that. Don't make it into a big deal. It's not, I swear.'

Felipe could see the anxiety in her eyes. He thought of the relief he had felt at being able to confide in

Paloma; he would never be able to admit that to Charlie. He checked the time. In another two hours he would have to set off for the airport. They always seemed to be saying goodbye to each other. Their relationship was certainly being tested.

As they came out of the brasserie a bunch of paparazzi blocked their way on the pavement, snapping away at them. They had been lucky and hadn't had any paps on their case . . . until now. Charlie managed to raise a smile, but Felipe hated paps with a vengeance. He scowled and lowered his head.

'Charlie, have you seen Felipe ride yet?' one of the paps called out.

So far any press coverage about them had focused on her living in the UK and Felipe living in Spain. The riding angle hadn't come up at all. But it seemed the press knew now.

'Have you got over your riding accident?' someone else shouted.

Felipe held on tightly to her hand and shouted back, 'It is none of your goddamn business. Now leave us alone. We are not asking for this attention.' And he pushed his way through the photographers to where Charlie's car was parked. He managed to open the door for her and then the passenger door, with the paps swarming around them.

'You have the worst press in the world!' he exclaimed as he slammed the door shut and the paps continued to take photographs of them. 'They are fucking scum!'

Charlie's hands were shaking so much she could hardly get the keys into the ignition.

'Why are they dragging up this story now? What does it matter to anyone except us?'

'Forget about them, Charlie, they're worthless. If you give them headspace, then they've won.'

But the press incident contaminated the remaining time Charlie had with Felipe. She felt on edge when they returned to the flat, as if she could still hear the yells of the photographers. She cried after they had made love, but hid her tears from him. Their weekend that had begun on such a high was ending on a low.

Chapter 18

Charlie hoped that Kris might be at the flat when she returned from taking Felipe to the airport, but her brother was out. She felt listless and blue, already missing Felipe. She had a horrible feeling of foreboding that she couldn't shake off, triggered by the nightmare and the intrusion of the paps. She curled up on the sofa and looked through all the photos she had of Felipe, wishing more than anything that he was there beside her.

Kris finally returned about half-past eleven, just as she was thinking of going to bed. He walked into the living room and threw his keys on the coffee table. He flopped down in a leather armchair and propped his feet up on the table, even though Charlie had asked him a million times not to. He had a big grin on his face.

'Good night?' she asked. It still felt slightly strange to be living with her brother and sometimes she felt a little bit like his mum, wanting to know that he had eaten properly and not had too much to drink.

'Great night. I went out with this gorgeous girl. She's classy too, before you say anything.'

'Is that why you're not back at her place?' Kris had a bit of a reputation for getting through women, something Charlie had pulled him up on in the past.

'Yeah, I don't want to rush things. I'm taking her out for dinner tomorrow night.'

This was a new development. 'Who is the lucky lady then?' Charlie teased him.

Another grin from Kris. 'You know her actually.'

She stared at him blankly.

'It's Darcy. Daft name . . . but what a beautiful girl.'

Charlie nearly fell off the sofa. The idea of her brother getting it together with Darcy was off the scale crazy! 'Darcy Stratton-Hensher?'

'Of course! How many other Darcys do you know?'

'But Darcy is only into rich men.' And other people's boyfriends, thought Charlie, thinking of the way Darcy had pretended that she and Felipe were an item. Since then the two women had just about managed to be civil to each other, but only just.

'Apparently not. I met her at your office and we hit it off straight away. It's pretty obvious I'm not some *Made in Chelsea* toff.'

Charlie looked at her brother, at his buzz cut and pierced ear, the tight white tee-shirt that showed off his biceps and bold tattoo of a black rose, and his low-hanging jeans. He looked tough and urban, definitely not as if he had been born with a silver spoon in his mouth.

'So what do you reckon then, Charlie? I really like her.'

Run away as fast as you can! she wanted to tell her brother, convinced that Darcy would only bring him grief. But he looked so happy, and he deserved to be happy, and she didn't want to be the one to disillusion him.

She shrugged. 'Just be careful. It's your first date since . . .' She didn't want to say prison. 'You might be feeling more vulnerable than you realise.'

'Nah! Everything's cool. I'm meeting that director tomorrow; things are definitely looking up. And Felipe's a good bloke. He gets my stamp of approval.'

There was a pause. *Please don't let Kris expect her to say that Darcy got hers – the words would choke her!*

'He really liked you too.'

'And it's great news about his place in the Olympics.'

'It's the best.'

'And do you think you might be able to watch him?'

God! Not Kris as well. ''Course. I have to be there for him.'

He seemed to register that Charlie looked pale and tired. 'Are you okay?'

It had always been her way to tough things out, and so now she didn't let on how upset she had been by the paps. 'Yeah, I'm fine. We got papped when we were out this afternoon and it wasn't very nice.' She didn't mention the questions about riding or how terrifying she found the very idea of watching Felipe compete in the Olympics.

'One of the drawbacks of being famous,' Kris commented, taking her at her word that she was okay. He stood up. 'And you don't have to worry about me, sis, I'm a big boy.' He stretched his arms up over his head and yawned. 'I'm off to bed. I want to be fresh for the meeting tomorrow. And for my night out.' He winked at Charlie and sauntered out of the room, whistling.

He seemed so cheerful and confident that of course Charlie was pleased for him. But Darcy! Oh, God, anyone but her! She wished she could ask Zoe's advice but it was too late to call now. It would have to wait until tomorrow. *Families* . . .

She left the flat before Kris got up the following morning, and had to go straight to a planning meeting that lasted until lunch-time so she didn't see Darcy in the office. But later she saw her in the canteen, flirting with Simon, one of the other presenters. So much for her liking Kris. Charlie hoped to get a sandwich and slip out without Darcy noticing her, but unfortunately the PA spotted her and made a point of sauntering over.

'Hi, Charlie, did Kris tell you about meeting me?'

Cue annoying pouty smirk.

Charlie could only manage a non-committal, 'Yeah.'

That wasn't enough for Darcy who ploughed on with, 'I can't believe that you two are twins, you look so different.'

'D'you look like your sisters then?' Charlie imagined a gang of tall, slim blondes with sulky expressions, designer clothes, and a shed load of disposable income.

'I guess I do look a bit like Bunny and Perdita.'

Charlie might have guessed her sisters would have equally pretentious names.

'So did you hear about Kris's meeting with the director?' the girl asked.

'Not yet.'

Darcy looked even more pleased with herself. 'He just texted me and said it went brilliantly. The director wants to cast him in a new detective series. They start filming next week. Isn't that awesome! I can't wait to see him tonight and celebrate.'

While Charlie was thrilled for her brother, she couldn't help feeling slightly put out that he hadn't texted her first. 'That is fantastic news,' she said quickly. Then she held up her tuna and sweetcorn sandwich as if it was a wand to banish the evil Darcy. 'Well, anyway, I've got to have a quick lunch and get back to work.' She couldn't bring herself to say 'enjoy your date with Kris'. It was just too freaking weird! And she couldn't believe that her brother had chosen to tell Darcy his big news over her, though when she checked her phone she saw that he had texted her. He must have sent it during the meeting so maybe he did text her before Darcy. She would try and be grown up about it. Though that didn't stop her from telling Aidan. She knew that he would understand how unsettling she would find Darcy getting up close and personal with her brother.

'No way!' he exclaimed. 'Darcy only goes for rich men. Are you sure?' They had gone outside to avoid being overheard.

'Believe me, I wish it wasn't true. But what can I do?'

'Absolutely nothing, I'm afraid, sweet pea. But chin

up, I'm sure it won't last. Your brother will soon realise what a nightmare Arsey Darcy is.'

Charlie could only hope that Aidan was right.

That night she had arranged to go to the cinema with Zoe to see the latest Ryan Gosling film. Charlie didn't usually find blond men attractive, but she was prepared to make an exception for the total hotness that was Ryan . . . While they waited for the film to start, they chatted and shared a bag of popcorn and inevitably Charlie confided in Zoe about Kris's date. 'I keep wondering if I should tell him what a total bitch she is. It's like watching a cute puppy going off with a big bad wolf. Nothing good is going to come of it.'

'Oh, for Godsake!' Zoe declared, grabbing a handful of popcorn. 'Kris is a grown-up, he can definitely look after himself. And, no, you can't say anything negative about Darcy. It will just backfire on you and Kris will think that you're the bitch.' She shared Aidan's view that the relationship would be short-lived.

'I'm sure Kris hasn't got enough money for madam's expensive tastes,' Charlie agreed dryly.

'Meow!' Zoe commented, adding, 'Have some more popcorn, it might sweeten you up.'

When Charlie returned home around eleven there was no sign of Kris. He must still be out with Darcy. Or maybe he had gone back to her place. Charlie didn't want to think about what that meant . . . She called Felipe and told him about Darcy, expecting him to side with her, but he agreed with Zoe that she shouldn't say anything and added that maybe Darcy had changed. As if . . .

Just after midnight, when Charlie had fallen asleep, she was woken up by the front door opening and the unmistakable sound of Darcy's drawling voice. Shit! Her brother had brought her back here. Darcy was the last person Charlie wanted in her home. She could just imagine the snotty cow looking at her small flat and possessions and turning her nose up. Why hadn't they gone back to her place? Not wanting to overhear anything, Charlie reached for her iPod and listened to music on her headphones, hoping that the sultry voice of Lana del Rey would calm her down. It didn't. She was so wound up that she found it impossible to relax or go to sleep. Why did her brother have to get involved with Arsey Darcy? If it had been any other woman Charlie would have been pleased for him.

In the morning she woke up in a foul mood as she hadn't had enough sleep. Her temper didn't improve when she walked into the kitchen after her shower to find Darcy perched on the kitchen table, *her* kitchen table, wearing a tee-shirt of Kris's and most likely nothing else. She was swinging her long tanned legs and giggling, while Kris made tea and toast. How like Darcy to be waited on and not lift a finger . . .

'Morning,' Darcy said, smirking. 'I hope we didn't keep you awake last night.' Another smirk.

Eeow! Charlie suffered a major sense of humour by-pass at the thought of this stuck-up bitch having her wicked way with her brother. 'Nope.' She was abrupt and offhand as she grabbed a yoghurt from the fridge and an apple from the fruit bowl.

'Okay?' Kris asked. He, at least, was not smirking. 'I know it's probably a bit weird for you as you work with Darcy. We agreed that we'll try and go to her place next time.'

Next time? Charlie had hoped it would all be over very quickly. 'Sure, whatever. I've got to run. Oh, I meant to say, it's brilliant news about the acting job. D'you have any more details?'

Kris smiled. 'I'm going to be playing a new TV detective and I've got you to thank for it. How about we go out and celebrate tonight? My treat.'

Charlie felt some of the bad mood lift. A night out with her brother sounded great. 'Where d'you want to go?'

'We thought about the Sanderson, d'you know it?' Darcy put in, adding, 'How about we meet up about half-seven?'

We! They'd only spent one night together, how could they be a *we*? And, no, Charlie didn't want to go out with Arsey Darcy. But if she said no she would seem like the most miserable old bag in the world. And the way that Darcy had asked her about the Sanderson! Of course she knew where it was. Patronising, stuck-up cow!

'Yeah, I know it.'

'Why don't you see if Zoe and Nathan can come too?' Kris suggested. Maybe he had already picked up on the negative vibe between her and Darcy and was thinking safety in numbers.

'Yep, good idea. See you then.'

*

Darcy waited until Charlie had left before commenting, 'I don't think your sister likes me very much.'

Kris put his arms around her waist and kissed her neck. 'How could she not like you? You're gorgeous. She probably just felt awkward because of work.' He kissed her on the lips. 'What time do you have to be in today?'

'Why?' Darcy asked coyly, knowing full well why.

'I thought we might have time to go back to bed.'

'What's wrong with right here?' Darcy asked, thinking it might add to the thrill to have sex on Charlie's kitchen table. But Kris shook his head. Scooping her up in his arms, he carried her into the bedroom.

Darcy was late for work. But it was worth it. Kris was a fantastic lover. He had such stamina and was *soooo* good at turning her on. It made her realise what she had been missing out on with Drew all this time.

'Don't let Nicky catch you,' Ruby warned when she noticed Darcy rushing in. Then she did a double take as she looked her up and down. 'Weren't you wearing those clothes yesterday?'

Darcy shook back her long hair, with its tousled bed head look, achieved because she had just got out of bed. 'Might have been.' Then she grinned and added, 'But it was worth it. Let's just say that it was a very satisfying night – and a pretty satisfying morning.'

Charlie walked past at that moment and overheard the comment.

'Too much information, Darcy,' she muttered, glaring at her.

'Sorry,' Darcy said breezily, not sounding sorry at all.

'Anyone want a coffee? I'm off to the canteen. I need a caffeine fix, I'm completely shagged.'

Charlie didn't say anything but sat at her desk with a face like thunder. Darcy smiled radiantly all the way up to the canteen.

Charlie's mood didn't improve when she saw the day's tabloids which all had the pictures of her and Felipe taken on Sunday. But worse still was the exclusive carried by the *Sun* which went into detail about her relationship with Felipe, and contained quotes from 'a friend' who said what a strain Charlie's phobia about riding was putting on their romance.

'Ouch!' Aidan commented, catching sight of what she was reading. 'Are you okay, Charlie? You mustn't take it to heart, you know, it doesn't mean anything.'

In fact Charlie was having to blink back tears of outrage at seeing her private life dissected like this.

'Why can't they just leave us alone?' she said quietly. 'And who is this "friend"? Some friend who would say those things.'

Realising how upset she was, Aidan put his arm round her. 'You know what the press are like. Say nothing, keep calm, and they'll move on to someone else.'

'But it's true, isn't it? They don't even have to make anything up. My phobia is putting a strain on my relationship with him.'

'You're having therapy; you'll get through this.' Aidan sounded confident, but it was a confidence Charlie didn't share. She had let him assume that she was having therapy. She hated to think of Felipe finding out about the news story; he didn't need that kind of stress now. Though she imagined his mother would be pleased. Yet more ammunition for her to use to prove what an unsuitable and bad girlfriend Charlie was.

Chapter 19

'Look at her,' Charlie whispered to Zoe when they walked into the courtyard garden of the Sanderson later that evening and saw Kris and Darcy sitting at one of the tables. 'I don't know why she's even bothering to wear that skirt, it's so short. It's a pussy pelmet!'

Zoe snorted with laughter. 'What's happened to you? You sound like my nan. *You* wear skirts as short as that.'

'No, I don't,' Charlie replied sulkily, unwilling to concede that Zoe was right.

'You are going to have to take a massive chill pill and deal with this. Kris likes her, which means she can't be that bad. And the two of you are going to have to get along, for his sake.' Zoe smiled, and patted her friend's shoulder. 'Cheer up, it won't be so bad. And at least you're not sitting at home worrying about what those wanker journalists have written.'

Kris gave her a big hug when they joined him and Darcy and asked Charlie if she was okay. Not wanting to talk about her feelings in front of Darcy, she side-stepped the question. 'Let's not talk about it now. This is supposed to be a celebration for you.'

But from the moment she sat down, Charlie found it fiendishly difficult to be nice to Darcy. The woman was so annoying – everything about her put Charlie's back up. True, it probably wasn't Darcy's fault that she sounded like a stuck-up cow with a plum in her mouth, but it *was* her fault that she was such a snob. When Kris suggested that he buy a bottle of house champagne, she immediately said, 'Oh, can't we get Krug? It's so much nicer.'

'It's also over twice the price,' Charlie couldn't stop herself from muttering. She knew Kris was broke at the moment.

'Sure,' he replied. 'It is a celebration and what else are credit cards for?'

Charlie raised her eyebrows at Zoe, who mouthed, 'Chill.'

While Kris ordered the champagne Darcy turned to Charlie. 'I was really sorry to see that story about you and Felipe. How's he taken it?'

'I haven't told him yet. I don't want to worry him. It was all made up crap anyway,' Charlie replied, somewhat abruptly.

'It must be hard having a long-distance relationship,' Darcy continued, appearing oblivious to Charlie's mood.

'It has its moments,' she replied, thinking of the time she had thought Darcy was seeing Felipe.

Kris's mobile rang then. 'It's Mum,' he said, 'I'd better speak to her,' and he got up and went into the lobby.

'So how Felipe's training going? I watched a film of him on his website. He really is an amazing rider, isn't he?'

'Amazing,' Charlie replied. What else could she say? Would Darcy shut up about Felipe now!

She frowned and mumbled, 'Oh, sorry, I guess you haven't seen him ride.'

'Not yet, but I'm hoping to soon. And I'll be watching him in the Olympics, of course.' But even mentioning it made Charlie feel sick to her stomach.

Darcy looked slightly hesitant as she continued, 'And I really hope that there aren't any hard feelings between us because of that misunderstanding? I never told anyone that I was seeing Felipe, I swear.'

'None at all.' Charlie could hardly admit to her true feelings.

Darcy was falling over herself to make conversation but Charlie could only come up with monosyllabic answers. Fortunately Zoe took over and managed to steer the conversation away from Felipe. By the time Kris returned they were on much safer ground, discussing the Ryan Gosling film that they'd all seen.

Charlie and Zoe stayed for a couple of glasses, then Zoe had to go off and meet Nathan and Charlie took the opportunity to leave as well. No way was she going to play gooseberry to the loved-up couple. She had a pounding headache from the champagne and no doubt the stress of the day.

'Don't you want to come and have something to eat?' Kris asked.

And spend any longer watching Darcy with her hands

all over him, smoothing his hair one minute, caressing his thigh the next? Such blatant PDAs were enough to put anyone off their food even if they weren't a close relative!

'I ought to have an early night, thanks,' Charlie replied, sounding as uptight as she felt.

'Yeah, sorry we kept you awake last night,' Darcy put in. 'We're going back to mine tonight, so it won't be a problem.'

Somehow Charlie forced a smile.

It was only when they were safely outside that she let rip. 'Fuck, fuck, fuck!' she exclaimed. 'Can you believe her?'

She expected Zoe to back her up so it was a shock when her friend took a different approach. 'Babes, you have got to calm down. She actually wasn't that bad and she seems to really like Kris. She can't help the fact that she sounds dead posh, just like you can't help your Manchester accent.'

'Aren't you forgetting that she was nearly responsible for breaking me and Felipe up?' Charlie was not in the mood for being reasonable.

'No, I hadn't forgotten, and she did apologise to you for any misunderstanding. Don't you think Kris deserves to be happy?'

'Of course I do. Just not with her!'

Zoe made a zipping motion across her mouth. 'Enough! You're winding yourself up.' Then she stuck her hand out and successfully hailed a passing taxi, calling out, 'Love you!'

Charlie waved back. Why didn't Zoe get it? Darcy

was bad news. And the only possible outcome was that her brother was going to end up hurt.

But for the next three weeks Darcy and Kris were inseparable, spending every night together. Kris made her feel so good about herself, which was an entirely new experience for Darcy. He was kind and thoughtful and wanted to know all about her. She found herself opening up to him about her childhood, the way she had always felt such a failure in her parents' eyes compared to her two elder sisters, the terrible time when she was expelled from school for taking drugs. She skimmed over her disastrous relationships – she certainly wasn't proud of those. They talked long into the night, after they'd made love. It seemed a waste to go to sleep . . .

She was lying next to Kris now, her head on his chest. She had lit tea lights on the mantelpiece and on her dressing-table which gave the room a cosy and intimate feeling. She suddenly wished they could stay in this room for ever and shut out the rest of the world. Darcy trailed her fingers along Kris's arm, feeling the curve of his biceps, his strong forearms, and settled on his wrist. There she felt the raised bump of a scar, which was usually covered by his watch.

'What's this?'

Kris had been so easy to talk to a minute ago, but now he clammed up. 'It's nothing.' He turned his head away from her as if the subject was closed.

'It's okay, you don't have to tell me. It's none of my business.'

For a few moments there was silence then he spoke. 'There was a time in prison when it really got to me and I didn't think I could take it any more.' He hesitated. 'I managed to get hold of a razor blade and – well, my cell mate found me.'

Darcy felt overwhelmed with sympathy for him. She raised his wrist to her lips and kissed the scar. 'My poor darling, but it's all going to be all right now.'

'Yeah, it feels like it is.' He paused. 'And what about your scars?'

Darcy had a series of pale criss-cross slashes on the inside of both arms and on the tops of her thighs. She was self-conscious about them and always tried to cover them up. If her past boyfriends had ever noticed them they had never commented.

Now she sat up and pulled the duvet around her. She had never talked about the period in her life when she had self-harmed, it had been her shameful secret . . . known only to her and to her family, though they had never mentioned it. She had always feared that people would be disgusted by it and end up loathing her as much as she loathed herself.

Kris reached out and gently stroked her back. His touch felt warm and comforting. As if he knew what she was thinking, he said, 'It won't change how I feel about you.'

Darcy had one of those now or never moments. Kris had confided in her and told her something deeply personal to him. She knew, even after this brief time they'd had together, that he was a man she could trust. 'I used to self-harm. It was just after I was expelled from school.' Her words were coming out in a rush and she couldn't bring herself to look at him. 'I felt like such a failure . . . everyone thought I was a failure. When I cut myself it felt like a release from all that. Sometimes I'm tempted to do it again, but I've been trying really hard not to.'

She tensed up, waiting to hear Kris express shock and disgust, but instead he sat up and put his arms around her.

'You're the most beautiful woman I've ever met and I can't believe how lucky I am that you're with me. Don't ever think that you're a failure.'

Darcy put her head on his shoulder, overwhelmed that he could be so accepting of her. They stayed like that for a while before he said, 'We should get some sleep.'

As they curled up next to each other, he said, 'You're the only person who knows about what happened in prison. Please don't tell Charlie, I know it would really upset her.'

'Of course not,' Darcy replied. Just a few weeks ago she would have revelled in knowing something that Charlie didn't, but now she only felt sympathy for Kris, a shared connection.

The following night she was due to meet her parents and sisters for dinner. She was running late, partly because a meeting over-ran and partly because she had taken too long getting ready, wanting as always to make a good impression. She was the last person to arrive, which earned her a disapproving look from her father, Gerard, who loathed unpunctuality.

'Last-minute script to type up?' Bunny enquired. Both of her successful sisters seemed to enjoy the fact that Darcy was the failure of the family. Maybe it made them feel more secure in their own Golden Girl status.

'No, a planning meeting on the Olympics over-ran.'

'Are you going to be on camera?' That was Mummy, ever hopeful that finally she might have something to boast about where Darcy was concerned. Her parents were hugely snobbish about the media and didn't think that she had a proper job at all.

Darcy shook her head and willed someone to change the subject. She picked up the leather-bound menu. She hated the food here; it was a carnivore's paradise, so meaty and rich. Her parents never seemed to remember that she was a vegetarian, or if they did, they didn't seem to care. They always booked a table at this French restaurant when they came up to London.

'Have you decided?' her father demanded. 'Because I'm keen to order. I don't like to eat after half past eight.'

Darcy might have been wearing a sack for all the interest her appearance seemed to generate in her parents. She had bought the new pearl grey fitted dress from L. K. Bennett, along with the black kitten heels, specially because it was the kind of thing her sisters wore. It had been a complete waste of money. She should have worn her leather trousers and to hell with it.

Why had she agreed to meet up? She might have known it would be like this. Her sisters raving about their work, her parents hanging on their every word, while she felt like the perpetual outsider. But she couldn't help clinging to a sliver of hope that one day she would be accepted, and then her parents would look at her with the same adoration that they lavished on Bunny and Perdita.

'I bet Darcy will have the asparagus tips in butter and then the goat's cheese salad,' Perdita put in. 'It must be so tedious always having the same thing. I'm going to have the escargots and then the braised lamb. They sound yummy.'

'Still veggie then?' her mother Eleanor said. 'It's such a bore having to cater for people who don't eat meat.' She was currently planning the wedding breakfast for Bunny, who was getting married in June.

'It is much better for the planet not to eat meat,' Darcy said quietly. 'All that land given over to cows when it could be used for growing vegetables. And did you know that cows are responsible for producing a massive amount of methane, which contributes to global warming?'

Her family ignored the comment.

'How's Hugo?' Eleanor asked Bunny, referring to her fiancé – a successful financier. Naturally he was successful, Darcy's sisters didn't date unsuccessful men. Perdita was seeing a successful corporate lawyer.

'Oh, he's great, but working flat out as ever.' She smiled slyly at her little sister. 'You should ask Darcy about her new boyfriend.'

Fuck! She might have guessed that it was a bad idea telling Bunny about Kris, but when she had emailed asking if Darcy was still seeing Drew – she was working out the seating plan for the wedding – Darcy didn't want to seem like a saddo singleton so she had mentioned Kris.

'Oh?' Her mother looked at her. 'And who is he?'

'He's an actor and he's lovely,' Darcy said defensively.

'An actor? Such a precarious profession. Has he been in anything I might have seen?' Her mother only watched classic dramas on the BBC and *Antiques Roadshow*, though she had managed to watch *Downton Abbey* even though it was on ITV.

Bunny smirked. 'I doubt it, Mummy. He's what you call a "rough diamond".'

Eleanor looked as if she had smelt something extremely distasteful wafting through the restaurant. 'Oh.'

'And he's just come out of prison,' Bunny said triumphantly.

Darcy glared at her. She hadn't told Bunny that. She must have Googled Kris.

'But he's done the time, paid for his crime,' her sister added. 'So no judgment.'

Gerard had been busy talking to Perdita but they both stopped talking at the mention of prison.

'What's this?' he demanded.

'Darcy's new boyfriend is an actor, just out of prison,' Eleanor said faintly, putting on what Darcy called her Dying Swan act. She was good at acting the martyr where Darcy was concerned. It was much easier than wondering if she might possibly have played some part in shaping her daughter's life. Gerard looked and sounded predictably disgusted. 'I don't know why you had to break up with Drew. He fitted right in. But oh no, as usual you have to go off and do something you know will upset your mother. What was he in prison for?'

Darcy wished she could leave right there and then. 'I think it was to do with receiving stolen goods. It was a one-off, a mistake. And I'm not seeing him to upset Mummy, and Drew broke up with me!' she replied, struggling to keep it together.

Their conversation was interrupted by the arrival of the first courses – asparagus tips for Darcy, steak tartare for her parents, escargots for Bunny and foie gras for Perdita. It was almost as if her family were setting out deliberately to upset her with their choice of food. She had once told Perdita that the idea of foie gras – where geese were force-fed corn – made her feel physically sick, and Perdita just laughed and said, 'But it tastes delish! When you can get something veggie to taste that good, let me know. Until then that's what I'm having.'

At least by now her sisters seemed to think enough attention had been given over to Darcy and had returned to their favourite subject – themselves and the plans for the wedding. Darcy was largely quiet during the meal, longing for it to be over.

'Are you free next week to have a fitting for your bridesmaid's dress?' Bunny asked her at one point.

'I'll have to check the rota.'

Bunny rolled her eyes. 'Well, let me know ASAP, I have to make the booking.'

Darcy wished that she didn't have to be a bridesmaid. In fact, she wished she didn't have to go to the wedding at all.

Before dessert she slipped off to the Ladies. She was tempted to have a sneaky fag, but knowing her luck she would set off the smoke alarm. She checked her messages and saw that there was one from Kris. *Am in the area. Do you want to meet up after your dinner? xxx* It was like seeing the sun come out after an unbelievably dreary day. Instantly Darcy cheered up and called him to suggest he meet her outside the restaurant in half an hour.

Knowing that she had that to look forward to, she let her family's comments wash over her for the remainder of the meal. She had planned to be the first to leave, but to her surprise, just as everyone was drinking coffee, Kris walked into the restaurant. Darcy was torn between the thrill that seeing him again always gave her and dread of him meeting her family.

He smiled and waved at her and strode over to the table. At least he looked smart in a suit. Well, actually, he looked stunningly handsome, but Darcy knew that his fate had already been sealed by the prison comment.

'Hiya,' he said, ducking down and kissing her. Darcy was aware of her family's eyes boring into them so she linked arms with him and said, 'This is my mother, Eleanor, and my father, Gerard, and my sisters Bunny and Perdita.'

Kris politely shook hands with everyone, while Darcy's parents looked at him as if he was a piece of low life about to steal their Cartier watches, and barely cracked a smile.

'I hope you don't mind me coming in but it was

pouring with rain outside and I didn't have an umbrella.'

Darcy waited for her father to suggest that Kris should draw up a chair and join them, as he would have done if one of her sister's boyfriends arrived. But no such suggestion was forthcoming, so she found one herself and ordered coffee for him.

'Have you all had a good dinner?' he asked politely.

'Very pleasant,' Eleanor managed to reply. 'Darcy tells us you're an actor.' She said 'actor' as if it was the equivalent of 'gigolo'.

'I am. I've just been doing a read-through for a new drama that I'm going to be filming. It'll be coming out early next year.'

'What part are you playing?' Bunny asked. Both Darcy's sisters had been blatantly checking him out. Darcy felt some satisfaction from knowing that he was massively better-looking than Bunny's fiancé, Hugo, who had a receding hair-line and didn't have the bone structure to look good bald. Perdita's boyfriend Simon, who was a keen rugby player, had a crooked nose and a bull neck.

'I'm the rookie detective who's trying to break away from his family who are all involved in crime.'

Bunny smirked. 'A case of art not imitating life then.'

Kris stared evenly at her, and she was the first to look away. 'That's all behind me now.' He turned to Darcy. 'Actually I'll skip the coffee, I've got an early start.' He stood up. 'It was good to meet you all.'

He received a series of half-hearted goodbyes in response. Darcy got up as well.

'Aren't you going to have your coffee?' her father asked.

'No, I'm going to leave with Kris. Thanks for dinner.' She kissed her father and mother and waved at her sisters. She wanted to get as far away as possible from them. She would get it in the neck tomorrow from her mother, but for now she just wanted to be with Kris. She held his hand as they walked out of the restaurant.

Outside it was still raining and there wasn't a taxi to be seen. Darcy didn't want to hang about near the restaurant in case her family came out. She suggested they get a bus.

'Your parents are dead posh, aren't they?' Kris commented. 'I thought I might have to pull my forelock . . . not that I've got one to pull.' He brushed his hand over his shaved head.

'Posh, cold and completely dysfunctional,' she agreed.

'I'm sure they're lovely when you get to know them.'

Darcy didn't bother to correct him. 'And I'm sorry that my sister came out with that comment. I didn't tell her, by the way, but she's the kind of person who always wants to know everything about everyone.'

He shrugged. 'I guess they would have found out eventually.' He put his arm round her and kissed her. 'So long as you're okay about it, that's all that matters to me.'

Darcy kissed him back. 'I'm more than okay about it and I don't care what anyone else thinks. You're the best thing that's ever happened to me.' And she meant it. She felt as if there was complete honesty between her and Kris, something she had never known with anyone else before.

'D'you want to come back to mine? Charlie's in Spain, so we'll have the place to ourselves.'

Darcy tried not to let on how pleased she was that Charlie wouldn't be around. She knew how close Kris was to his twin.

Chapter 20

Charlie stretched out on the bed, blissfully happy to be with Felipe again after three long weeks apart. Their reunion had been as passionate and intense as ever and now she was in the mood for talking.

She turned and looked at him. His eyes were closed. 'Thanks for getting the new bed.' Paloma's fancy silver rococo model had been replaced with a solid oak sleigh bed, which was much more to Charlie's liking.

'You're welcome,' he murmured, but didn't open his eyes.

'Kris seems to be getting serious with Darcy. He sees her all the time.'

'Lucky thing. I mean, I wish I saw you all the time.' Now Felipe opened his eyes, but he still seemed exhausted. He yawned as if proving the point. 'I'm sorry, Charlie, I'm going to have to go to sleep.'

'Sure, I understand,' she replied, and in the time it took her to fetch a glass of water from the kitchen, Felipe had fallen into a deep sleep. She snuggled up next to him and put her arms around him. They had the whole weekend together; it didn't matter if he slept now.

Felipe was still tired the following morning, but it was more than physical exhaustion; he also seemed unusually subdued. They were having breakfast outside at a café in the old town. It was a beautiful morning and the May sunshine was a perfect temperature. 'Is everything okay?' Charlie asked him, realising that she had been chatting away about work and her brother while Felipe had barely said a word.

'Fine,' he replied. 'It's just been full on and . . .' He hesitated. Charlie had the feeling that he must have been about to say something about riding but had stopped himself.

'What?'

He shook his head. Reaching into his shirt pocket, he pulled out a packet of cigarettes. Charlie looked at him in surprise as he lit a cigarette and inhaled deeply.

'I didn't know you smoked.'

He shrugged. 'I do sometimes. I'll give up again soon.'

'God, I hope so!' she said with feeling. 'It's a disgusting habit.'

Felipe abruptly stood up. 'Fine, I'll go and sit somewhere else, if it offends you that much.'

She had never heard him snap like this before. She reached out her hand to stop him. 'Stay, don't be silly.'

He sat back down, and ran a hand through his hair. 'I'm sorry, Charlie. I'm just exhausted. Running on empty.'

'Really? Are you sure there isn't something else bothering you?' He seemed so on edge.

'Just tired.'

'Maybe I shouldn't have come this weekend.'

'Of course you should have! This has been the one thing I've been looking forward to.' He ground out the cigarette in the ashtray. 'There, I'll try not to smoke when you're here and I promise I'll quit again soon. You're right, it is a disgusting habit.' He smiled at her, but Charlie could sense the tension within him. Was it just down to the pressure of training and competing? She wasn't sure if she believed him.

After breakfast Felipe said he had something to collect. They strolled through the picturesque narrow streets and ended up at an expensive-looking jeweller's – the kind of establishment where you had to ring a bell to be admitted, and a uniformed security guard stood by the door. Charlie imagined that Felipe was picking up a peace offering for his mother – she knew that things had remained strained between them.

'Which one do you prefer?' he asked as the jeweller showed off two pendant necklaces, both beautiful. One was a diamond-studded love heart pendant, the other an aquamarine.

'I think the love heart.' Surely a diamond necklace would melt even Vittoria's ice-cold heart?

'Good. I thought so.'

Charlie idly looked round the display cases as Felipe paid. The jewellery here was so expensive that none of it carried a price tag. She smiled as he walked over to her. 'I'm sure your mother will love it,' she commented.

He frowned. 'What are you talking about? It's for you.'

'Oh, no! I mean, oh, wow! You didn't have to buy me anything!'

'I wanted to. I chose it last week but I wanted to be certain you liked it. Will you wear it now? I missed you so much and you had the press to deal with on your own.'

Felipe had found out about the story in the paper. Charlie had deliberately underplayed how much it had upset her, but he had obviously realised.

'Thank you,' she replied. 'It's the most beautiful present I've ever been given.'

'Better than anything TFB ever gave you?' he teased.

'He bought me a Chanel bag. I sold it on Ebay when we split up. Someone got a bargain.'

She looked in the mirror as Felipe fastened the necklace around her neck and was struck again by how drained he looked. Something wasn't right. Even though he had just given her this stunning present, she felt there was a distance between them that hadn't been there before, as if he were keeping something from her.

They headed back to the apartment, stopping off to buy champagne as they were going to Luis and Mariana's house for lunch. Charlie insisted on paying for the champagne and Felipe stayed outside the store to take a call. She stared up at the rows of bottles, wondering which one to choose.

'The Perrier-Jouet is Felipe's favourite,' a familiar

voice said. It was Paloma. Instantly Charlie felt self-conscious in her skinny jeans and tee-shirt as Paloma stood there looking as if she had stepped off the red carpet in a bright yellow fitted dress and a pair of sky-high gold sandals – did the woman ever dress down? Charlie felt a stab of insecurity that Paloma still knew more about Felipe's tastes than she did.

'How are you, Charlie?' As ever Paloma had impeccable manners. Even if she loathed the sight of her, she kissed Charlie on the cheek and acted as if she was genuinely pleased to see her.

'Good, thanks.'

'And how is Felipe? I was so very sorry to hear about Audaz. I do hope he is going to be okay. It will be devastating for Felipe if he cannot ride him for the Olympics. Of course he has other horses, but Audaz is the best he has ever competed with.' She looked at Charlie enquiringly, clearly expecting her to know the answer.

Something had happened to Felipe's horse? Why hadn't he told her? Charlie was reeling inside but didn't want to reveal that she knew absolutely nothing about any of this. Somehow she managed a non-committal, 'Felipe's fine, he's outside if you want to talk to him.'

She watched as Paloma swept out of the store and approached Felipe. Charlie saw their animated conversation, saw Paloma give him a sympathetic hug, and felt utterly excluded. Felipe hadn't been able to tell her this crucial news about his horse because of her phobia. No wonder he was so preoccupied and on edge.

By the time she had paid for the champagne, Paloma

had left and Felipe was having another cigarette – so much for him trying to quit, but now at least Charlie understood why. As soon as he saw her he threw the cigarette down and ground it out with his heel.

'We should hurry or we'll be late.' He noticed the champagne. 'Ah, my favourite, that's very clever of you.'

'Paloma told me. It's just one of the many things she knows about you that I apparently don't.'

She thought that might be the prompt for Felipe to tell her what had happened, but he shrugged and said, 'None of those things are important.'

Charlie couldn't bear the fact that he was trying to pretend everything was okay, when it so clearly wasn't. She wanted to tell him that she knew but now wasn't the time as they hurried through the narrow streets, trying to avoid other shoppers. It was only when they arrived back at the apartment that she felt she could broach the subject.

'I'm so sorry about Audaz. You should have told me.'

They were both in the bedroom, gathering together their swimming things, as the plan was to have a swim in Luis and Mariana's pool during the afternoon.

'I didn't want to upset you. There is no conspiracy,' Felipe told her, but he still seemed closed off.

'It was upsetting having to hear about it from Paloma.' Charlie hadn't intended to sound resentful but that was what Felipe detected as he immediately snapped back, 'Paloma knows because of my mother, for no other reason. Please don't be jealous. I hate jealousy. It stifles everything and ruins relationships.'

'I'm not jealous of her,' Charlie protested. 'I feel so excluded from your life. And that's not your fault, it's mine. Please tell me what happened?'

Felipe sighed. 'We were jumping and Audaz hit one of the fences quite badly. He's damaged one of his tendons and we're waiting to find out the extent of the injury.'

He looked so bleak Charlie hardly knew what to say. She walked over to him and put her arms around him. 'I'm so sorry.'

'I know you are, and hopefully he will be okay, but it just adds to the pressure. I'll have to work even harder with Valiente, one of my back-up horses.'

'Shouldn't you be at the stables now, checking how he is doing?' Charlie asked, feeling guilty that Felipe had taken this weekend off to see her.

'No, Daria, my groom, is more than capable of looking after him. I had to spend this time with you. Besides, what will be will be, whether I am there or not.' He kissed her lightly. 'Now come on, we should go.'

They were both quiet on the drive over to their friends' house. Once again Charlie found herself replaying in her mind Vittoria's words about how unfair it was on Felipe that he couldn't confide in his girl-friend about his sport. Suddenly she was gripped with a dark feeling of pessimism. She and Felipe had been living in a bubble of unreality these past months, lost in their passion for each other. They had both been pretending that her not being able to talk about riding was not a problem. They were deluding themselves. It was a huge problem, and Charlie feared it was only going to gain in momentum the closer they got to the Olympics.

Luis and Mariana lived some twenty minutes outside Marbella, in a luxurious hillside villa, with stunning views of the Mediterranean. The couple were their usual easygoing selves when they saw them, which only seemed to throw the tension between Charlie and Felipe into sharper relief.

'Charlie, how wonderful to see you!' Mariana exclaimed, hugging her affectionately. 'We're going to have lunch on the terrace by the pool. Luis is in charge of the barbecue so I hope you aren't hungry, it could take some time. A very long time. We asked you for lunch, but it may well be for dinner.'

Luis overheard his wife and smiled. 'Don't listen to her, Charlie. I am the barbecue king, whatever she says. But you ladies go and sit down and I will bring out the drinks as I am also an excellent waiter.'

'I'll help you,' Felipe put in, and Charlie wondered if he wanted to update his friend on Audaz.

Mariana led her through the comfortably furnished living room. Charlie paused to look at some of the photographs on the wall. These ranged from the early days of Mariana and Luis's romance, with quirky pictures with them pulling funny faces in photo booths, right through to the elegant black-and-white photographs of their wedding day. Felipe had been their best man and Charlie's gaze was drawn to one photograph of the three friends, arms round each other, laughing. Felipe looked so carefree then.

Mariana saw what she was looking at. 'Don't worry, we airbrushed Paloma out of all the pictures. She's so tiny that it was very easy.' She intended it to be a joke, but it barely raised a smile from Charlie.

'Felipe looks so happy,' she said quietly.

'That's because he knew that I would have killed him if he didn't look happy at my wedding!'

There was still no smile from Charlie.

Mariana linked arms with her. 'Come on, let's go outside and you can tell me all your news.'

They settled down at a table on the terrace, under the shade of a large white parasol. Mariana wanted to hear how Charlie's brother was getting on. She answered the questions as best she could but it didn't take Mariana long to realise that there was something wrong.

'Has something happened, Charlie? You don't quite seem yourself.'

She thought about pretending that everything was fine, but she hated not being honest so she told Mariana about running into Paloma and her revelation.

'Oh, Charlie, you mustn't be upset that Felipe didn't tell you. He had the best of intentions.'

Charlie felt even worse. Clearly Luis and Mariana too had known about Audaz. Everyone had known, except her.

'Felipe should have been able to tell me, though. I feel that I am letting him down.'

'Don't be so hard on yourself.' Mariana smiled warmly. 'Things will work out, I'm certain of it. Felipe is very happy with you. Truly, I've never seen him so happy in a relationship before.'

Luis and Felipe came out of the house to join them and Charlie noticed that Felipe still seemed subdued. The heart to heart with Luis clearly hadn't helped much. Luis was carrying a tray with the bottle of champagne, glasses and a jug of water. He poured a glass for Charlie and was about to pour a glass for his wife when she stopped him. 'Oh, yes, water for you, of course!' he exclaimed. He beamed at her.

Charlie and Felipe exchanged glances and Charlie wondered if he was thinking what she was, but they didn't have to wait long as Mariana rolled her eyes and said, 'Luis, you are the most unsubtle man I know! You could have poured me a glass of champagne and I could have pretended to sip it. But instead you make a big performance and draw attention to the fact that I'm not drinking.'

'I'm sorry,' Luis said again, 'I'm just so happy. I feel as if I will burst if I don't say something.'

'I thought we weren't going to tell anyone yet,' Mariana replied.

'Tell anyone what?' Charlie asked, though she had a pretty good idea.

Luis put his arm round Mariana. 'We're having a baby!'

'Congratulations!' Charlie and Felipe exclaimed, and hugged and kissed their friends.

'We wanted to wait until after the twelve-week scan, which we've just had. You two are the first to know,' Mariana told them.

Felipe proposed a toast to the couple and conversation focused on when the baby was due (November) and whether the couple wanted a boy or a girl (they didn't mind). Charlie was thrilled for them and their good news did something to disperse the dark cloud that had been hanging over her since her earlier encounter with Paloma. But she couldn't help noticing as the afternoon progressed that Felipe seemed increasingly distracted. He didn't want to go in the pool and barely said a word. He half-heartedly helped Luis with the barbecue, but seemed to prefer having a cigarette at the far end of the garden. Charlie guessed he was worrying about Audaz. He had barely touched his lunch when suddenly he stood up and announced, 'I'm going over to the stables to check on him. I won't be long.'

'I'll come with you,' Charlie said quickly. 'I could always wait in the car or in the house.'

'No, no, I won't be long, I promise.' He kissed the top of her head and practically jogged to the front of the house, clearly desperate to leave.

'He'll feel better once he's seen Audaz,' Mariana said sympathetically, seeing the strained expression on Charlie's face.

'Be honest with me, how bad is it?' she asked Luis.

He looked as if he wished she hadn't asked the question. 'It's not good is all I can say. The vet thinks that there is only a fifty-fifty chance that he will be fit for the Games.'

'Oh, God, Felipe didn't tell me it was that bad!' Charlie felt even worse. She should be with him, supporting him.

*

Two hours went by and there was still no sign of Felipe. Charlie insisted on clearing away all the lunch things and loading up the dishwasher. She couldn't handle inactivity while she was so anxious. She tried calling Felipe but there was no reply. Mariana and Luis did their best to distract her but Charlie couldn't stop thinking about him and wondering where he was. Finally, when she couldn't take it any longer, she turned to Luis and said, 'Would you drive me to the stables?'

He and his wife exchanged worried glances. 'Are you sure that's a good idea, Charlie?' Mariana said gently. 'You said yourself that you hadn't been near a horse since your accident.'

'I know, but I have to do this for Felipe. Please take me, or if you'd rather not, could you call me a taxi?'

The couple saw that Charlie had made her mind up, and Luis agreed to take her.

She called Felipe again on the journey over but he still didn't pick up. It was a half-hour drive to his house through spectacular countryside with rolling hills and clusters of picturesque white-washed villages on the hilltops. They were called *Los Pueblos Blancos*, Luis told her, or the white towns of Andalusia. He kept on making conversation, trying to distract her from where they were going. The breathtaking, unspoilt scenery was a world away from the busy, built-up Costa del Sol. But Charlie was oblivious to the beauty. I can do this, she was telling herself over and over again. There is nothing to be afraid of. As if sensing her mood, Luis stopped talking and instead put on the radio.

But by the time he stopped outside the impressive

wrought-iron gates leading to Felipe's estate and equestrian centre, Charlie was sweating and her mouth felt cotton-wool dry. As Luis keyed in the security code she looked out at the fields surrounding the house and centre. There was a mare and her foal in one, several horses grazing in another, a series of jumps in another. Felipe's *cortijo* was a beautiful honey-coloured building built around a bougainvillaea-filled courtyard. It was elegant but also looked homely. Not offputtingly grand like his parents' home.

Luis parked alongside a vast silver horse lorry which looked as if it could fit at least six horses and which Charlie knew from experience would also have a kitchen, living-room area and bathroom.

Luis said, 'Are you sure you want to go through with this? We could leave now. Felipe wouldn't have to know that we had come.'

'I'll be okay, thanks,' Charlie replied, feeling anything but as she opened the car door.

Luis linked arms with her. 'Come on, Charlie, it's this way.' Everything, from the freshly painted wooden fences to the yard floor, was in pristine condition. There wasn't a speck of manure or strand of hay to be seen. Ahead of them was the impressive stable block, built in the style of an airy American barn. They passed a smaller building which Luis told her housed an office, and living accommodation for five grooms. Then they passed a tack room, filled with saddles and bridles, each and every piece polished and gleaming and perfectly arranged. Charlie used to adore the smell of leather, preferred it to any perfume, but since the accident it aroused very different feelings. Almost immediately she felt a prickle of anxiety as she breathed in the familiar rich smell of freshly polished leather. *Keep going*, she urged herself, desperate to prove that she could do this one thing for Felipe.

Luis paused outside the stable building. 'Are you sure you want to go in?'

Charlie could hardly trust herself to speak. In spite of the blazing sunshine and a temperature in the mid-twenties she suddenly felt freezing. But she nodded and followed Luis into the stables. These were far and away the grandest she had ever seen. There were stalls to either side, accommodating some twenty horses. As she and Luis approached, several of the occupants stuck their heads over the doors, curious to see who the visitors were and whether they might have any treats with them.

Pre-accident Charlie would have gone straight up to them without hesitation, now she could hardly bear to look at them.

'Audaz is at the end,' Luis told her, adding, 'you're doing fantastically well.'

That wasn't how Charlie felt. A young woman in jodhpurs and a green polo shirt with the equestrian-centre logo came out of one of the stalls and called out something in Spanish to Luis.

'Daria says that we've just missed Felipe. He's gone to meet up with the Chef d'Équipe.'

Charlie knew that this was the person who managed the national eventing team.

'How's Audaz?' she asked.

Luis quickly rattled something off to Daria and her downbeat expression said it all.

'It's not looking good,' he told Charlie. 'He will need at least twelve weeks' rest. And that means . . .'

'Felipe can't ride him in the Olympics.'

He stopped talking as if expecting that Charlie would want to leave then, but she carried on walking to the end stall.

A magnificent chestnut stallion was standing in the corner; his hind fetlock was strapped up with a bandage and bent forward to take the weight off it. He looked very sorry for himself, as if he knew that he wouldn't be taking part in the competition of a life-time.

'Poor boy,' Charlie said out loud. At the sound of her voice Audaz lifted his fine head and limped over to the door. She found herself closer to a horse than she had been since the accident. By now Luis had joined her and made a great fuss of Audaz, gently pulling his ears and patting his neck while the horse whickered in appreciation. Charlie stood rigid, hands clenched, trying to keep herself together. Audaz gently butted his head against her side. Ace was always doing that, ever hopeful that there might be a Polo coming his way.

'It's all right,' Luis commented, noticing Charlie's tense expression. 'He's just looking for treats, he's a big softie.' Somehow she managed to unclench her fists and stroke Audaz's head, where there was a brilliantly white blaze down the middle of his face. He had huge brown intelligent eyes, just like Ace. Before Charlie could stop herself she was remembering the last time she had seen her horse, his eyes rolling in terror as he looked to her for help. And suddenly she felt the insidious, wretched feeling of a panic attack, building up inside her. She felt as if she couldn't breathe, couldn't get enough oxygen into her lungs.

'Are you okay?' Luis was asking. His voice sounded a long way away.

Charlie tried to speak, but couldn't get the words out. Then she was running out of the stables, desperate to get away. She tripped and fell in her haste, grazing her knee on the concrete. Luis quickly helped her up. 'Take my arm, we'll go to the house. It's all right, Charlie, you're safe.'

She was overcome with despair as she slumped back on the sofa, struggling to get her breathing under control, while Luis anxiously asked her if there was anything he could do. She had been so convinced that she was strong enough to overcome her fear, but it was hopeless, she was never going to get over what had happened. What an insane idea to think that she could even watch Felipe compete at the Olympics.

'I'm so sorry,' she said finally, when she could speak, 'I really thought I could do this for Felipe.' She put her hands over her eyes and sobbed, 'But I can't, I just can't, not even for him.'

Luis sat next to her and put his arm around her. 'Charlie, have more faith in yourself. You suffered a terrible trauma, and these things take time to get over.'

That's the one thing I haven't got, she thought. The idea of being with Felipe suddenly seemed as fanciful as a fairy tale. His mother had been right, it was incredibly selfish of her to get involved with him. He needed to be with a partner who could share his passion for riding, not someone who practically went into melt-down at the mention of . . . never mind actually seeing . . . a horse. She thought of what Paloma had said at the party about how involved she had been in Felipe's riding. How he must have valued her support. What good was Charlie to him?

'Please don't tell Felipe about this, will you?' she pleaded with Luis. 'He has so much to deal with right now.'

Luis frowned. 'Charlie, he would want to know, he would want to help you.'

'I beg you, Luis, please don't tell him. You saw how exhausted and stressed he is.'

Luis looked at Charlie. She was beautiful even when she was distraught, but she seemed incredibly vulnerable. He didn't want to make such a promise but knew he would have to, for her sake. 'Okay,' he said reluctantly, 'I promise I won't tell him.'

Charlie stood up; she still felt shaky but she didn't dare stay here any longer in case Felipe returned. Even in her distressed state she registered how beautiful the house was. It was stylishly and comfortably furnished with big squashy sofas and armchairs strewn with brightly coloured cushions, gorgeous silver Arabian-style candle holders, richly patterned Oriental rugs scattered on warm terracotta tiles. It was designed to be cool in summer with all the downstairs rooms opening on to the courtyard or terrace, and cosy in winter with wood-burning stoves in all the rooms. She could just imagine Felipe and herself here, snuggling up beside the fire in the winter. It was far more to her taste than the achingly chic Marbella apartment. But somehow she didn't think she would be seeing it again.

Charlie wanted to wash her face and Luis directed her to one of the bathrooms upstairs. She passed what had to be Felipe's bedroom on the way. It was a lovely room with a four-poster bed in the centre hung with white muslin drapes, and windows overlooking the fields and hills in the distance. She couldn't resist walking in. On the beside table she saw that he had framed a photograph of them together, taken on the beach in Barbados. They had their arms round each other and were smiling away at the camera. Her heart ached to see how happy they both looked. It had been a fairy tale meeting. But it felt to her as if the fairy tale was over.

Luis insisted that she have a glass of water before they leave and Charlie followed him into the kitchen. There, by the door, she noticed a recycling box full of empty wine and whisky bottles. She had no idea that Felipe even drank whisky. Luis noticed what she was looking at, and sighed. 'When Felipe gets stressed he has a tendency to drink. I try and keep across it as much as I can, but I can't be with him all the time. And lately it's been getting bad again.'

'I bet Paloma stopped him, didn't she?' Charlie said quietly.

Another sigh from Luis. 'Charlie, don't do this to yourself. Felipe wants to be with you.'

She didn't reply.

*

Felipe ended up staying at his house. He told Charlie that he needed to ride Valiente. He sounded despondent. All riders at his level had several horses that were trained to take part in the Olympics and other important competitions, but Audaz had been special and Felipe needed time to adjust. True to her word, Charlie didn't tell him about her panic attack at the stables. She just hoped that Daria would have more important things on her mind than telling Felipe that she had seen Charlie.

She spent a quiet night with Mariana and Luis. After supper, which Charlie had no appetite for, she pretended she had a headache and went up to her room very early. She knew that Mariana and Luis were concerned about her and wanted to talk to her about what had happened, but she couldn't deal with their sympathy. They would only tell her that everything would be okay. It wasn't and it never would be.

Once in her room she booked herself a flight for the following morning and a taxi to pick her up at half-past six. She felt awful making the arrangements behind the couple's back, but she knew if she told them they would only try and stop her.

She hardly slept for agonising over what to do. She was in love with Felipe, but she couldn't be with him. It was no use pretending otherwise. If she told him about the panic attack he would insist that it didn't matter. But at what price to himself? Anyone could see the enormous pressure he was under. Her phobia was adding to that pressure. She couldn't do that to the man she loved, she couldn't be that selfish.

She got up around six, just as the sun was rising and it was promising to be another beautiful day, and let herself out of the house to await the taxi at the end of the drive. She had left Mariana and Luis a note saying that she'd had an urgent call from the studio and had to get back to the UK. She sent Felipe a text, saying the same thing, just before she boarded her flight.

When she arrived back in London Felipe called her and she carried on her pretence that something had come up at work. While he was surprised by her sudden departure, he was so preoccupied with training that he didn't press her for details. He sounded so down. It broke Charlie's heart knowing that she couldn't help him, and that made her even more determined. She took off the diamond pendant, put it in its case and shut it away in the bottom drawer of the jewellery box, which she rarely opened. She knew what she had to do. All the same she felt sick when she sent TFB the message.

Chapter 21

Drew hadn't contacted Darcy for over a month and she had been so happy with Kris, she hadn't given him another thought. So it was a shock on Sunday night, as she and Kris were snuggled up on the sofa watching *True Blood*, to receive a booty text from Drew. *How's my head girl? Fancy coming over? x* The thought of it made her skin crawl.

She ignored it. But half an hour later there was another text. *Are you coming?*

This time she turned her phone off. Kris hadn't commented on the texts, and nor had Darcy told him about Drew. But suddenly she felt the need to wipe the slate clean and be completely honest with him. 'Those texts were from my ex.'

'Should I be worried?'

Darcy shook her head. 'After we split up . . .' She hesitated. No, she was going to be totally honest. 'Okay, after he dumped me, he'd call me every few weeks wanting to have sex. And I always ended up saying yes. I guess I hoped that he would want me back.'

'And that's what those texts were about?'

She nodded, wondering how she would feel if Kris suddenly received such texts from an ex.

'Are you tempted?' he asked.

Darcy looked at him, taking in the handsome face and the brown eyes that were so full of warmth. 'Not in the slightest.'

'Then I'm not worried. And tomorrow you'll be meeting my mum as she's staying at Charlie's. I would have hated to disappoint her by saying that you'd dumped me.'

Darcy kissed him. 'That is never going to happen.'

They were in bed when the doorbell rang.

'D'you want me to see who it is?' Kris asked.

'No, it's okay, I'll go.' Darcy had a suspicion that she knew exactly who it was. She slipped on a tee-shirt and padded over to the front door. Sure enough when she looked at entry-phone screen there was Drew.

She picked up the phone. 'It's after midnight, Drew, what are you doing here?'

'Why didn't you answer my texts?'

He sounded pissed.

'Because I was busy.'

'Can I come up? I really need to see you, Darcy. Everything's shit at work.'

Was he expecting her to be sympathetic? 'I'm sorry, I can't.'

Drew couldn't have looked more surprised if she had slapped him. 'Why not? Oh, is *he* up there with you?

Yeah, your sister told me you were seeing some guy who's just got out of prison. Enjoying your bit of rough, Darcy?'

'Good night, Drew.' She hung up the phone and turned to go back to bed. But Drew had other ideas and rang the bell again. In fact, he kept his finger pressed firmly on it. Fuck! What was she supposed to do now? Kris came out of the bedroom. He'd pulled on some jeans. 'Do you want me to go down and tell him to go?'

'Let me deal with him,' Darcy replied, knowing what a mean drunk Drew could be. She opened the front door and ran downstairs to the main entrance. Drew was still ringing the doorbell; at this rate he would wake the entire block. Then again, consideration for others had never been his strong point. She opened the door and glared at him. 'Will you stop doing that!'

'Can I come up then?'

Whatever had she seen in him? It was one of his off days so he hadn't shaved and he'd put on yet more weight. He looked bloated and unhealthy.

'No, you've got to go. I'm seeing someone else. I don't want to see you any more.'

Now he decided to switch tactics, 'Please Darcy, I've really missed you.'

Yeah, right! He missed someone who would drop everything for him, including their knickers, and be there when he wanted them – and out of sight when he didn't. She had played that role for too long.

'Like Darcy said, it would be better if you left.' Kris had come downstairs. He stood on the doorstep, arms folded across his chest. He was at least four inches taller than Drew.

'Is this him?' Drew demanded, jabbing his finger at Kris. 'Why don't you fuck off, mate? We're having a private conversation.'

'No, we're not,' Darcy replied. 'I don't want to see you any more and that's it.'

'You'd seriously rather see him than me? He's just a chavvy nobody with a pumped-up body. Do you know what your family think of him? How upset your mother is because you're seeing a criminal?'

Kris stepped forward, causing Drew to shout out, 'What are you going to do? Hit me?'

Darcy put her hand on Kris's arm, as if to restrain him.

'Don't worry, Darcy, I wouldn't touch him.'

In spite of the tense stand-off, she stood on tiptoes and kissed Kris's cheek. 'I know. He isn't worth it and I completely trust you. I know that you would never do anything to hurt me.'

Suddenly Drew seemed to realise that Darcy meant what she said. Muttering, 'You're making a fucking huge mistake, Darcy. Don't expect me to be around when he's finished with you,' he turned and walked unsteadily away.

The following day Darcy had to have the fitting for her bridesmaid's dress. She met up with her sister at a chic and wildly expensive boutique on the King's Road in Chelsea. As she was shown upstairs to the fitting room, she thought yet again what a pity it was that she wasn't close to her sisters. Then this would have been a fun event, whereas now it felt like a chore. Bunny and Perdita were already there. Perdita was dressed in her bridesmaid's dress and the designer was making last-minute alterations. Bunny was going for a very traditional wedding. Her attendants' dresses were long, strapless creations in ice-blue silk taffeta. As cold as her family relationship, Darcy reflected.

'About time!' Bunny exclaimed as Darcy kissed her hello. 'You're late for everything. Please say you won't be late for my wedding? That's *my* prerogative.'

'The dress looks good,' Darcy forced herself to say.

'Well, come on, you have to get yours on now. I'm meeting Hugo's parents at the Connaught for cocktails.'

'Oh, yeah, Simon will try and get along for one drink before dinner,' Perdita drawled. Then she exchanged glances with Bunny and both sisters looked faintly guilty. Darcy realised that she had not been invited.

'I was going to ask you of course,' Bunny put in, 'but Hugo has asked Drew and I thought it might be awkward.'

Before she'd met Kris, Darcy might have felt hurt that she was being treated like this. Now she couldn't have cared less. She shrugged. 'It's okay, I'm busy anyway.' And, picking up the dress, she walked over to the cubicle and pulled across the pale pink silk curtain. It was the first time she had tried on the dress and while the colour made her blue eyes seem bluer, the style exposed her arms, which she usually kept covered up. It was going to be impossible to hide the scars unless she kept her arms clamped to her sides, which was hardly a good look. Her sisters must be aware of the scars, though they had never mentioned them.

She pulled back the curtain and stepped outside.

'Oh, fab, it fits really well. Hardly needs any alterations,' Bunny commented, while the seamstress got to work putting in pins to indicate where the fabric could be taken in.

'Your hair is going to be styled in a sleek French twist,' Bunny continued, 'with a pearl tiara.'

If Darcy hadn't been feeling so tense about her arms she might have smiled as the look was so far from the one she would go for on her own wedding day. If she mentally channelled Kate Moss, her sister was more of a Kate Middleton. Glossy, perfect, unthreatening. And – if Darcy was feeling bitchy – bland.

'Um, I wondered if I might be able to have a wrap round my shoulders, maybe in the same material?'

Bunny frowned. 'No, it will ruin the look and it won't be cold so you won't need it.'

'I wasn't thinking of the cold,' Darcy said quietly, 'I meant because of my arms.' She turned her right arm up, showing off the scars she usually kept hidden. Then quickly turned it back.

'Fuck! I'd completely forgotten about those.' Bunny looked aghast.

'I know, it was very inconsiderate of me to have been so unhappy that I once self-harmed.'

'There's no need to be sarcastic,' Perdita put in, backing up Bunny as always. 'What about a wrap, Bunny? It's not a bad idea.'

But Bunny had turned into Bridezilla, and shouted back, 'I wanted simple, elegant lines. It's so typical of you, Darcy, to end up ruining everything! Drew was thinking of getting back with you, did you know that? But oh no, you blew that by seeing that low-life Kris! Do you know how upset Mummy is? You're *so* selfish.'

The designer muttered something about needing extra pins and tactfully left the room.

Darcy looked her sister in the eye. 'Drew treated me like shit. Now I've met someone who makes me feel good about myself, and you don't like that, do you? I'm sorry I'm not the sister you want. You're not the sister I want either.' And she swept into the changing room and pulled off the hated dress, leaving it on the floor. Bunny was sobbing with Perdita comforting her as Darcy walked out of the room. She heard Bunny say, 'It's my wedding day . . . why does *she* have to spoil it?'

Darcy might have put on a tough image in front of her sisters, but in the taxi she cried all the way to Charlie's flat where she was seeing Kris. Thankfully he was the one who opened the door to her, and not Charlie. Darcy didn't think she could deal with anyone else being horrible to her.

'Hey, what's the matter?' he asked. The concern on his face made her cry even harder. He put his arm round her and led her to his bedroom where she blurted out every humiliating and hurtful detail about the disastrous dress fitting.

'I don't even want to go to her wedding,' she finished

up. 'And Bunny wouldn't care if I wasn't there anyway.'
She sniffed and brushed the tears away.

'I'm sure that's not true and I'm sure she regrets
saying what she did,' Kris replied.

He didn't know her sister! 'Bunny would never admit
to being in the wrong. She always has to have the
fucking moral high ground.'

'Why don't you send a text telling her you didn't
mean what you said?'

'But I *did* mean it!'

Kris sighed. 'It will be stalemate then. And it seems
to me that you're the only one in your family with any
sensitivity. If you don't make the first move, then they
won't. It *is* her wedding day, people get stressed.'

Through her hurt Darcy could see that Kris was
talking sense, but part of her wanted to dig in her
heels, say it was all Bunny's fault and that *she* should
be the one to apologise. But maybe that's what she
had been doing for far too long. If Darcy made the first
move, then she could let go of the hurt. She could move
on, rather than being permanently stuck as the
wronged sister.

'How did you get to be so wise?' she asked, leaning
her head against Kris's shoulder.

'I'm great at giving advice, not so good at acting on
it,' he replied, planting a kiss on the top of her head.
'My mum's going to be here in a minute, are you going
to be okay?'

'I'll be fine now, thanks.'

'I'd better go and help Charlie with supper.' He
paused in the doorway, 'D'you know if anything has

happened at work to upset her? Or if she had a row with Felipe? She seems really down. I tried asking her what was wrong but she just said she was tired. It's not like her at all.'

Darcy shook her head, 'Not that I know of.' She didn't add that Charlie would never confide in her.

In the kitchen Charlie was busy grating Parmesan cheese. She muttered 'Hi' when Darcy and Kris walked in, but didn't stop what she was doing.

'Can we do anything to help?' he asked.

'No, thanks, it's all under control,' Charlie replied. She turned to Darcy. 'Is mushroom risotto okay with you?'

'Fantastic, thanks. I'm vegetarian, so it's perfect.'

Kris was right, Charlie did seem down and she looked exhausted. Darcy wondered what could be wrong with her. She had a brilliant career, a gorgeous boyfriend and a lovely family. Hers was the perfect life, wasn't it?

'Are you sure we can't help?' Darcy asked again, feeling bad about leaving Charlie to do all the work and wanting to make a good impression on Lori.

But Charlie shook her head. 'I'm fine, really. Go and have a glass of wine. You might need it before Mum arrives.' She gave Kris the briefest of smiles. 'Have you warned Darcy what Mum's like when she meets someone new?'

'Not yet,' he replied, 'I was just about to.' He turned to Darcy. 'Mum is going to ask you shed loads of questions. She can't stop herself, but she means well.'

Darcy thought of her own mother, who had made

no effort to be polite to Kris on first meeting him. No one could ever accuse Eleanor of being well-meaning.

From the moment she arrived Lori did not stop talking and asking questions. But it was impossible not to warm to her. She was so funny and generous with her compliments, telling Darcy that she was beautiful, teasing Kris for having landed such a looker for a girl-friend.

'You're just like a model!' she exclaimed. 'Look at your gorgeous skin! You'll have to tell me what you use on it.' She couldn't have been more different from Darcy's own mother as she flitted around the flat, wearing leggings and a brightly patterned tunic. The only time she seemed slightly lost for words was when Kris asked how his dad was.

'He's fine, busy with work and the cricket team. He sends his love.'

'Does he?' Kris asked. He didn't sound convinced.

'Yes,' Lori insisted. 'And he's really pleased about the acting job, we all are.' But she quickly asked him what the rest of the cast was like, to avoid any more questions about his dad.

Charlie stuck her head round the living-room door then. 'Supper's ready.' Lori waited until she was out of earshot before saying, 'Is everything okay with Charlie? She seems a bit out of sorts.'

'I wondered that, but she says everything's fine.'

Lori raised her eyebrows. 'That sounds like Charlie – always good at putting on a brave face. Maybe she's just missing Felipe.'

Charlie was in torment. She had been in torment

ever since she had decided what she had to do. And what made it even harder was that she felt she couldn't confide in anyone. She knew that her friends and family would only try and persuade her that the riding phobia didn't need to affect her relationship with Felipe, but they were wrong. Charlie kept thinking of the look of anguish in his eyes when he finally told her about Audaz. It wasn't fair that he couldn't confide in her. She couldn't be responsible for putting him under that pressure on top of everything else. And she knew that she would never be able to watch him compete in the Olympics. It would be so much better if she ended it now.

Usually she loved seeing her mum but tonight she was finding it incredibly hard to be around her.

'So how's Felipe? You've hardly mentioned him,' Lori commented, as they were halfway through dinner. Well, everyone else was halfway through the risotto, Charlie had only managed a couple of mouthfuls.

Please! Not this, not now. Charlie avoided eye contact.

'I think he's okay. Obviously he's got a lot on his mind with the Olympics.' She paused, willing herself to go through with the lie. 'To be honest, I'm feeling a bit bored. He's so obsessed with his sport, there's not much left over. It takes over his whole life, and you know that I'm not interested in riding any more.'

Lori, Kris and Darcy all stopped eating and looked at her in disbelief. 'This is a bit sudden, isn't it? I thought you were getting on brilliantly.' That was Lori.

Charlie couldn't look her mum in the eye as she replied, 'Not lately.'

'Did something happen last weekend?'

God! Her mum knew her so well.

'Nothing, that's just it. I think some of the spark might have gone.' She was desperate to change the subject now, knowing that she couldn't keep up the pretence for much longer.

'He must be under a huge amount of pressure with his training . . . I mean, can you imagine what it must feel like to be picked to compete in the Olympics? Of course he's going to be obsessed. But he's a good bloke, Charlie, and he really likes you,' Kris put in.

Shut up! Shut up! Shut up! Charlie wanted to scream at them.

'You'll work it out, love,' Lori said optimistically.

They had no idea. Then, thankfully, Darcy of all people seemed to realise that Charlie was suffering and asked Lori about her job. It felt like a rare flash of empathy, and Charlie was grateful. For the rest of the evening Felipe wasn't mentioned. When Charlie went to bed she saw she had several messages from him. She didn't reply and made herself switch off her phone.

In the morning she was hoping to leave for work before anyone else was up – specifically Lori. She couldn't face any more of her mum's questions and hated having to lie to her. But Lori was already up, dressed and having breakfast in the kitchen. Typically she had made herself at home. She had switched on the radio and changed the station from Radio 1, which Charlie usually had on, to Radio 2. Chris Evans was nattering away cheerfully. It was far too upbeat for Charlie's dark mood.

'Morning, love! D'you want a cup of tea?' Lori called out happily. She could match Chris Evans for enthusiasm first thing.

'Just a quick one, Mum, I don't want to be late.'

'I've made a fruit salad – it will be great with some natural yoghurt and honey, and you look like you could do with a vitamin C boost. You seem tired.'

'I've been busy at work is all.' Charlie had no appetite but she forced herself to accept a bowl of fruit salad from Lori.

'Darcy's a sweetheart, isn't she? I thought you said that she was posh and stuck up?'

Charlie shrugged as she toyed with a slice of kiwi fruit. 'That's the vibe she gave off at work, but yes, she's much nicer than I realised.'

'And Kris seems so happy with her, doesn't he? He's almost back to his old self. So now I've just got to worry about you.' Lori was looking at her daughter with concern. 'Are you going to tell me what is going on between you and Felipe?'

This was exactly the conversation Charlie had wanted to avoid.

'It's what I told you, Mum – riding is everything to him and I'm bored by it.'

Lori hesitated. 'And this has nothing to do with your accident?'

'Of course not – I'm totally over it now,' Charlie almost snapped back.

'So you haven't had any more panic attacks? Because you can tell me, love. I am your mum, you don't have to pretend.'

'No, I'm fine.' Charlie knew how defensive she sounded so she stood up abruptly and said, 'I know you love Chris Evans but I'm not old enough to listen to Radio 2,' and switched over to Chris Moyles.

'Don't be cheeky! I'm not old either. I'm younger than Madonna, don't you forget that!'

Charlie blew her a kiss. 'Just don't think that gives you the right to parade around in thigh-length boots and a pointy bra.'

'Ooh, and there was I thinking I'd wear that on my next night out with your dad!' Lori shot back.

'And on that bombshell, I've got to go to work, Mum.' She gave Lori a quick hug. Just as Charlie was thinking that she had escaped any further questions, her mum said, 'You would tell me if there was something wrong, wouldn't you?'

Charlie hated having to lie, but somehow she managed to say, 'You know I would.'

Chapter 22

Charlie avoided speaking to Felipe for the next two days by screening all her calls and texting him that she was frantically busy at work. She knew that if she spoke to him she wouldn't be able to go ahead with her plan, and she *had* to go through with it. It was killing her, but she saw it as proving her love for Felipe. She also managed to avoid speaking to Zoe, who had a sixth sense for knowing when something was up with her friend.

It was Thursday night. Earlier on Charlie had tipped off a paparazzo about where she was going and who she was going to be seeing. It seemed the paps had their uses after all. She felt sullied after the call, as if she was turning her private life into a sideshow, but she couldn't see any other course of action. Now all that remained was to get ready. Smoky eyes check, black body-con dress check, her highest leopard-print heels check – all in all, the look that her ex had loved. Her make-up was perfect, her body had never been in better shape, but as she looked in the mirror Charlie wanted to cry.

Tonight she was meeting Aaron for dinner. God, she must remember to call him that and not TFB. She had it all planned out. When Felipe confronted her about it – as he would once the story had broken in the press – she would tell him that she couldn't help it, that she was in love with Aaron and always had been.

They were meeting at Nobu, a favourite haunt of celebrities and, because of that, the paps. Charlie felt sick with anxiety on the taxi ride over to Mayfair; the closer they got to their destination, the more she longed to tell to the driver to turn round and take her home. How could she go through with this? But then she thought of Felipe, having to keep the most important thing in his life to himself because she couldn't share it, and her resolve strengthened. If she could do this then he would be free from her.

Aaron was already sitting in the stylish restaurant when she walked in. He stood up as soon as Charlie approached the table and all she could think of was that he didn't compare to Felipe. True, he was very good-looking, with his perfectly styled short brown hair and deep blue eyes, but his looks seemed so boyish compared to Felipe's strong handsome features. But there was no going back now.

'Charlie, it's been too long,' he murmured as he kissed her. 'I love you in that dress.'

'I thought you would,' she replied, somehow managing to smile though she knew it didn't reach her eyes. They sat down opposite each other. It felt so wrong to be here. The waiter poured her a glass of champagne and Charlie took a long sip. Usually she adored champagne, now it tasted bitter and acidic in her mouth. Aaron leant forward and treated her to one of his intense, sincere gazes, his *you're the only girl in the world for me* look. It used to work on Charlie. It didn't any more. She thought he looked cheesily insincere.

'I can't believe you're here, after all this time. I've missed you so much, babe. And I'm sorry about what happened. I was a total dick.'

He'd got that right. 'Yep, you were.'

He gave a cheeky grin. 'That's the Charlie I remember. Never afraid to speak your mind. That's why I liked you so much.' He paused. 'That's why I still like you so much.'

Another pause. Maybe Aaron was expecting her to say that she still had feelings for him. She couldn't do that. Instead she replied, 'I know. Greg told me.'

'I haven't been in touch because I thought you were seeing that Spanish guy. I read about it. It seemed serious. So what happened?'

Charlie shrugged. 'We broke up. It was only ever a holiday romance. It passed its sell-by date.'

When she had tried something like this before with Kyle, she had ended up bursting into tears, but this time Charlie was not going to give the game away. It helped that she barely touched any alcohol, and with iron determination managed to smile and flirt her way through the rest of dinner.

Aaron had drunk the best part of a bottle of champagne and was now having a brandy. He was becoming more emotional, though whether it was the alcohol loosening his tongue or his true feelings, it was hard to tell. He reached out for her hand. Charlie looked down at his fingers around her own, instantly comparing them unfavourably with Felipe's elegant strong hands. Aaron hadn't kicked his childhood habit of biting his fingernails and his nails looked ragged and short, making his fingers look stubby. She wanted to yank her hand away, but forced herself to leave it there.

'We had some good times, Charlie, didn't we? Until I blew it.'

She was racking her brains to think what those good times might have been. The way he had cheated on her with the lap dancer had effectively blanked out any positive memories.

'I swear I'd never cheat on you again. Not ever. I know what's important now.'

Charlie just stopped herself from saying, *Is that a real promise, or a footballer's promise?*

'It's a big *if*, Aaron,' was the best reply she could come up with. 'I really need to see how it goes.'

'I'll prove it to you,' he replied, and gave her his best heartfelt look. She almost felt guilty for using him like this, but not enough to stop. And if she had to use someone, then it may as well be Aaron who had treated her, and no doubt scores of other women, so badly.

They left the restaurant together. Aaron draped his arm around her, holding her possessively close to him. Even that gesture made her feel suffocated. She didn't know how she would manage the next thing she knew she had to do.

'I'm so glad you called me,' he told her, gazing into her eyes. 'I just know we can be good together again.'

And as he saw her into the taxi Charlie kissed him on the lips . . . a lingering kiss that was captured by the lurking pap, ready and primed for the moment.

As the taxi sped away, Charlie sat back in a daze. There were so many conflicting emotions churning away inside her. She fumbled in her bag for her phone. There was a text from Felipe: *Miss you like crazy. Call me when you get in, it doesn't matter how late.* With her eyes blurred with tears, Charlie deleted it.

Felipe picked up his phone yet again. There was no still reply from Charlie. It seemed strange that she hadn't called him – usually she replied to his messages straight away, as he did to hers. He thought about texting Zoe, and then dismissed the idea; he didn't want her to think he was keeping tabs on Charlie. God knows, he remembered what that was like from when he was seeing Paloma who had wanted to know where he was at all times, and exactly what he was doing.

But by midnight he was starting to feel on edge about Charlie's lack of response, especially when he called her again and only reached her voice mail. This just wasn't like her. It was frustrating being so far away! He left yet another message and then forced himself to go to bed – he had to be up at five for training. He slept badly and kept reaching out to check his phone. Still nothing from Charlie.

Usually he was the kind of early-morning riser who could leap straight out of bed and into the shower, already anticipating and relishing the prospect of working with his horses all day. But the following morning he felt jaded and worn out, especially when he realised that Charlie hadn't called or texted him. He finally dragged himself out of bed at half-past five and was grumpy with his grooms when he arrived at the stables.

After an intensive jumping session with Valiente he was ready to snatch a quick breakfast and hopeful that he might finally be able to talk to Charlie. He left Daria in charge of exercising the horses in the walker – a huge contraption that looked exactly like a gigantic merry-go-round, which they would walk in for an hour. All of them had to be in the absolute peak of condition.

'I'm sure she will have called you back by now,' Daria called out to him. She knew Felipe well enough to realise what was up.

'Concentrate on those horses!' he shouted back, but his dark mood had lifted after the workout and he was convinced that he would speak to Charlie soon and there would be a perfectly rational explanation.

But there was still no message. He sat outside on the terrace with an espresso and decided to email her some of the photos his brother had sent him, taken when they were out on the yacht. Seeing them might prompt her to call him, he reflected. He smiled as he looked at the shot of them sitting with their arms around each other, leaning against the side of the boat, Charlie with her head on his shoulder. They looked as if they were meant to be together.

He heard the sound of the security gates swinging

open and looked up to see a silver Alfa Romeo slowly
approaching the house. It was his mother's car. What
the hell did she want? He had finally seen Vittoria the
week before, but she hadn't apologised for her comments
to Charlie and Felipe was still furious with her, so it had
been a somewhat frosty encounter. It was totally out of
character for her to be making such an early visit; usually
she didn't get up before half-past ten. It was just after
eight now. It must be something to do with his sister or
his father, and she wanted to vent at him, though God
knows why she couldn't have picked up the phone.

Even at this time in the morning Vittoria was immaculately made up, and wearing an exquisitely cut white
trouser suit.

'Felipe, are you all right, my darling?' she asked
breathlessly, as soon as she reached the terrace. 'I came
as soon as I could.'

He had no idea what she was talking about – no
doubt some drama of her own invention. He stood up
and gave her the obligatory three kisses. 'Why wouldn't
I be okay, Mama?'

'Oh, my darling, you do not have to pretend to me.
I am talking about the pictures of Charlie with that
other man. I cannot believe that she would do this to
you. It is so hurtful and cruel.'

'What pictures are you talking about?' he said warily.
His mother was quite capable of blowing something
out of all proportion.

'The pictures of Charlie with another man. They are
all over the UK tabloids and on their websites. You can
see for yourself.' She gestured at the laptop.

A sick feeling of dread uncoiled in the pit of his stomach. Trying not to betray any emotion, Felipe logged on to the *Sun's* website and was met with an image of Charlie kissing her ex-boyfriend. The sick feeling intensified. *Charlie Scores with Aaron!* screamed the headline, as if to hammer the message home. But even faced with the evidence, Felipe refused to believe there was anything more to it than a friendly kiss good-night. There had to be a perfectly innocent explanation. And so what if she had met up with her ex? He saw Paloma and it didn't mean anything. He was about to say as much to Vittoria when his mobile rang. Charlie at last! Grabbing his phone, he strode back into the house and away from his mother.

'Charlie! I've left you so many messages, what's going on?'

'I'm sorry, I should have told you before now. I didn't want it to come out like this.'

He was stunned, both by what she was saying and the cold, detached tone of her voice.

'Didn't want what to come out?'

'I've been seeing Aaron.' There was no emotion in her voice at all. But this had to be some kind of joke, didn't it? She was teasing him – he'd annoyed her in some way and she was getting her own back with this charade. It didn't sound plausible but Felipe was desperate for there to be an innocent explanation.

'You are joking, aren't you? Is it because I've been neglecting you? I know that I've been preoccupied with training, and I'm sorry. I can take some time out. We could go away somewhere.' He was clutching at straws here. 'You're just trying to make me jealous, like you did before with that other footballer.'

'No, Felipe, it's not like that time. I'm seeing Aaron.' She definitely didn't sound as if she was joking.

'What are you talking about?' he exclaimed passionately. 'How can you be seeing him again? You told me you *never* wanted to see him again. What do you call him – that total fucking bastard!'

'I was lying when I told you that. Please, Felipe, I don't want a big row. We had a good time together but it's over. I'm back with Aaron now.'

Felipe felt as if he had been catapulted into a nightmare. This simply could not be happening, and yet Charlie was calmly telling him it was all over between them. He still refused to accept it.

'Charlie, I don't know what's going on but we can work this out. I'll try and get a flight this afternoon. I have to see you . . . we have to talk.'

'There is nothing to talk about, Felipe. I'm in love with Aaron, I always have been, I was just trying to pretend to myself that I wasn't.' She hesitated. 'I guess I used you. The closer it got to the Olympics, I realised I couldn't do that to you any more. I'm sorry.'

'I don't believe you!' Felipe was shouting now. 'You *can't* love that man after what he did to you! And you can't turn your back on what we have. It's a once-in-a-lifetime thing. I love you!' There, he had come out with it, the words he should have said ages ago, the words he'd known to be true within days of meeting her.

'You can't love me. I'm sorry, Felipe, I've got to go now.'

Was it his imagination or had there been a trace of hesitation in her voice then, and a touch of warmth which had previously been missing? But before he had the chance to say anything else, she hung up. And when he tried to call her back, Charlie had switched off her phone.

Felipe slumped on to the sofa, head in his hands. He could barely take in the enormity of what had just happened. It was so shocking, he felt as if he had been punched. Why hadn't he told her he loved her before? He had wanted to but had held off, worried that it might be too much, too soon. And now this – the discovery that their entire relationship had been a lie. And yet, he still couldn't believe that . . .

His mother walked cautiously into the living room. 'Luis is on his way over, I thought you might want to talk to him.'

Felipe raised his head. 'Did you have something to do with all this?' he demanded aggressively. 'It seems too much of a coincidence that this should happen mere weeks after you laid in to Charlie at the party.'

Vittoria looked taken aback. 'Of course not, my darling! You know I had my reservations about her, but I would never do anything to hurt you.' She approached him tentatively and seemed to want to comfort him.

She was probably telling the truth, but he didn't want her around him.

'Please go now, Mama,' Felipe replied wearily, as if the fight had gone out of him. 'I need to be on my own.'

Vittoria remained where she was. 'Felipe, something

must have happened to make Charlie behave like this. She had strong feelings for you, I'm sure – anyone could see that.' She hesitated. 'And I know what you felt for her.'

'Really?' He was sarcastic now. 'Well, all l can see is that you never liked her. She was devastated after your party. And then there was that story in the press . . . I wouldn't put it past you to have ordered your lackey Enzo to have leaked it.'

His mother was silent and Felipe took that as an admission of guilt. She had indeed got her lawyer to tip off the British tabloids.

'Please go now,' he repeated.

'Are you sure I can't get you anything first?' she asked. He shook his head and was relieved when she finally left.

Charlie cried for much of the rest of the day. She had phoned in sick to work – she had never done that before. At this rate she would lose her career as well as her relationship, but everything about the job that had once seemed so important to her, now didn't seem to matter at all. Kris was out, so she had the flat to herself and her misery. She ignored all calls from Zoe, her mum, Luis and Aaron. Every time she thought of weakening and calling Felipe to tell him that it was all a mistake, she thought back to the incident at the stables. It was killing her but she had to do this for him. He had told her that he loved her and that made her even more determined, because she loved him and she was making this sacrifice for him.

When Kris returned home, Charlie pretended to be asleep in bed. The following morning she got up earlier than usual, wanting to get to work before he woke up. Once there she went straight to Nicky's office. Her boss was already at her desk, hard at work at her computer. She looked up when she noticed Charlie in the doorway,

'Oh, hi, Charlie. Are you better now?'

She sounded concerned and Charlie felt even worse about lying. She was lying to everyone. Her whole life was one big fat lie.

'I'm fine. Nicky, I need to tell you something.'

Nicky looked faintly embarrassed – she was great on work issues, not so good on the personal stuff. 'If it's about you breaking up with Felipe, I saw the papers and it's none of my business. It's no one's business but yours.'

'It's not that. I should have told you this before . . . I can't work on any of the Olympic equestrian events. I had a bad riding accident a year ago and since then I haven't been able to ride. I've developed a phobia.' Shit, she had a horrible feeling that she was going to cry! She clenched her fists and dug her fingernails into her palms.

Nicky gave a small cough and fiddled with some of the documents on her desk. 'Actually, Charlie, I already knew. I read about the accident when you joined the channel, and I saw the press picked up on it last week. I would never ask you to report on any riding events until you're ready.' She smiled at Charlie. 'Is there anything else?'

Charlie shook her head.

'Good. Well, I'll see you at the planning meeting.' And Nicky turned her attention once more to her screen.

But as Charlie walked back to the office, she didn't feel relieved. She felt numb. Darcy was sitting at her computer; she smiled hesitantly at Charlie. 'Are you okay?'

'Yes, why wouldn't I be?' Charlie replied coolly.

Darcy looked embarrassed. 'Um, well, I saw the story in the *Sun* this morning. They've blown something out of nothing, right?'

Here goes. Time to lie again. 'Wrong. I'm back with Aaron. It's over with Felipe.'

Darcy couldn't have looked more stunned if Charlie had slapped her. 'But why? You seemed so good together. You seemed so happy.'

It was killing Charlie to pretend, but somehow she managed to shrug as if this was all boring to her. 'Like I said before, the spark's gone.'

'Do Lori and Kris know that it's over?'

God! Was Darcy ever going to give up?

'Not yet. Go ahead and tell them if you want.' And then because she couldn't stand another minute of Darcy's interrogation, Charlie made an excuse about needing to talk to a researcher, and locked herself in the disabled loo and sobbed.

Somehow she got through the live show in the afternoon. Aidan took on all the interviews. Usually Charlie would have made sure that she did as much as he did as she didn't want to be seen as a piece of eye candy for sports fans, but today she was grateful that Aidan carried the show. She checked her phone as she hurried out of the lifts – more missed calls from her friends that she had no intention of answering. But she had reckoned without Zoe's persistence. Just as she was about to leave the reception area through the revolving glass door, she saw her friend sitting on one of the sofas, obviously waiting for her. Reluctantly Charlie walked towards her.

Zoe stood up. 'What's going on, Charlie?'

She bit her lip. The last thing she wanted to do was fall out with Zoe, but she couldn't handle her questions now.

'Nothing's going on. I split with Felipe; I'm seeing Aaron. It's no biggie.' She hated herself for sounding so cold.

'It fucking is a biggie!' Zoe exclaimed, her voice echoing round the glass-walled reception area so everyone could hear. Great, that was all Charlie needed.

She reached for Zoe's arm. 'Can we at least go outside?'

Charlie led the way to a bench where she sat down and folded her arms, steeling herself for the conversation.

'I haven't got long, Zoe. I'm going out tonight and I need to get ready.'

Zoe curled her lip. 'You're not seeing *him*, are you?'

'If you mean Aaron, then yes, I am. He's taking me to Hakkasan for dinner.'

'I'm surprised you could have any appetite at all sitting opposite that wanker. Come on, Charlie! What's happened to you? It's like *Invasion of the Body Snatchers* – you look like Charlie, but you're behaving like a total stranger. Felipe adores you, and you adore him. I know you do.'

Somehow Charlie forced herself to meet Zoe's gaze. 'I did. I don't any more. Why can't you accept that the spark has gone for me? It's not about you, Zoe, it's about me. Now can we drop this?' She looked at her watch. 'I've got to go. D'you want a lift anywhere?'

It was a shock when Zoe shook her head. 'No, thanks.' She stayed sitting on the bench while Charlie hurried away, desperately trying to blink back the tears.

Chapter 23

Felipe didn't give up and called her every single night, leaving urgent, pleading messages which Charlie didn't return. She felt as if she was sleepwalking through her life, her head felt thick with misery, but somehow she found the strength to continue with her plan. She met up with Aaron for another date and made sure the paps were there to photograph them. The pictures then duly appeared in the press. Her friends and family were stunned by this turn of events. No one could believe that she had broken up with Felipe. But Charlie insisted that she was in love with Aaron, that she always had been, and that was that.

It will get better, she kept telling herself. But she cried herself to sleep every night. As if to vindicate her choice, the nightmares about the accident returned as badly as they had in the days immediately following it. These surely were the proof that she couldn't be with Felipe.

Aaron kept hassling her to sleep with him. But

whatever Charlie might pretend to her friends, there was no way she wanted to and every time he kissed her it took all her will-power not to run away. She came up with yet another lie – after such a big lie to Felipe, what were these smaller ones to Aaron? – that she needed time before she could trust him again. If after a month he could prove that he wasn't seeing anyone else, then they would take their relationship further. She was sure that by then Felipe would have given up on her, and she could come up with some excuse to Aaron and end things quietly.

It was a Friday night in the middle of May and she was meeting him for dinner at Sanctum Soho hotel. As she hurried through the lobby, she saw a familiar figure. It was Felipe. *My only love!* She longed more than anything to throw her arms around him and bury her face in his shoulder. To feel his arms around her. She had missed him so much. He looked shattered, unshaven, with dark shadows under his eyes. She steeled herself for what was coming next as he strode towards her.

'I had to see you, Charlie. Zoe told me you would be here.' His beautiful brown eyes were burning with intensity and passion. He was close enough for her to smell his familiar aftershave.

'Zoe had no right to tell you anything,' Charlie replied, trying to keep the emotion out of her voice.

'She told me because she cares about you. And Luis told me about your panic attack at the stables. Is all this something to do with that? Because you know I will do whatever it takes to help you overcome your fear.'

He sounded so sincere, so heartfelt. She forced herself to reply, 'I'd already forgotten about that thing at the stables. It isn't about that.'

'Tell me to my face that you don't want to see me any more because I don't believe you, Charlie.'

Every fibre of her being was calling out for him, longing for him, dying for him. 'I'm sorry, Felipe, you've had a wasted journey. It really is over.' Charlie didn't know how she was keeping it together.

He took a step towards her. 'I don't believe you. You can't just turn your back on the connection we had and pretend it was nothing – just a fling.'

She shrugged. 'To me it was. I didn't feel it as much as you did, I'm sorry.' Charlie didn't think she could go on with this pretence a moment longer. But then Aaron walked into the lobby and made a bee-line for her. He looked cocky, arrogant, a jack-the-lad. She had never disliked him more than when he put his arm around her waist, claiming possession, and kissed her in front of Felipe.

Somehow Charlie managed to smile and slide her arm around his back, aware of Felipe's hawk-like gaze still fixed on her. 'This is Aaron. Aaron, Felipe.'

Aaron put out his hand, but Felipe ignored the gesture and said, 'If this is really what you want, Charlie, then I'll go and you'll never have to see me again.'

No, no, no! Charlie was screaming inside.

'It is.' She felt as if she had turned to stone as Felipe gazed at her one last time then strode away, violently shouldering open the glass door.

He was lost to her now.

'Bit of a coincidence him pitching up, wasn't it?' Aaron commented. 'Looked a bit rough, didn't he?' He was never the most perceptive man when it came to emotions.

It was taking all of Charlie's will-power not to run after Felipe. Her heart felt as if it was breaking. She knew then that she loved Felipe more than she had ever loved anyone before, and that she would never love like this again. Ignoring Aaron's remark, she said, 'Let's get a drink.'

Felipe was in a daze all the way back to the airport. Zoe had called him and begged him to come and stay with her, but he couldn't face anyone, seeing the pity in their eyes, dealing with all the questions. How could he have got it so spectacularly wrong with Charlie? She had looked at him so coldly and seemed so glad to see that idiot footballer with his diamond earrings and stupid designer jacket. And she was even dressed differently, like a WAG, in a tight white low-cut dress, with far more make-up on than he had ever seen her in before. She had still looked beautiful, but so hard.

He downed several whiskys on the flight back, even though he had vowed that he wouldn't drink again until after the Olympics. He craved some respite from the agony of knowing that Charlie was lost to him.

He walked through arrivals with his shoulders hunched and his head lowered, trying to ignore the happy scenes of couples hugging each other, the smiles on the faces of families being reunited. He had waited for Charlie here so many times; he remembered the feeling of anticipation before she walked out, the sheer joy of seeing her, their passionate embraces. Suddenly he realised that someone was waving at him. It was Paloma.

'Felipe, I just wanted to see if you were all right.' Her beautiful face was aglow with sympathy. He thought about giving her the brush off, pretending that he was fine, but then the prospect of returning to an empty house with only his thoughts of Charlie for company was too much. He could do with a friend right now.

'Not really. I don't understand what has happened. I don't know why Charlie has broken up with me. Nothing makes any sense.'

Paloma reached out and lightly touched his arm. 'Come, let me drive you home, you look exhausted.'

He was silent on the drive back to his house. It was strange sitting next to Paloma. She had driven his car many times in the past, and seeing her at the wheel almost made him feel that they had never split up. Maybe they never should have. Life with her would be easy and straightforward. Also dull, but at least he wouldn't hurt the way he did now.

Once they arrived at the house she made him a bowl of spaghetti Napolitana, refusing to listen to his protests that he wasn't hungry. 'I know you won't have eaten anything all day. And you must keep your energy levels up.'

Felipe managed a couple of mouthfuls, before pushing the plate away. He had no appetite. He longed to drink, anything to numb the pain, but when Paloma saw him pour a glass of whisky, she said, 'Felipe, that is not the answer. You've already had some on the flight.' She clearly expected him to obey her, like a good little boy, and he remembered how infuriatingly bossy she could be, wanting everything to be done her way. He picked up the glass and took a large gulp of whisky.

'Thank you for your concern, Paloma, but I will be the judge of what I do or don't need. And right now, believe me, this is what I need.'

Paloma looked as if she had plenty to say, but managed to stop herself. She adopted a different tactic. Sitting down on the sofa next to him, she smoothed back his hair.

'Would you like me to give you a massage?' Her hands moved to his shoulders. God knows he was tense. He closed his eyes as Paloma's slim fingers skilfully kneaded the knots in his shoulders. What was Charlie doing now? he wondered, torturing himself with images of her with that stupid footballer. Was he unzipping that slutty dress, kissing her breasts, caressing her between her legs, fucking her? The images were like scorpions in his head. He couldn't bear it. He opened his eyes. Reaching for Paloma, he pulled her on to his lap and began kissing her, forcing his tongue into her mouth, caressing her breasts, sliding his hands along her thighs. Her skin felt cool to his touch. Against his will he remembered the heat rising from Charlie's body, the way she always responded to his touch. Caressing Paloma was like touching a beautiful statue. But maybe this would help him break the hold Charlie had over him.

He was brought sharply back to reality when Paloma murmured breathlessly, 'Oh, my darling, I've missed you so much. But now we can be back together, can't we?'

She was gazing at him with adoration and Felipe felt any desire for her fade away. He was deluding himself. He didn't want Paloma; he didn't want anyone other than Charlie.

'I'm sorry, Paloma, I don't think that's a good idea.' He gently removed her from his lap.

'What do you mean? You're free from your infatuation with that girl now. You've seen her for who she really is – a slut. A common little slut.' The adoration had gone, to be replaced by cold fury.

'All this time, Felipe, I have been waiting for you. Do you know what it felt like, seeing you with that girl? We are meant to be together, it's what everyone thinks.'

'Everyone? Do you mean my mother? And please don't speak of Charlie like that.'

'I'll say whatever I want about that stupid whore! She wasn't good enough for you. And what is she doing right now? On her knees sucking the cock of some footballer. It'll be a different one next week.'

Felipe was already tormented with images enough of his own without Paloma giving him any more. He sprang up from the sofa and shouted furiously, 'Get out now.'

Paloma realised that she had gone too far and desperately tried to backtrack. 'I'm sorry, Felipe. It's only because I can see how badly she has hurt you.' Her attempt to be his friend and confidante again failed dismally. Felipe could see straight through that act.

'Call yourself a taxi, I'm going to the stables. I want you to be gone by the time I return.'

He grabbed the bottle of whisky as he left. After checking on the horses, he went into the office and slumped back on the sofa. There he poured himself a large glass of whisky and couldn't stop himself from looking at the pictures of Charlie on his mobile, torturing himself once more as he recalled how close they had been. What had happened to his beautiful girl? Had she really not shared his passion? Round and round the questions chased each other in his head. He drank half the bottle, and then mercifully the alcohol took hold and he passed out on the sofa.

Charlie fumbled to get her keys in the lock and almost lost her footing once she opened the door and staggered into the hallway. She was drunk. She had broken her promise to herself not to drink when she was with Aaron. Somehow alcohol had seemed like the only way to get through the night after seeing Felipe.

'What the fuck do you think you're doing?' It was Kris. He stood in the doorway of the living room, arms folded, looking the picture of disapproval. Who did he think he was? Her mum!

'I'm walking into my flat. *My flat*. What does it look like?' She was aware that she was slurring her words.

'I'm talking about your life. You're wrecking it, and I want to know why.'

'I don't know what you're on about. I'm going to bed.' Charlie attempted to walk past him but he grabbed her arm and marched her into the living room where she collapsed on to the sofa.

'Right, you've been avoiding me this past few weeks – avoiding everyone. But now you're going to tell me what the hell is going on with you,' he insisted.

Even in her drunken state Charlie knew that Kris was only trying to help her but she couldn't deal with his concern. She couldn't afford to let her guard down for an instant.

She shrugged. 'There's nothing going on. I broke up with Felipe; I'm seeing Aaron. That's it. End of.'

'That's not it – you were so happy with Felipe. I've never seen you like that with anyone before.'

'It was an infatuation. It didn't last.'

He looked at her, taking in the revealing dress, the smudged make-up. 'Just look at the state of you. You look like a tramp.'

Charlie managed to shrug. 'Good. It's the look Aaron likes.'

Kris shook his head. 'I'm getting you a glass of water and some painkillers. You're going to feel like shit tomorrow.'

There is nothing that can kill my pain, Charlie thought bleakly. She bent down to unfasten the straps on her sandals and as she did so noticed that Kris had stacked up her post on the coffee table. Top of the pile was an envelope. It was another poison pen letter. She ripped it open and pulled out a picture of Felipe, torn out from the pages of the Spanish magazine *Hola!* Across it was scrawled, *Too good for you, bitch.* She threw it down in disgust.

'What's that?' Kris asked, as he put down the glass of water.

'A message from someone who doesn't like me very much.'

Kris picked up the picture and frowned as he read what was written on it.

'Have you had any more of this kind of thing?'

'Four or five.' Charlie was sounding blasé though she didn't feel like that.

'Have you told anyone at work about it?'

'It's no big deal. Aidan's been getting them too. It's someone who's jealous of us, that's all. Some sad little person who wants what we have.' And then, as if she had her finger firmly pressed on self-destruct, Charlie added, 'For a while we thought it might be Darcy.'

'Now hold on there! I hope you haven't been going around saying things like that? Of course Darcy wouldn't send that kind of letter.' Kris sounded very protective and Charlie should have left it there. Should have, but didn't.

'She's always been jealous of me, it's obvious.'

'She's not jealous of you! You don't know her like I do. I think I'm in love with her.'

There was a stunned silence for a moment, then Charlie burst out with, 'How can you love that spoilt little rich girl? She's so full of herself, I'm surprised she even noticed you. But I guess you're a better shag than her wanker banker boyfriends, because seriously, don't delude yourself it's anything more than that. You're her bit of rough.'

She didn't know why she was being so cruel to her brother. It wasn't his fault that she had ended her relationship with Felipe and that she was heartbroken. And it wasn't as if lashing out at him made her feel any better. If anything it made her feel worse.

'I don't know what your problem is, Charlie, but you are way out of line.' Kris looked disgusted by her outburst. 'You'd better apologise in the morning, when you've sobered up.'

'And you're wrong about me, Charlie.' Darcy had come out of Kris's bedroom and was standing there in a tee-shirt of his, looking very upset.

Shit! Charlie hadn't wanted her to hear those things. She could only hope Darcy hadn't overheard the comment about the poison pen letters.

'Your brother means more to me than anyone in the world.'

'Oh, please! You hardly know each other.' Charlie hated herself for being such a bitch but she couldn't stop. If she did they might discover what she really thought about Felipe, and she couldn't let that happen.

She managed to drag herself up from the sofa. 'I'm going to bed. I'll leave you two to plan your wedding.'

Kris shook his head as if he couldn't even bring himself to reply, which spurred Charlie on. 'Maybe it would be better if you stayed round at your girlfriend's for the next few weeks. I could do with the space.'

He stared at her. 'If that's what you want?'

Charlie managed, 'Yeah, it is.' And ignoring Kris and Darcy while trying to walk straight, she made her way to her bedroom and slammed the door shut.

Charlie woke up on Sunday morning with a horrendous hangover. Her head was pounding and she had a foul taste in her mouth. The night was coming back to her in a series of hideous flashbacks – Aaron snogging her in the back of his chauffeur-driven Range Rover and then being pissed off when she wouldn't go back to his house; her shouting at Kris, saying those terrible things about Darcy; the look of disgust on her brother's face. In a way Charlie was almost glad that she felt so bad. She *deserved* to feel bad after last night. She dragged herself into the shower, turning the water temperature up as hot as she could stand it. She could hardly bear to look at herself in the mirror, she felt such a deep sense of shame.

She pulled on her running kit and, on her way out to the gym, paused outside Kris's door. She gently knocked on it, fully intending to apologise. There was no reply. She waited for a few seconds and knocked again. Still nothing. She opened the door and discovered the room was empty and the bed hadn't been slept in. When she opened the wardrobe she saw that Kris had taken all his clothes. She really was on her own now.

Chapter 24

Two days later Darcy studied Charlie as she worked at her computer. She looked exhausted and had none of her usual spark. There was yet another story in the tabloids about her relationship with Aaron. This time Charlie had been photographed leaving the footballer's house early in the morning. She might as well have been waving a banner saying, *I've just shagged Aaron!* What the hell was going on with her? Darcy wondered. She seemed intent on destroying all the good things in her life – apart from her career. Darcy knew that Kris was worried about his sister, but he also possessed a stubborn streak like Charlie so hadn't tried to make things up with her after their appalling row.

Darcy was wary around Charlie after hearing the things she had said about her, but also felt sorry for her as she was clearly so desperately unhappy. Something happened to make her behave in this self-destructive way and Darcy was convinced it could all be traced back to the riding accident. Checking that Charlie was engrossed in her work, Darcy Googled the article about the accident and quickly re-read it. It was every bit as horrific as she had remembered. She closed the article and then looked over at Charlie again. It was no wonder that she had such a terror of riding – every time she looked at a horse, it must remind her of what had happened.

Aidan approached Charlie's desk and Darcy couldn't help overhearing their conversation.

'Have you seen Dr Mackay lately?' he asked.

Instantly Charlie seemed defensive. 'There's no reason to as I'm not seeing Felipe any more. I've told Nicky that I can't cover any of the equestrian events and she's cool with that.'

Aidan frowned. 'But you were making progress with therapy, weren't you? You shouldn't stop now.'

'What I need is for people to let me get on with my life, the way I want to,' Charlie snapped back.

He looked completely taken aback by her tone of voice.

'I'm sorry, Aidan, but the therapy didn't work and I'd rather forget all about it.'

And with that Charlie got up and abruptly left the room.

Darcy was shocked by the way Charlie had spoken to Aidan, knowing how close they were; she really was pressing self-destruct. And what was all that stuff about therapy? She was sure Charlie hadn't seen anyone. Darcy looked up in surprise as Aidan sat down at the desk opposite hers and, instead of logging on to the computer, leant forward and said quietly, 'Do you know what's going on with Charlie?'

'She's hardly my number one fan,' Darcy replied. 'So, no.' She hadn't meant to sound so dismissive – it was her default mode in front of Aidan. She quickly added, 'But I'm worried about her. She seems so lost, and Kris won't talk to her after the row they had.' She paused. 'I've been wondering if there was anything we could do to help her.'

Aidan almost did a double take. 'Wow! I didn't expect you to say that.'

'Why? Because you think I'm a spoilt little rich girl like Charlie does?'

He looked uncomfortable. 'Let's not go there. If I did think that, I was obviously wrong. So let's have a fresh start. How about we meet up with Zoe? She knows Charlie better than anyone. It's time we staged an intervention.'

'Sure, just let me know when and where.'

'I'm thinking about tonight.' He glanced up as Charlie came back into the room, looking as downcast as ever. 'We have got to do something.'

The three of them met upstairs at a pub on Dean Street in Soho. Darcy bought the first bottle of wine – everyone agreed that alcohol was essential – and they settled down at a table in the corner to talk about what was going on with Charlie. Zoe, in particular, seemed very upset.

'We've always been so close, I don't know what's happened to her. It's like she's shut down. She doesn't return my calls, and when I do manage to speak to her and suggest we meet up, she always says she's busy.'

She slammed her hand down on the table. 'And I just can't believe that she is seeing TFB again! That man is such a dick. I can't fucking stand him! Nor can Charlie. She loves Felipe . . . I know she does. And he loves her. They are meant to be together!'

'I agree,' Aidan said, when he could finally get a word in. 'It's like she's hell-bent on self-destruction. But why, and what can we do about it?'

Darcy had been largely silent up until now – both Aidan and Zoe knew Charlie so much better than she did and she didn't want to step on their toes – but now she spoke up. 'I think Charlie could be suffering from post-traumatic stress disorder. I've been doing some research online and she seems to have all the symptoms – the panic attacks, the flashbacks. I'm sure she'll be having nightmares as well.'

'But she said she was having therapy and the therapist I recommended is really good,' Aidan insisted.

Darcy shook her head. 'I don't think she is having therapy. I think she just wanted you to believe she was.'

'I suppose it's possible,' he replied. 'But then why break up with Felipe? He didn't put any pressure on her about riding or watching him ride. She told me they never even talked about it.'

Zoe and Darcy looked at each other, both clearly thinking the same thing. Zoe was the first to speak. 'I think she felt awful because she couldn't give him any support. Luis told me that she had a massive panic attack when she went to Felipe's stables. He said she was in a terrible state, he'd never seen anything like it. Apparently she begged him not to tell Felipe as she was worried about giving him any more to cope with.'

'And I think that she knew that she wouldn't be able to watch him at the Olympics,' Darcy added. 'And hated herself for it so much that she ended the relationship, even though she still loves him.'

'Oh my God! This whole thing with TFB was to distract Felipe from that, wasn't it?' Zoe burst out. 'Because she knew that if she told him it was all to do with her riding phobia, he would say it didn't matter. She's done all this for him, precisely because she loves him!'

'Bloody hell, you women are complicated, complex creatures. It's exhausting. Give me a simple man any day of the week! They're only ever after one thing,' Aidan said, injecting the first bit of humour they'd had all night.

He went up to the bar and returned with another bottle of Sauvignon Blanc – their third. Concern about Charlie had caused them all to knock back the wine. And he bought a huge bag of pick and mix sweets: Haribo fried eggs, love hearts, cola bottles, jelly babies, and giant chocolate buttons with sprinkles.

'God, I shouldn't be eating these!' Zoe said, shoving three fried eggs into her mouth. 'I just fucking love them. Sorry,' she added. 'The swearing always gets bad when I'm feeling emotional. And I am feeling *very* emotional.'

For a few minutes the trio felt more optimistic, buoyed up by Sauvignon Blanc and a sugar rush. Everything would be all right now they knew what Charlie's problem was. That was until Darcy said, 'So what do we actually do?'

'We should go straight round to Charlie's. Tell her she has to have therapy, and that we'll help her.' That from Zoe.

Aidan shook his head. 'We're all a bit squiffy, I don't think it will go down well. And you know how defensive Charlie can be. If she sees the three of us coming at her, it will make her shut down even more.'

'I think you should talk to her, Zoe,' Darcy suggested, 'and I'll try and persuade Kris to go with you. You're her best friend, and even though she and Kris had this row, I know he will want to help her.'

Zoe got up from her seat and enveloped Darcy in a hug. 'You're right, you're so right!' She turned to Aidan. 'I love this girl!'

He smiled at Darcy. 'Yeah, she's okay.'

'Once you can get past the stuck-up rich part?' Darcy said dryly.

Aidan held up his hands. 'I won't be so quick to judge again. Cross my heart.' He paused then added, 'Oh, and FYI, I'm gay.'

'I pretty well knew that,' she replied. 'I'm stuck-up and rich, not completely stupid. Your nails are far too good for any straight man and I've seen you reading *Grazia* . . . I mean *properly* reading it, not just flicking through to the pictures to ogle the models. Or at least not the girls.'

'She's got your number,' Zoe commented.

'Actually I'm coming out on Twitter,' he replied. 'All the important people in my life know, like my family and close friends, but I'm sick of pretending at work. And it will wind up the little fuck who's been sending me and Charlie poison pen notes!'

'What's this?' Darcy asked. Aidan quickly explained what had been going on.

'You have to speak to someone at work,' she insisted. 'For all you know other presenters could have been targeted.'

'Maybe, but I'm still coming out on Twitter. I should have done it a long time ago.'

They tumbled out of the pub at last orders, slightly tipsy but full of good feelings about their plans to help Charlie and sort out the poison pen letter writer. And as she took a taxi home Darcy felt a glow of happiness. She had never felt part of anything before. Her phone beeped with a text message. It was from Bunny.

Thanks for your text. I'm sorry too. About being a bride from hell and being such a bitch to you. I really want you to be at my wedding and of course you can wear a wrap. And I would like to invite Kris. You were right about Drew. He's a shit.

Darcy hadn't expected this. If her sister could change, anything seemed possible.

It was only a small story and Charlie nearly didn't see it as she was all set to read the sports coverage. And how she wished that she hadn't. It was a tiny piece on the show-business page of the *Mirror: Charlie's Ex Goes Back to his Ex*. There was a picture of Felipe and Paloma – one that had been taken long before Felipe and Charlie got together, but the article stated that the Spanish couple were back together and likely to announce their engagement any day now. She should hardly be surprised, given that she had done everything she could to push him away. But of course it hurt. She had succeeded in her plan, but at what price? She had lost the man she loved.

Charlie closed the lid of her laptop and curled up on the sofa. Even the knowledge that she had done the right thing couldn't relieve the deep pain she felt. She was so lost in thought that she didn't hear the front door open and nearly jumped out of her skin when Kris and Zoe walked into the living room. She hastily rubbed away the tears that were streaking her cheeks. The last thing she needed was for them to ask her what was wrong – she just couldn't go there.

'Hiya,' Zoe said, sitting down next to her. 'You look like shit.'

'Thanks a lot, Zoe. You really know how to make a girl feel good about herself.' Charlie tried to seem light-hearted but knew how dismal she must sound.

She looked up at Kris who had remained standing and seemed ill-at-ease. She had to apologise. It had been a week since their argument and he hadn't replied to any of her messages – they had never had such a bad row before.

'Kris, I'm sorry I said those things. I didn't mean them. I was drunk. And you were right, I was out of order.'

'Yeah, well, you were out of order, and I'm still pissed off with you, but Darcy said I had to make it up with you – that you didn't really mean what you said.'

Charlie managed to stop herself from saying it was none of Darcy's business.

'Anyway, let's forget it now,' he added and sat down in an armchair. Both he and Zoe were looking at her closely. God knows what was going on.

'We've got something to say to you, and you've got to hear us out.' Zoe was speaking now. 'We know why you broke up with Felipe.'

Not this! 'I told you – it wasn't working out between us. Why do you keep going on about it? Change the fucking record, can't you?'

'Because that's not the reason!' Zoe said passionately. 'We know it's because you couldn't bear to let him down by not going to the Olympics. You only pretended to feel something for TFB so Felipe wouldn't realise it was all to do with your riding phobia.'

Kris picked up the explanation there. 'And we're going to help you. You're going to make an appointment to see Aidan's therapist, and then you're going to call Felipe and tell him what you did. We are not going to sit back and watch you ruin your life like this.'

Charlie hated to think that her friends had been discussing her, picking over her life, analysing her, and was instantly on the defensive. 'There are just a couple of flaws in your little plan. I'm not going to have therapy because it won't work, and Felipe is now back with Paloma and they're probably going to get married.'

'No way!' Zoe exclaimed. 'He doesn't love her.'

Charlie shrugged. Leaning forward once more, she opened her laptop where the story about Felipe and Paloma was still on the screen.

'You know what the press is like,' Kris said after he'd

quickly read the article. Neither he nor Zoe wanted to admit defeat.

'And Aidan said his therapist is brilliant,' Zoe persisted. 'Look, I've brought along all the information about the kind of therapy she specialises in – it wouldn't be like last time.'

'No! I told you, it didn't fucking work. Why won't you get the message? I'm not going through that again.' Charlie's *I couldn't care less attitude* had been replaced by one of passionate anger. At her friends for interfering, at herself, at the total fuck up that was her life. She stood up. 'And now I've got to get ready, Aaron is picking me up in half an hour.'

Kris and Zoe looked helplessly at each other, their plan of action in ruins.

'Don't you mean TFB?' Zoe said, 'Because he won't have changed. What are you *doing* with him? You don't even like him. I know you well enough to know that.'

But Charlie was already walking out of the room. 'I'm going to have a shower. You can let yourselves out, can't you? Unless you want to stay and say hi to Aaron.'

In fact Charlie had no intention of seeing him. Tonight was the night she was going to dump him, by text. She never wanted to see or speak to him again. By the time she returned to the living room Kris and Zoe had left. She felt terrible at treating her brother and best friend so badly. Her mum rang but Charlie ignored the call.

It was a beautiful evening and it would have been the perfect opportunity to sit outside on the decking, catching the last of the sun's rays with a glass of wine, having a good gossip with Zoe, but now all Charlie wanted to do was hide herself away. She poured herself a large vodka. She had run out of tonic but didn't care. She couldn't even face going to the shops to buy any. There was no food in the house either, and usually Charlie would have made herself a healthy supper. But nothing seemed to matter. Felipe was back with Paloma, and she had alienated everyone who was close to her.

She was halfway through her second vodka when the doorbell rang. God, it wouldn't be Aaron, would it? She'd planned to send the break-up text late at night, specifically to avoid any confrontation. She ignored it but whoever it was kept ringing. Finally Charlie got up and stomped to the front door. She flung it open and got the shock of her life when she discovered Luis standing on her doorstep.

Chapter 25

What the hell was he doing here? Charlie looked at him in astonishment.

Luis smiled warmly. 'Hello, Charlie. I really need to talk to you.'

'Did Felipe send you?' Even mentioning his name caused a lump in her throat.

'No, he doesn't know I'm here.'

'Was it Zoe?'

He shook his head. 'No, it was something I planned along with Mariana and – this may surprise you – Vittoria. Now, is this interrogation over? Can I come in?'

Vittoria! What the hell did the Ice Queen have to do with this? Trying to collect her thoughts, Charlie showed him through to the living room.

'This is a very pleasant flat,' Luis commented, as he sat down on the sofa.

The half-empty bottle of vodka stood on the coffee table and Charlie waited for him to notice it. But he didn't mention it.

'So how are you, Charlie? We've all missed you.'

She sat at the opposite end of the sofa.

'Fine. Busy but fine. And I've missed you too.' Charlie attempted to sound upbeat, but realised it must be blindingly obvious that she was anything but. She knew how rough she looked. Her hair, which needed a wash, was scraped back into a ponytail, she had dark shadows under her eyes and wasn't wearing any make-up. And seeing Luis again was causing the memories of Felipe to flood back into her mind.

'How's Mariana?'

Luis beamed. 'She is blooming. But I haven't come here to talk about her.' He leant forward and clasped his hands together. 'Vittoria came to see me last week.'

'How nice for you,' Charlie commented sarcastically.

Luis ignored the comment and pressed on. 'She was very upset about you breaking up with Felipe.'

'Yeah, right!' The sarcasm went up a notch.

'I know it's hard to imagine. She admitted that at first she hadn't wanted your relationship to work, that she wanted Felipe to get back with Paloma *and* that she had her lawyer tip off the British press about your riding phobia.'

Charlie frowned. She had suspected as much.

'But when Vittoria saw how devastated Felipe was, she had a change of heart . . . well, about pretty much everything, but especially you. She insisted that I fly over and tell you that you are making a terrible mistake.' He paused. 'To tell you that whatever has been going on, it's plain you love Felipe. And he loves you.'

Charlie had been so strong these past weeks, hidden

her true feelings, built up her defences, but Luis's words were battering them down. She tried to speak, to come out with a denial, but tears were blurring her eyes. She couldn't pretend any more.

'You broke up with him because you loved him,' Luis continued. 'Because you didn't want your fear of riding to distract him in any way. That's right, isn't it?'

Charlie nodded; the tears were falling freely now. Instantly Luis moved next to her and put his arm around her. At the feel of his friendly embrace, she finally gave in to her emotions. Luis let her cry herself out. When Charlie could finally speak, she said, 'But Felipe's back with Paloma, he won't want me after what I've done.'

'He's not seeing her again. That story was entirely of her invention. She is bitter because he rejected her. In her heart she knows Felipe loves you. You *have* to go back to him.'

For a tantalising instant Charlie allowed herself to believe that this might be possible. Then she had a reality check. 'No, I can't do that. It's better that we don't see each other again.'

'That's where you're wrong, Charlie. Felipe is your soul-mate. He's the man for you, just as you are the woman for him. You belong together.'

'But my fear of riding is always going to get in the way. Vittoria was right when she told me that it wasn't fair on Felipe that he couldn't share the most important thing in his life with me.'

'Well, she now thinks she was wrong, and she wanted me to tell you that. Charlie, you can overcome this – you can have therapy.'

'I tried before but it didn't work!'

'My dear Charlie, from the little I have learnt from Felipe, it seems you had an unfortunate experience with therapy. There are other experts out there who can help you. You just have to be open to it. Believe me, if you turn your back on Felipe, you will regret it for the rest of your life.'

Charlie was in turmoil. 'But I've destroyed my relationship with him. He believes I'm in love with Aaron. He will never forgive me.'

'He doesn't believe that, and he will forgive you.'

Part of her longed to get a flight there and then, Luis made it sound so wonderfully easy. But Charlie knew she had a major obstacle to overcome first.

'I can only see him again if I have therapy and it works. If I am with him, I want to be with him one hundred per cent. I want him to be able to share all his life with me.'

'Can you at least tell him that this is what you are doing?'

Charlie shook her head. 'No, absolutely not, in case it doesn't work.'

For a moment it seemed as if Luis might keep trying to persuade her; then he smiled and stretched out his hand. 'Do we have a deal then?'

Charlie hesitated, then reached out and firmly shook his hand. 'Yes, we do.'

Luis smiled. 'I don't know about you, but I could do with a drink.'

'I've only got vodka and no tonic,' Charlie replied, gesturing to the half-empty bottle of Smirnoff.

'Perfect. We can have a toast to the future – to your future with Felipe. And then I can call Mariana and tell her the news. She will never forgive me if I don't – she has been so worried about you.' Luis hesitated, 'And would you mind if I told Vittoria?'

'If you must,' Charlie replied. She still found it hard to have any warm feelings towards Felipe's mother, even if she had realised that she'd been wrong.

'I must,' Luis told her. 'Maybe this will make you feel differently about her – she has finally accepted Eduardo's marriage to Ricky and is throwing them an anniversary party.'

'Oh my God!' Somehow the news gave Charlie a feeling of optimism, as if anything might still be possible. She hesitated before she asked, 'Do you really think Felipe will want me back?'

Luis smiled. 'Of that I have no doubt. He has never stopped loving you. Everything is going to be okay.'

Charlie hugged him tightly. 'Thank you so much, Luis.'

'You are very welcome. I have just one request: that you name your first child after me . . . even if it's a girl. Actually two requests. Have you got anything to eat? I am starving.'

'It'll have to be pizza, unless you want some out-of-date hummus and a wilted carrot?'

'Let me think – pizza, please, my dear Charlie. But please don't tell Mariana . . . I'm supposed to be on a low-carb diet.'

'For you, Luis, anything,' she replied, hugging him once more.

*

Felipe jumped off Valiente and handed the reins to Daria. Both rider and horse were sweating after the intensive training, but Felipe was quietly pleased with how the session had gone. He was still feeling shattered by Charlie's betrayal, but instead of hitting the booze and wallowing in despair he had channelled everything into his riding. He had won his last three eventing competitions; was at the top of his game. A medal at the Olympics seemed more than a possibility.

He unstrapped his crash hat and pulled it off, running a hand through his hair. He looked fit and lean, ready for the competition, but there was a definite sadness about his eyes. He'd intended to have a quick break before resuming training and was surprised to see his friend standing waiting by the entrance to the stable yard.

'Luis, I wasn't expecting you. Did we have something arranged?'

'I thought I'd come by and see if you had time for dinner tonight? Mariana is cooking one of her famous *Arroz con pollo*.'

Felipe hesitated; he felt he was better on his own right now. He wasn't good company. He tended to ride until at least eight at night, have something to eat, and then fall into bed exhausted by ten.

'Come on, you need a break. We haven't seen you for ages. And let's have a coffee now,' his friend suggested.

The two men sat down in the welcome shade of Felipe's terrace. It was only 11 a.m. but already the sun was burning hot and the temperature in the high-20s. Felipe asked Luis about work and about how Mariana was doing. He was intent on avoiding any personal questions, but Luis wasn't going to let him get away with it.

'So how are you?'

Felipe shrugged. 'Fine. Busy. You know how it is.'

Luis gave a quiet cough, always a sign that he was anxious about the impact of what he was about to say. 'Do you think you might try and see Charlie when you go to London for the Olympics?'

Felipe hadn't been expecting this. He kept all thoughts of Charlie firmly locked down, buried. He could not, *would* not, go there. He shot Luis a furious look. 'Why the fuck would I want to see *her* again? She made her choice very clear to me the last time I saw her.' He gave a mirthless laugh. 'I don't think I'll ever forget the expression on her face. It made me wonder if I really knew her at all.'

'I'm sure that's not true. Maybe there has been some kind of crisis in her life that you don't know about.' Luis sounded so hopeful and optimistic. And totally misguided.

Felipe shook his head. 'No, Luis. If you must know, I regret ever having met her.'

His friend seemed stunned by his bitter words. Felipe drained his espresso and stood up. 'Look, Luis, I know you liked her, but she isn't the woman you thought she was. She's manipulative and selfish – and she broke my heart. But d'you know what? Maybe she did me a favour, because I sure as hell won't be falling for someone so easily again. And now I've to get on.' Felipe grabbed his hat and started heading back to the stables.

'What time shall I tell Mariana to expect you?' Luis called after him.

'I'm sorry, Luis, I won't be able to make it. Send her my love though.'

Felipe couldn't believe that his friend had brought Charlie's name up. It was going to take all his will-power to push her to the back of his mind again. But he was determined to do it and he was certain of one thing: he never wanted to see Charlie Porter again.

Chapter 26

Charlie walked twice past the beautifully maintained Edwardian terraced house in Richmond, with its smart navy blue door, the colour of Dr Who's TARDIS, before plucking up the courage to approach. She half wished the house were the TARDIS, all set to transport her somewhere else, anywhere but here. It was her first appointment with Dr Rosie Mackay, the therapist Aidan had recommended, and Charlie was incredibly nervous. Aidan had offered to come with her but she had refused – if she couldn't even manage to get here on her own then there was no hope for her. She didn't know what to expect and was terrified that instead of helping her overcome her fears, it would bring the accident back and cause her to relive every single agonising moment, even though Aidan had promised her that this wouldn't be the case.

Charlie knew very little about therapy and was convinced it would be the kind where she lay on a black leather couch and had to pour her heart out while the earnest-looking therapist took notes and didn't say anything. Or worse, came out with disturbing comments like the very first therapist she'd met, about how she must have been abused as a child. So it was a very pleasant surprise when an attractive woman in her late-forties, wearing a stylish dark green wrap dress, opened the front door.

'Charlie, do come in,' she said warmly, 'I'm Rosie.'

The surprises continued as she showed Charlie into a comfortably furnished room that was more like a living room than a consulting room. There was a desk, but Rosie chose not to sit behind it and instead took one of the armchairs, while Charlie sat down on the sofa. Rosie began the session by explaining how she worked and giving an overview of how Cognitive Behavioural Therapy or CBT worked. Put very simply, she explained, the way you perceive a situation influences your emotional reaction to it and then the way you behave. Because Charlie had had the accident, every time she saw a horse she would think about a horse dying horribly and believe she couldn't cope. She had tried to mask these feelings from herself by avoiding horses and everything to do with riding, which ultimately had made the fear worse.

'But do you think I can get over this?' Charlie asked.

'If you put in the work, I've no doubt at all. It's about us working out the links between your thoughts and your feelings,' Rosie told her, 'and then trying to break the destructive ones and establish more helpful ones.'

There were tears, of course, and it was painful, but Charlie left two hours later feeling that she had made some progress. Rosie had diagnosed that she was suffering from post-traumatic stress disorder and had given her a series of exercises to work through. The point about CBT was that it was an active therapy, she had to work hard to re-programme the way she thought about the accident and horses. Equally it wasn't a miracle cure. She was going to have to commit to twice-weekly sessions for the next two months. Charlie had told Rosie that her goal was to see Felipe compete in the Olympics. If she could do that, then she thought they might possibly have a future together. *If.* A great deal was hanging on that word . . .

Zoe and Kris were waiting at the flat when she got home. Both of them looked at her expectantly when she walked into the living room and she knew that they were dying to find out how it had gone. She sat down next to Zoe. 'It was good,' she said, and promptly burst into tears.

'Oh, babes!' Zoe put an arm round her. 'You've been so brave. We're so proud of you for going.'

'I don't know why I'm crying. I suppose it's because, for the first time, I feel I can do this . . . I can get better. And that I'm not stupid or mad.' Charlie sniffed and brushed away the tears. The relief at starting to unlock the feelings she had suppressed for so long was almost overwhelming.

She looked over at Kris. 'Where's Darcy?'

'She didn't know if you would want to see her.'

'Phone her up and tell her to come over! I want to tell her how sorry I was for being so vile to her. And then I'm taking you all out for dinner. I know what a bitch I've been and dinner isn't going to make up for it all, but it's a start. And I'm going to phone Aidan too.' She hesitated. Felipe's name was the one she longed to include in that list, longed with all her heart.

'Why don't you call Felipe and at least tell him how it went?' Zoe said quietly.

Charlie shook her head. 'Not yet, in case this was a one-off. I want to prove to myself that I can get through this. I can't let him down again.'

But when she went into her bedroom to get changed for dinner, she rescued the diamond necklace from her jewellery box and put it on. And when she returned to her flat later that night, she switched on her laptop and began pouring out her feelings to Felipe in an email that she didn't send, but saved in the draft folder.

Charlie had her second therapy session just three days later. She had been working through all the exercises in the meantime and thought she was doing well. Rosie seemed to think so too as she suggested that they watch a film of someone riding. Maybe it was because it was too soon, or because the horse was black, just like Ace, but minutes into the film, Charlie felt the onset of a panic attack. Realising that something was wrong, Rosie stopped it and began taking her through her relaxation exercises. But Charlie was too upset to continue.

'This is stupid! If I can't even look at a film, I'm wasting everyone's time. I knew it wouldn't work.'

Charlie grabbed her bag. Before Rosie could stop her, she ran out of the house. She heard Rosie calling after her as she pounded down the street, but ignored her.

Back at her flat Charlie was all set to shut herself away in her bedroom, depressed by what she saw as her own failure, but Darcy was in the living room.

'Hi, Charlie. I hope you don't mind, but Kris said it was okay if I borrowed his key to let myself in? India has got a hot date with this sexy gardener, and I wanted to give them some space.'

'No problem,' Charlie replied.

'Is everything okay? You seem a bit upset.'

Just a few weeks ago, Darcy would have been the very last person Charlie would ever have considered confiding in. Now she found herself sitting down and telling her what had happened at the therapist's house.

'It only goes to show that I was right to split up from Felipe. I'll never get over this, and I'm just going to have to live with it.'

'I'm no expert,' Darcy said quietly, 'but it was only your second session and you have to give therapy time to work properly. Maybe you need to take some medication as well . . . just a low dose to help you through. You'll be able to come off it again, once you don't need it any more.'

Charlie looked at Darcy. She had said that she wasn't an expert, but she seemed pretty clued up. 'D'you really think that?'

Darcy didn't reply straight away but rolled up her shirt sleeves and held up her arms so Charlie could see a number of scars running up the inside of her arms. They were long-healed, but still looked awful. Charlie winced in sympathy.

'I used to self-harm. And when I had therapy and

medication, it helped. There have been times when I've wanted to do it again, when I was feeling worthless, but then I remember what my therapy taught me and I get through it somehow. You'll get through it too, Charlie.'

She realised Darcy had been courageous in showing her the scars, and in getting through what must have been a dark time in her own life. Along with a newfound respect for Darcy, Charlie felt a flicker of hope for herself. She phoned up Rosie and apologised for running out, arranging to see her the following day.

One month later
'It's so good to be out of the city,' Rosie commented as Charlie drove along a country lane, deep in the heart of Surrey. It was a deliciously sunny morning in the middle of July – the kind of day which seems full of possibilities. The sky was a blissful blue, and beyond the lush green hedges there were fields of ripening crops and stately horse chestnut trees. It was on just such a country lane that Charlie had been riding when the accident occurred and because of this for a long time she had avoided trips into the country at all costs. But this was her second time out with Rosie as part of her intensive therapy and so far she hadn't experienced any flashbacks. Since the disastrous session when Charlie had fully expected never to go back, she had been making good progress; she could now look at pictures of horses and watch films of people riding without feeling any anxiety. She still occasionally had one of the nightmares, but was better able to deal with

them. She no longer felt overwhelmed by the experience.

Now she was facing her biggest challenge so far as they were on their way to a stables. She turned along the private road that led there. To either side were fields with horses grazing in them.

'Okay, Charlie?' Rosie asked as they pulled into the car park.

'I'm feeling nervous, but yes, I'm okay,' Charlie replied honestly.

Rosie smiled. 'That's perfectly normal, but you know I'm with you.'

They met up with the owner in the office-cum-tackroom at the front of the yard. Miranda was a cheery woman in her late-forties, dressed in black jodhpurs and a red tee-shirt. Charlie knew the type – someone who lived for their horses and to ride – knew it because she used to be something like that herself. Miranda had been briefed on why Charlie was visiting and she already knew Rosie as her daughter kept a horse at livery here. They chatted for a few minutes about the glorious weather and Charlie's TV work – Miranda asked if she would sign an autograph for her teenage son. Part of Charlie wished that they could stay here making small talk. But then Rosie looked at her and asked, 'Are you ready?'

Charlie nodded. The nerves were increasing now, and she was hyper-conscious of the smell of leather from the saddles and bridles neatly stored in the room, but she had been consciously practising the relaxation breathing technique that Rosie had taught her. It was now or never, she felt, as they followed Miranda into the yard.

This place was nothing like as grand as Felipe's equestrian centre; it was more like the stables where Charlie used to keep Ace: clean but a little shabby, though the stable doors were freshly painted in pale green. Charlie imagined that all Miranda's spare money went into the horses.

Several of them stuck their heads over the stable doors as the three women approached. Without hesitating Charlie went up to the first one – a handsome bay with a narrow white stripe running down the middle of his face.

'That's Basil,' Miranda told her.

Charlie reached out and tentatively patted him on the neck. He felt reassuringly solid to her touch. He was alive and vital. She stroked his pale pink nose; she had forgotten how velvet-soft the skin was there. She realised that she felt fine. No, more than fine, she felt good. The plan had been to see a horse at close hand, but now she felt she wanted to push herself further.

She turned to Miranda. 'Is there any chance that I could have a ride?'

If she could do this, then maybe she could make it to the Olympics and see Felipe. She had hardly dared let herself consider this might actually be possible . . . even though it was what she longed to do. She saw Miranda look over at Rosie for her approval. She nodded.

'Come on then,' Miranda said briskly. 'Help me get him tacked up.'

Charlie's hands were shaking slightly as she fastened the girth on the saddle, but she didn't falter. She put her foot in the stirrup and swung herself up into the saddle. Her Converse sneakers and white skinny jeans didn't make for ideal riding attire, but they would have to do. For a second she felt giddy being so far from the ground, uncertain that she could go through with this. Briefly she touched the love heart necklace she always wore now, as if to draw strength from it, then she gathered the reins and gently pressed her heels against Basil to get him to walk on. Miranda opened the gate to the paddock with the well-trodden circular track in the field beyond.

'Just walk him round to start off with, Charlie,' Miranda told her, taking up position in the middle of the circle. 'Get the feel of riding again. You're doing great.'

Charlie was acutely aware of the powerful horse beneath her, the creak of the saddle, the feel of the reins rubbing against her hands. She rode twice at walking pace round the circle and then, at Miranda's command, urged Basil into a trot. From there it was easy to progress to a smooth canter. She could feel Basil raring to go faster. In the past she had loved that feeling; it was like sitting on a rocket charged with sheer energy, and then she couldn't wait to take off into a furious gallop. Now she felt a stab of anxiety that she wouldn't be able to stop him, that he would be too strong for her, that he'd jump over the fence and end up on the road . . . But she controlled her fears and easily reined Basil in; there was nothing to be afraid of.

'Okay, when you're ready, bring him back down to a walk,' Miranda called out.

By the time she rode Basil back into the yard Charlie was feeling exhilarated. In less than a week she would see Felipe again.

Chapter 27

The atmosphere in the Olympic arena in Greenwich Park was electric. The stands were packed with thousands of spectators all buzzing with excitement to be there for the thrilling finale of the Olympic eventing competition – the show jumping. It was the most awe inspiring location, within the majestic beauty of Greenwich Park with a view of central London and the docklands skyline shimmering in the distance through the heat haze.

Charlie was sitting some five rows from the front, next to Rosie and her daughter Millie, a horse-mad fourteen-year-old who wanted to be an event rider herself and had kept up a detailed running commentary on how every rider was doing. Charlie was grateful for Millie's non-stop chatter as she was possibly more nervous than she had ever been in her entire life – nervous for Felipe competing, and nervous that he wouldn't want her after everything that had happened. True to her word, she hadn't contacted him directly, she didn't want do anything that might distract him from his Olympic goal, but it had been the hardest thing she had ever done and there were many, many times when she had nearly caved in and picked up the phone, longing to speak to him.

'The German Jonas Wulf is up next,' Millie said cheerfully. 'He's one to watch. He hardly had any penalty points in the dressage and he did fantastically at the cross-country too. And then the last rider is Felipe.' She looked across at Charlie and grinned. Rosie had told her something of Charlie's relationship with Felipe and Millie thought it was the most wildly romantic thing she had ever heard, nearly as romantic as Edward and Bella in *Twilight*, as she had told Charlie several times.

Charlie's heart skipped several beats. Just knowing that Felipe was nearby made her feel faint with longing. She wondered what was going through his mind right now as he prepared for the ride of his life. She knew that he would have walked the course first thing this morning, trying to determine which were the hardest jumps and how many strides he should allow Valiente to take before tackling each of them. And he would have been obsessively watching the other competitors, too, to see how they handled the course.

At the enclosure at the back of the arena, Felipe heard the roar of the crowd as Jonas Wulf completed his round with just four faults. It was a very impressive score and he was going to be hard to beat. Valiente was raring to go, keen as his rider to show what he could do in the ring. Daria, who had been his rock during the Olympics and in all the training, was standing by Valiente's noble head and giving him one last pat for luck. She caught Felipe's eye and smiled. 'You can do it.'

Yes, Felipe felt that he could. It had been the toughest time of his life, especially these past two weeks when he had been in London. Even with his focus on the Games, he couldn't help thinking of Charlie, wondering where she was, how she was, whether she ever thought of him . . . His mother had told him that she had split up with the footballer and, while he had pretended that the news meant nothing to him, inside he was filled with longing for her.

Then he heard his name being called out. He was cantering into the ring, and there he emptied his mind of everything except the daunting task before him.

Charlie held her breath as Valiente's fetlock rapped against the bar of the final jump, and the loud noise on the metal seemed to ring out in the hushed arena. Everyone was on the edge of their seats, captivated by the sheer brilliance of Felipe's riding. If it didn't fall Felipe would have a clear round. The bar stayed where it was.

'A clear round! He'll get silver!' Millie whooped, leaping out of her seat with excitement, to be joined by Charlie and Rosie. Charlie had tears in her eyes. She was so proud of Felipe for his incredible achievement, and so thrilled that she had been able to watch him compete. She longed to go to him, to throw her arms around him and tell him that she loved him, tell him why she had broken off their relationship. But she knew it would be impossible to get anywhere close because of the incredibly tight security. She hadn't even told him that she was going to be here. However agonising the wait, she would have to be patient, for just a little longer. And she also knew that she might find he didn't want her any more.

The crowd were whipped up into a frenzy as GB had taken the gold, but Charlie only had eyes for one rider. Felipe rode Valiente into the ring and then dismounted along with the other medallists and handed Valiente's reins to Daria while he stepped on to the podium. Charlie was waving and cheering for all she was worth. She willed Felipe to notice her but he was looking up at the crowd and didn't see her. She felt a sharp pang of disappointment – she wanted him to know that she had been here for him. But beside her Rosie, to Charlie's total astonishment, unfurled a poster of a huge red love heart, inside which was written: *Charlie loves you!* She saw Felipe notice the flash of red, pause to take in the message and then his eyes locked on hers. Would he still want her? Felipe looked as if he couldn't believe the evidence of his own eyes, but then he smiled and placed his hands on his heart and held them out to her. Charlie repeated the gesture back to him.

Outside the arena Millie took Charlie's hand. 'Come on, we'll get to the riders' enclosure this way.' She purposefully wove and dodged her way through the crowds. But at the entrance there were six security guards and only people with accreditation were allowed in.

'But we have to see Felipe Castillo de Rivas!' Millie said urgently, when a burly guard told them that without the right documents they weren't getting any further, adding, 'Yeah, you and most of the women here apparently. He's got quite a following, that one.'

'It's okay,' Charlie told Millie, 'I'll text him.' Even as she said it, she thought how ridiculously trite it sounded. She wanted to push past the security guards, who all looked as if they had been eating too many take-outs, and find her lover! Nonetheless she scrabbled through her bag to find her phone.

'O.M.G! You don't need to bother. He's here!' Millie exclaimed excitedly. Charlie looked up. Felipe was standing in front of her, still in his riding gear. Everything and everyone else seemed to recede into the distance as they stared at each other.

'You are the last person I expected to see here,' he said.

Charlie's heart was hammering in her chest as she replied, 'I've been having therapy, and it worked. I couldn't see you again until I knew that it would.'

'I thought you didn't want me any more?'

Charlie shook her head. 'I wanted you so much.'

'So the message was true?'

'Yes. I love you,' she told him, gazing into his brown eyes, willing him to believe her. 'I always have.'

He reached out for her and pulled her into his arms. 'I love you too.' And then, to the delight of the onlookers, they kissed, oblivious to the phones being whipped out as people took pictures of them.

Four hours later
Charlie was lying in Felipe's arms after the most amazing make-up sex. If he was shattered after competing in the Olympics, it was safe to say that it hadn't shown. She lifted her head and kissed him, feeling that she couldn't get enough of him but unable to resist teasing him. 'I know you've just won a silver, but that was a gold performance.'

'Well, we've got all that lost time to make up for!' he replied, then glanced across at the clock on the bedside table. 'I guess I should get back for the press conference.'

She couldn't bear to think of being separated from him again so soon. As if sensing that, he added, 'You're coming with me. And I think I've just got time to see if I can improve on that performance. You know what a perfectionist I am.' And he started kissing her once again.

Six months later . . . Barbados
'Wake up, sleepy head, it's time to get up!'

Charlie opened her eyes and saw that Felipe was already dressed. She was still feeling jet lagged and wanted nothing more than to stay in bed, preferably with him beside her.

'Come back to bed,' she pleaded. 'What's the rush?'

'I've arranged to meet the others – we should get going.' They had come away with Zoe and Nathan, Luis and Mariana and their adorable baby girl, Pia. Kris and Darcy had been going to come but Kris had an audition that he couldn't miss and so they pulled out. If you had asked Charlie a year ago if she could ever possibly imagine going on holiday with Darcy, she would have thought the question was insane, but the two women had become good friends. Darcy had been the one to find out that the poison pen writer had been one of the former sound engineers at the channel, who had haboured a grudge against several presenters when he was sacked. Her relationship with Kris had not been the short-lived affair Charlie had once predicted. The couple were now living together. And what's more, Darcy's family had accepted Kris – especially after Drew had been arrested for fraud involving pension funds. He was awaiting trial and likely to be sent down for considerably longer than the five months Kris had served for a one-off mistake.

'I thought this was supposed to be a holiday,' Charlie grumbled. 'You're ruining my erotic fantasy.' She grinned and stretched her arms up above her head, deliberately kicking off the sheets with her feet to show off her naked body. 'I had this wonderful dream that I made love with this handsome man in the morning. He was so sexy and so hard for me . . .'

She had Felipe's full attention now. 'What did this man look like?' He sat down on the bed.

'I didn't really see his face,' Charlie said cheekily. 'Only his gorgeous body.' She slipped her hands under Felipe's tee-shirt and caressed his smooth skin. 'Yep, his abs were like yours. But I really need to see everything before I can say whether it was you or not.' She undid the buttons on his shorts. 'And I mean *everything*.'

'We're going to be so late!' Felipe groaned, but he was already pulling off his tee-shirt.

Half an hour later the couple were on their way to the beach. 'You are so naughty, Charlie, we've kept everyone waiting,' Felipe told her.

'Yeah, but wasn't it worth it?'

'You know it was. I can never resist you.'

Six months on from their passionate reconciliation their relationship was stronger than ever. There was still the fact that they lived in two different countries, which made every moment they could spend together even more precious, and when the eventing season began again in February, Felipe would be travelling all over Europe to take part in competitions. But this part of his life was no longer closed off from her. Nowadays Charlie frequently went along with him and watched him compete. The therapy had helped to heal her. She was no longer paralysed by fear. There were still times when she could feel a panic attack looming or she had one of her nightmares, but she could deal with them. Therapy had given her the tools to work through her emotions and feel in control. She had even started riding again. Felipe had bought her a beautiful grey mare called Estrella.

'About bloody time!' Zoe called out. 'I'm the only one who is allowed to be late around here.' The group of friends were sitting under the shade of two large parasols.

'Sorry, it was my fault, I overslept,' Charlie said.

'Yeah, right.' Zoe's raised eyebrow showed that she knew the real reason.

'Well, you are here now and that's all that matters,' Luis put in, ever the peace-maker.

'So what are we doing?' Charlie asked.

But her question was answered when she noticed Captain Jack waving enthusiastically at them from his boat, moored further along the little wooden jetty. 'Come aboard, my friends!' he called out.

'I'm staying here with Pia and Luis,' Mariana said. She was wearing a white maxi-dress and motherhood had given her beauty an extra glow. 'We'll catch up with you later.' She blew Felipe and Charlie a kiss. 'I want to hear all about it – every single detail.'

It seemed an odd thing to say and it got odder when Luis hugged Felipe and said *'Buena suerte'*. Why was Luis wishing him good luck? They were only going on a boat trip, it was hardly *Mission: Impossible*! She was about to say as much when Felipe picked up the beach bags and began walking briskly towards the boat.

'I knew I would see you two again!' Captain Jack told them as he helped them aboard. 'And I am never wrong about these things. Never.' Clearly he hadn't changed in the year since they had last seen him.

'And here is beautiful Zoe with the boyfriend who forgot her birthday!' he exclaimed, shaking them both warmly by the hand.

'Oh, man, did you have to bring that up again?' Nathan joked. 'It cost me enough. And I'm not talking about the money, I'm talking about the emotional grief.'

'Still got your balls though, haven't you?' Zoe put in cheekily. 'Captain Jack said that his wife would have lopped his off and worn them as earrings if he'd forgotten her birthday!'

'Zoe!' Nathan muttered, shifting awkwardly in his seat. Captain Jack let out one of his trademark loud laughs.

'It's okay.' Zoe linked her arm through his. 'If you hadn't forgotten my birthday then I never would have come on holiday here with Charlie and she would never have met Felipe. So we're all pleased you forgot it.' She paused. 'That one time.'

Charlie squeezed Felipe's hand – she didn't like to think of their meeting being so random, so dependent on Nathan's big mistake. And nor did Captain Jack as he declared, 'Nonsense! These two were destined to be together, they would have met somehow.'

Felipe lightly kissed Charlie and whispered, 'I believe that too.'

They motored along the coast and then dropped anchor at the idyllic bay where Charlie remembered swimming with the turtles on their last visit. 'Brilliant!' she exclaimed. 'I really wanted to come here again.' She stood up and stripped down to her bikini, all set to put on the snorkel mask and hit the water. She had turned her back on everyone to get changed and was suddenly aware that conversation had stopped.

'Charlie, I've got something to say to you.' It was Felipe speaking.

She turned round. He didn't seem his usual confident self. What was going on? She looked across at Zoe and Nathan who were smiling.

'You were right about us, Captain Jack,' Felipe said.

'I love this woman, more than anything in the world
. . . more than life itself. And to prove it,' he knelt
down on one knee, 'Charlie, will you marry me?'

She gazed at him. The man who was wrapped around
her heart, the man she loved with every fibre of her
being. There were still obstacles in their relationship
– the question of where they were going to live and
their respective careers. But this was not the time for
any ifs, or buts, it was the time for one word.

'Yes!' Charlie exclaimed. 'Oh, yes! I would love to
marry you!'

Captain Jack couldn't resist chipping in with, 'I told
you, I'm never wrong! Some people are just meant to
be.'

Felipe stood up. He took Charlie in his arms and
kissed her. 'Yes, they are,' he murmured, adding, 'You
don't mind that we had an audience? It felt right to
propose here.'

'It was the perfect place,' she told him.

'Congratulations!' Now Zoe and Nathan got in on
the act and hugged and kissed the couple.

'But haven't you forgotten something, Felipe?' Zoe
said. And when he looked blank, she gestured at her
ring finger.

'Of course! The ring.'

Zoe turned to Nathan. 'Just so you know for future
reference, I want to see the ring before I give my answer.'

Everyone laughed, though knowing Zoe she probably
wasn't joking.

Charlie watched as Felipe took out a small red velvet
case from his pocket and held it out to her. 'It's yes

whatever the ring is like,' she told him. Though she gasped when she snapped open the case and there was the most breathtaking ring she had ever seen – a dazzling emerald-cut diamond in a brilliant-cut diamond setting. It was beautiful and unique. Felipe slipped it on to her finger where it fitted perfectly and glittered extravagantly in the bright sunshine. Even Zoe was momentarily speechless. But then Captain Jack popped the cork on a bottle of champagne and poured out glasses for everyone.

'When did you know you wanted to marry me?' Charlie asked quietly, so that only Felipe could hear.

'Two days after I met you. But you would have thought I was crazy, right?'

'I think I felt the same.'

'You *think!*' Felipe exclaimed.

'I *know* I did.'

'Smile!' Captain Jack ordered, 'I need a picture for my album. This proves that I am never wrong. I might have to re-name this boat – *The Love Boat.*'

Angel

Katie Price

A sparkling and sexy tale of glamour modelling, romance and the treacherous promises of fame.

When Angel is discovered by a model agent, her life changes for ever. Young, beautiful and sexy, she seems destined for a successful career and, very quickly, the glitzy world of celebrity fame and riches becomes her new home.

But then she meets Mickey, the lead singer of a boy band, who is as irresistible as he is dangerous, and Angel realises that a rising star can just as quickly fall . . .

'The perfect sexy summer read' *heat*

'A page-turner . . . it is brilliant. Genuinely amusing and readable. This summer, every beach will be polka-dotted with its neon pink covers' *Evening Standard*

'The perfect post-modern fairy tale' *Glamour*

arrow books

Angel Uncovered

By Katie Price

Angel Summer looks as if she has found her happy ever after. She's married to the love of her life, sexy footballer Cal, they have a beautiful baby girl and Angel is Britain's top glamour model. But all is not as it seems and there is heartache in store.

When Cal is transferred to AC Milan, Angel feels isolated being so far away from her family and friends instead of embracing the WAG lifestyle of designer shopping and pampering. Surrounded by beautiful people, will Angel and Cal pull together or will they turn elsewhere to seek comfort? Angel's worst nightmares come to life when an old flame of Cal's comes back on the scene and suddenly Angel is fighting to save her marriage, and herself . . .

'Glam, glitz, gorgeous people . . . so Jordan!' *Woman*

'A real insight into the celebrity world' *OK!*

'Brilliantly bitchy' *New!*

arrow books

Paradise

Katie Price

It's six months since beautiful model Angel Summer found herself having to choose between a life with Ethan Turner, the laid-back Californian baseball player, or giving her marriage to football star Cal Bailey another go. Her friends and family were stunned when she picked Ethan, but it looks like Angel made the right decision: Ethan loves her and she loves him.

But nothing is perfect. Ethan has secrets in his past that could threaten their relationship and when he faces financial ruin the couple are forced to star in a reality TV show about their life together. Despite everything, though, Angel is convinced that Ethan is the man for her. So why can't she stop thinking about Cal?

As the tabloids have always been quick to point out, the path of true love has never run smoothly for our sexy celebrity, and when her dad falls dangerously ill Angel rushes back to England to be by his bedside, throwing her and Cal back together. But Ethan loves her, Cal has a girlfriend, and Angel has made her choice. It's too late to go back now . . . isn't it?

'A fabulous guilty holiday pleasure' *Heat*

'Peppered with cutting asides and a directness you can only imagine coming from Katie Price, it's a fun, blisteringly paced yet fluffy novel.' *Cosmopolitan*

arrow books